His V

*These powerful men are helpless to resist
a virgin mistress*

His Virgin Lover

MISTRESS ON LOAN
by
Sara Craven

THE MISTRESS DEAL
by
Sandra Field

A PASSIONATE
PROPOSITION
by
Susan Napier

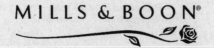

MILLS & BOON®

MILLS & BOON and MILLS & BOON with the Rose Device are registered trademarks of the publisher.
Harlequin Mills & Boon Limited,
Eton House, 18-24 Paradise Road, Richmond, Surrey, TW9 1SR

HIS VIRGIN LOVER © by Harlequin Enterprises II B.V., 2006

Mistress on Loan, The Mistress Deal and A Passionate Proposition were first published in Great Britain by Harlequin Mills & Boon Limited in separate, single volumes.

Mistress on Loan © Sara Craven 2000
The Mistress Deal © Sandra Field 2001
A Passionate Proposition © Susan Napier 2001

ISBN 0 263 84642 3

05-0106

Printed and bound in Spain
by Litografía Rosés S.A., Barcelona

Sara Craven was born in South Devon, and grew up surrounded by books in a house by the sea. After leaving grammar school she worked as a local journalist, covering everything from flower shows to murders. She started writing for Mills & Boon® in 1975. Apart from writing, her passions include films, music, cooking and eating in good restaurants. She now lives in Somerset. Sara has appeared as a contestant on the Channel Four game show *Fifteen to One* and is also the latest (and last ever) winner of the Mastermind of Great Britain championship.

MISTRESS ON LOAN

by

Sara Craven

CHAPTER ONE

It was the time of day that Adrien loved best—those quiet, early-morning hours when she had the house completely to herself. Before the painters arrived, and the joiners and plasterers, and work began again to restore Wildhurst Grange to its former glory.

She liked to move slowly from room to room, opening shutters and flinging back the drapes from the newly curtained windows to admit the pale late-summer sun. Letting herself move forward in her imagination to the time when she and Piers would be married, and living here, and she would no longer be simply the interior designer but the mistress of the house. And Piers's wife.

That was the best part of all, and the thought always made her slightly breathless—as if she could hardly believe her own luck, the way her life had fallen so sweetly into place.

Because there was a wonderful symmetry about it all. About the way they'd met at Wildhurst all those years before, when he'd come to her rescue when she was in trouble, and then how the house had brought them back together, when Piers had inherited the neglected property from his late uncle, Angus Stretton, and needed a designer to help plan the restoration.

And soon, she thought, it would be finished, and theirs to share as man and wife. Bringing the chain of events full circle.

Her only regret was that Piers wasn't there to watch the regeneration of his future home, but was working in Portugal.

'I'm sorry too, my darling,' he'd murmured as he held her on their last evening together. 'But it has to be done. Quite apart from all the work it needs, the Grange won't be a cheap proposition to run, and I have to make sure the money's there, that we don't have to scrimp and make do with second best. I want you to have everything.'

'But I don't need everything,' Adrien had protested, slightly troubled. 'And we could start slowly—just doing up the rooms we're going to use.'

But Piers wouldn't hear of that. He wanted the whole house finished—'so that we're not living with workmen and out of boxes for the next ten years, my sweet.'

He had a point, Adrien supposed, with a sigh. And she wrote to him every week, sending a concise progress report, including colour charts and fabric samples, while he telephoned and sent e-mails and faxes.

But it wasn't the same as having him there.

'Once the company's established, I won't leave you again, I promise,' he'd whispered. 'And just think what a marvellous showcase the Grange will make for your talents,' he'd added cajolingly. 'Business will boom when we start entertaining.'

Adrien had laughed and hugged him, but inwardly she was determined that the Grange would be first and foremost their home—their private sanctuary.

In any case, she wasn't sure she could cope with a boom, she thought wryly. Before she'd met Piers again, and fallen in love, and become involved with the restoration project, her business had already been thriving.

It was basically a two-woman operation—herself, as designer, and Zelda March, who was a local girl and a brilliant seamstress. A to Z Design hadn't lacked for work since it had opened its doors.

Although it certainly wasn't what she'd had in mind when she'd completed her training, she admitted. Coming back to the quiet country town where she'd been brought up hadn't been part of the plan at all. But her mother's sudden death three years ago had caused her to rethink her future completely.

Adrien, rushing down from London, had had to face the fact that she was now alone in the world. But she'd also inherited Listow Cottage, and some money from her mother's life insurance, which had given her a measure of independence for the first time.

Her life, she had realised bleakly, could change. But she hadn't seen how until she'd run into Zelda at the funeral.

It had been a long time since they'd seen each other. They'd been in the same year at school, but not on the same track. Zelda had been the local wild child, always in trouble with the authorities for smoking, under-age drinking and hanging round with boys. In her final year she'd amazed everyone by winning the Home Economics prize with a baby's wooden cradle, which she'd trimmed with handmade curtains and a beautiful embroidered quilt, as well as making a complete set of baby clothes.

Before she was seventeen she was pregnant by a local garage mechanic, and their hasty marriage had been followed by an even speedier divorce.

Adrien had been surprised to see her in the congregation at the church, and, on impulse, had invited her back to the cottage.

'I thought the world of your mum,' Zelda confided, when the other mourners had departed. She looked sadly round the sitting room. 'It was only a couple of months ago that I made these loose covers and curtains for her.'

On the surface, Zelda didn't seem to have changed much. The dark spiky hair was still much in evidence, and so was the nose stud. But as they talked Adrien sensed a new, quiet maturity about her. A strength to the set of her thin shoulders that impressed Adrien. And the workmanship on the soft furnishings was superb.

'Do you work freelance?' Adrien questioned.

Zelda shook her head. 'I wish. I do customer orders for Beasley and Co in Enderton, but the pay's rock-bottom. I've tried doing some work at home, but I'm back living with Mum and Dad and the kids, and there just isn't room. Not with Smudge too.'

'Smudge?'

'That's what I call my son. His real name's Kevin, like his father, but I don't want to be reminded.'

'I suppose not.' Adrien bit her lip. 'It seems a shame that you can't work for yourself. You're really good.'

'There's no chance of that.' Zelda shrugged. 'Dad goes mad when the sewing machine comes out. And he's not too thrilled to have Smudge around anyway, so I try not to rock the boat.'

It was only a brief exchange, but it stuck in Adrien's mind.

During the days that followed, she set about working out a business plan. There was undoubtedly a gap in the market. Beasley's were no real competition, and there was no one else within miles who could offer a complete interior design service. She could pinpoint all the genuine craftsmen in the area to use as sub-contractors, and with Zelda to cover the soft furnishing side...

Premises might be a problem, she realised. Until she took a good look at the cottage. It wasn't large, and it needed modernisation, but around its rear courtyard there were old stables and outbuildings, unused for years and ripe for conversion. There was space for workrooms, an office, and a self-contained flat.

'Are you serious about this?' Zelda asked huskily when Adrien finally put the plan in front of her. 'Really serious? Because it sounds too good to be true.'

'I mean every word,' Adrien assured her. 'And the flat will have two bedrooms, so there'll be plenty of room for you and Smudge,' she added, knowing that they were currently sharing one small room with bunk beds.

'A place of our own,' Zelda whispered. 'It's like a dream. I keep waiting for someone to pinch me, and wake me up.'

The dream rapidly became a nightmare while the building work was being done. It threw up all kinds of unforeseen problems, and cost far more than anticipated. Adrien remortgaged the cottage, and raised a bank loan on the strength of her plan, while Zelda, overwhelmed at finding herself a partner, insisted on contributing the small settlement she'd received from her ex-husband.

Their faith in themselves seemed justified, she had to admit. The enquiries came in steadily from day one, and they had to rent some temporary work-space to cope with the demand. Soon they'd been in their new premises for nearly two years, and were already employing extra help with the sewing.

'Maybe we shouldn't have downsized,' Adrien joked. 'Perhaps we should have looked to expand, and put in a bid for the Grange instead.'

'Except that the Grange isn't for sale,' Zelda said, frowning over some fabric catalogues. 'What a shame—a lovely house like that, just standing empty.'

'Yes,' Adrien sighed. 'When I was a child I used to go there all the time, while my father played chess with Mr Stretton.'

'What did you do?'

Adrien shrugged. 'Oh—read books from his library, played in the garden.'

'All by yourself?'

Adrien hesitated, hearing faint alarm bells ring in her mind. 'Not all the time,' she returned. 'Mr Stretton's nephew, Piers, was there sometimes. His mother had married someone Mr Stretton disapproved of—a Brazilian—and there'd been a big row. But I suppose Mr Stretton had eventually to accept the fact that Piers was going to be his heir, and invite him to stay, although he'd still have nothing to do with his brother-in-law,' she added, frowning. 'My parents said he really hated him. Called him "a thoroughly bad lot".'

'Families.' Zelda wrinkled her nose. 'Do you think Mr Stretton will ever come back?'

'I shouldn't think so. He moved to Spain for the climate, and seems settled there.' Adrien sighed again. 'I couldn't believe it. The Grange has been in his family for years. And he'd just got to know Piers properly, too.'

'Perhaps he thought he was a bad lot as well.'

'He couldn't have done.' Adrien drew a stormy breath. 'He's one of the kindest people I ever met. Saved me from pneumonia—or hypothermia, or worse.'

Zelda put the catalogue down. 'How?'

Adrien bit her lip. 'Oh, there was a treehouse in the wood at the back of the house. I climbed up there once when I was about nine and got stuck, and he found me. But I'd been there for hours, and I was frozen and sick with fright. I'm hopeless on ladders to this day.'

'But that's not all,' she added. 'When I was eighteen, Mr Stretton gave a party for me at the Grange, and he presented me with a garnet pendant, very old and very pretty. During the party it was stolen, and Piers—found it. But it was dreadful. It ruined my birthday. And he was so sweet and understanding.'

'Well, let's hear it for Piers—the hero of the hour,' Zelda said drily. 'What happened to him?'

'Oh, it was shortly afterwards that Mr Stretton closed up the house and went to live in Spain. I guess Piers went back to Brazil.'

'Shame,' said Zelda. 'By the way, who pinched the pendant?'

'One of the servants,' Adrien said shortly. 'No one important.'

Piers would be thirty-two now, she found herself thinking. And so would the other one. The one whose name she wouldn't speak. The one who'd caused all the nightmares…

Well, all that was in the past, and the past couldn't hurt her. Firmly, she slammed the gate of memory shut again, regretting that she'd allowed it to open even fractionally.

It was only ten days later that news came that Angus Stretton had died at his villa in Spain, and would be buried out there.

The vicar, however, decided to hold a memorial service at the parish church, and, to Adrien's astonishment, Piers arrived to attend it.

It was assumed locally that, having done his duty, he'd simply put the place on the market and get on with his life elsewhere.

But how wrong we were, Adrien thought—smiling to herself as she walked down the long corridor which led to the master suite.

He came—we saw each other again—and suddenly everything was different and wonderful.

She opened the door and stepped into the main bedroom. It was a large room, with doors leading to its own dressing room and a bathroom, both of them completely remodelled.

There was no furniture yet in the bedroom, which smelled of fresh paint and newly papered walls, now the colour of thick cream. The floor had been sanded and polished, and a square of deep green carpet laid.

Adrien couldn't help wishing that Piers had kept some of his uncle's furniture. Much of it was old, and she suspected valuable, and it had suited its surroundings.

But he'd insisted on a clean sweep. And since then, of course, she'd found the bed.

She'd discovered it at a country sale, lying in pieces in an outbuilding. A genuine four-poster bed, needing a lot of restoration work, admittedly, but she'd got it cheaply and handed it over to Fred Derwent, who specialised in such things and who'd received it with a delight bordering on reverence.

Soon, Adrien thought dreamily, it would be installed—the centrepiece of the room—and of their marriage.

And Zelda had unearthed some fabulous fabric, incorporating a heavily stylised pattern in blue, green and gold, from which she was making the hangings for the bed and the windows.

Three months from now, she thought, I'll be sleeping in that bed with Piers.

Happy colour rose to her face, and she laughed softly to herself.

She would still keep this morning tryst with the house, however. Only she'd wear the peignoir in ivory silk and lace that she'd bought on her last trip to London instead of the jade towelling robe which had seen better days, she thought, giving it a disparaging look.

And her dark auburn hair would be cascading over her shoulders instead of hauled up into an untidy topknot.

She would save this room until last, as she'd always done. Keeping it special. And once the new window curtains were pulled back, and she'd looked out over the wide lawns at the rear of the house, she'd go over to the bed and kiss Piers awake. And he would draw her down into the shadowed softness, back into his arms.

So far it was only a fantasy that stirred her blood and brought her senses to trembling life. But very soon now it would be reality.

She walked slowly to the window and looked out at the view she'd come to love.

And stopped, gasping, her hand flying to her mouth.

A man was standing in the middle of the expanse of grass, looking up at the house. A man dressed all in black, with an overcoat hanging from his shoulders like a cloak and early mist coiling round his legs, giving him an air of unreality, as if he'd come from another age and been caught in a time slip.

He was so still that for a moment she thought he wasn't human at all, but a statue that someone had placed there during the night as some kind of bizarre joke.

But then she saw the breeze lift the skirts of the coat and ruffle the dark blond hair, and realised that, whatever else, she was confronted by flesh and blood.

She thought, But not Piers, and her heart plummeted, shock replaced by disappointment. Piers wasn't quite as tall as the figure below, and his hair was raven-dark. And yet— just for a second—she'd experienced this curious sense of familiarity.

Who is he? she asked herself. And what is he doing here?

The Grange had its share of visitors, most of them driven by curiosity to see how the work was progressing. But they didn't come at sunrise, and usually they asked first.

Adrien swallowed. A visitor who came unannounced this early in the day had to be an intruder. Someone who was up to no good. A potential burglar casing the place? she wondered frantically. She'd heard of empty houses being stripped to the bone, their fixtures and fittings carried off. And downstairs there was a brand-new kitchen, as well as Angus Stretton's library, its walls still lined with books.

She said fiercely under her breath, 'But this house isn't empty. And you're not taking anything.'

She turned and ran to the door, tearing along the corridor to the wide oak staircase, launching herself downwards.

The drawing room was also at the rear of the house, to take advantage of the view, and French windows led on to the terrace. She ran towards them, grabbing the keys from the pocket of her robe.

It was the stark chill of the stone flags under her bare feet that startled her into awareness of what she was doing. She hesitated, staring around her, scanning the now-deserted lawn, recognising that the black-clad intruder was nowhere to be seen.

And at the same time she heard in the distance the sound of a departing car. He must, she thought, have parked at the side of the house, where he wouldn't be seen. But how had he known that?

Adrien realised she was holding her breath, and released it, gulping as common sense belatedly intervened.

What on earth did she think she was doing? she asked herself. Charging down here like a maniac, with only a bunch of keys for protection. Quite apart from wearing nothing except an elderly robe. Hardly confrontation gear, she acknowledged, tightening the belt protectively round her slim waist. And just as well the stranger had disappeared.

But why the hell hadn't she stayed in the house and used her mobile phone to call for assistance? How could she possibly have taken such a stupid risk?

After all, he could have been violent, and she might have ended up badly injured, or worse.

He must have assumed she wasn't alone, or else he'd have stood his ground.

Because he'd known she was there. She was convinced of it. Certain that he'd seen her, somehow, standing in the window. And that his dark figure had stiffened.

But that's crazy, she thought, beginning to shake inwardly at the realisation of her narrow escape. He couldn't possibly have picked me out from that distance. I'd have simply been another shadow inside the house.

And I couldn't have noticed such a detail either. I'm letting my imagination run away with me.

She straightened her shoulders and stepped back into the drawing room.

It was over, she reassured herself, and nothing had happened. But she would play safe and report the incident to the local police station, although there wasn't much they could do without a detailed description of a car number.

He'd invaded her privacy, she thought, as she trailed back upstairs to shower and dress. Spoiled that first golden hour of her day. Made her feel edgy and ill at ease, as if a storm was brewing.

Oh, pull yourself together, she adjured herself impatiently. You're reacting like a spoiled child. And you'll have tomorrow and all the days to come to treasure, so you're hardly deprived.

And he was probably some poor soul who'd been driving all night and had turned in at the wrong gate through tiredness.

She gave a small, fierce nod, and turned on the shower.

She dressed for action, in a tee shirt under a pair of denim dungarees, and secured her hair at the nape of her neck with an elastic band.

Over a breakfast of toast and coffee, she reviewed what the workmen would be doing when they arrived, making notes on her clipboard as she ate.

There was some tiling to complete round the new Aga in the kitchen, and plumbing to install in the laundry room. They'd converted the old flower room into a downstairs cloakroom, and if the plaster was dry that could be painted. The panelling in the dining room was finished, but the ceiling needed another coat of emulsion.

Most of the bedrooms were finished, apart from the one

with the camp bed that she was occupying at the front of the house.

She decided she would make a start on that, peeling off the layers of old wallpaper with the steam stripper. It was a messy process, but she enjoyed it.

Remembering how immaculately the house had been kept in Mr Stretton's time, Adrien could have wept when Piers had taken her back there to see what needed to be done. The plaster had been flaking, and there had been damp patches on some upstairs ceilings. In addition, her practised nose had warned her that dry rot was present.

'My God,' Piers had muttered. 'It might be easier just to pull the place down.'

'No.' She'd squeezed his hand. 'We'll make it beautiful again. You'll see.'

And she'd been as good as her word, she reflected, with satisfaction. The Grange was looking pretty wonderful already. Most of the work that was left was cosmetic—adding finishing touches—so that the final bills should be relatively modest.

At least compared with the last batch that she'd just paid, she remembered, shuddering.

She was making good progress with the steam stripper when it occurred to her that her small workforce was uncharacteristically late. She finished the section she was working on, then unclipped her mobile from the belt of her jeans.

But before she could dial it rang, making her jump and swear under her breath.

She said crisply, 'A to Z Design. Good morning.'

'Is that Miss Lander?' It was the boss of the building firm she was using. 'It's Gordon Arnold here.'

She gave a sigh of relief. 'I was just about to call you, Gordon. No one's turned up yet. Is there some reason?'

'You could say that.' His voice was slow and deliberate. 'We've had a bit of a problem.'

Not another vehicle breakdown, Adrien thought with a faint irritation. Gordon should get himself a van that worked.

She said briskly, 'Well, try to get it sorted quickly. There's still plenty to do here.'

'That's it, you see, Miss Lander.' He sounded odd, embarrassed. 'We did the work, and you paid us for it, same as always. Except this time the bank sent the cheques back.'

Adrien was very still for a moment. This was a room that caught the early sun, yet she felt suddenly deathly cold.

Rallying herself, she said, 'There must be some mistake.'

'That's exactly what I said.' He sounded almost eager. 'A mistake. So I got on to the bank, but they wouldn't talk to me. Said I had to refer to you.'

Adrien groaned. 'I'll get on to them myself,' she said. 'It'll probably be a computer error,' she added confidently.

'Dare say it will,' he said. 'Generally is. I'll leave it with you, then, Miss Lander. Only, we can't really do any more work until we know we're going to be paid, and there's other jobs waiting.'

'Yes, of course,' she said. 'I'll have it put right by this afternoon, Gordon. Cheers.'

But she didn't feel very cheery as she switched off the phone and put it back on her belt.

Something had gone badly wrong, she thought, as she went to her room to retrieve her bag and, because she was still feeling cold, a jacket.

It was a mistake. It had to be. Yet somehow she kept getting an image of that dark, silent figure standing unmoving in front of the house, like some symbol of ill omen.

Don't be silly, Adie, she reproved herself, using the childish version of her name she'd coined when she was small. Just go to the bank and get it sorted.

It was a simple enough system that she and Piers had
devised. He'd opened an account at a local bank, with a
chequebook in her name, and each month she sent him an
itemised account of her spending and he deposited sufficient funds to cover it.

'You're too trusting,' she'd told him.

'I love you,' he'd returned. 'Love can't trust too much.'

For the past four months the system had worked like a
charm. But this time, when some of the heaviest bills had
to be paid, a hiccup had developed.

I suppose it had to happen eventually, Adrien thought,
as she set her Jeep in motion. Nothing's perfect, especially
when it's automated. But why did it have to be this month?

The bank was busy, but as Adrien waited at the enquiry
desk she had the curious feeling that people were watching
her. That a couple of the cashiers had exchanged glances
as she walked in.

They probably realise they've screwed up in a big way
and are wondering how to apologise, she decided, with an
inward shrug.

The enquiry clerk looked nonplussed when she saw her.
'Oh—Miss Lander. The manager has been trying to contact
you at home, but we only got your answer-machine.'

'That's right.' Adrien's brows lifted in slight hauteur. My
God, she thought, she sounds almost accusing. 'I'm staying
at the Grange so that I can oversee the final stages.' If it's
any business of yours.

'Oh—that explains it. Will you take a seat for a few
moments? Mr Davidson needs to talk to you urgently.'

Adrien was glad to sit down, because her legs were trembling suddenly and her stomach was quaking.

Because those were not phrases that indicated grovelling
on the bank's part. On the contrary...

She wished that she'd taken the trouble to change, to put
on a skirt and blouse, or even a dress, some heels, and some

make-up. Because she had the oddest feeling she was going to need all the help she could get. She was also aware that in her present gear she looked about sixteen.

'Miss Lander?' Mr Davidson was standing beside her. 'Come into the interview room, won't you?' His smile was pallid and his gaze slid away. A very different reaction from his enthusiasm when the account was being set up.

She wished, not for the first time, that Piers had used her own bank, where she was a known and valued customer.

While he closed the door, Adrien took the chair he indicated. 'Mr Davidson, I understand you've returned some of my cheques.'

'I've had no choice, Miss Lander. There are no funds to meet them.'

Her throat tightened, and her heart began to pound. She heard herself say with unbelievable calmness, 'Then payment must have been delayed for some reason. Perhaps you could give me a little leeway here, while I contact my fiancé.'

'I'm afraid not, Miss Lander. You see, we've been notified that no further deposits will be made. Did Mr Mendoza not warn you of his intentions?'

'No more deposits?' Her lips felt numb. 'But that's impossible.'

'I fear not.' He paused, as if choosing his words carefully. 'I have some other bad news which I must pass on to you. I have just learned that Mr Mendoza is no longer the owner of Wildhurst Grange. That he has sold it to a property development company.'

There was a strange buzzing in Adrien's ears. The room seemed to be swimming round her.

She said hoarsely, 'No—it's not true. It can't be. He—he wouldn't do that. Not without telling me—discussing it...'

'I'm afraid it is perfectly true. I have the head of the

company in my office now, and…Miss Lander—where are you going?'

The metal handle slipped in her damp grip, but she wrenched the door open and ran out.

The door to the manager's office had been left slightly ajar. She pushed it wide and went in, knowing what she was going to see. Fearing it…

A man was standing by the window. He was tall, and dressed in beautifully cut black Italian trousers and a matching rollneck sweater in fine wool. The long overcoat had been discarded, and was lying across a chair. His dark blond hair, expertly layered, reached the collar of his sweater. His face was lean, with a beak of a nose and strongly marked mouth and chin. The eyes that met hers across the room were as grey as a northern sea, and about as warm.

And at the edge of one cheekbone there was a small triangular scar.

Adrien recognised that scar, because she'd put it there. She'd been just nine years old, and she had been cold, hungry, and hysterical. Because he'd deliberately left her on a flimsy platform in a tall tree for hours. To punish her. To make her think that she'd be left there for ever. That she'd die there.

So she'd picked up a stone, and flung it at him. He'd gasped and thrown back his head, but it had hit him, and she had seen a small trickle of blood on his face and been glad, because she'd hated him. She'd wanted to hurt him.

He'd looked at her then with those cold grey eyes just as he was looking at her now. With contempt and a kind of icy arrogance. And without pity.

She'd been frightened then, and she was frightened now. Too scared to speak or to run. Although she was no longer a child. Or an eighteen-year-old whose birthday had been ruined by theft and betrayal.

All these years she'd blotted him out of her memory, even though the legacy of those traumatic days was still with her. Haunting her each time she had to climb a ladder or stand on a chair, and found herself assailed by nausea and giddiness. Piercing her when she opened her jewellery drawer and saw the empty velvet box which had once held the garnet pendant.

But she'd managed to convince herself that she would never see him again. That she could bury the past.

And that he would have done the same.

But she was wrong, because here he was.

And once again she was stranded and terrified, with no means of escape.

CHAPTER TWO

'IT'S been a long time, Adrien.' His voice had deepened, but she would have recognised that husky timbre anywhere.

She would not—*not*—allow herself to go to pieces in front of him. Not again. Not for a third time.

Instead she lifted her chin defiantly. 'My God.' She kept her tone just this side of insolence. 'It's the Haddon boy.'

'No,' he said. 'Not any longer. I've become the Haddon man. A distinction I advise you to observe.'

'A threat,' she said. 'But then you were always good at them.'

'And an accusation,' he said. 'For which you had a positive genius. Even when you were in pigtails. And later.' The grey eyes made a leisurely and nerve-jangling inspection of her. 'You haven't changed a great deal—over the intervening years.'

Her throat tightened. 'I'm afraid I can't say the same for you. I would never have known you.'

He laughed softly. 'Are you quite sure about that, Adie? Wasn't there just a glimmer of recognition this morning when you were staring down at me from your ivory tower?'

His use of her childhood name grated. As did the confirmation of her earlier suspicion that he'd known she was there.

She said shortly, 'You were the last person in the world I ever expected to see again. And you didn't hang around to introduce yourself.'

'No,' he said. 'I had business elsewhere. And besides, I knew we'd be meeting again very soon. I didn't want to anticipate such a pleasurable moment. The first, I hope, of so many more to come,' he added silkily.

She bit her lip. 'So—what are you doing here? Why have you come back? I don't understand…'

'You're not required to.' His smile chafed her nerve-endings. 'Perhaps I just wanted to surprise you.'

He looked past her as Mr Davidson peered anxiously into the room.

'Is everything all right, Mr Haddon?'

'Everything's fine, thanks.' The sudden switch to power and charm made Adrien reel inwardly. 'Could you give us five minutes? Miss Lander and I would like to renew our old acquaintance.'

'Yes—yes—of course.' Mr Davidson began to back out of the room.

She wanted to cry out, Don't go. Don't leave me with him. But she couldn't allow herself to betray such weakness.

Instead, she stood in silence and watched the door close. Shutting her in with him. Her enemy.

'How very deferential of him,' she threw into the sudden silence. 'I'm surprised he didn't call you sir.'

'He probably will—given time. I'm about to become a very important customer at this bank.'

'Does he know you were the housekeeper's son?' She cringed inwardly at the crudity of the query. Despised herself for voicing it too. Because she'd liked Mrs Haddon, who'd always been warm and kind to her on Adrien's visits to the Grange with her father.

She had a sudden memory of the well-scrubbed kitchen table, being allowed to scrape the remains of the cake mixture from the bowl. And being given fresh-baked cookies, with her initial picked out in chocolate chips.

'I've no idea.' His voice was calm. 'But it would make

no difference. Because money talks—and it has a louder voice than your outdated notions of snobbery.'

Faint colour rose in her face, but she stood her ground. 'Then you've come up in the world. How odd.'

His brows lifted. 'I've worked hard. I've found it pays off. And I intend to go on working so I can have what I want in life.'

'Wildhurst Grange, for instance?'

'Among other things, yes.'

'Well, I don't believe it,' she said. 'Piers would never sell his inheritance—and especially not to you.'

'Piers would sell his own grandmother to get out of the kind of mess he's in.'

She said thickly, 'How dare you say that? After the way you've behaved. You always hated him—you were always jealous...'

'I had no reason to like him.' The grey eyes glittered at her. 'But I wasn't jealous. He had nothing that I wanted— not then.'

'And now you want the Grange. So you've stolen it from him—somehow.' She lifted her chin contemptuously. 'Well—once a thief, always a thief.'

'What a depressingly commonplace mind you've developed, Adie,' he drawled. 'It must be through associating with Mr Mendoza. But I'm sure you'll recover.'

'I don't have to,' she said. 'Or did you think I'd dump Piers because he doesn't have the Grange any more?' She moistened her dry lips with the tip of her tongue. 'If so, you're wrong. Because that was never the attraction. Piers and I are going to be together, no matter what's gone wrong. As soon as I get home I'm going to call him and...'

'Well, make sure you get the time zones right.' He looked at his watch. 'It's probably the middle of the night in Brazil. And you wouldn't want to disturb him on his honeymoon.'

The sudden silence in the room was almost tangible. Adrien could feel it beating against her eardrums, constricting her heart.

She looked at him numbly. He seemed to have retreated to a great distance, his dark figure swimming in front of her. Swimming…

'Sit down.' His voice was suddenly incisive, authoritative. 'Put your head between your knees and breathe deeply.'

She obeyed for no better reason than her legs no longer seemed capable of supporting her.

When the dizziness had passed, and she could speak again, she said, 'You're lying.'

He said slowly, 'No, it's true. He'd been seeing this girl out in Portugal, and made her pregnant. Her father is Brazilian, and powerful, and insisted on marriage. And Brazil was a safer option for him than London or Lisbon.'

He paused. 'Will you believe, Adrien, that it gives me no pleasure to tell you?'

'No.' She raised her head to glare at him. 'I don't believe it. You've waited a long time for your revenge, Chay Haddon. Waited to punish me for having you sent away all those years ago. I just wish with all my heart that you'd gone to jail instead.'

'Only to jail?' he came back at her mockingly. 'I was certain hell would be the preferred destination.'

'Hell's too good for you.' She pushed back a strand of hair that had escaped its confinement and got to her feet, swaying slightly as she fought off the last remnants of dizziness.

'Be careful.' He went to take her arm, and she recoiled.

'Don't touch me,' she said hoarsely. 'Don't ever *dare* to touch me.'

'A threat, an accusation, and now a challenge.' He was actually smiling. 'What a pity I have neither the time nor

the inclination to take you up on it. At present,' he added
silkily. 'I gather you're terminating our reunion. May I ask
where you're going?'

'Yes,' she said. 'I'm going to find Piers and talk to him.
Show you up for the liar and cheat that you are.'

'I wouldn't have so much to say about cheating.' There
was a note of grimness in his voice. 'Not when you owe
money all over the area. And don't even think of going to
Brazil, Adie, always supposing you could find the fare. I'm
sure your creditors wouldn't like it, quite apart from Piers's
wife.'

He opened the door and held it for her. 'I'll see you
around.'

To answer, Not if I see you first, would have been simply
childish rudeness. Instead Adrien did not even glance at
him as she walked out of the office.

She heard Mr Davidson saying, 'Miss Lander—Miss
Lander, I need to talk to you,' but she ignored him too,
breaking into a run as she headed for the door of the bank.

She could only think of Piers, and the necessity to contact him. To disprove the monstrous things that Chay Haddon had been saying. Nothing else mattered, or could be
allowed to matter.

The next hour was a nightmare. She tried faxing Piers in
Portugal, but found his outlet had been closed down and
that the same thing applied to his e-mail address. The telephone line she'd always used seemed to be disconnected.

Panic was closing her throat and making her fingers
clumsy as she pressed the buttons on her receiver, trying
every number he'd ever given her.

Eventually someone answered—a man speaking
Portuguese. She asked haltingly for Piers, and heard him
say something in a muffled voice, as if he'd covered the
phone with his hand, which was followed by a burst of

laughter, as if other people in the room were responding to his remark. To a joke that her query had triggered.

Adrien found she had bitten her lip so hard she could taste blood.

When he spoke to her directly, he made her understand in fractured English that Piers had gone to Brazil and would not be coming back. Nor could he tell her where she could contact him.

Amid another shout of laughter, he added, 'Good luck.'

She put the receiver back on its stand and stared into space, aware that her heart was thudding erratically against her ribcage.

However unacceptable she might find it, it seemed that Chay Haddon had been speaking the truth after all. That Piers had indeed sold him the Grange, and vanished.

She could feel pain ready to explode inside her, but she dammed it back. She could not deal with her personal anguish and betrayal now, because there were other overriding considerations.

Thanks to Piers, she was now in debt for thousands of pounds, over and above her mortgage and bank loan. All over the area there were people who would soon be demanding their money, and she had no means of paying them.

She looked around her at the pleasant sitting room, with its familiar furniture and ornaments. They'd always been part of her life, but soon all of them could be lost for ever, along with the cottage, and the business.

She was without illusions about what she could be facing. Bankruptcy was staring her in the face, and it would touch everyone around her too. Zelda and Smudge could end up homeless. And there were the women in the workroom as well, who thought they were in secure employment and had taken on extra obligations as a result.

And all because she'd fallen in love.

A sob rose in her throat.

She'd trusted Piers and he'd defaulted, crudely and cruelly. Her name was on the empty account and the chequebook, and she was responsible. She had no contract or written guarantees. Nothing that could support her in law, even if Piers could be found.

He'd arranged it that way, quite deliberately, and because she loved him she'd agreed. And her naivety could cost her everything.

And it wasn't as if she hadn't been warned. Zelda had been openly unhappy about taking on such a big project that would absorb all Adrien's time and energy.

'People aren't going to wait while you sort out the Grange,' she'd argued. 'They'll go elsewhere. Tell people we're never available. And word soon gets round. We shouldn't put all our eggs in one basket like this.'

But she'd wanted to be totally involved in the Grange's restoration, she thought achingly, because it was going to be her home, and she didn't want anyone else imposing their ideas. Intruding on the idyll she was creating.

Moving like an automaton, she went through to the kitchen, filled the kettle and set it on the stove to boil. She needed some strong black coffee to clear her head while she made a list. She needed to know the entire extent of her obligations and also what work A to Z had in the pipeline.

She would also have to go back and face Mr Davidson, as well as her own bank manager. Try and arrange an overdraft facility or a further loan. And then work her way out of trouble.

She swallowed, aware that she had a hard furrow to plough.

But she had to start somewhere. See if she could pull some of the irons out of the fire before Zelda and the others got to hear the rumours that would already be flying...

They depend on me, and I can't let them down, she thought, catching her breath convulsively. I can't…

She fetched a notepad and a pencil and began to write.

In spite of her brave front, backed up by business suit and briefcase, all her worst fears had been confirmed by mid-afternoon.

Her own bank manager, while sympathetic, had told her that her borrowing limit was already fully extended, and he couldn't agree another loan. And Mr Davidson had sighed heavily, looking down his nose, and had asked how she proposed to pay off her present unauthorised overdraft.

Even more dauntingly, both of them had recommended her to consult an insolvency expert 'without delay'.

She had also been reminded that, as the Grange now belonged to Haddon Developments, she was in effect squatting, and should remove her personal effects immediately and hand over her keys to Mr Haddon's lawyers, Frencham and Co, in the High Street.

So there was no reprieve, Adrien thought as she climbed wearily back into her Jeep. And the execution would take place as scheduled. She was shaking inwardly, and her facial muscles ached from the effort of hanging on to her self-control.

In a few short hours she had been transformed from a girl happily in charge of her own life, with a successful business and a future with the man she loved, into some kind of grotesque puppet, capable of movement only when someone else jerked the strings.

And the worst part of it all—the realisation that flayed her skin and made her stomach quiver with nausea—was that Chay Haddon was the one holding the strings.

And each time she'd encountered him he'd brought trauma with him, she thought shivering.

What in the world could have brought him back? That

was what she couldn't understand. Because his own memories of the Grange could hardly be happy ones. The housekeeper's son, she thought, who'd been sent off to boarding school for marooning her in a tree, then banished from the house for ever for stealing her garnet pendant.

Was he seeking some kind of posthumous revenge on Angus Stretton, who'd been responsible for exiling him from the house and had also, in the aftermath, sacked his mother, who'd given such quiet and faithful service for so many years.

If so, there was a real sickness there, she thought, wrapping her arms protectively around her body.

But it was a comprehensive and sweeping retribution that he was exacting. Piers had lost his inheritance, and she—she was facing financial ruin.

As he was already well aware, she realised, recalling his jibe about her creditors. He knew exactly what he was doing. The thief had returned as a robber baron, and this time he'd stolen her whole life.

She wanted to run and hide. Seek some dark corner where no one would ever find her. But she couldn't do that. She had to be strong—to stand her ground and fight back with whatever weapons she could get.

But first she had to say farewell to the Grange. She still couldn't deal with the more personal loss, although she'd have to do so soon. She'd have to admit that Piers had deserted her and married someone else. Endure the inevitable gossip and speculation. Local people were kind, but only human, and her downfall would be sensational stuff. Plus, there would be resentment from those who'd worked on the Grange, and were owed money as a result.

When businesses went bust there was often a knock-on effect, and the local economy couldn't afford it, she thought worriedly.

Gordon and his sub-contractors would be the main victims.

I'll pay them back somehow, she vowed silently. Even it takes the rest of my life.

A life that stretched before her as bleak and empty as a desert—and, she realised, with a pang, just as dangerous.

The Grange looked beautiful in the late-afternoon sun, the mellow brickwork glowing.

Adrien swallowed past the sudden constriction in her throat and drove round to the side of the house.

To her limitless relief, there were no other vehicles around.

Don't look too closely at anything, she adjured herself, as she left the Jeep. You can't afford to be emotional. Not yet. Just grab your things and get out while the going's good.

Usually when she walked across the wide entrance hall, and up the sweep of oak staircase, she felt all the pride of ownership glowing inside her. Today she couldn't even afford a glimmer of satisfaction in a job well done.

Because Chay Haddon wasn't just getting a house. He was getting all the heart and soul that she'd poured into it. All the love.

And she was only sorry she couldn't tear it down, brick by brick, with her bare hands, and leave him with a pile of rubble.

Instead she was the one with the handful of dust—and the nightmares.

She walked slowly to the side door and stood for a moment, trying to control her flurried breathing. She had the key in her hand, so what was she waiting for?

She needed to go in—to get the whole thing over and done with—then be on her way. For the last time.

Gagging suddenly, she turned and ran, stumbling in her

haste. She by-passed the lawn, where Chay Haddon had
stood that morning, opting for the gravelled path which led
to what had once been the enclosed kitchen garden but
which now resembled a jungle on a bad day.

She closed her mind to the plans she'd made to transform
this riot of weeds into a thriving vegetable plot again and
kept running, until she reached the gate at the far end, and
the area of woodland beyond it.

It was so long since she'd been here. She'd deliberately
shunned this part of the grounds for sixteen years. But now,
in the face of the greatest crisis of her life, she needed to
confront that old childhood fear and defeat it.

She was looking for the only oak tree—an ancient, massive specimen, with room in its spreading branches for a
whole terrace of treehouses.

'So where does he go all day?' Down the years, Piers's
voice returned to haunt her. 'The housekeeper's son. Where
does he hide himself? Do you know?'

And she, eager to please this glamorous dark-haired boy,
paying his first visit to his uncle, had said, 'Yes—I'll show
you.' At the same time knowing, guiltily, that she
shouldn't. That it was not her secret to share.

Now, for a moment, staring up into the branches, she
thought she'd picked the wrong tree. She'd been convinced
that time would roll back, and she'd find herself, just nine
years old, in shorts and tee shirt, her hair in the plaits she'd
hated, looking up longingly at the wooden platform that
had been Chay's hidden place.

An elderly ladder had been propped against the lower
trunk, and after that you'd climbed up through the branches
until you reached the treehouse.

It had had a roof of sorts, and three walls constructed
out of timber oddments, but to Adrien it had been a magic
place—a castle, a palace, a cave where anything could happen.

She had known, because he'd let her look through his
binoculars, that Chay went there to watch birds mostly, but
sometimes he'd come to read or just think. He'd kept books
up there, and a sketchpad, and a tin of biscuits.

She'd asked once, 'Isn't it funny—being all on your own
here?'

He'd looked at her thoughtfully, not smiling. 'It's good
to be alone sometimes. You need to be comfortable in your
own company before you can be happy with other people.'

Adrien hadn't been sure what he meant, and her face
must have shown it, because he'd laughed suddenly, and
reached out, tugging gently at a plait.

'Is it so awful, Adie—the thought of having no one to
talk to?'

'I'd hate it,' she'd said, shivering as a breeze stirred the
leaves and made them sigh. 'I'd be frightened. Up here by
myself.'

I actually told him that, she thought. I put the weapon
in his hand and he used it against me. Used it to punish
me. Unforgettably. Unforgivably.

There was no ladder there now, or platform, no flapping
roof. No trace of the little girl who'd knelt there, crying,
for all that endless time, convinced she'd been deserted and
forgotten.

It was just—a tree.

His voice reached her quietly. 'It's been gone a long
time, Adie. Angus had the gardener dismantle it and put it
on a bonfire. I had to watch it burn.'

She spun round, her hand flying to her mouth. 'What are
you doing here?' She'd had no inkling of his approach until
he spoke.

'You have a short memory,' he said. 'I own the place
now—remember?' He looked her over, absorbing the dark
grey linen suit and the white silk camisole beneath it. 'What
happened to this morning's Pollyanna?'

She said shortly, 'Pollyanna grew up—fast. And I meant how did you know where I'd be? Because I never come here.'

'Your Jeep was there,' he said. 'But the doors were still locked. I—obeyed an instinct.'

She supposed she had done the same thing, and it irked her. She lifted her chin. 'I'm—trespassing. I apologise. I came to clear out my stuff.'

He glanced round, brows raised. 'You've been camping in the wood?' he enquired. 'How enterprising.'

'No,' she said. 'It's in the house. I—I'll go and fetch it—if that's all right.'

He shrugged. 'Be my guest.'

She offered him a frozen smile. 'I think that's carrying hospitality too far.'

'As it happens,' he said slowly, 'you've already been under my roof for nearly a week.'

She swallowed, forcing her legs to move, walking back down the track. 'The sale went through that long ago? And I wasn't told? Oh, but I suppose it all happened in Portugal.'

'No,' he said. 'I was in London, and so was Piers. He came over to sign the necessary papers before leaving for Brazil.'

For a moment she couldn't speak. She certainly couldn't move as she digested this latest blow.

Piers had been in England, she thought with anguish, and she hadn't known. He'd been here, and he hadn't warned her. She wanted to sink to her knees and howl her misery to the sky.

Chay watched her. He said, 'Obviously he didn't make contact.'

It was a statement, not a question. But then, he'd been able to observe her shock and desperation at close quarters earlier that day. He knew how brutal the deception had been.

Adrien straightened her shoulders and set off again. She said coolly, 'That's understandable. After all, I might have taken it badly—learning I'd been jilted as well as saddled with a mountain of debt. Far better to let me find out once he was at a safe distance. I suppose Brazil could be considered a safe distance. Besides, he knew what fun you'd have, breaking the news to me in person.'

His mouth twisted. 'You have a weird idea of what I find enjoyable. But I'll say this for you, Adie, you're not a whinger.'

'Give me time,' she tossed back over her shoulder. 'I'm planning a whinge of cosmic proportions. Would you like to buy a ticket? It seems I need every penny I can get. And you don't have to follow me,' she added with aggression. 'I'm not planning to rob the place.'

'Don't be paranoid,' he said. 'We just happen to be going in the same direction.'

'No,' she said forcefully. 'No, we don't. Not now, not ever. Could you wait somewhere, please, while I collect my things? Then I'll be out of your face.'

'Sorry.' He shook his head. 'I want to look over the Grange—see what's been done and what's left to do.'

'I have the whole thing on computer,' she said. 'I'll send you a print-out.'

'It might be useful.' He was walking beside her now. The track was narrow, and it was difficult to avoid contact with him. 'But I'd prefer a guided tour and a detailed breakdown of the renovations process from the person responsible. You.'

She halted, lips parting in a gasp of outrage. She'd transformed the Grange for Piers and herself. Her hopes and dreams were woven intimately into the fabric of each room.

Too intimately to share with an interloper. She felt as if he'd asked her to strip naked.

She said jerkily, 'I have a better idea. Hire another design team and let them fill in the missing pieces. Although you could probably sell it as it stands, if you want a fast profit.'

He gave her a hooded look. 'What makes you think I'm going to sell?'

My accountant, she thought. She'd telephoned him earlier—asked, trying to sound casual, what he knew about Haddon Developments.

Chay, she'd learned, was a mover and shaker. 'His speciality,' Mark had told her, 'is identifying major building projects that have run into financial difficulties, buying them for bottom dollar, then selling them on after completion for megabucks. He's good at it. Why are you asking?'

'Oh,' she'd said. 'Someone was mentioning his name, that's all.'

Mark had laughed. 'Friend or foe?' he'd enquired. 'Word has it he's a good man to have on your side, but a bad one to cross. Generally he doesn't arouse lukewarm opinions.'

She'd said lightly, 'Thanks for the warning.' Adding silently, It's only sixteen years too late.

Now, she looked back at her adversary. 'Because that's what you do. You move in, clean up, and move on.'

'Not always,' he said. 'And not this time. Because I'm going to live here.'

'But you can't.' The words escaped before she could stop them.

'Why not?'

'You already have somewhere to live.' Mark again. 'You have a flat in a converted warehouse by the Thames, and a farmhouse in Suffolk.'

'You've really done your homework,' he said appreciatively. 'When interior design palls, you could always apply to MI5.'

She shrugged. 'Local boy makes good. That's always news. Even if it's the housekeeper's son.'

'Especially when it's the housekeeper's son,' he said mockingly.

She glared at him, and walked on. When he spoke again his voice was quiet, 'I was sorry to hear about your parents, Adie. I know how close you all were.'

She said tightly, 'Clearly I'm not the only one to do homework.' And they completed the rest of the walk back to the house in silence.

Outside the side door, Adrien paused and drew a deep breath. 'If you want to make your inspection in privacy, I can come back another day for my things.'

'No,' he said. 'Get them now. That is, if you're sure you won't come round with me.'

'I'm certain.'

'Don't you want to boast of your achievements?'

She shrugged. 'I don't feel particularly triumphant. Anyway, you're the expert,' she added with edge. 'I don't need to point out a thing.'

'You used to like company.'

'That,' she said, 'would depend on the company. I'll see myself out when I've finished.'

Once inside, she headed for the stairs, and the room she'd been using. She hadn't brought much, and her travel bag was soon packed. She was just rolling up the sleeping bag she'd been using when Chay appeared in the doorway.

'So you chose this room?' He looked round, brows raised quizzically as he took in the narrow camp bed. 'I'd have thought the master bedroom was the appropriate place for the mistress. Don't you find this a little cramped for passion? Or did Piers like you to keep still?'

Her face flamed. 'You bastard. You know nothing about it—nothing. Piers and I were engaged.'

His glance skimmed her bare left hand. 'Really? Well,

at least you don't have to send the ring back for—er, re-cycling.'

There was a silence, then she said huskily, 'That was an unforgivable thing to say.'

'Yes,' he said. 'But so much between us, my sweet, has been unforgivable. And unforgiven.'

She snatched up the travel bag and walked towards the door which he was still blocking.

She said, 'Will you let me pass, please?'

'In a moment. I have a proposal to put to you.'

My God, Adrien thought. He's going to ask me to finish the house.

Naturally, she would refuse. It would break her heart to go on working here, with all the might-have-beens. Yet—if she agreed—she could charge him a fee that would en-able her to start paying her creditors. Could she really af-ford to turn down such a chance?

She said discouragingly, 'Well?'

Before she could guess what he was going to do, or take evasive action, his hands had slid under the lapels of her jacket, pushing them apart, while the grey eyes made a slow, lingering survey of the swell of her rounded breasts under the clinging camisole.

He said softly, 'Very well. Quite exquisite, in fact. You've grown up beautifully, Adie.'

'Don't call me that.' Shaken to the core by the sudden unprovoked intimacy, she pulled away, horrified to realise that behind their silken barrier her nipples were hardening in swift, shamed excitement.

'And don't handle me either,' she added, her voice quiv-ering. 'You have no right…'

His mouth twisted unrepentantly. 'Not even the *droit de seigneur*?'

'You bought a house,' she said. 'I was not included in the price. Now, let me past.'

'Only because Piers didn't think of it.' His voice was reflective, and he made no attempt to move. 'But as you've raised the subject, Adrien, what value do you put on your services?'

She said slowly, hardly daring to hope, 'Are you offering to pay for the work I've done?'

'That would rather depend,' he drawled. 'You see, it occurs to me that this house lacks something. And so do I.'

She drew a deep breath. 'You mean that it isn't quite finished. But it wouldn't take much…'

'No,' he said. 'That isn't what I mean at all.'

'Then what?' she asked defensively, hating the way his grey gaze held hers, yet somehow unable to look away. Or walk away.

'It needs a mistress,' he said softly. 'And so do I. And you, my sweet Adrien, are the perfect candidate. So, maybe we can do a deal. What do you say?'

CHAPTER THREE

SHE said thickly, 'Is this some kind of sick joke?'

'Do you see me laughing?'

No, she thought, swallowing. The grey eyes meeting hers in challenge were cool, direct—even insolent. The firm mouth was equally unsmiling. No—it seemed he was shockingly—incredibly—serious.

'So you're just adding insult to injury.' She tried to laugh, but the sound choked in her throat. 'Time hasn't mellowed you, Chay. You're still a bastard.'

He smiled. '"Now, gods, stand up for bastards!"' he quoted softly. 'However, I see myself more as a white knight riding to your rescue.'

'Very chivalrous.' Her voice bit.

'No,' he said. 'I'm a businessman. You claim to be a businesswoman, and you're in financial trouble. I'm offering you a lifeline.' His gaze touched her parted lips and travelled down to her breasts. 'A very personal loan,' he added softly.

Adrien bit her lip. She said savagely, 'Mr Davidson needs to learn some discretion.'

'Mr Davidson didn't tell me a thing.' Chay propped a shoulder against the doorframe. 'He didn't have to. I could sense the shock waves as soon as I arrived. And when I was here earlier today, a plasterer and an electrician turned up waving major bills which had been refused payment. I'd make an educated guess that they're just the tip of the iceberg. That you're facing serious trouble.'

Adrien lifted her chin. 'And if I am,' she said curtly, 'I'll manage. I can survive without your particular brand of knight errantry.'

'Then I wish you luck,' Chay said silkily. 'But I hope you're not counting on a bank draft arriving from Brazil. You'd do better to rely on the National Lottery.'

'You utter swine,' she said unevenly. 'You've got everything you've wanted, haven't you? How you must be enjoying your moment of triumph.'

'I've had to wait long enough,' he said. 'But they say that revenge is a dish best eaten cold.'

'I hope it poisons you,' she flung at him. 'Now let me out of here.'

He straightened. Moved out of the doorway. 'You're not a prisoner,' he pointed out mildly.

'No,' she said. 'Nor do I intend to be, either.'

'Do you imagine I'm going to keep you chained up like some sort of sex slave?' He had the gall to sound amused. 'What a vivid imagination you have, darling.'

'Don't you dare laugh at me.' Her voice shook. 'You can't pretend what you're suggesting is a normal arrangement.'

'On the contrary, very little in your life would change.' He sounded the soul of reason, she thought incredulously.

'After all, you're already living here,' he went on.

'That,' she said swiftly, 'was just a temporary convenience.'

'Which would become a permanent one.' The return was incisive. 'But you'd have your debts paid, plus a free hand to finish the house exactly as you want, and staff to manage it for you. You'd go on running your business quite independently. And when I have guests you'd act as my hostess.'

'And that's all there is to it?' Adrien enquired ironically.

'No,' he said equably. 'My work takes me abroad a great

deal. I'd expect you to accompany me sometimes. But not always.' He paused. 'I take it your passport's in order?'

'Of course,' she said, staring at him. 'And this conversation is totally surreal.'

'Before commencing any project I like to establish the ground rules,' he said silkily. 'When I'm away, you'll be free to come and go as you please. Entertain your own friends. Live your life.'

'It sounds too good to be true,' she said. 'Which of course it is. Because when these business trips were over, you'd come back.'

'Naturally.' He was smiling faintly.

'Expecting precisely what?'

'You're no longer a child, Adrien.' There was a sudden harshness in his voice. 'Or a romantic teenager, dreaming of first love. I'd expect you to fulfil your side of the deal.'

'Just the idea,' she said, 'makes me physically sick.'

'Once,' he said slowly, 'you didn't feel like that.'

'What do you mean?' She stiffened defensively.

'It was your birthday,' he said. 'You were eighteen, and you looked as if someone had lit stars behind your eyes. I wished you many happy returns of the day, and you came flying across the room and offered me your mouth to kiss. Or had you forgotten?'

There was a brief, loaded pause. Then, 'A moment of weakness,' she said. 'And a long time ago.'

'Ah,' he said softly. 'So you do remember?'

His glance brushed her mouth in overt reminiscence, and she felt her skin warm suddenly.

She said between her teeth, 'And before I discovered what a treacherous, money-grabbing sneak-thief you really were.'

'Ouch,' Chay said thoughtfully. 'Well, at least neither of us will be embarking on this liaison with any illusions

about each other. That bodes well for our future, don't you
think?'

'You don't want to know what I think. And, thanks to
you, I don't have a future.'

'How do you reason that?'

She spread her hands, then realised there was an element
of weakness in the gesture and let them fall to her sides
instead.

'You say I could live my life, but that's rubbish. What
kind of existence would I have, living here as your kept
woman? Who the hell would want to know me under those
circumstances?'

'Get real,' he said wearily. 'You're not some Victorian
virgin, ruined by the wicked squire. What difference will it
make to anyone?'

'It will make a hell of a difference to me,' she threw
back at him.

'You didn't mind selling yourself to Piers Mendoza.' The
casual contempt in his voice cut through the uneasy turmoil
of emotion within her, bringing only swift, searing anger
burning to the surface.

She said, 'Bastard,' and her hand came up to slap him
across the face.

But his fingers caught her wrist, not gently, before the
blow could reach its target.

'I see time hasn't soothed that temper of yours,' he remarked with a touch of grimness as he released her. 'Keep
the fires damped down, Adrien, and don't trade on your
gender. It won't work.'

She rubbed her wrist, staring at him with resentful eyes.
'I thought that was exactly what you wanted me to do.'

'Perhaps,' he said. 'But on my terms, not yours.'

'Which I'm not prepared to meet. So, buy someone else
to share your bed. Because I'm telling you to go to hell,'
she added fiercely.

He shrugged, unperturbed. 'That's your privilege, Adie. Go off—explore what other avenues you like. But don't be surprised if they all lead back to me.'

'I'm sure you'd like to think so,' she said. 'But if I have to degrade myself, I'd prefer to do it in my own way.'

'As you wish.' He paused. 'My offer stands, but it has a time limit. So, if you decide to change your mind, don't wait too long to tell me. I can be reached at the King's Arms.'

'Slumming at a hotel, Mr Haddon?' Adrien asked with contempt. 'I thought the new lord of the manor would have taken immediate possession.'

His glance went past her to the camp bed, standing forlorn and solitary beneath the window. His brows lifted mockingly. 'On that, darling? I prefer comfort—and room to manoeuvre.' He watched sudden colour invade her face, and laughed softly. 'I'll be waiting for your call.'

She lifted her chin. 'Don't hold your breath,' she advised scornfully, and walked past him, out of the room.

He said, 'You'll be back.'

'Never.'

'If only,' he continued, 'to collect this bag you've packed with such care.'

Adrien swung round, mortified, to find he was holding it, his mouth curved in amusement.

'Here,' he said. 'Catch.' And tossed it to her.

She clutched it inelegantly, caught off-balance in more ways than one, then gave him one last fulminating look before turning and heading for the stairs.

Walk, she told herself savagely, as she descended to the hall. Don't run. Don't let him think for one minute that he's got to you—even marginally.

But for all her bravado she was shaking when she got into the Jeep. She sat gripping the steering wheel until her hands ached, fighting for her self-control.

She thought, There must be something I can do. Oh, God, there just *has* to be…

Somehow she had to find a way out—a way of escape. But her immediate priority was to start the engine and get away. The last thing she wanted was to give Chay the satisfaction of finding her, sitting there as if she'd been turned to stone.

She drove home with immense care, using every atom of concentration she possessed. Not relaxing until she found herself turning the Jeep into the parking area at the rear of Listow Cottage. As she switched off the engine a small group of women came out of the workroom and walked past her, laughing and talking. When they spotted her, they gave a friendly wave.

And one day soon I'm going to have to tell them that they're out of work, Adrien thought, feeling sick as she lifted a hand in response. As she climbed out wearily, a football bounced towards her, with Smudge running behind it. His small, rather pale face was alive with excitement.

'Adie—Adie, guess what? We're getting a puppy. Mum says we can go and choose it this weekend.'

Adrien paused, forcing her cold lips into a semblance of a smile. 'Well—that's terrific,' she said, trying to ignore the sudden hollow feeling inside her.

Zelda had hesitantly asked a couple of weeks before if Adrien would mind her acquiring a dog.

'Smudge would really love one,' she'd said wistfully. 'And so would I. Dad would never let me have a pet of any kind when I was little.'

'I think it's a great idea,' Adrien had immediately approved. 'Have you any idea about breeds?'

Zelda laughed. 'I guess it'll be strictly a Heinz,' she'd said cheerfully. 'They've got a couple of litters at the animal sanctuary that'll be ready soon.'

I'll have to talk to Zelda straightaway, Adrien thought now, her heart sinking. Warn her that she may not be able to stay on here. That the whole place could be repossessed.

Zelda's door was standing ajar, so Adrien tapped and peeped round it, scenting the aroma of freshly ground coffee. Zelda was chopping vegetables at the table, but she looked up with a welcoming grin.

'Hi, stranger. I saw Smudge nail you. It is still all right about the puppy?'

She waved Adrien to a chair, set a couple of mugs on the table, and checked the percolator.

It was an incredibly warm and welcoming kitchen, Adrien thought, looking round. Zelda had chosen rich earth tones to complement the stone-flagged floor, and homely pine units. Smudge's paintings occupied places of honour on the terracotta walls, and several of them, Adrien saw with a pang, featured dogs.

Zelda had changed her own image too. The dark hair was now cut sleekly to her head, and she was wearing the black leggings and tunic that comprised her working gear. She looked sophisticated and relaxed, Adrien thought, a young woman in control of herself and her environment. But what would happen to her new-won confidence if she had to go back to the crowded family house and her father's unceasing complaints and strictures?

And how would Smudge cope? He'd been a quiet, almost withdrawn little boy when Adrien had first met him. A child who'd never had his own space. Who'd not been allowed to play in the garden in case he damaged the prize-winning begonias that his grandfather exhibited with such pride at the local flower show. A kid whose every word and action had been subject to restriction.

'Are you OK?' Zelda was staring at her. 'You're very quiet.'

Adrien smiled constrainedly. 'I've got a lot on my mind.'

'You certainly have.' Zelda grinned at her. 'The Grange to finish—a wedding to plan. In between it all, can you bend your mighty brain to the Westbrook Hotel? They've accepted my estimate for redoing all the bedroom curtains and covers, but now they're looking at a total revamp for the lounge and dining areas. Maisie Reed says she can't live with all those Regency stripes any longer. I said you'd go to see them.'

'Oh—fine.' Adrien rallied herself. 'When would they want the work doing?' If it was this autumn, she thought hopefully, and there was other work on hand too, she might be able to stave off the creditors for a while. Look for another lifeline.

'They're planning to close for January and February.' Zelda unwittingly dashed her hopes. 'Have a grand re-opening next Easter. It would be a good advertisement for us.'

'Yes,' Adrien said. 'Yes, it would.'

'Well, don't turn cartwheels.' Zelda brought the percolator to the table, with a jug of milk. 'There is a real world outside the Grange, and we need it.'

'I'm sorry.' Adrien steeled herself. 'It's just—there's a problem.'

Zelda gave her a long look, then poured the coffee carefully into the mugs. 'Major or minor?'

'Fairly major.' Adrien gulped down some of the black, fragrant brew to give her courage. 'The Grange has been sold—to a property developer called Chay Haddon.'

'Who plans to pull it down and build a theme park, I suppose.' Zelda reached a commiserating hand across the table. 'Love, I'm so sorry. I know all the time and effort you've put into the place. You must be gutted.' She paused, her eyes narrowing. 'When did Piers tell you?'

'He didn't.' Adrien withdrew her hand, clamping icy fingers round the mug instead. 'He left that to Chay Haddon himself—and the bank manager.'

Zelda said a short, sharp expletive. 'And where is Piers now?'

'In Brazil,' Adrien said tonelessly. 'Apparently on his honeymoon. I—I don't expect to hear from him.'

Zelda said, 'Oh, God,' and there was a brief, loaded silence. 'Honey, you won't believe me if I tell you that you're better off without him, but it's true. So who's this other bird?'

Adrien managed a shrug. 'Some rich Brazilian lady. I gather he's in financial trouble,' she added.

There was another pause, then Zelda said carefully, 'Is all this as bad as it sounds?'

'It's worse.' Adrien swallowed some more coffee. 'He—he cancelled his deposit to the payment account, and the bank's returned all the cheques. As my name's on the account, I have to carry the can. So—I'm broke.'

All Zelda's colour had faded, leaving a faint sprinkling of freckles across her nose.

She said, 'The new owner—isn't he liable? Couldn't he be...?'

Adrien bit her lip. 'No. And I've pulled out of the—the Grange project anyway. But he isn't going to pull it down. He plans to live there.' She forced a smile. 'On the whole I'd prefer demolition.'

'Chay Haddon,' Zelda said thoughtfully. 'The name's familiar.'

Adrien stared fiercely into her mug. 'He used to live at the Grange years ago,' she said. 'His mother was Mr Stretton's housekeeper.'

'I remember now,' Zelda said slowly. 'He used to come into town sometimes. Blond, sexy, but didn't say much.'

'His powers of speech seem to have expanded over the years.' Adrien's voice was wintry.

'But you must have known him quite well,' Zelda persisted, 'if he was at the Grange when you used to visit?'

'Yes,' Adrien said tightly. 'But we were never—friends.'

No, she thought, but for a while—when I was a little girl—he was my hero. And I worshipped him.

'Pity,' was Zelda's dry comment. 'It could have been handy.' She paused. 'So, what are we going to do?' She swallowed, her glance flickering round her clean but cluttered domain. 'Sell up and start again?'

'Oh, I hope it won't come to that,' Adrien said quickly, without any optimism at all. 'I'll find some way out. But I felt I ought to tell you before the rumours started flying.'

'Yes.' Zelda smiled with an effort. 'Thanks, babe.'

It was as if a light had been switched off inside her, Adrien thought wretchedly as she walked over to Listow Cottage and let herself in.

And Smudge had been even worse. He'd come dashing in, talking nineteen to the dozen about his puppy, and Zelda had put an arm round him and said gently that he might have to wait a little while longer.

Most children would have thrown some kind of tantrum, but Smudge had simply gone silent, his small face closed off and stoical, as if disappointment was nothing new to him.

It shouldn't be like that, Adrien thought angrily. He doesn't deserve it. And nor does Zelda.

She noticed without surprise that the answer-machine was winking furiously. The calls were from contractors who'd worked on the house, or suppliers, and without exception they wanted to know when they would be paid. And a few of them sounded frankly hostile.

She couldn't believe how rapidly she'd gone from being a valued colleague to a potential enemy.

She listed down their names and set them to one side.

There was no point in calling them back until she had a solution to offer, and at the moment there wasn't one.

Or nothing that she was prepared to contemplate, she amended stonily.

She tried to do some sums, but none of the numbers seemed to make sense, and the eventual total horrified her. It appeared that even if she was able to sell the business, plus the cottage and the outbuildings, including Zelda's conversion, there would still be a shortfall.

I'm ruined, she thought blankly. We all are. And it's Chay Haddon's fault. Forcing his way back into our lives. Using his money like a sledgehammer to get what he wants.

Shivering, she wrapped her arms protectively round her body.

Piers, she thought with anguish. Why didn't you tell me that you were in financial trouble? I could have stopped work on the house. Why didn't you warn me…?

But it wasn't simply the money, a small, cold voice in her head reminded her. There was also the personal betrayal of the affair in Portugal, and she couldn't reasonably blame Chay for that, although she wished she could.

But it had been entirely Piers's own decision to dump her and run. To leave her abandoned and practically destitute while he married someone else without even a word…

Up to that moment she seemed to have been numbed by disbelief. Now, pain came over her like a black wave, swamping coherent thought, constricting her throat and dragging her mouth into a rictus of grief. She heard herself moan, and found, suddenly, that she was free-falling into some dark chasm of hurt and fear.

She groped her way to a chair by the table, put her head down on the smooth wooden surface, and began to weep without restraint, her whole body convulsed by the sobs that tore through her, so that she ached with the force of them.

When, at last, they began to subside, she stayed where she was, her face buried in her folded arms, an occasional shiver curling down her spine. She felt utterly drained, and when she got to her feet her legs were shaky.

Not altogether surprising, she reminded herself, as she'd had nothing to eat since breakfast, and those two slices of toast now seemed to belong to another lifetime.

She felt empty, but at the same time the thought of food was repulsive. She felt hot and disorientated, and her bout of weeping had left an odd metallic taste in her mouth. She filled the kettle and set it to boil, then realised she didn't really want tea or coffee either.

I need something stronger, she thought, and headed down to the cellar, emerging a few minutes later with a bottle of white burgundy.

She found the corkscrew and took a crystal glass from the wall cupboard in the dining room, then carried them all into the sitting room.

It was showing signs of her absence. There was a film of dust on the polished surfaces, and a vase of dead flowers on the table below the window.

She sat down in one of the big chairs that flanked the fireplace, and leaned back against the cushions.

Outside, the light was fading rapidly, and there was a faint chill in the air which spoke of autumn. *The days are drawing in.* That was what people said, and they hung heavier curtains at their windows, and lit fires in the evening, and started to make plans for Christmas. All the usual, normal things.

Only this year it would not happen. Not for her, or Zelda.

In the course of one day her life had changed for ever. All its certainties gone.

By Christmas, heaven only knows where we'll all be,

she thought bleakly, and drank some wine. Its crisp, cold fruitiness filled her mouth and caressed her dry, aching throat, and she savoured it gratefully.

There were tall shelves in the recesses beside the fireplace which had been filled with books and ornaments. There was a radio just beside her, and she switched it on, turning the dial until she found a station playing classical music.

The sound filled the room, haunting and wistful—an orchestral version of Debussy's 'Girl with the Flaxen Hair'.

Adrien closed her eyes as the music washed over her, seeing the girl, her blonde hair shining in the sunlight, walking through a meadow, dreaming, perhaps, of her wedding, as she made her way back to some solid French farmhouse. Her life, she thought, would be safe, and secure, and full of hope.

Whereas I—I have no hope at all. I'm going to lose everything I've worked for. Every dream I ever had.

Maybe I should change my hair to blonde, she thought with bitter self-mockery. They say blondes have more fun.

She drank some more wine, and refilled her glass.

So much of her future had been wrapped up in Piers it seemed impossible that he was no longer part of her life. She'd created this image of their relationship in her mind, and invested all her emotional energy in it.

He dazzled me, she thought, from the first moment I saw him, even though I was only a child. He was so glamorous, and so different. And, after Chay let me down, he made me trust him.

And he knew it. My God, when he came back, I must have been a sitting duck. I just accepted everything he told me—went along with his schemes. Walked blindly into his trap.

But now that he'd gone she felt strangely numb—hollow—as if nothing mattered any longer, she thought, almost dreamily. As if every bit of emotion had been drained out of her, leaving only a shell. As if the girl she had been simply didn't exist any more.

She drank again, feeling the wine spreading warmth through her chilled veins. Seeing the difficulties surrounding her with a new clarity.

Because, she realised with cool finality, she didn't have to be a loser. She had a choice. Not an enviable one, but a serious option.

Piers didn't want her, but there was another man who did. All she had to do was agree to his terms and her problems would be solved. Well—most of them, anyway, she amended, wincing.

He'd offered her a business arrangement, so she didn't have to pretend to be in love with him—or even to want him. He could have the shell—the empty husk she'd become. Because there was nothing else.

She emptied her glass, staring into space. She would loan herself to him for a set time—a finite term. That was the only way she'd be able to bear it: if she could remind herself each day—and each night—that the situation was temporary. If she could know for certain that she would eventually be free of him, and that he would have no further claim on her.

She shivered violently. It all sounded so—cold-blooded. Yet that was the deal he'd suggested, and that was the bargain she'd made. No more and no less.

That way the business would be safe, and so would this house. And Zelda and Smudge would be secure too.

So many good reasons for degrading herself. For offering herself for sale. For going against every principle she possessed.

But I can't afford principles, she reminded herself harshly, refilling her glass again. I have to be pragmatic. Do the expedient thing.

And I must do it now. While I still have the courage.

She got up so quickly that her head swam, and made her way to the telephone, dialling the King's Arms hotel. Not giving herself time to think—to change her mind, or clutch at sanity.

A girl answered, briskly polite. 'King's Arms—Reception. How may I help you?'

Adrien cleared her throat. 'You have a Mr Haddon staying with you. May I speak to him, please?'

'I'm sorry, madam, Mr Haddon isn't here at the moment, although we're expecting him to return for dinner. May I take a message?'

Yes, thought Adrien, feeling a crazy giggle trying to escape. Tell him I'll sleep with him if he pays all the debts on the Grange.

Aloud, she said, rather more sedately, 'Will you tell him that Miss Lander called, please?'

'Of course, madam. Is he expecting to hear from you?'

There was a pause, then, 'Yes,' Adrien said with difficulty. 'Yes, I—I rather think he is.'

And gently she replaced the receiver.

She lifted her head and stared at herself in the wall mirror above the telephone table. Her face was white, except for a trace of hectic colour on her cheekbones, and her eyes were blurred with weeping.

'Some bargain,' she derided herself shakily. 'But I've done it now—and I can't afford to turn back. The stakes are too high.'

She lifted her glass in a parody of a toast.

'To the future,' she said huskily. And drank.

CHAPTER FOUR

ADRIEN had picked up the splinter on her climb to the tree-house. The sliver of wood was now embedded firmly in her knee, with dark drops of blood welling up around it.

'Let me have a look.' Chay sat her down on his rolled up sleeping bag and scrutinised the damage with faint impatience. 'I can get it out,' he said, at last. 'But it's going to hurt. Can you keep very still while I do it?'

She nodded mutely, biting her lip hard, because it was already hurting, but reluctant to let him see. He might decide she was a nuisance, and never let her come up to the treehouse again. Never let her use the field glasses to watch birds and rabbits and squirrels, or give her a sheet from his sketching block and show her how to draw a tree or a flower.

He opened the old biscuit tin she thought of as his treasure box. It held a compass, a magnifying glass, pens and pencils, a wonderful knife, with all sorts of blades that she wasn't allowed to touch, and a pair of tweezers.

He was quick and deft, but when he'd finished her eyes were filled with tears although she hadn't made a sound.

He looked up at her, and his thin face softened. 'You were very brave,' he said, and her lips trembled into a smile. 'But it really needs bathing, and maybe a tetanus shot.' He produced a clean handkerchief from the pocket of his jeans and tied it round the little wound. 'You'd better go home and let your mother have a look at it.'

He saw her droop with disappointment, and stood up briskly. 'And don't look as if you're being punished,' he cautioned sternly. 'The house will still be here tomorrow.

And so will I.' And he touched her cheek gently and fleetingly with his finger…

'My God,' Adrien whispered, shooting bolt-upright in her chair, her heart thumping. 'I must have been dreaming.'

But was it a dream? she wondered uneasily, as she stared round the sitting room. Or a long-buried memory that suddenly, and for no good reason, had come swimming to the surface of her consciousness?

And 'swimming' was the appropriate word, she thought, shaking her head. She felt positively fuzzy.

Slowly, she pulled up the hem of her skirt, and looked down at the tiny silver scar on her knee. It had been there so long—so much a part of her physical make-up—that she never really registered it any more. Or hadn't done so. Until now, when she'd suddenly remembered how she'd acquired it.

But I know why I forgot, she thought slowly. Because the next time I went to the Grange Piers was there—and everything changed. The treehouse stopped being a sanctuary and became a nightmare. And Chay wasn't my hero or my friend any more, but my enemy.

Besides, a splinter in the knee was nothing to the other wounds she'd suffered at Chay's hands, then and afterwards. The scarring was hidden, internal, but still potent, she realised bitterly.

And he hadn't finished with her yet.

Shivering, she rose to her feet, and paused, aware that she felt hollow and still faintly dizzy. While she'd been dozing, or whatever, it had got dark. And cold too. Perhaps she was catching a chill, and that was why she felt so shaky.

Moving gingerly, she lit the lamps, and had started towards the window to draw the curtains when the brisk sound of the doorbell halted her in her tracks.

She stood for a moment, aware that her mouth was suddenly dry and her pulses drumming. Also that she was swaying slightly where she stood. And that her head seemed stuffed with feathers.

If she hadn't switched on the damned lights she could have pretended she wasn't there. As it was, she might as well have been standing in a goldfish bowl.

Reluctantly, she felt her way into the hall, and opened the door, gasping as a blast of cool air hit her.

'Good evening,' Chay said. 'I got your message. May I come in?'

'What do you want?' She wrapped her arms defensively round her body.

'I think that's really my question. You called me—remember?'

'Yesh,' she said, and swallowed. 'Er—yes, I did.' She propped herself against the doorframe. 'You certainly don't waste any time.'

He gave her a searching look. 'Not very welcoming, darling. Have you had a change of heart?'

In spite of her sense of fragility, Adrien sent back a challenging stare. 'No,' she said. 'I—I rang because I've decided to accept your offer.'

'I thought you would,' he murmured.

She glared at him, hating him. 'And the victor's here to claim his shpoils.'

His smile was ironic. 'I think it's pronounced ''spoils''. And also that it's a little early to claim total victory.' He gave her a moment to digest this. Then, 'Do you plan to conduct this entire interview standing on the doorstep?'

Adrien gave him a mutinous glare. 'It's thish way.' She started towards the sitting room, pausing to touch base with the wall and the hall table as she went.

Chay caught up with her and took her arm. 'Let me help.' But she pulled away.

'Leave me alone. I can walk round my own housh.' She frowned, drew a breath, and enunciated 'house' with great clarity.

She gestured towards the wine bottle. 'Would you like a glass of wine?' Pleased with herself, she repeated, 'A glass of wine?' She picked up the bottle and held it up to the light. 'Oh,' she said. 'There's none left.'

'Now, why does that not surprise me?' Chay gave her another long look. 'When did you last eat?'

She gave the matter frowning consideration. 'I don't remember. And what hash it to do with you, anyway?'

'Just kindly concern for your well-being, Adie.'

'Kindly concern?' Adrien repeated. 'Isn't that a little out of character?'

He laughed. 'Prompted entirely by self-interest, darling, I assure you. After all, I've no wish for you to die of malnutrition before we've had the chance to consummate our bargain.' He paused. 'Tell me, were you in this condition when you called the hotel?'

She said with dignity, 'I don't know what you're talking about. I don't have a condition.'

'No?' He looked amused. 'Now, I'd have said you'd been drowning your sorrows, and to some measure.'

'Well, I'm not likely to be shelebrating.' She frowned. 'I mean...'

'It's all right,' he said. 'I get the idea. I think I'll continue the funereal theme with some black coffee. I presume the kitchen's through here?'

Adrien followed, watching with a kind of mute indignation as he deftly filled the kettle, and set it to boil, then found the coffee jar and two beakers.

She said freezingly, 'Make yourself at home.'

'Thanks.' He remained calmly unfrozen. Even slanted a smile at her.

'What exactly are you doing here?' Adrien demanded.

'I felt we'd better sort a few important details. When you're sober enough to deal with them, that is.'

'I'm not drunk,' she denied with emphasis.

'No,' he said soothingly. 'Just a little fuzzy round the edges. And I'd really prefer you to be thinking straight.'

She drew a stormy breath. 'And your wishes, of course, are paramount.'

He said softly, 'So you've come to terms with that already. Excellent. I thought you'd find it far more of a hurdle.'

'Actually, I was being—' She considered 'sarcastic' then opted for safety with 'ironic'.

'I'd never have guessed.' He poured boiling water on to granules, and handed her a beaker. 'Try this. Have you got any eggs?'

'No,' she said blandly. 'The cupboard is bare. Don't forget, I've been staying at the Grange.'

'How could I forget?' Chay said softly. 'It's fragrant with your presence.' He shrugged. 'But it doesn't matter about the food. I'll ring that French place in Market Street and get them to send us something.'

'If you mean Ma Maison,' Adrien said sharply, 'they don't do takeaway.'

He smiled at her. 'Then I'll just have to talk them round.'

The coffee was strong and scalding, and one mouthful cleared her head and steadied her tongue. The second put new heart into her. She lifted her chin. 'Has it occurred to you that I might not want to have dinner with you?'

'Yes,' he said. 'But I dismissed the idea. We have to take that first step together some time, and it might as well be sooner rather than later.'

She put the beaker down on the worktop. She said carefully, 'When you say "first step"…?'

'I mean dinner,' he said. 'Just that. Only that. What, in other circumstances, might be termed a date.'

Adrien raised her eyebrows. 'Except that I would never go on a date with you. Under any circumstances.'

'Then I'm glad I never asked you.' He grinned at her. 'Imagine the dent to my pride.'

She said with sudden fierceness, 'And the role you have planned for me? The fact that you're—buying me, when you know I'm in love with someone else? Do you have pride in that?'

'Upon which I'm supposed to hang my head in shame and slink back into the night?' Chay's smile widened. 'Nice try, darling.'

'Don't you have any scruples?'

He gave a negligent shrug. 'I've managed pretty well without them up to now. And I didn't think they were a priority with you, either, if your ex-boyfriend is anything to go by.'

'Don't you dare criticise Piers,' she said thickly. 'At least he's not a rapist.'

'And nor am I,' he said softly. 'As I shall have exquisite pleasure in demonstrating to you before too long.' He paused, to allow his words to be assimilated. 'And now I'll order us some food. I hear their lemon chicken is good.'

'I don't want any bloody chicken.'

'You'd prefer the cassoulet?'

'No.' Her voice rose. 'Don't you care that I still love Piers?'

'I admit it doesn't say much for your critical faculties,' he said. 'But look on it as an illness. Something childish and unpleasant, like measles. You'll get over it.'

'Perhaps I don't want to,' she hurled back recklessly.

He said quietly, 'Now you're being ridiculous. You were always blinkered where he was concerned, but that's carrying things too far.' He paused. 'However, if that's really how you feel, why did you call me?'

'Self-interest,' she said. 'I hear there's a lot of it about.

Besides, you didn't leave me much choice.' She squared her shoulders defensively. 'I decided I wasn't prepared to lose everything I've worked for, particularly when there are other people involved who'd go down with me, and you were the only person to offer a solution. But that doesn't mean I have to like it.'

'"Like" is a pallid word,' he said musingly. 'I prefer— "enjoy".' He smiled at her. 'As you will.'

'Never.' Her voice was passionate. 'Never in this world.'

He sent her a meditative look. 'I strongly advise you to try. You'll find it much easier that way.' He paused again. 'Anyway,' he added softly, 'I don't think you know what you like.'

Her heart missed a beat. 'What,' she said 'is that supposed to mean?'

'I'm sure you can work it out.' His tone was dry. 'Now, get your coat. I've decided that we'll eat at the restaurant instead.'

'I don't want to go out,' she said defiantly.

'You'll find it safer.' The winter eyes swept her, stripping her naked with one devastating glance. 'The urge to take you to bed and teach you several much needed lessons is becoming almost overwhelming.' He watched the rush of hot colour into her face and nodded. 'Besides, it's good policy for us to be seen in public together,' he went on. 'It may stop your creditors beating the door down.'

Adrien bit her lip. 'Yes,' she said unevenly, angry to find she was trembling. 'Yes, I—I can see that.'

The room seemed suddenly to have shrunk to claustrophobic proportions, making it difficult for her to breathe properly.

She took another gulp of coffee, steadying herself.

She said, 'Does it—have to be Ma Maison?'

'You don't like it there?'

'I—used to go there a lot.'

He sighed. 'With Piers?'

'Naturally.'

'And now you're going with me,' he said. 'And soon that will seem equally natural.'

'There's an Italian place in the Square…'

'Adie,' he said. 'I'm not going to waste time avoiding places you might have visited with your ex-lover. Life is too short. Now, fetch your jacket.'

She said bitterly. 'Yes, my lord. To hear is to obey.'

He laughed. 'Now you're getting the idea. And hurry, please. It's a long time since I ate, too.'

She glanced down at her creased blouse and rumpled skirt. 'I really should change.' She made it tentative.

'Fine.' His tone was equable. 'I'll wait for you here.'

She walked past him, across the hall to the stairs, turning on the bottom step and posing, hand on hip, her whole body a deliberate challenge.

'You mean you're not planning to watch?' She mimicked astonishment, her eyes flashing contempt.

'Why, yes,' he said. 'But only when I choose to do so. I'm setting the scenario here, darling. Not you. Try and remember that.' He paused. 'So, don't keep me waiting or make me fetch you, because you could seriously regret it.'

'Don't worry,' Adrien threw over her shoulder. 'I already have all the regrets I can handle.'

'I shouldn't count on that,' Chay sent grimly after her.

Reaching her bedroom, Adrien was sorely tempted to lock the door, but she knew it would be a waste of time. Chay's body might be lean, but it was strong and muscular. Any physical contest between them he would win effortlessly, even if there was an elderly door in the way.

She looked at herself in the mirror, swallowing convulsively as she saw the pale face and hunted eyes.

Her decision to change her clothes had been purely an excuse—a temporary escape route from the ordeal of confrontation. She'd begun to feel stifled downstairs—totally trapped. Yet she had no one but herself to blame.

Finding herself alone with Chay had brought the true implications of her decision forcibly home to her. So far he had barely laid a hand on her, but all too soon that would change. And she would have to accept it.

Although something warned her that Chay would not settle for mere acceptance. She had agreed, after all, to be his mistress—his partner in passion. Which was almost funny under the circumstances, except that she didn't feel like laughing.

And if Chay came upstairs and found her, in her underwear, staring into space, she might have even less to be amused about, she thought drearily, treading across to the wardrobe.

Most of her things were working gear. The few play clothes she possessed she'd bought for Piers, loving to dress up for him and hear his voice murmur in approval.

None of them seemed—appropriate for this occasion. Except for one outfit, which she'd bought but never worn. She'd been saving it for Piers's next visit, she realised, wincing.

She took it out and surveyed it. It was a top and skirt in silvery grey voile, overlaid with a pattern in black. The filmy skirt was knee-length, and fluted at the hem, and the top had tiny cap sleeves and a deep vee neck. Too deep for the workaday bra she was wearing, she decided, rooting through her drawer for the only one she possessed with sufficient plunge. But it wasn't there, and she thought, To hell with it, and slid the top over her head.

It was a good choice, she decided, the lines discreetly fluid, the skirt flowing round her slim body. She used blusher and eyeshadow swiftly and deftly, then ran a brush through her hair, tying it at the nape of her neck with a black silk scarf. She thrust her feet into low-heeled black kid shoes, grabbed up a matching purse and a black silk-knit jacket.

When she got downstairs, Chay was standing in the sitting room doorway, leaning one shoulder against its frame.

'I was just starting to get impatient,' he commented, his brows lifting as he surveyed her. 'Now I'm impressed.'

'Don't be,' Adrien said brusquely. 'I haven't dressed for you. I'm certain that tongues will already be wagging about my financial problems. So, whatever the outcome of tonight's negotiations, I don't intend to look like a loser.'

'You doubt that our deal will be concluded to our—mutual satisfaction?' The mockery in his tone scratched across her nerve-endings.

'It takes two to make a bargain,' she returned coolly. 'And I have certain stipulations of my own.'

'I'm sure you have,' he murmured, straightening. 'Shall we go?'

Ma Maison wasn't very large, but the intimate ambience and the quality of its food ensured that it was always busy.

Adrien had secretly hoped that they'd be politely but regretfully turned away. It would be good, she thought vengefully, to see Chay thwarted, even in such a minor way. But instead they were met with smiles and shown to a secluded corner table, sheltered from the rest of the room by a large weeping fig tree.

There was also an ice bucket, containing a bottle of Moët et Chandon and two champagne flutes.

Adrien took her seat and looked at her companion across the table. She said, tight-lipped, 'When did you actually make this reservation?'

'Not long after you made your outraged departure from the Grange. I'm glad I judged the situation correctly,' he added silkily.

She said between her teeth, 'My God, you're sure of yourself.'

'No,' he said. 'Just good at assessing the variables. That's why I've prospered, whilst Piers is in Brazil with a woman who'll soon tire of him, even though she is pregnant.'

She looked down at the immaculate white cloth. 'I don't want to hear about that.'

'Rubbish,' Chay said briskly. 'You're only sorry I haven't got photographs. Now you can tell me I'm totally insensitive—or are you still slurring your words?'

Adrien stared at him. She said, 'You bastard.'

'Well, that was clear enough.' The grey eyes glinted at her. 'But smile when you say it. We're being watched.' He handed her a menu. 'And don't tell me you're not hungry,' he added. 'You need something to soak up that bottle of wine.'

'Thank you,' Adrien said, putting down the menu without a glance. 'I'll have fillet steak and a green salad.'

'Just as you wish,' he said equably. 'It's your loss, not mine. But, as you've come here to negotiate, a degree of co-operation might serve you better.'

There was a silence, then Adrien, biting her lip, reached for the menu.

He was right about them being the centre of attention, she realised, sheltering behind the dark brown leather covers. Although, if she was honest, it was Chay who was attracting the sideways glances and murmured comments, not herself. Because it was the other women in the restaurant who were looking, their eyes lingering and speculative, and, in some cases, envious.

If only they knew, she thought bitterly.

And yet—and yet—if she was seeing him for the first time—encountering him as a stranger, with no past or hidden agenda—what would she think?

He had a powerful physical presence, she admitted unwillingly. The silent, rather shy boy had been left behind long ago. And the cool eyes now held a world of experience in their mocking gaze.

Perhaps this was what those other women sensed. He might be wealthy, but he would never need money as an aphrodisiac because he already possessed a potent sexual charisma.

She might resent it, but she had to be aware of it. And she had to fear it, she thought, swallowing.

'Have you decided?'

She said huskily, 'It—it seems so.' And was glad that the menu was hiding her from him, so that he could not see her eyes.

Food was a kind of salvation. A note of normality in a reeling world. In the end they both chose the terrine, after which she had the lemon chicken while Chay opted for the cassoulet. She even drank some of the champagne when it was poured into her glass, and listened to Chay making light, amusing conversation with a smile that felt as if she'd nailed it there.

Several people came across to the table to greet her—a couple of former clients and the rest barest acquaintances—all of them wanting to be introduced to Chay.

Adrien, face and voice expressionless, explained that he was the new owner of the Grange, and saw interest mount.

Wait until they find I've moved in there, she thought wearily. They'll have a field-day.

She supposed she could only be thankful that her engagement to Piers had never been made official—or public. Local people had speculated, naturally, but no one, apart from Zelda, had known that Piers had indeed asked her to marry him.

'I want to do it in style,' he'd told her. 'Throw an enormous house-warming party and invite the whole county. Until then let's keep them guessing.'

Adrien had chafed at the restriction, but now she was thankful. The rumours already flying about her financial status were bad enough, but they'd be dispelled soon by even more fascinating gossip. Somehow to have it known she'd been tricked and abandoned—and to be pitied or laughed at—would have been infinitely worse.

Whereas here she was, dining out with a new man, seemingly without a care in the world. So let them think and say what they liked. Now and for ever.

The main course was served, the wine poured, and the waiter left them alone.

'So,' Chay said softly. 'Shall we talk business?'

'Perhaps we should.' Adrien chewed a piece of her delectable chicken as if it was the sole of an old boot, and swallowed it with difficulty. 'From what you said this afternoon, you're prepared to pay the debts I've incurred over the Grange, and allow the remaining work to be finished, if I—make myself available to you. Is that right?'

'Yes.' The candlelight made his eyes glitter oddly.

She concentrated on cutting another morsel of chicken. 'So—how long would this—arrangement last?'

'I beg your pardon?' His voice was quiet.

She gestured with her fork. 'Weeks—months—a year? How long before you'd consider the debt paid and let me go?'

'That's difficult to assess,' he said after a pause. 'I'd expect my money's worth.'

She stared rigidly at her plate. 'Yes.'

'Have you worked out how much cash you need.'

'Approximately,' she said huskily, and named the figure. It sounded outrageous—and maybe it would be. Perhaps, even at this late stage, he'd decide she wasn't worth it after all.

But he nodded, apparently unfazed. 'You'd better let me have an exact rundown of all the people you owe, and the amounts. I'll arrange for my PA to have the money transferred to the account you've been using.'

'When?' Adrien asked baldly.

He said softly, 'When you've fulfilled your part of the bargain, Adrien—and to my complete satisfaction.' He smiled at her. 'So the timing is entirely down to you.'

'That's not fair.' Her voice sounded stifled. 'I can't guarantee to—be what you want—to please you.'

'Come now, darling,' he said mockingly. 'Don't tell me that the fire in that beautiful hair of yours is all bad temper. I'm sure Piers didn't think so.'

Her back stiffened. 'But that's totally different. I—I loved Piers.'

'And you hate me. Is that what you're trying to say?'

She said curtly, 'You can hardly blame me.'

His mouth twisted. 'Love and hate, Adie. Opposite sides of the same coin. And in bed, believe me, the distinction can become very blurred.' He paused. 'But I've been patient for a long time. I can wait a while longer for you to accept the situation.'

'A year,' she said. 'Whatever happens, you have to let me go after a year. That has to be my absolute limit. Do you agree?'

He shrugged a shoulder. 'If that's what you want. But has it occurred to you, Adie, that a year might be too long? That six months might be a more realistic target? After all, I get bored very easily,' he added softly. 'So your ordeal may be over sooner than you think.'

She said hoarsely, 'Six hours—six minutes—would be too much for me. And I want my own room—my own space. Somewhere that I can pretend none of this is happening.'

'You can have a whole suite,' he said. 'But you occupy

it while I'm not there. When I'm staying at the Grange you share my life and my bed. Understood?'

Mutely, she nodded.

'Then it's all settled. Now eat some of your chicken before it's cold.'

She said, very distinctly, 'Another mouthful would choke me.'

He grinned. 'You wish.'

She said slowly, 'How do you know that I won't simply empty the account and vanish?'

'I don't,' he said. 'I'm counting on your regard for your colleagues and creditors outweighing your resentment of me. They'd have to bear the brunt if you went, and I know you don't want that.'

'No,' she said. 'Damn you.'

'If ever I thought I was irresistible, tonight would be one hell of an eye-opener,' he commented sardonically. Then his voice became businesslike again. 'My furniture will be arriving during the week. I'd like you to supervise the unloading and arrangement, and complete the outstanding work on the house. There isn't that much left to do.'

'You mentioned staff...'

'My present housekeeper will be joining me. I'd like you to engage local cleaners, and contractors to handle the gardening. If you have a problem, talk to my PA. Her name's Sally Parfitt, and you can reach her here.' He handed a Haddon Developments business card across to her.

'I shall be in Brussels until the end of the week,' he added. 'But I'll be coming down to the Grange on Friday evening.' He paused. 'And I expect to find you there, Adie. Warm and welcoming. No excuses.'

She said tonelessly, 'I'll—be there. I've said so.'

'I'd prefer a little more conviction—and commitment,' he said silkily. 'But I can wait. And now shall we shake hands on our bargain—for the sake of our audience?'

She stared down at the table as his fingers closed round hers, only to glance up, startled, as he turned her hand over and bent his head to drop a kiss on to its palm.

For one searing moment she felt the flicker of his tongue against her soft skin, and her body jerked in shock at the brief intimacy of the contact.

He straightened, his eyes glinting as they took a leisurely toll of her, lingering on her parted lips and the hurried swell of her breasts.

'You taste like Paradise,' he told her softly. 'Friday just can't come soon enough.'

'For you.' The words were barely audible. 'But not for me.'

She pushed back her chair, and got to her feet, collecting her jacket and bag.

She said, clearly and calmly, 'Goodnight, Mr Haddon. And—thank you. I—look forward to working with you. Have a pleasant trip.'

And with a smile that acknowledged the other diners, Adrien, her head held high, walked to the door and out into the chill of the night.

CHAPTER FIVE

SHE was breathless when she reached the cottage, almost flinging herself through the front door. She snapped on the central lamp in the hall, then found herself running from room to room, pressing light switches with feverish energy until the whole ground floor was lit up like a Christmas tree.

Anything—*anything*—to dispel the darkness that seemed to be closing around her. The darkness that Chay Haddon had brought.

And that other inexplicable darkness inside her that had responded to the brush of his mouth on her flesh.

Adrien shivered, wrapping her arms round her body, her throat tightening convulsively.

He took me by surprise, she thought defensively. That's all it was. I was startled. In future I shall be on my guard. And stone-cold sober. All that wine—and then champagne. That was the problem.

She nodded fiercely as she started towards the kitchen. More black coffee was what she needed. And what did it matter if it kept her awake? After the events of the past twenty-four hours she was unlikely to sleep anyway.

She'd just filled the kettle and set it to boil when the tap came at the back door.

Zelda must have seen all the lights go on and popped across to check that she was all right. Only Adrien wasn't sure she wanted to talk right now. She was afraid that she might say too much—alert her partner to what she was planning. Because, no matter what the consequences might be, Zelda would forbid her to do it. She knew that.

71

She hastily put the coffee jar away and took down the packet of herbal teas instead. She'd claim she was tired, and making a bedtime drink. Send Zelda away reassured.

Bracing herself, she opened the door and found herself staring up at Chay Haddon's unsmiling face.

'What are you doing here?' Her voice sounded unnaturally husky.

'Don't play games.' He stepped into the kitchen, kicking the door shut behind him. 'It was a terrific exit, Adie, but you didn't fool anyone, least of all me. I can't wait until Friday, and neither, I suspect from your reaction, can you.'

'Get out of here,' she said, her throat tightening. 'Get out of my house.'

He shook his head. 'You don't mean that, and you know it. Because you're as curious as I am—wondering how it'll be between us.'

'No,' she said. And again, desperately, 'No—we had an agreement...'

'It's a dangerous world out there,' he said. 'And a lot can happen in a week. I might not come back. You might run after all. And I need to know, Adie. I need to know how long you'll maintain those stony defences of yours once your clothes are off. How your body's going to feel against mine—under mine. Whether your mouth will be honey and musk—just as I've always dreamed.'

He took a step towards her and she backed away, lifting her hands in front of her in a futile effort to ward him off.

'Please...'

'Why not?' His brows lifted.

'It's too soon,' she said hoarsely. 'I—I'm not ready.'

He shrugged. 'Sooner—later. What real difference does it make? You gave your word, Adie. Are you reneging on your promise.'

'No.' Adrien bit her lip. 'But by Friday I'll have had a chance to think it all through. To prepare myself.'

Chay shook his head. He said softly, 'I disagree. I say it's time you stopped thinking—and started feeling instead.'

He took another step forward, and she retreated again, only to find herself blocked by the work surface behind her.

'Poor Adie,' he said. 'Nowhere left to run.' He was close to her now, but still not touching. She could almost feel the warmth of his skin. Sense the tautness of his muscular body. She stared up at him, aware that her legs were shaking.

And he looked back at her, his mouth twisting in something that was not quite a smile.

He said quietly, 'Close your eyes, darling.'

'Why should I?' Her voice sounded thick.

'Because it's the first barrier, and I want it removed.'

He made it sound totally reasonable, and after a pause she obeyed, feeling an enervating weakness spreading through her body as the chilling inevitability of it all began to invade her conscious mind.

He was going to kiss her, she thought. And that was not new. She'd briefly known the touch of his mouth on hers already.

But what would follow was totally outside her experience, and she could feel panic closing her throat.

His arm went round her, drawing her forward, gently but quite inexorably, and she swallowed, golden lights dancing behind her closed eyelids and she waited for his lips to take hers.

Instead, she was aware of his fingertips, light as gossamer, on her hair as he stroked it back from her face, before moving slowly over her temple and down to her cheekbone. The brush of his fingers followed the shape of her face, then discovered the faint hollow below her ear, where they lingered, tracing a gentle, tantalising spiral. That was, she realised, shocked, almost enjoyable.

As enjoyable, in fact, as the delicate movement of his other hand against her spine, making the silk of her top shiver against her skin.

A faint, insidious excitement was sending its first tendrils through her being, drying her mouth and sending her pulse-beat ragged.

Her voice didn't sound as if it belonged to her. 'Why are you doing this—please…?'

'Hush.' His mouth just touched her parted lips in a caress so fleeting she might have imagined it. 'You don't look. You don't speak. Speech is the second barrier.'

She could just capture a trace of the cologne he wore— expensive, but elusive. Seductive enough to tempt her to put her face against his tanned skin and breathe it deeply.

But she couldn't afford any more temptation, she realised breathlessly. Not while she stood, blind and silent in his arms, her whole body tingling with awareness of those tiny patterns his fingers were drawing on her flesh. And not just awareness. Arousal.

A slow, sensuous warmth was spreading through her veins, drugging her, blotting out all sensation but the sub-tlety of his caresses.

And just as she thought that she couldn't bear any more, that she'd have to beg him to stop, his hand moved down-wards, skimming the slender line of her neck and throat, to the smooth angle of her shoulder. Where he paused.

A small sound rose in her throat, to be instantly stifled, and in return she thought she heard him whisper, 'Yes.'

His fingers slid beneath the neckline of her top, pushing aside the flimsy edge as he began to explore the delicate line of her collarbone, so minutely that he might have been committing it to memory.

Adrien was dimly aware that her stance had changed. That she was no longer rigid within his encircling arm but leaning back, her body gently slackening, allowing him to support her. And that under the silky top her breasts were tautening in anticipation of the moment that would come when he… Ah, dear God, the moment that was here—now.

Her breasts seemed to blossom and flower at his touch, the nipples erect and eager for the flutter of his fingers against their hardening peaks.

Her back arched in sensuous joy and demand, all thought of resistance finally ebbing away. She felt the edge of the wooden worktop pressing against her back as his other hand moved slowly down in its turn, smoothing its way over the curve of her flank and lingering over the slender pliancy of her thigh. Leaving her on some knife-edge of bewilderment and need, her body hot and fluid in anticipation of his touch.

Her nipples were aching, on fire with pleasure. She wanted him to kiss them—longed to experience the balm of his tongue.

Her thighs had already parted—inviting his exploration—pleading with him to discover this intense molten desire for him in a demand more potent for being silent.

Her breathing was in tense abeyance, her lower lip caught between her teeth in an attempt to balance the pain of this unlooked for yearning.

And then, like the lash of a whip across her senses, it was over. Chay released her, straightening her clothing in one practised movement.

'I think you have a visitor.' His voice was cool, even expressionless, as if he was some stranger with whom she'd been exchanging thoughts on the weather, Adrien thought dazedly.

Then, instantly, she heard Zelda's voice outside the back door, calling, 'Adrien—are you there! Are you all right?'

By the time she'd opened the door and walked in Chay was on the other side of the kitchen, attending to the kettle which had come unnoticed to the boil.

'Oh.' Zelda checked in obvious embarrassment when she saw him. 'I'm sorry. I saw all the lights come on and wondered… I didn't realise…'

'Everything's fine.' His smile was relaxed, charming. As if she was the one person in the world he'd wanted to see, and at that particular moment, Adrien thought with a silent gasp of outrage. 'I was on the point of leaving, anyway,' he added, adding fuel to the flames. 'I just had—a few final details to settle with Miss Lander.'

'Well, if you're sure,' Zelda began doubtfully.

'Totally.' He nodded for emphasis, then turned to Adrien, his expression cool—even impersonal. 'I think that little discussion has made things much clearer, don't you? I look forward to continuing our dialogue next Friday. Please don't move,' he added quickly, as she took a half-step forward, her lips parting indignantly. 'I'll see myself out.'

He favoured them both with another swift smile, and was gone.

'Well,' Zelda said, with a wealth of meaning. 'So, what was that all about?'

'I don't know what you mean,' Adrien said evasively, wondering if she could walk across the kitchen without her legs collapsing under her. Her body, subjected to the sexual equivalent of cold turkey treatment, had gone into shock.

Zelda gave her an old-fashioned look. 'Who are you kidding? You could cut the atmosphere with a knife. I thought I'd walked into a force field.'

'Nonsense.' Adrien found her way to the cupboard and took down two beakers and a jar of coffee, moving busily, even fussily, to cover her complete disorientation and her seriously flurried breathing. 'We were simply talking business.'

'That's the kind of business I like.' Zelda gave her a cat-like grin. 'So that's the new model Chay Haddon. Actually, he hasn't changed much. Still blond, still sexy, but definitely more outgoing.' She paused, giving Adrien a speculative glance. 'And you're looking good yourself. Isn't that your new outfit?'

Adrien bit her already sore lip, and winced as she spooned coffee into the beakers and brought the kettle back to the boil. 'We've been out to dinner. I felt I'd better make an effort—that's all.'

'Well—did it work?' Zelda asked with painful intensity.

Adrien stirred the coffee, and tried to get her mind in gear. 'I suppose it did,' she said quietly. 'At any rate he—he's going to pay for the work on the Grange—settle all the bills—and let me finish the project. So, we don't have to worry.'

'Oh, God.' Zelda closed her eyes. 'There is a Santa Claus.' She took a breath, then gave Adrien another penetrating look. 'So, what's the snag?'

'Why should there be one?' Adrien handed over a beaker and took a scalding mouthful of her own brew.

'Because I don't believe in Santa Claus,' Zelda said grimly. 'So, what's the worm in the apple—the fly in the ointment?'

Adrien hesitated. She hadn't time to invent a story, so a half-truth would have to do.

She shrugged, trying to look nonchalant. 'He wants me to move back into the Grange while I'm sorting it out.'

Zelda frowned. 'Why?'

'It's nothing new.' Adrien took another gulp of coffee, hoping that would explain the sudden rush of colour into her face. 'After all, I have been staying there for the past couple of weeks.'

'Yes,' said Zelda. 'But that was when you thought you and Piers were going to be married and the Grange semi-belonged to you. That's not the case any more. So, what gives?'

'There's still quite a bit of work to be done,' Adrien parried. 'And he has his own ideas as well. So he wants me on the spot to make sure everything's done properly.'

'Can't he do that for himself?'

'He's away a lot.' Adrien bit her lip. 'Anyway, by paying off the contractors he's got me off the hook, so if he wants a favour I can't really argue about it. I—I owe him.'

'Gratitude is one thing,' said Zelda. 'Although I hope what I interrupted tonight wasn't you simply being grateful,' she added drily. 'But the guy can't expect to own you, body and soul. Remember that.'

Adrien forced a smile. 'Now you're being silly,' she said, surreptitiously crossing her fingers in the folds of her skirt.

But he does own me, she thought, her mind shuddering away from the events of the past half-hour. He does—and there's not a thing I can do about it...

She still could barely believe her reaction to his advances. She had nothing but dislike and contempt for him, and yet she'd stood there and let him do what he wanted without a word of protest, and, but for Zelda's arrival, she would probably be having sex with him at this moment.

I'm as bad as he is, she thought, wincing with distaste.

Zelda spoke, her voice gentle. 'Adie—if you don't want to accept Chay Haddon's offer, say so now. We'll manage somehow. It's not too late.'

Oh, but it is, Adrien thought. It was too late from the moment I saw him standing there, looking up at the house.

'Everything's fine.' She lifted her chin. 'Living at the Grange won't be particularly convenient, but it's only a temporary measure. Soon—very soon—life will be back to normal again.'

And she wished with a kind of dread that she could believe her own reassuring words.

*   *   *

Just a few more hours, Adrien thought, turning the Jeep into the Grange's drive. When the day ended, her life would have changed for ever.

It had been a strange week. The days short, as she'd struggled to finish the Grange. The nights all too long, as sleep had proved elusive.

Do what she would, she had not been able to forget her last encounter with Chay—or forgive herself for it either.

And something told her that she was going to pay dearly for those long moments of self-betrayal in Chay's arms.

She should have insisted that they adhere to the original terms of the bargain—made him leave. Oh, she could see it all now. Why hadn't she been as wise at the time—instead of melting like some sex-starved idiot? she berated herself savagely.

Yet wasn't that exactly what she was?

I'm a throwback, she thought. A total, pathetic anachronism. I don't belong in the twenty-first century.

Looking back, she could see that Piers's determination to postpone the physical consummation of their relationship until they were married hadn't been the act of a chivalrous romantic at all.

He had to sweet-talk me to get me to restore the Grange for him, she thought bleakly. But that was as far as it was ever going to go. The rest of it was my imagination.

She'd lain in the darkness, night after night, trying to remember how Piers's arms had felt—his kisses. And to recall her own responses.

She'd been in love with him, she thought wonderingly, yet, to her shame, not one of his embraces had ever stirred her as Chay's lightest touch had done.

She shivered. How had Chay been able to exert such power over her, and with such consummate ease, too? It seemed too glib to tell herself that he was just a very experienced man toying with the senses of a relatively innocent young woman. But what other explanation was there?

It was almost as if she'd been bewitched.

But next time he wouldn't find her mental and emotional defences so fragile, she promised herself grimly.

She'd found it easier to cope in the daytime. There'd even been times when work on the house had taken her over again. When she'd been able to lose herself in the pleasure of restoration, watching the Grange coming to life again. When she could look around her and allow herself to bask in the satisfaction of a job well done.

All the contractors had returned to work, presumably on Chay Haddon's guarantee, and although she'd been aware of curious glances from some, and an air of constraint from others, no one had referred to the returned cheques, or even to the new ownership. At least not in her hearing.

Sometimes she'd even been able to relegate the price she had to pay for Piers's defection to the back of her mind. Until something would occur to remind her of the new regime, and how intimately she'd soon be involved with it.

The arrival of the phone company to install extra lines and points had been the first thing, and that had been followed by a van-load of high-tech office equipment.

And today she'd been told to expect the arrival of another consignment of furniture.

The first load had arrived the previous day. She'd watched the men carry in chairs and sofas, with luxurious feather cushioning and brocaded covers in sapphire, ivory and jade. They looked good in the formal surroundings of the long drawing room, but she'd been in no mood to admire Chay's taste.

The beds, too, were all brand-new, and ostentatiously large, Adrien had noted, tight-lipped, as she'd directed which rooms they were to be placed in.

She'd chosen a relatively modest queen-size bed for her own quarters, a bedroom with its own tiny shower room and an adjoining sitting room, at the opposite end of the house to Chay's suite.

And today she would complete the furnishing of her little suite. She'd brought an easy chair from the cottage yesterday, but she still needed a chest of drawers and a night table. However, a number of small items of furniture that Piers had deemed not good enough to be auctioned had been relegated to the cellar, so she might find something down there.

Inside the house, the contractors were clearing up and preparing to leave. She'd been astonished at the amount of work they'd got through lately, until she'd heard one of them say that Chay Haddon had promised them all a bonus if they finished on time.

How nice, she thought, to have that kind of money, and to be able to wield that kind of power.

She went into the kitchen and put the kettle on, then took the cellar key from the hook and went off to investigate.

The cellar had once been Angus Stretton's pride and joy, but now it looked more like an explosion in a junk yard, she thought without pleasure, as she switched on the single lightbulb. His collection of wine had been the first thing Piers had sent off for auction.

That should have warned me that he could be short of cash, she thought with an inward sigh. But I believed him when he said he didn't want to live in the past.

But then—what hadn't she believed?

Moving carefully, because the entire place was thick with dust and the spiders had been having a field-day, she began to sort through the hotch-potch of chairs, stools and occasional tables. One of the first things she found was the little davenport that had once stood in the morning room, with one of its delicate pillars snapped off.

That could easily be repaired, she thought, touching it

with a protective finger. Maybe she should make an inventory of everything that was down here.

Underneath a box of odd cups and saucers she came upon a small circular mahogany table, its veneer chipped and scratched but otherwise intact, and a matching chair needing a replacement seat cover. Nearby she unearthed a three-drawer chest, also in mahogany, the bottom draw lacking a handle.

Chay would hardly begrudge her any of those, she thought.

She manhandled the small table up the cellar steps, and was just catching her breath when a voice said, 'Miss Lander?'

She was confronted by a small, rather plump woman in a neat navy suit, with smartly cut grey hair and bright dark eyes.

She said briskly, 'I'm Jean Whitley. I believe you're expecting me.'

Adrien, very conscious of her elderly tee shirt and paint-stained dungarees, gave a constrained smile. 'Yes, of course. Er—welcome to Wildhurst Grange.'

'It's certainly a lovely house.' Mrs Whitley gave her surroundings an appraising look. 'I can see why Mr Haddon feels so strong about it.' She nodded, then picked up the leather suitcase beside her. 'If you'd be good enough to show me my quarters, I'll get settled in. The rest of my things are in the car.'

She looked at her watch. 'Lunch will be ready in an hour and a half, madam. Only soup and sandwiches, I'm afraid, but I'll be back in my stride by this evening.'

She looked at the table. 'And where is that to go?'

'In my room. There are a couple of other things as well,' Adrien said. 'I'm going to ask one of the workmen to bring them up for me.'

'No doubt they'll need cleaning.' Mrs Whitley clicked

her tongue. 'What a shame to let nice things go to rack and ruin. But all that can stop here and now.' She nodded again, rather fiercely. 'Now, where am I to sleep?'

Adrien took her up to the small self-contained flat on the second floor which the Grange housekeepers usually occupied.

I wonder if she knows that Chay used to live there? she wondered as she returned downstairs, feeling as if she'd been caught in a small whirlwind.

The soup was a home-made vegetable broth, and the sandwiches were smoked salmon.

'That was delicious,' Adrien said with complete sincerity when Mrs Whitley arrived to collect her tray.

The housekeeper snorted. 'Nothing but a snack,' she declared, and ran a martial eye over Adrien's slender figure. 'You need feeding up, Miss Lander,' she added, and withdrew.

Did she? Adrien wondered, glimpsing her reflection in the drawing room window. Her week of snatched meals and sleepless nights had emphasised her cheekbones and made her eyes look shadowed and wary. Perhaps Chay would take one look and decide she was past her sell-by date, she thought, her lips twisting wryly.

Mrs Whitley's head reappeared round the door. 'The furniture van's just coming up the drive, madam. Mr Haddon said you'd give the men their orders, as you know where everything goes.'

'I know?' Adrien repeated in bewilderment, following her into the hall. 'I don't understand.'

But comprehension soon came as the first pieces of furniture were carefully unloaded and carried into the house.

She said numbly, 'But those are Mr Stretton's things. That cabinet—and the table and chairs. And there's his big desk from the library.' She shook her head. 'But that's impossible.'

'Not if you know where to look, madam. And Mr Haddon was keen to have the house just as it was in the old days.'

Adrien felt her throat close in shock. My God, she thought, but he's been thorough. He's even got the Persian carpets—and most of the oil paintings too, by the look of it. And the silver…

She opened the nearest crate and found herself looking down at Angus Stretton's chessboard, its ivory and ebony squares gleaming. And next to it was the familiar box of matching chessmen. How many times, she wondered, had she seen Mr Stretton and her father sitting opposite each other in the study, intent on their next moves? And this was the board she'd learned on too.

It's not just the house—or me, she thought, feeling cold. He wants the whole of Piers's inheritance. He hasn't missed a thing. Not the slightest detail.

All these years he must have been waiting. And this is his revenge—on both of us.

She lifted her head, staring into space. Ruthless, she thought. He's totally ruthless. And soon—very soon now—he'll be here. For me.

CHAPTER SIX

'YOU really don't have to do this,' Zelda said.

Adrien fastened the lid of her suitcase. It had been mid-afternoon before the furniture was finally in place at the Grange, leaving her free to come back to the cottage for her clothes. A task she'd left to the last minute. Like a condemned person hoping for reprieve, she thought rue-fully.

She said lightly, 'Oh, but I do. It's a job, just like any other.' She paused. 'My goodness, you didn't make all this fuss when I moved into the Grange last time.'

'That was different,' Zelda said grimly. 'I know it, and you won't admit it.'

'Well, don't look so glum,' Adrien said bracingly, as she hefted her case off the bed. 'I'll be back before you know it. This is our workbase, after all. Besides, I have to see Smudge's puppy.'

'Adie,' Zelda said. 'Tell me you're not doing this so that my son can have a dog.'

'It's work,' Adrien said determinedly. 'Just another assignment. Purely temporary. So don't worry about a thing.'

When Zelda had made her reluctant departure, Adrien carried her case down to the Jeep. She hadn't packed very much, partly because her wardrobe was limited, and far too utilitarian for a tycoon's mistress, she decided with irony, even if she was only on loan. No slinky evening dresses, designer casuals or see-through lingerie anywhere. But perhaps Chay intended to buy her those kind of things, she thought with a grimace.

That could be just one of the many hurdles confronting

her. She still wasn't sure what conclusions Mrs Whitley was drawing about her place in the household, but it hadn't taken long for her to discover that Chay could do no wrong in his housekeeper's eyes, and that she probably wouldn't have turned a hair if Adrien had been lead concubine in his harem.

But she seemed prepared to go along with the fiction that Adrien was just another employee, and had, in a brief time, transformed the rooms Adrien had chosen for herself.

When she got back to the Grange Adrien found the bed made up, two charming watercolours on the sitting room walls, and the reject furniture polished to within an inch of its life. There was a cushion in the easy chair, and a bowl of late roses on the table. Mrs Whitley had even found time to fix new handles to the chest of drawers.

Adrien said, 'It all looks wonderful.'

Mrs Whitley beamed. 'Mr Haddon said I was to make sure you were comfortable and had everything you needed.' She glanced at her watch. 'Now I must make a start on dinner.'

It didn't take long to unpack, and then Adrien found herself at a loose end. It was disturbing to walk round the house and find it almost the same as it had been in Angus Stretton's day. For a small child it had been like a treasure house—an enchanted castle with Mr Stretton as the kindly wizard, talking to her about the pictures on the walls, opening the cabinets of curios so that she could hold them while he told her their history. And always Chay had been there, a quiet, watchful presence on the edge of her vision.

Mr Stretton was so good to him, Adrien thought wretchedly. It must have broken his heart to find that he was a thief.

Thank God he can never know that Chay was just biding his time, she told herself with bitterness. That he's stepped in and stolen everything.

The afternoon seemed endless, moving slowly but inevitably to the moment when Chay would return.

She tried to keep herself occupied, using the computer in the office to draw up a new design for the kitchen garden, but got to a point where the walls of the room seemed to be closing in on her. She was glancing at her watch every few seconds, every nerve on edge and screaming, so that at last she said, 'To hell with it,' and went out for a walk instead.

She went up through the trees, steadfastly ignoring the place where the treehouse used to be. She had to dismiss that part of her childhood—relegate it to some distant corner of her mind—even though the sense of betrayal—of desertion—would always haunt her.

What Piers had done to her was infinitely worse, yet some strange instinct told her that his defection would not linger nearly as long in her mind. And that made no sense at all.

The sun was still warm on her back, but there was a crispness in the air which signalled autumn. It was her favourite time of year, and one of the busiest too, as people decided to have rooms redone for Christmas. But now Chay Haddon had the right to the lion's share of her time.

But I can't allow the business to suffer, she told herself. I'll need something to go back to when—all this is over.

She bit her lip and increased her stride. It was the present she needed to worry about, she reminded herself grimly. The future—well, that would have to look after itself.

It was over an hour later when she got back to the house, and Mrs Whitley met her with an air of faint reproach.

'Mr Haddon called,' she said. 'He's been slightly delayed, so I've put dinner back to eight-thirty.' She paused. 'Would you like me to run you a bath, madam? And bring you a glass of sherry, perhaps?'

My God, thought Adrien. She thinks I'm going to do the

whole bit. Soak in a hot tub, rub in body lotion, varnish my toenails, and put on something glamorous and revealing. Prepare myself for the master's return.

Well, no chance. That's not for me. In my case, what you see is what you get.

She smiled at Mrs Whitley. 'Thanks, but I'm just going to have a quick shower. And I'll have a glass of white wine—Chardonnay, for preference—when I come down.'

'Just as you wish, madam, of course. But I thought…'

'I'm sure you did,' said Adrien, and ran lightly up the stairs.

So she wasn't deceived at all, she thought, wondering just how many others Mrs Whitley had pampered in this particular way…

Wrinkling her nose, she went into her room and banged the door with unnecessary force.

She showered and washed her hair, then pulled on a pair of white jeans and a black silky sweater with long sleeves and a round neck before piling her still-damp hair into a loose topknot. She put on moisturiser, added a coating of mascara to her lashes, and a pale coral lustre to her lips.

Tidy, she decided, giving herself a critical look. And that was all the effort she was prepared to make.

Reluctantly, she went downstairs, into the drawing room. The lamps had been lit and there was a fire burning in the hearth, dispelling the faint chill of the evening. The whole room seemed to be glowing a welcome, Adrien thought cynically, taking a seat on one of the jewel-colour sofas. And the only discordant note was herself.

Now that the moment of truth had finally come, she could feel tension coiling inside her. She could rationalise what she was doing until the crack of doom, but the fact remained that tonight she had a debt to pay. And the transaction would take place in Chay's bed. In Chay's arms.

And she wasn't sure she could cope. If she could bear the reality of it.

As if, she thought bitterly, she had a choice.

She was grateful for the wine that she'd found cooling on a side table. It was cool and fragrant against her dry throat, but she wasn't going to drink too much of it. That had been the cause of her problems last time, she told herself with conviction, and she couldn't risk another loss of control like that.

While she was getting ready, she'd reached a serious decision. Chay would have the access to her body that he'd paid for, but nothing more. Because her heart and soul belonged to herself alone. That was the only way she could survive. By closing off her mind, by divorcing herself from everything but the physical act.

Endurance, she thought, staring at the restless flames curling round the logs in the dog crate. That was the word to focus on. To cling to.

Mrs Whitley came bustling in, smiling. 'Mr Haddon has returned, madam. He's gone up to change. Perhaps you'd like to take his drink up to him. He has whisky with a little spring water,' she added confidentially.

She paused expectantly, and Adrien, whose lips had started to frame a blistering retort, found herself subsiding, the furious words bitten back.

This, she thought, was how it began. What she had to expect. And there was no point in protesting. It was, after all, only what she'd agreed to.

She swallowed hard. 'Very well,' she said tonelessly, and took the heavy cut-glass tumbler which Mrs Whitley was holding out to her.

'And do you still wish me to serve dinner at half past eight, madam?' The question was delicately put but the implication was clear, and Adrien felt her face burn.

She said coolly, 'Yes, that will be fine, thanks,' and started for the door.

Her legs were like lead as she mounted the stairs and walked along the passage to the master suite at the end.

She would knock, she thought, leave the whisky on his night table, then make herself scarce. And Mrs Whitley could read what she wanted into that.

She tapped gently at the door, and opened it a fraction. The bedroom appeared to be empty, and she could hear the sound of running water coming from the bathroom.

The coast was clear, she thought, treading quietly across the room. She was just about to place the whisky beside the bed when Chay spoke from behind her. 'Good evening.'

Adrien jumped violently, spilling a few drops of spirits on the carpet, then turned warily to face him.

He was standing in the bathroom doorway, towelling his shoulders and upper arms. And, apart from another towel draped casually round his hips, he was naked.

Against the white towel, his skin looked very brown. It was the kind of all-over tan he certainly wouldn't have acquired in Brussels, she thought, biting her lip.

She said huskily, 'You—you startled me.'

'I seem to make a habit of it,' he returned drily, running his fingers through his water-darkened hair. 'And you're quite a surprise yourself. Is that drink for me? How sweet and thoughtful of you.'

'It isn't— I mean, I didn't...' Adrien stumbled to a halt, resentfully aware of the amusement lurking in his grey eyes. 'Mrs Whitley asked me to bring it.'

'Ah,' he said softly. 'But Jean always did have a romantic streak.' There was a note of laughter in his voice, and something else, less easily definable.

He tossed the towel he was using for his hair back into the bathroom and took a step forward. Adrien froze.

He paused, his mouth twisting wryly. He said, 'Adrien,

I'm going to comb my hair. That's all. And it may comfort you to know that I never ravish women on an empty stomach. You're safe until after dinner.'

She said unevenly, 'You bastard—how dare you laugh at me?'

'I was trying to be reassuring—as the sight of me seems to have turned you to stone.' He walked to his dressing table and picked up a comb. 'You'll have to get used to it, Adrien.'

'Used to what?'

'Having me around—with or without my clothes.' He was watching her in the mirror. 'Or have you changed your mind about our bargain?'

She lifted her chin. 'I'm here, aren't I?'

'Ah, yes,' he said. 'But that's not the same thing at all. You've had nearly a week to think again.'

She said shortly, 'I can't afford second thoughts, and you know it.'

'Well, you're honest.' He put the comb down and turned. 'So, bring my drink over here, please—and say hello to me properly.'

Reluctantly, she complied, heart sinking, stomach churning, and mouth as dry as a desert. Chay took the tumbler from her hand and put it down, then let his fingers curl gently round the nape of her neck, drawing her forward.

His skin smelt cool and damp, the fragrance of soap commingling with the sharper essence of some cologne.

He said softly, 'You can fake your orgasm later, darling. For now, just pretend to be glad to see me.' And his mouth took hers.

She stood in the circle of his arms, steeling herself against the gently insidious movement of his lips on hers, her body taut as a bowstring under the skilful glide of his hands.

He lifted his head and stared down at her, the grey eyes

glittering. He said, 'I told you I'd expect my money's worth, Adrien. And so far you haven't earned a penny. So—relax.'

He put up a hand and took the clips from her hair, letting it fall to her shoulders, his fingers teasing the damp, silky strands. Then he took her hands, lifting them to his shoulders.

He said softly, 'Touch me.'

Swallowing, Adrien obeyed, her fingers spreading over the smooth skin, feeling the hard muscularity that lay beneath. A tacit reminder of how helpless she really was. Of how easily he could subdue her if she tried to fight...

Chay kissed her again more deeply, parting her unwilling lips with his and exploring the softness of her mouth with his tongue.

His hands slid down to her hips, pulling her against him, letting her experience the strength and heated power of his arousal.

The thin layers of cloth which separated them were no barrier—no barrier at all, she thought, as her breathing quickened and her lashes swept down to veil her eyes.

When he lifted his head, he was smiling faintly. 'You see,' he said. 'This is not going to be as impossible as you think.'

Adrien stared up at him. She felt strangely dizzy, as if she'd taken some powerful drug.

She said, her voice shaking, 'I hate you.'

He nodded, unperturbed. 'I can live with that. At least you're not claiming to have fallen madly in love with me. Because that could mean serious trouble.

'And leave your hair loose,' he added sharply, as Adrien dived to retrieve her clips from the floor. The look he sent her was sardonic. 'It will give me something to fantasise about while I'm dressing.'

She glared at him. 'Am I free to go now?'

'The choice, as always, is yours, my sweet.' He picked up the tumbler of whisky and lifted it in a mocking toast. 'But if you stay, dinner could be delayed indefinitely. My appetite seems to have changed.' He swallowed some whisky and put the glass down again, his eyes quizzical as his hands moved to discard the towel round his hips.

He said softly, his gaze holding hers. 'Well, Adie, what's it to be?'

She gasped in outrage and whirled round, making for the door. And as she fled, to her chagrin, she heard his laughter following her.

She was still ruffled some twenty minutes later, seated tensely on the edge of one of the sofas, the stem of her wine glass gripped so tightly it was in danger of snapping.

How could he do this? she asked herself despairingly. How was it possible that, just for a fleeting moment—barely more than a second, indeed—she'd been tempted? That she'd actually wondered, to her shame, what it would be like to have that potent male force sheathed inside her...?

And he—Chay Haddon—had evoked this unlooked for sexual curiosity in her. Had deliberately initiated this need to know—and be known.

'Damn him,' she said raggedly under her breath. 'Oh, damn him to hell.'

'I hope I haven't kept you waiting.' Right on cue, he was there, watching her from the doorway.

Adrien stared back, lifting her chin insolently. 'Please don't apologise,' she said. 'It must have been quite a fantasy.'

'The best.' Chay strolled across to the drinks table and replenished his glass. 'Remind me to share it with you some time.' He indicated the bottle of Chardonnay. 'Some more wine?'

She said hurriedly, 'No—thank you.'

He said silkily, 'I'm sure you're wise.'

She raised her eyebrows. 'You want me sober?'

'Not necessarily,' he said. 'But conscious would be a bonus.'

As he walked across the room, Adrien tensed involuntarily, but he made no attempt to join her, choosing instead the sofa on the opposite side of the fireplace.

He moved well, she acknowledged unwillingly, his body lean and graceful. But even as a boy he hadn't been subject to the usual adolescent gaucherie.

Only, they weren't children any longer. And he was a predator with his prey in sight. She had to remember that.

He'd gone for the casual look, too, in blue denim, the shirt open at the neck to reveal the faint shadowing of chest hair that she remembered had felt like springing silk beneath her fingers. The cuffs were turned back negligently over tanned forearms, and his legs in the close-fitting jeans seemed to go on for ever.

She watched him lean back against the cushions, very much at ease, his dark blond hair gleaming like silk in the lamplight. Making himself at home, she thought, igniting anger and resentment inside her and letting it burn slowly, driving out the trembling weakness which the sight of him had induced.

The intruder, she whispered silently. The usurper. Something else she could not afford to forget.

He said softly, 'So you're still here.'

She stared down at her empty glass. 'Did you doubt it?'

'I wasn't totally certain.' A smile played round his mouth. 'That's one of your great charms, Adie. Your ability to surprise me.'

She said curtly, 'I must try to become more predictable.'

'You just did,' he murmured, and she subsided, biting her lip.

There was a silence as he sipped his Scotch and took a long, appraising look round the room. He said, 'The house looks good. Thank you.'

Adrien shrugged. 'It wasn't difficult to achieve.' She paused. 'I have a good memory.'

'If a selective one,' he murmured.

'You seem to have instant recall, too,' she went on doggedly, deliberately ignoring his interjection. 'You've hardly missed a thing. How on earth did you do it?' She gave a small, harsh laugh. 'You must have been stalking Piers for weeks.'

'I didn't have to.' He lifted his glass, studying the amber of the whisky with a kind of detached appreciation. 'I knew what he would do, and the probable markets he would use. After that, it was simple.'

'Easy pickings,' she said stonily. 'Like everything else you've taken from him. He really didn't stand a chance.'

He drank some whisky. 'I didn't exactly hold him at gunpoint.' His tone was unexpectedly mild. 'He chose to sell. And I'm a little surprised to find that you're still defending him.'

'I'm not,' Adrien denied. 'I just don't understand why you should have gone trawling through the salerooms for Angus's furniture. What were you trying to prove?'

'Not a thing. I simply wanted his things back where they belong. I thought if he knew, he'd be pleased.' He paused. 'I thought you'd be glad, too.'

'Pleased that you rescued them? When you abused the roof he put over your head?' Her voice bit. 'When he barred you from his house for thieving?' She shook her head. 'I think it would make him sick to his stomach to know that you're here—pretending to be the master.'

'And is that how you feel, too?'

Across the space that divided them their eyes met and clashed. His gaze was like grey ice, but there was something darker, deeper, that quickened her breath, shivering along her nerve-endings, and Adrien was the first to look away.

She said hoarsely, 'What else?'

'Then that's unfortunate,' he said softly. 'Because I am the master here—be in no doubt of that, Adrien.' He paused, allowing his words to sink in, watching her pupils dilate in confusion as she absorbed them.

'Now,' he continued coldly, 'I've had one hell of a day, and a bastard of a journey, so I really don't need this.'

He flung the remains of the whisky down his throat and got to his feet. 'Shall we go to dinner—or are you planning a hunger strike?'

For a crazy moment she was tempted to do just that. To run. To take refuge in her room and lock the door.

But something told her that he would follow, and that might precipitate a disaster which could haunt her for the rest of her life.

Not in anger, she thought, swallowing convulsively. I—I couldn't bear to be taken in anger.

She stood up, lifting her chin, because she didn't want him to sense the naked panic twisting inside her, and went with him, in silence, to the dining room.

CHAPTER SEVEN

THE CENTRAL leaves had been removed from the big dining table, and candles had been lit to provide a more intimate atmosphere. Mrs Whitley was a determined woman, Adrien thought without amusement. Or perhaps she had her orders…

Chay saw Adrien to her chair, then seated himself opposite.

'Not quite two sword lengths apart,' he observed drily. 'But you should be safe enough.'

Adrien concentrated on shaking out her table napkin. 'Safe,' she thought, was not a word she could ever apply to her present situation.

It's a business transaction, she reminded herself forcibly, adding the mantra she'd been whispering to herself all week. Nothing lasts for ever…

Mrs Whitley had provided a marvellous meal—a home-made country pâté, followed by duck with a dark cherry sauce, and crème brûlée to finish with.

To her surprise, Adrien found she was enjoying the food, and the claret that accompanied it. Ironic, she thought, that her appetite should have chosen this of all days to return.

It wasn't a silent meal, although Chay initiated most of the conversation, talking lightly about his trip to Brussels, and the problems with European bureaucracy. At any other time she'd have been intrigued and animated, leaning forward to ask questions, or expand on a point he'd made.

We could always talk to each other once, she thought with a sudden pang. But that was while I was a child, and didn't know any better. When I trusted him. Before everything changed…

She found herself wondering how she would feel if they had just met for the first time. If she was here with him now simply because she wanted to be, without the past like a shadow at her shoulder.

But she couldn't let herself think like that. It was stupid—and could be dangerous, she reflected with a slight shiver.

'Are you cold?' He didn't miss a thing.

'No—I'm fine.' It was the usual all-purpose lie, and it was a relief when Mrs Whitley appeared to clear the table before Chay could probe any further.

The housekeeper returned briefly, to bring in coffee and armagnac, and then withdrew, wishing them goodnight.

'She's very discreet,' Adrien said, after a pause. 'But I suppose she'd had a lot of practice.'

Chay sighed. 'What do you want me to say?' he asked wearily. 'That I've been celibate all these years? It wouldn't be true.'

'And, naturally, you're the soul of honesty,' she said bitterly.

'But there hasn't been a constant procession of women through my life either,' he went on, as if she hadn't spoken. 'A major part of my time has been taken up by work—getting the company established abroad as well as here.'

'Oh, don't let's forget for a minute what a dazzling success you are.' Her voice was heavy with sarcasm. 'Yet you never seemed particularly ambitious in the old days.'

He shrugged. 'Perhaps I was still deciding what I really wanted.'

'And it just turned out to be Piers's inheritance.'

His smile was cold. 'Piers was only ever interested in disposable assets. Haven't you grasped that yet?'

'He was in trouble, and you dangled a small fortune in front of him. What was he supposed to do?'

'In his place, I wouldn't have sold.' He paused, then added more gently, 'And nor would you, Adrien.'

She found his use of her name disturbing. The way his voice seemed to linger over the syllables sent an odd, unwelcome frisson down her spine.

She looked down at her cup, aware that his eyes were on her, feeling her heart begin to bang unevenly against her ribcage.

He said, 'Shall we take our coffee into the drawing room?'

She touched the tip of her tongue to her dry lips. 'It's fine here—isn't it?'

'You mean with a yard or two of solid oak between us?' He was openly amused. 'Believe me, my sweet, the barricade you're trying to build in that stubborn mind of yours is far more effective.'

She flushed. 'I don't know what you're talking about.'

'Don't lie, Adrien.' Chay leaned forward. There were little silver sparks dancing in his eyes, she noted confusedly, or was it just some trick of the light? 'Right this moment, there's a battle going on between your heart and your body. That's why you're spitting venom at me with every other breath.'

She said very clearly, 'Of course it couldn't be that I just don't find you attractive?'

'In that case,' he said, his voice almost meditative, 'why don't you wear a bra when I'm around?'

She gasped, and her colour deepened fierily. 'How—how dare you? I do as I like.'

'But not all the time.' He slanted a grin at her. 'You were wearing one that first day, but not later—when we went out to dinner. I—er—noticed particularly,' he added, his grin deepening reminiscently. 'And you're not wearing one tonight either. Interesting, don't you think?'

'Only if your mind's in the gutter,' she hit back.

'Why, Adie,' he said gently. 'What a little hypocrite you are.' He picked up his coffee and got to his feet. 'Now, I'm going to sit in my new drawing room and listen to some music. I suggest you go to bed.' He paused. 'In your own room.'

Her lips parted in sheer astonishment as she stared up at him. 'But I thought... I don't understand.'

Chay shrugged. 'What's to understand?' he countered. 'This is your own private war that you're fighting, darling, and although I'm naturally interested in the outcome, I haven't the patience tonight to become personally involved. For which you should be grateful,' he added with grim significance. 'As I said, I've had a bastard of a day, and I'm not turning my bed into a battlefield. So, when the fight's over let me know which won—your mind or your body. Because it matters quite a lot.'

He paused on his way to the door and swung round, his eyes raking her mercilessly. 'And forgive me for not kissing you goodnight, my sweet. I think it's best to keep my distance, or I might forget myself and show you that the top of that table isn't quite the defence against passion that you seem to think. Catch my drift?'

He nodded to her with a kind of remote courtesy, and left, closing the door behind him quietly but very definitely.

Leaving her sitting there. Staring after him. Trying to make sense of what had just happened.

There were a number of emotions struggling for dominance inside her, but disbelief was ahead on points.

All evening he'd been making love to her with his eyes, his voice, his smile. She'd assumed he'd be offering a more physical expression before long, and had been gearing herself up for passive resistance. And now—nothing.

So, what sort of game was he playing?

She shouldn't ask questions, she thought, as she pinched out the candles and walked slowly to the door in her turn. She should just be thankful. But gratitude didn't seem to feature too strongly in her inner turmoil.

She could hear music from the drawing room as she crossed the hall. Rachmaninov, she recognised, passionate and plangent. Not the cool jazz she'd expected.

But let's face it, Adie, she told herself. You don't know what to expect any more. And she went upstairs to her room. Alone.

That night she dreamed about the treehouse again. The same dream as always, where she knelt on rough boards, peering, terrified, over the edge, searching for a way down. But the ground, hundreds of feet below, was shrouded in clouds and mist, and she knew she was seeking a safety— a reassurance—that no longer existed. Knew, too, that it wasn't simply the isolation or distance from the ground that was scaring her...

She could hear herself crying, but barely recognised her own voice. There were other voices too, raised in anger, but she couldn't catch the words as a rising wind took the little house and shook it, sending it tumbling down into crumpled matchwood. And her with it.

Adrien awoke with a start, to find tears on her face. She sat up shakily and looked at her alarm clock, and saw it had just gone one a.m.

She drank some water from the carafe on her night table, then got out of bed, wandering across to the window seat.

Tucking her feet under her, she leaned her forehead against the cool pane and stared sightlessly into the darkness.

It was time, she thought, to lay some ghosts to rest. To force herself to remember exactly what had happened all those years ago and then wipe it from her mind. If she could.

Young as she'd been, she'd sensed instantly the hostility between Chay and Piers from the first day the glamorous newcomer had spent at the Grange, and had been distressed by it. Chay had been her friend, but Piers was exciting, almost alien, with his expensive clothes and easy charm.

'So this is the demon chess-player,' he greeted her at their first meeting. 'My uncle's told me all about you. I shall have to watch my step.'

And when they played, and she beat him, he praised her extravagantly, making her glow. Each time she went to the Grange after that he sought her out, behaving as if she was the one person he wanted to see.

She tried her best to bring the two boys together. She wanted them to like each other so that she wouldn't feel disloyal when Piers monopolised her company, as he undoubtedly did. But Chay stayed aloof.

And it wasn't Piers's fault. He was clearly interested in Chay, continually asking questions about him. And, eventually, Adrien succumbed to his pressure and showed him the treehouse.

She knew at once it was a mistake. She stood, awkward and upset, while Piers prowled round, examining everything with contemptuous eyes, rifling through the precious biscuit tin, tossing the neat pile of sketches on to the plank floor.

'Field glasses.' He snatched them up. 'Good ones too. Where did he pinch these from?'

'Mr Stretton gave them to him.' Adrien looked apprehensively at the entrance. 'Let's go down again, please. Chay will be angry if he finds us here. It's his special place.'

'Chay has no right to any place at all.' There was a note in his voice that scared her. 'He's nothing—just the housekeeper's son.' He looked down at the field glasses. 'As for these…' His arm went back, and he hurled them into the nearby trees. She heard a crash and a tinkle as they landed.

She said with a little wail, 'You've broken them,' and began to scramble down. But when she reached the ground Chay was waiting, his face like stone and his eyes bitter with anger and condemnation as he looked at Adrien.

She tried to say something, but he cut her short. 'Go back to the house, Adie. Go now.'

Tears streaming down her face, she ran. Behind her, she could hear angry voices, then the violent sound of a scuffle. As she came out of the trees she saw her father standing with Angus Stretton by the gateway to the kitchen garden, clearly looking for her. She reached them breathlessly.

'Chay and Piers are fighting,' she gasped through her tears. 'Oh, make them stop—please.'

Mr Stretton said grimly, 'I'll deal with it,' and broke into a run.

'We'd better go home,' her father said, trying to hustle her gently away, but she resisted.

'No, Daddy, please. I want to see Chay. I want to see he's not hurt.'

She watched them come down from the trees, with Angus Stretton bringing up the rear.

Piers, looking thunderous, had a split lip and a torn shirt, while Chay, staring in front of him, his face set, had the beginnings of a black eye.

Adrien twisted free of her father's restraining hand and ran up to him. 'Chay.' Her voice was urgent. 'Chay, I'm sorry. I didn't mean it to happen—any of it.'

He didn't look at her, and his voice was barely more than a whisper. 'Go away from me, Adie, and keep away. I'm warning you.'

But she had to see him, she thought as she lay in bed

that night. She had to talk to him properly and explain. Tell him how sorry she was that their secret place was spoiled.

The next morning she told her mother she was going to play with a schoolfriend, who lived at the other end of the village, and set off on her bike, taking the back road to the Grange instead.

She left her bike in a deserted corner of the rear yard and set off to the wood, expecting to find Chay already there, clearing up.

By the time she reached the tree the sky had darkened, and misty rain was falling. Usually he helped her to climb up, but this time there was no answer when she called, so she had to struggle up as best she could, her feet slipping on the damp rungs.

Chay had already been there, she saw with disappointment, because all his things had gone. The little structure looked deserted and forlorn. All that remained was one sketch, torn in half and lying face-down on the floor.

When Adrien picked it up she realised it was a drawing of herself, lying on her tummy with her chin propped in her hands. She hadn't even known he was sketching her, and now he didn't want it any more, she thought desolately.

She was standing staring at it, tears pricking at the backs of her eyes, when she heard a scraping noise from down below. Puzzled, she went to the edge and peeped down cautiously, only to see the ladder lying on the ground and someone walking away. A figure in a grey waterproof hooded coat as familiar to her as her own green anorak.

Bewildered, and frightened, she shouted to him. 'Chay— I can't get down. Come back—oh, please come back.'

But he didn't even look round. Just kept going until he was lost to view among the trees. And although she went on calling until her voice was hoarse, her only answer was silence.

When Piers found her at last, hours later, Chay was with

him, still wearing that betraying grey jacket, and somehow that was the worst thing of all.

She screamed at him, 'You did this! I saw you! I hate you!' And she picked up the stone and threw it at him.

She saw the blood on his cheek, and the grey eyes turn to chips of ice. And realised she had lost her friend for ever.

Adrien came back, shivering, to the present, to find that her arms were wrapped protectively round her body. Each memory, it seemed, still had claws to tear her apart.

How could he do that? she asked herself stormily. I was a thoughtless child. I didn't deserve that. He didn't care that I was frightened. Didn't think that I could have fallen and hurt myself badly—or even been killed.

She'd been taken home and fussed over, given a hot bath and warm milk, and been tucked into bed. But she hadn't been able to sleep, and she'd got up and gone to her parents' room. The door had been ajar, and she'd heard them talking in low voices.

'The boy's dangerous,' her father had been saying. 'Angus has always been afraid of something like this.'

She hadn't been able to hear her mother's response, only her father's incisive, 'Oh, he'll be sent away, of course. There's no alternative.'

And the next day Chay had been gone from the Grange. She'd told herself she was glad. That she never wanted to see him again.

But he'd come back, of course, bringing different trouble with him.

And now he was here to stay, and more dangerous than ever. Because she was in his power, trapped again, with no means of escape apart from the terms he himself had offered.

Terms she'd accepted, and now had to fulfil. Before it

was too late, and his patience was exhausted. Or his transient desire for her passed…

She slid down from the seat, her face fixed and set. Nothing could change the past, but she needed to make sure her future was secure. Too much depended on the deal she'd made with Chay, and now she had to keep her side of it.

The peignoir she'd bought for her honeymoon was in the wardrobe, swathed in tissue. Without giving herself time to think again, Adrien pulled her cotton nightshirt over her head and dropped it on the floor. The gossamer ivory peignoir spilled into her hands for a long moment.

So fragile, she thought. So transparent. Wearing it, a woman would have no defences. Seeing it, a man would have no doubts.

Swallowing, she put it on, tying the ribbons that fastened it at throat and waist.

The silk whispered round her as she left her room and went silently down the corridor.

He would probably be asleep, she thought, with self-derision. And her grand gesture of capitulation would be totally wasted.

But he was awake, propped up on one elbow and reading. The dark green coverlet had been pushed back, and a sheet just covered the curve of his lean hip. Beneath it he was clearly naked, and it occurred to her that she'd never seen a naked man before. Apart from pictures, she amended dizzily, and no amount of paint or film could ever have prepared her for the warm, living reality.

She thought she hadn't made a sound, but his head lifted instantly, sharply, and he stared at her, marking the place in his book with a finger.

He said softly, 'Insomnia would seem to be catching.'

'Yes.' Her voice was husky. She felt heat rise in her face, flood through her body under the sensuous intensity of his gaze.

'The hot drinks are in the kitchen,' he said after a pause. 'I don't use sleeping pills. So, what can I do for you, Adrien?' It sounded like a civil question. The courteous host enquiring after the well-being of a guest. Only she knew differently...

'Chay.' Her voice broke huskily. 'Don't make this more difficult than it has to be.'

He leaned back against the pillows, watching her from under lowered lids. 'The problem's all in your mind, Adrien. It always has been. Ever since you decided I was your enemy.'

'I was a child,' she said. 'A little girl.'

'Not you, my pet. You were a woman the moment you were born. I watched you grow up—remember?' He touched a hand mockingly to his cheek. 'It scarred me for life.'

'You're not the only one with scars,' she said. 'Those hours I spent in the treehouse still give me nightmares. I— I had one earlier tonight.'

'If you've come here to be comforted,' he said, with a touch of harshness, 'think again.'

She said steadily. 'You know why I'm here.'

His smile mocked faintly. 'You look like a bride on her wedding night. But appearances can be deceptive.'

Her throat tightened. 'That cuts both ways. I don't know who you are any more. Or what you are.'

He shrugged a tanned shoulder. 'I'm a man whose money you need. I thought we'd established that.'

He closed his book and put it on the night table with a certain finality, then took one of the pillows from behind him and tossed it on to the bed at his side. Turned back the edge of the sheet in invitation.

He said softly, 'Well, make your move, darling. I'm all attention.'

She paused helplessly. 'Will you—turn off the lamp—please?'

'No,' he said. 'I want to look at you. You can't walk in here wearing something as revealing as that exquisite piece of nonsense then play the modesty card. So take it off, my lovely one, and walk towards me. Slowly.'

'You don't understand.' She hesitated, her hand on the ribbon at her throat. 'I've never—I mean, I'm not into casual sex.'

'Who said this was going to be casual?' The grey eyes seemed to burn into hers. 'Now come here, or do I have to fetch you?'

She'd never been naked in front of a man before either, she thought as she loosened the ribbons. And she'd been crazy to think she could stay detached—treat this as some routine task.

She wanted it to be dark, so that she didn't have to see the stark hunger in his face. She wanted silence, so she couldn't hear the sudden harsh breath he drew as she let the peignoir fall from her shoulders. She wanted it finished, so that she would never feel so helpless and so—stupid again.

She was aware of every hammering pulse-beat in her body. Could feel the dark race of her own blood as she walked to the bed. There was an iron bar constricting her chest—or was that just because she was holding her breath?

When she reached the bed, she sank down on to it, her hands gripping the edge of the mattress. She bent her head, letting her hair fall forward and shield her flushed face. And waited.

She thought she heard him sigh, then sensed movement and realised that he was kneeling behind her. She tensed, but his fingers were gentle, brushing her hair from her neck, exposing the sensitive nape to the warmth of his lips. She moved restively, surprised—disturbed—at the shiver of reaction that feathered through her, and felt his hands close on her shoulders, stilling her.

His mouth moved slowly downward, covering the taut skin over her shoulderblades, then beginning to trace, softly and sensuously, the long, delicate line of her spine.

Adrien released her pent-up breath in a gasp that was only part shock, her back arching in response to his caress. He pulled her back towards him so that she was leaning against him, the heat of his body penetrating her frozen inner core of panic and shame, dissolving it slowly away.

His arms encircled her, his hands sliding down to enjoy the involuntary thrust of her breasts, the long fingers moulding their softness while the palms moved in aching provocation against her hardening nipples.

Her head fell back on his shoulder, allowing him to kiss her throat, and she felt the hot flicker of his tongue in the whorls of her ear.

She was trembling in earnest now, but not with fear, consumed by a maelstrom of other far more unwelcome emotions. Her throat muscles were quivering under the caress of his mouth. Her breasts were swelling, blossoming with excitement under the subtle play of his fingers, and this wasn't how she'd planned it at all.

She hadn't bargained for her own curiosity, she thought dazedly. For the frustrations of her relationship with Piers. It was those dreams, those longings which had awoken her. It had to be.

Because it couldn't be the hands and lips of the man who was holding her. Who was turning her gently in his embrace, lowering her to the pillow so that she was lying beside him—beneath him—his nakedness grazing hers. Whose mouth was seeking hers, caressing her lips, then coaxing her lips apart to accept the heated silk of his tongue.

His hands clasped hers, raising them above her head so

that he could feast on the satin skin of her underarms, while his leg slid across, covering both of hers, pinning her to the bed, so that she could not have moved even if she'd wanted to.

Making her realise, to her shame, that it was the last thing she wanted.

Then he began to kiss her breasts, adoring their scented roundness, letting his lips tug softly at her nipples, sending shafts of sensation racing like tiny flames through her restless body.

She found she was lifting herself towards him, mutely begging for the sweet agony of his tongue against the rosy engorged peaks.

Chay sighed again, this time with soft satisfaction, his breath fanning her heated skin as he pleasured her.

He'd released her hands, and now she felt the lingering whisper of his fingers on her body, discovering every curve and angle on their slow downward path.

His hands moulded her hipbone, then slid inward to the soft pulsating hollow, where he paused.

She was caught, held tantalisingly on some unimagined brink. She tried to say, No, but all that emerged was a tiny sound like a whimper, while that too was stifled by his kiss.

His hand was at the junction of her thighs, stroking the silky triangle of hair, silently teasing her into allowing him the more intimate access he wanted. And she could feel her body melting, the responding rush of scalding heat that welcomed the first devastating glide of his fingers.

The breath came sobbing from her lungs as his exploration of her deepened, creating a need—a reaction—that she could not control. Her body was opening for him, demanding him, so that when he moved across her—over her—his hands lifting her hips to meet the burning force of his possession, denial was impossible.

It was so right, so totally imperative, that Adrien had no

inkling that her inexperienced flesh might resist this initial invasion. The sudden unexpected pain jolted her into a small shocked cry, her eyes dilating as she tried, too late, to push him away from her.

He said, 'Adrien?' his voice harsh and urgent, then the bewilderment in his face changed to a kind of horrified comprehension.

He groaned her name again, but this time it was a plea for forgiveness as his driven body, establishing its ownership beyond question or control, was impelled towards the point of no return.

She closed her eyes, pressing a clenched fist against her mouth as, at last, she felt the frenzied spasms tearing him apart, and heard him cry out in a kind of agony.

Then it was over, his body sinking against hers in heavy quietude, the hoarseness of his breathing slowing to normality.

She lay, unmoving, unable to differentiate between the ache of her wrenched body and the sharper pain of disappointment twisting inside her, and a single tear squeezed from under her closed lid and burned its way down her cheek.

She saw him wince, then silently take the corner of the sheet and wipe the tear away. Then he lifted himself away from her, putting space between them on the bed.

There was a long pause, then he said very quietly, 'Why didn't you tell me, Adie?'

'I didn't think you'd know.' She bit her lip. 'And I thought it wouldn't matter.'

'But you're wrong,' he said. 'Because it makes one hell of a difference, and in all kinds of ways.'

'I—I don't see how.' She drew a quick, shaky breath. 'This was what we agreed.'

His mouth tightened. 'I could at least have made it— easier for you.' There was another silence, then he said slowly, 'I assumed, you see, that you'd slept with Mendoza.'

'He said we'd wait.' Her voice trembled. 'He said he wanted a white wedding—and a wedding night that meant something.'

He nodded, his face like a stone. 'And that's what you should have had, Adie.' He sighed harshly. 'Oh, God, what a bloody mess.'

She turned her head on the pillow and looked at him. He was so careful, she thought, not to touch her. Yet she needed to be touched. Held. Comforted—and loved...

Dear God. What am I saying? What am I thinking?

She kept her voice expressionless. 'He didn't mean it. He just wanted someone to work on the house for him and keep costs down. He didn't love me—and he didn't want to make love to me either. I see that now.'

'Then we're both marginally wiser than we were an hour ago.' Chay flung off the tangled sheet and swung himself off the bed, causing Adrien to look away hastily. Nothing was ever going to erase the memory of his body, naked against hers, but she didn't need any visual reminders to go with it.

He disappeared into the bathroom, reappearing a few minutes later tying the belt of a white towelling robe.

He said, 'I'm running you a bath. How badly did I hurt you?'

She tried to smile. 'I'll live.' She paused, her eyes searching his face. 'Chay—it had to happen some time. It's—not important.'

'There we disagree.' He bent and picked up the crumpled peignoir. 'I was right when I said you looked like a bride.' The grey eyes were chilly. 'I presume you bought this for Piers?'

'Yes.' Adrien lifted her chin. 'But I wore it for you.'

'Strange.' His mouth twisted. 'I only remember you taking it off. I'll go and check your bath.'

'I don't need a bath,' she said. 'But I'd really like to sleep for a while.'

'If that's what you want.' He put the peignoir down on the bed beside her. 'You'd better put this on.'

'To sleep in?' She was bewildered.

'No,' he said. 'To wear back to your own room.'

She stared at him, her heart beating a little faster as she huddled the peignoir around her. 'You—you don't want me to stay here?'

His smile was wintry. 'I think enough damage has been done already—don't you? Besides, virgin sacrifices have never been to my taste.' He tied the ribbons for her, his fingers impersonal, almost brisk. 'So it's best if you leave the Grange tomorrow.'

She sat very still, staring up at him. 'But—but Chay…' Her voice trembled into silence as she tried to find the right words.

His brows lifted. 'You're concerned you won't be paid if I go back on our deal?'

No, she thought blankly, that hadn't even entered her mind. Her attempt at protest had been on far more complex grounds, which she was still struggling to understand. Which she was frightened to face.

She lifted her chin. 'Of course,' she said. 'What else?'

'Well, don't worry, darling.' His tone was almost casual. 'You'll get your money.'

If he'd slapped her face she couldn't have felt more hurt, or more humiliated. She'd expected reassurance, and instead she was faced with rejection.

Piers hadn't wanted her, she thought numbly. And now Chay was turning her away too. And suddenly—for some unfathomable reason—she felt as if she was dying inside.

Dear God, she thought, swallowing. What's happening to me?

But she couldn't think about that now. Because the important thing—indeed, the only thing—was to get out of this room somehow, with what little remained of her pride. Before she said something—made some plea—that she would regret bitterly later. Or even broke down and cried like a baby.

He mustn't know how I feel, she thought. He must never find out.

From some hidden store of courage she conjured up a smile, and she rose to her feet and straightened her shoulders.

'Thank you,' she said, lightly. 'Somehow that makes it all—almost—worthwhile.'

And she walked to the door and went out, without looking back.

CHAPTER EIGHT

ADRIEN walked slowly and steadily to her room, but once the door was closed behind her she collapsed against it, gasping for breath as if she'd just run a marathon.

The pressure of the past week had got to her at last, and she'd gone slightly crazy. That was the only feasible explanation.

She could rationalise until she was blue in the face. She could come up with a whole range of excuses. But the truth was she'd gone to Chay tonight because she'd wanted him. And not just with her body, she admitted bleakly. Her heart and mind had surrendered too.

Even reliving the childhood trauma he'd inflicted on her hadn't deflected her even for a minute.

I was never able to remember it before, she thought wonderingly. Not in its entirety. I didn't want to examine the pain he'd caused too closely.

So why did I choose to do it—tonight of all nights? Why did I torture myself all over again? It makes no sense.

Yet even with all those memories—all that cause to hate him—she'd gone to him. Offered herself and been taken.

And then sent away.

And that, she thought, was the ultimate act of cruelty. None of the other things he'd done to her even came close.

It was pointless to remind herself that she was now free to leave. That, in essence, she'd beaten him. Because if this was victory, she never wanted to face defeat.

She stripped off the peignoir and threw it, rolled into a ball, to the back of the wardrobe. She never wanted to see it again. Tomorrow it would go in the firebox of the Aga.

Her body felt alien. She was wearing the scent of his skin, and if she was ever to close her eyes in peace again she had to rid herself of it. Along with some even more potent memories.

She'd allowed herself to be haunted by the past for far too long already. Now she would have the remembrance of Chay's hands touching her, the heat of his mouth on her eager flesh, to colour her dreams and twist her waking hours into helpless longing.

She hadn't known it was possible to want someone so badly, she realised. And telling herself that she was just a chronic case of sexual frustration, that any man would have done, was simply self-deception.

Because Chay had always been part of her life. He'd been her friend, her enemy, and, tonight, her lover.

It was as if every moment in her existence had been preparing her—leading her up to this. And now it was over.

She stood under the shower, using a body scrub until every inch of her tingled. She towelled herself dry, then put on the old jade bathrobe. Comfort-dressing, she thought, her mouth twisting.

She felt too restless to go to bed, and curled up in the armchair, tucking her feet under her, breathing in the faint drift of fragrance from the roses. Trying to calm herself. To make some kind of plan.

Her future was settled, she reminded herself. She had her home. The business was safe now, and they could continue to build on their success. And that was what she'd wanted to achieve.

But she'd had to pay an agonising price for her new-found security.

And now she had to consider her future peace of mind, with Chay living almost on her doorstep.

Avoiding the Grange physically shouldn't be too diffi-cult, she thought determinedly. True, it stood on the main road out of the village, but there were other routes—slight detours—which she could take, especially at weekends when Chay would be there.

That wasn't the problem.

Somehow she had to accept it was no longer part of her life. That everything that had happened to her under its roof, and the man who was responsible for it, belonged to the past.

And could not be allowed to matter.

Or she would spend her life thinking of all the 'might have beens'. Which would be intolerable. Unbearable.

She repeated, 'Unbearable,' and only realised she'd spoken aloud when she heard the note of utter desolation in her own voice.

She eventually fell asleep towards dawn, and woke, cold and cramped, to the splash of rain against the window.

My God, she thought, catching sight of her little carriage clock. It's nearly ten o'clock.

She dressed hastily, flinging on a black knee-length skirt and a matching long-sleeved blouse, and ran downstairs.

'I'm sorry I'm so late,' she apologised, encountering Mrs Whitley in the hall.

'Mr Haddon said you were to have your sleep out, madam.' Mrs Whitley's eyes were shrewd, assessing Adrien's pale face and heavy eyes. 'What may I get you for breakfast?'

'I—I'm not hungry. Just some coffee, please.' Adrien hesitated. 'Where is Mr Haddon?'

'He went out first thing, madam. And he didn't say when he'd be back.' Mrs Whitley sounded disapproving. 'I'll bring your coffee to the dining room.'

When she did so, Adrien wasn't surprised to find it accompanied by a plate of creamy scrambled eggs and some crisp toast, which she ate obediently because it was marginally less trouble than arguing.

When she'd finished, she got up from the table and wandered to the window, standing irresolute as she watched the driving rain.

'Such a nasty day,' said Mrs Whitley, bustling in to clear the table. 'I hope the weather improves next weekend for Mr Haddon's visitors.'

'He's expecting guests?' Adrien turned, surprised.

'Oh, yes, madam. Some business acquaintances, I understand. It's been planned for some time. When Mr Haddon gives you the final list, we can decide on bedrooms and menus.' She nodded happily, as if she'd just bestowed a longed-for treat, and disappeared.

I should have told her, Adrien thought with a sigh, returning to her contemplation of the rain. I should have warned her that I won't be here.

Not that it really mattered, of course, she added drearily. Mrs Whitley could cope with a whole houseful of people with one hand tied behind her back.

And I, she thought, squaring her shoulders, I shall be living my own life again. And, as it can't start soon enough, I'll begin my packing right now.

She'd no idea what she was going to say to Zelda, of course, she mused as she went towards the stairs. Some carefully edited approximation of the truth, perhaps. After which the subject would be taboo.

A loud peal from the front doorbell halted her in her tracks. She called, 'It's all right, Mrs Whitley. I'll get it.'

There was a furniture lorry parked on the drive, and a man in waterproofs beaming at her. 'Nice to see you, Miss Lander. I've brought your bed.'

For a moment she stared at him uncomprehendingly, then realisation hit her like a brick.

'Oh, God,' she said. 'The four-poster. I—I'd forgotten all about it.'

That was what had been nagging at her all week, she thought. The bed she'd bought all those weeks ago for Piers and herself. Which Fred Derwent had now restored and was now trying to deliver. Which she'd forgotten to cancel.

She forced a smile. 'Fred—I should have contacted you. There's been a change of plan, I'm afraid. The Grange has been sold, and the new owner doesn't want a four-poster bed, so I'd like you to sell it for me—in your showroom.'

Fred's ruddy face drooped. 'Well, that's a pity. It's a fine bed, and I've made a good job of it, if I do say so myself. Is the gentleman sure he doesn't want it?'

'Absolutely certain.' She looked at him beseechingly. 'Fred, you'll have no trouble selling it—'

'Selling what?' Chay's voice interrupted brusquely. He'd arrived unnoticed from round the corner of the house, and was standing on the gravel, hands thrust into the pockets of his trench coat.

Fred Derwent turned to him eagerly. 'A beautiful four-poster bed, sir. A genuine antique that Miss Lander found and meant for this house. For the master bedroom, I understand. And if you're the new master that makes it yours, I reckon,' he added with a chuckle.

Chay's eyes rested dispassionately on Adrien, framed in the doorway, her face flushed, her eyes wide with trouble.

There was a pause, then he said, 'Of course. Will you bring it in, please? Perhaps your men could move the existing bed up to the attics?'

'Glad to, sir,' Fred said heartily. 'You've made the right decision.'

Chay's smile did not reach his eyes. 'I'll take your word for it Mr—er—Derwent,' he added, glancing at the side of the lorry. 'Now, let's get out of this rain. I'll ask my housekeeper to make us all some coffee.'

As he walked past Adrien her hand closed on his arm, halting him. Mr Derwent had returned to his lorry to superintend the unloading, and there was no one to overhear as she said quietly, urgently, 'Chay, you don't want it. You can't...'

His brows lifted. 'Why not? Because you planned to consummate your passion for Piers in it?' He shook his head, almost scornfully. 'That won't disturb my dreams, Adrien.'

Her hand dropped to her side. 'Then there's nothing more to be said.'

'Now there I disagree.' His tone was cool and brisk. 'Come to the library in fifteen minutes, will you? And tell Jean about the coffee, please. I'm going to change out of these wet things.'

It was the voice of a man who was used to being obeyed giving orders to a junior employee, Adrien realised furiously, finding herself trailing off obediently in search of Mrs Whitley. Not someone who'd held her naked in passion the previous night.

Apparently he was even readier to forget the whole disastrous episode than she was herself.

Well, that's good, she thought defiantly. Excellent, in fact.

She supposed he wanted to give her some kind of formal notice, or to finalise any outstanding payment arrangements.

Well, that was all right too. If she tried she could be out of the Grange before lunch.

She spoke to Mrs Whitley, then went up to her room and began dragging things out of the wardrobe and tossing them into her case, closing her ears to the sounds, at the other end of the corridor, of a four-poster bed being brought upstairs and assembled.

When fifteen minutes had elapsed, she went down to the library and knocked at the door.

Chay's 'Come in' held a note of weary exasperation.

He was seated behind Angus Stretton's big desk, scanning through the morning's mail delivery, and as he looked up Adrien checked, her hand going to her throat.

The firm mouth tightened. 'Good God, Adie, I can't have startled you this time,' he rasped. 'You knew I was here.'

'I'm sorry.' She steadied herself. 'It's just—seeing you there, where Angus always sat. For a moment I felt as if I were seeing a ghost.'

He glanced back at the letter he was reading. 'I didn't know the Grange was supposed to be haunted.' He sounded coolly indifferent.

'It's not,' she said. 'And that's not what I meant...'

'Ah, yes,' he said. 'I have no real right to be in this house, or at this desk, and if there was any justice I'd be serving a life sentence without remission for traumatising your childhood and stealing from you on your eighteenth birthday.' He delivered the words with stinging contempt. 'Isn't that the way it goes?'

She bit her lip. 'Believe it or not, I didn't mean that either. I—I came to tell you that I'm ready to leave within the hour. If that's all right.'

He put the letter he was holding down on the desk, crumpling the envelope and tossing it into the waste basket. Then he looked at her, the grey eyes expressionless.

He said, 'Take a seat, Adie. I think we need to talk.'

She remained standing. 'Everything necessary was said last night. You said I should leave.'

'And now I'm asking you to work a month's notice.'

'I'm sorry,' she said. 'I'm afraid the terms of employment are unacceptable.'

'I suppose that's a reference to last night's sexual fiasco,' he said softly. 'However, as I've already indicated, I can safely promise there'll be no repetition of that.'

He paused. Then, 'I think Jean told you I'm having people to stay next weekend. These are men I do business with, and their wives. I need a lady of my own to meet them, and act as my hostess. I'd like you to do this for me.'

'Give me one good reason why I should.'

He said gently, 'I could mention thousands. But I'd like to think you were generous enough to help me out here.'

'Make it a week's notice,' she said. 'And I'll consider it.'

Chay shook his head. 'It has to be a month. That's not negotiable.'

'But why? I want to get on with my life.'

'And I want to ensure that you can.' He paused again. 'Tell me, Adie, are you on the Pill?'

Her brows snapped together. 'Of course not—' she began, then halted, her lips parted in sheer consternation as she met his sardonic gaze. She said, 'No—it's not possible. It can't be…'

Suddenly she needed to sit down. She groped for the chair he'd indicated and sank on to it.

Chay shrugged. 'We had unprotected sex, Adrien. Again, I hadn't bargained for your extreme state of innocence,' he added drily. 'I thought if you were sleeping with Mendoza, you'd be geared up accordingly.'

'How—dare you?'

His mouth twisted. 'It was an honest mistake, Adie. I only wish you'd been equally candid.' He allowed her to digest that for a second, then went on, 'But, as you can see, I have good reason for keeping you here until I can be sure I haven't made you pregnant.'

'If I am,' she said, 'it'll be my problem, and I'll deal with it.'

'No,' he said. 'It concerns me too, so cool the display of fighting spirit.' He sent her a mocking glance. 'I know you have red hair, Adrien. You don't need to keep demonstrating the fact.'

She glared at him. 'My hair is auburn,' she began, and then realised she'd fallen right into his trap. Remembered with heart-stopping clarity how he'd used to call her 'Ginger' and 'Carrots' all those years before, winding her up until she launched herself at him in fury.

She saw his mouth soften into a grin of pure appreciation, and found, astonished, that she was smiling reluctantly in response.

She said, 'You brute.'

'Well, that's almost a term of endearment compared with some of the names you've called me recently.' He leaned back in his chair, watching her from under his lids. 'So— are you going to stay, Adie? Naturally, I don't want to pressure you...'

'But you will if you have to,' she supplied bitterly.

'Perhaps,' he said. 'But I'd rather you agreed of your own accord. Is it really so much to ask?'

More than you can ever know. The thought swam into her mind, and was instantly banished.

She looked down at her tightly clasped hands. 'I—suppose not. And, anyway, you'll only be around at weekends.'

Oh, God, she thought immediately. Why did I say that?

Glancing apprehensively at Chay, she saw his face harden.

'I shall be here,' he said, his voice biting, 'just as often as the mood takes me. This is now my home, and I'm not staying away to spare your feelings, Adrien. However, I'll take your response as grudging consent.'

He paused. 'After all, I now have an extra bill to pay— for the bed you so conveniently forgot about.'

She said in a stifled voice, 'You didn't have to keep it. I was quite prepared to send it back.'

'You were positively eager to do so.' His mouth curled. 'Poor Adrien. Did it revive too many unhappy memories?'

'It didn't revive any memories at all,' she said. 'As you know.'

Again, she wished the last words unsaid as soon as she'd spoken, but he only nodded.

He got to his feet and walked round the desk, standing looking down at her, his expression unreadable.

He said quietly, 'Are you all right, Adie?'

Colour warmed her face. 'I'm fine,' she said quickly. 'Now, can we forget about it, please?'

His mouth twisted without humour. 'You can, I'm sure. I shan't find it quite so easy.'

He allowed the words to die into a tingling silence, then reached behind him and picked up a sheet of paper from the desk. 'Is this your work?'

'Yes,' Adrien said, swallowing, glad to move to the impersonal. 'It's something I was working on yesterday—a plan for the kitchen garden. I shouldn't have left it around.'

'It's good,' he said. 'When the contractors arrive next week, I'd like you to show it to them—get them to work on it.'

'The kitchen garden's a long-term project,' Adrien said hastily, getting to her feet. 'I—I really shouldn't get involved.'

He gave her a swift, wry smile. 'But you already are involved, Adrien,' he said softly. 'You know it, and so do I.' He went back to his chair and picked up another envelope. 'I'll see you at lunch,' he added casually.

Adrien closed the library door behind her and took a deep breath. It seemed, in spite of everything, she'd committed herself to another month under Chay's roof. Four weeks, she thought. Hardly a lifetime. Unless…

For a moment her hand strayed tentatively to her abdomen.

No, she told herself with determination. It's not true. *It can't be true.*

But, at the same time, she wouldn't have a quiet moment until she finally learned the truth. And maybe not then, she reminded herself painfully, and went slowly back upstairs to take her clothes out of the case.

As she reached the head of the stairs, Fred Derwent hailed her cheerfully. 'Your bed looks wonderful, Miss Lander. This room really sets it off.'

'Oh—good.' Adrien gave him a fleeting smile and turned towards her own room, but he was not to be gainsaid.

'Come and have a look,' he urged.

Reluctantly, she walked to Chay's bedroom doorway and peeped in. Mrs Whitley was there, busying herself with sheets and pillowcases.

'Beautiful, isn't it?' She ran an approving hand over one of the carved posts. 'What it really needs, of course, is curtains, and one of those canopy things.'

'They'll be coming,' Mr Derwent assured her. 'Miss Lander's partner was making them special. Isn't that right?'

Aware of their expectant glances, Adrien nodded feebly.

'When will they be ready?' Mrs Whitley asked eagerly.

'They—they're already finished,' Adrien admitted. 'I—could go and fetch them.'

'That would be wonderful.' Mrs Whitley beamed. 'The exact finishing touch.'

'Then I'll go now.' Adrien glanced at her watch. 'Would you tell Mr Haddon I won't be here for lunch, please?'

The rain had stopped and a watery sun had broken through the clouds when she arrived at the cottage.

She'd been gone for less than twenty-four hours, but already the cottage had an oddly disused air about it.

Only a month, Adrien comforted herself. And then it will belong to me again. And I'll come over as often as possible. Put fresh flowers around. Open the windows.

She collected her post, listed the messages on the an-

swering machine, and made herself some coffee to drink
with the ham roll she'd bought at the village shop.

Then she locked up, and walked across the courtyard to
Zelda's flat.

Zelda opened the door to her knock. 'Hi.' Her voice was
surprised. 'I didn't expect to see you today.'

Adrien smiled constrainedly. 'I thought I'd come and
collect the curtains and canopy that you made for the four-
poster bed. It—arrived today.'

Zelda stared at her. 'Didn't you cancel it?'

Adrien bit her lip. 'I forgot.'

Zelda's face broke into a grin. 'I think that's what they
call a Freudian slip.'

'Nothing of the kind,' Adrien said with a faint snap. 'I
just had other things on my mind. Now, may I have the
keys to the workroom, please?'

Zelda went with her, and helped her load the heavy bun-
dles of fabric into the Jeep.

She said, frowningly, 'Are you all right?'

'Fine. Never better,' Adrien lied. She nodded. 'It's all
going really well.'

'Really?' Zelda gave her a measuring look. 'Why don't
I come back with you and help you hang these things? You
know how you are with ladders.'

'Not any more,' Adrien said briskly. 'I've put all that
nonsense behind me now.'

'Then let me come for moral support.'

Adrien climbed into the Jeep. 'Isn't this the day Smudge
gets his puppy?'

'That could wait till tomorrow.'

Adrien shook her head. 'No,' she said. 'He's waited quite
long enough. I'll be over to see you all very soon.'

'One day,' Zelda said grimly, 'I expect you to tell me
exactly what's going on.'

I wish I knew myself, Adrien thought, as she put the Jeep in gear and drove off with a cheerful wave.

The Grange seemed deserted when she got back. It took several trips to take the bulky material up to Chay's room, and then she had to search the outbuildings for a pair of suitable steps.

Not too high, she reassured herself as she carried them upstairs. Start in a small way, and build on that, and you'll be fine.

With her bottom lip caught in her teeth, she climbed up carefully, the swathe of fabric over her shoulder.

'Don't look down,' she muttered under her breath. 'Just don't look down.'

Ten minutes later she was wondering what had made her think this was a job for one pair of hands. Despite her best efforts, the heavy canopy refused to stay in place while she fixed the corners.

'Damn the thing,' she muttered, leaning over further to tug it straight, only to feel the steps begin to wobble as the balance of her weight altered.

She gave a little cry, and clutched at the nearest bedpost to steady herself.

And heard Chay's voice say grimly, 'What the hell do you think you're doing?'

She looked down and saw him beside her. Below her, looking up. And suddenly the old nightmare took possession again, and the green carpet was grass, and she was a terrified child, realising how far she could fall.

'Don't touch me.' Her voice rose hysterically. 'Don't touch the ladder.'

He said grimly, 'Don't be a fool, Adie. I've got you. Down you come.'

'No.' As his hands gripped her waist she kicked out at him.

Chay swore, lifting her away from the steps, turning her

in his arms so that she was pinned against him, her breasts crushed against the wall of his chest, her dilated eyes staring into his. Holding her there until she stopped struggling and the small dry sobs died away, leaving only the hurry of their breathing to disturb the tense silence.

He said harshly, 'You just don't get it, do you, Adie?'

Then, infinitely slowly, he began to lower her to the ground, still watching her, letting every inch of her body linger tellingly against his.

She felt the first dark shiver of arousal ripple through her. Heard herself whimper softly as her head fell back and her lips parted, inviting his kiss.

Then, abruptly, there was the quick tap of approaching footsteps, a gasp and a murmured apology, and Adrien turned her head to see Mrs Whitley beating an embarrassed retreat.

Chay said, 'Jean—wait a minute.' He set Adrien gently and unhurriedly down on the floor, then turned to the housekeeper hesitating in the doorway.

He said, 'Jean, you can hang these curtains, please?' He paused, adding silkily, 'Miss Lander has no head for heights.'

He divided a swift, impersonal smile between the pair of them, and walked out of the room.

Mrs Whitley came forward, tutting. 'You should have come to me, madam,' she said reproachfully. 'Why, you're as white as a sheet.'

'I thought I'd fall,' Adrien said, half to herself, still staring at the door. Still seeing the image of Chay walking away from her, with that long lithe stride that she knew so well. It wasn't the first time, she thought, so why should she suddenly find it so disturbing?'

'Then I'll stand on the steps and you can hand everything up to me,' Mrs Whitley said firmly. She stroked the material. 'Such lovely colours—and beautiful workmanship.'

She chatted quietly and inconsequentially as the curtains were hung round the bed and at the tall windows, and while the canopy was adjusted, and Adrien replied at random, her thoughts whirling as she tried to rationalise the feeling of unease which Chay's abrupt departure had triggered.

When everything was finished, and admired, and Mrs Whitley had disappeared to restore the steps to their usual place, Adrien escaped to her room. She curled up on the window seat, looking down at the sodden garden.

She'd given herself a fright, but it was over now, and anyway, Chay had been there to rescue her. Just as he had been all those years before, guiding her down from the treehouse, she recalled. Trying to make belated amends, she had supposed bitterly, for stranding her there. Or pretending that he hadn't been the one to do it, not knowing that she'd looked down and seen him—walking away.

Except—except that it was all wrong, she realised, frowning. The figure walking away from her, imprinted in her mind, had had a much shorter stride. Had held himself differently. Hadn't been as tall.

She thought, with a kind of anguish, I know Chay. I know everything about him and I always have. I've carried that knowledge with me all these years, no matter how it hurt. So how could I not have seen that it wasn't him at all—but someone wearing his grey jacket?

It had to have been Piers, of course, she recognised with an odd calm. Piers—the Grange's future owner—who had resented Chay as an interloper. Piers, who'd deliberately smashed Chay's field glasses and had been determined to wreck his private sanctuary too. Who had wanted Chay blamed and sent away.

But why? she asked herself in bewilderment. Why such an extreme reaction over the housekeeper's son?

'You don't get it,' Chay had said to her.

But I do now, she thought. I know exactly how it happened.

And maybe Chay himself could tell her why.

She had to find him, explain to him the self-deception she'd been practising all this time. And ask him—somehow—to forgive her.

And there was no time like the present, she thought, steeling herself as she got up from the window seat.

She ran lightly downstairs, not giving herself time for second thoughts, and tapped on the library door. There was no reply, and she knocked again more loudly.

'Miss Lander?' Mrs Whitley spoke from behind her. 'I was just coming to tell you that I've put some tea for you in the drawing room.'

'Oh, thank you,' Adrien hesitated. 'Has Mr Haddon gone out again?'

'Yes, madam.' Mrs Whitley's pleasant face took on a faintly wooden look. 'Unfortunately, he's had to go back to London. He asked me to make his apologies and say he'll see you next weekend.'

'When his guests are expected,' Adrien said quietly. 'Yes, of course.' She mustered a smile. 'Thank you, Mrs Whitley.'

The tea looked delicious. Tiny triangular sandwiches, a sponge filled with jam and cream, and a plate of home-made biscuits. But Adrien could not have eaten a crumb.

Because Chay had not simply walked away. He'd walked out.

She thought, in desolation, I've left it too late—and now he's gone. I've lost him. And tasted tears, hot and scalding, in her throat.

CHAPTER NINE

'IF WE'RE not careful,' Zelda said gleefully. 'We're going to have a full order book.'

'Seems like it,' Adrien agreed, brows furrowed as she checked an estimate. 'What's caused this sudden flurry of activity?'

'Christmas cards in the shops,' Zelda told her solemnly. 'People realise that, although it's only September, the countdown to hell has started, and they want to rethink the decor in their houses before the relations start arriving.'

She paused. 'At least there isn't that problem at the Grange. I hope Chay's guests will be duly impressed.'

'So do I,' Adrien said drily. 'But I doubt it. They all seem pretty high-powered.' She sighed. 'Chay's PA has faxed me details of all their interests and likes and dislikes, so that I can plan their entertainment with more precision.'

'Ouch,' said Zelda. 'Rather you than me.'

'Oh, it's not too onerous.' Adrien slid the estimate into an envelope and sealed it. 'The men want to play golf, which is easy. As for the wives, one of them is mad about tennis, another likes to swim, and the third collects antiques. So I've arranged temporary membership of the Country Club for the entire weekend, and a visit to the antiques fair at Lower Winkleigh on Sunday morning.'

She frowned slightly. 'On Saturday evening some of the local people have been invited to a drinks party.'

'Anyone interesting?'

'Sally Parfitt sent out the invitations from the London office some time ago. They're mostly the older generation,

131

I think. People who knew Angus Stretton.' Her frown deepened. 'Which is odd, really.'

'Or a shrewd move. Wooing the people who matter?'
Zelda suggested. She put down the book of fabric samples
she'd been examining. 'Anyway, I hope the master of the
house appreciates your efforts. When does he plan to return?'

Adrien shrugged. 'Around lunchtime tomorrow, I suppose,' she said neutrally. 'The guests will be arriving during
the afternoon, and he'll want to be there to welcome them.'
She hesitated. 'I feel as if I'm leaving you in the lurch, now
that all this work has started to come in. But it won't be
for much longer.'

Zelda sent her a half-smile. 'I'll take your word for it,
honey.'

Adrien picked up the pile of envelopes from the desk.
'I'll take these to the post, then get back. I have to sort out
something to wear at dinner tomorrow evening.' She pulled
a face. 'I'm not expected to compete, so I guess my all-
purpose black will do.'

'I'd like to think it had some purpose,' Zelda said, and
dodged, laughing, as Adrien threw a ball of crumpled paper
at her.

Out in the courtyard, Smudge was playing with his
puppy, an eager, bright-eyed bundle with ominously large
paws, whom Zelda had christened Bugsy Malone in tribute,
she said, to his criminal tendencies.

Smudge was a different kid these days, Adrien thought,
pausing to watch them affectionately. So perhaps some
good had come out of the past fraught few weeks after all.

She'd waited the rest of last weekend, hoping for a message of some kind from Chay, explaining his abrupt departure. But there'd been nothing. And the only contact this
week had been through his PA.

'Adie—watch.' Smudge had spotted her. 'Bugsy can do a trick. He can roll over.'

Adrien hid a smile as the puppy lay on his back, waving his paws in the air. 'Wow,' she said, crouching down to tickle the velvety tummy with a gentle hand. 'He's a very intelligent dog.'

'He's got to have injections,' Smudge said. 'I can take him for walks. Will you come too, Adie?'

'Whenever I can,' Adrien told him, rising to her feet again.

'You live at the Grange now,' Smudge persisted. 'Why do you? I liked it when you lived in the cottage. When are you coming back? I miss you.' He put his arms round her and buried his face in her skirt.

Adrien touched his hair. 'I miss you, too. And I'll be coming back very soon.'

She heard a slight sound, and looked up. Chay was standing a few yards away, watching her, his expression cold and bleak.

She said, aware that her pulses had begun to behave erratically, 'What are you doing here? You're a day early...'

'You weren't at the house,' he said. 'I came to make sure you hadn't run out on me.'

Adrien gently detached Smudge's clinging hands. 'You said I could continue with my business,' she reminded him. 'It won't manage itself.'

'I haven't forgotten. However, this weekend is important to me, and your primary role is as my hostess.'

'You've bought my services,' she said. 'And you won't be short-changed. I think you'll find everything in place.'

'I hope so.'

Oh, why are we sniping at each other? she asked herself in anguish. This isn't how I planned it at all.

But then Chay's unexpected arrival had wrong-footed her completely.

'Are you going with that man?' Smudge suddenly demanded.

'I have to,' she told him. 'He's my boss.'

Smudge turned a mutinous look on Chay. 'Why can't you leave Adie alone?'

'Because I need her,' Chay said. 'To work for me.'

'When she's finished work, can she come back here?'

'I think,' Chay said quietly, 'we'll have to wait and see.' He looked at Adrien. 'Are you going straight to the Grange?'

'I have to go to the post office first.' Adrien waved to Smudge as she turned away.

'Then I'll walk with you.' Chay fell into step beside her.

He looked tired, she thought. She wanted to kiss the tautness from his mouth and close his eyes with her fingertips. She wanted to hold him. To draw his head down to her breast and let him sleep.

The longing to touch him twisted inside her like a knife in a wound.

He said, his tone expressionless, 'You have an admirer.'

She forced a smile. 'He's a terrific kid. Things haven't been easy for him.'

'He was one of your concerns when you agreed to our arrangement.' It was a statement, not a question.

She bent her head. 'Yes.' There was a silence, then she said, 'Why did you come to look for me?'

'Just protecting my investment, darling.' His voice was light and cynical.

'You didn't need to come down today,' she said carefully. 'Mrs Whitley and I have everything under control.'

'You mean you'd find it more convenient if I only showed for a few hours at the weekends.' His tone hardened. 'The Grange is my home, Adie, and I'll visit it when I want.' He paused. 'And if that's a problem for you, then deal with it.'

'That isn't what I meant.' She bit her lip. 'Chay—let's not have any more misunderstandings. The weekend's going to be difficult enough without us being at each other's throats.'

'I thought everything was arranged.'

'Not that,' she said. 'I'm wondering how your guests will regard me. As I'm living in your house, they're bound to make assumptions.'

'Would you like me to wear a badge?' His tone bit. '"I am not sleeping with this woman"?'

'Now you're being ridiculous,' she said wearily. 'Just forget I said anything. And here's the post office.'

'Ah,' Chay said derisively. 'I thought it looked familiar. And across the road is a café. Why don't we share a civilised pot of tea together while we figure a way to lessen your embarrassment?'

'"Civilised",' she said, pushing her envelopes into the mailbox, 'is hardly a word I'd use to describe our relationship.'

His mouth twisted into a smile. 'Maybe you bring out the barbarian in me, Adie. But I want this weekend to be relaxed, and it won't be if you're seething with resentment.'

'Perhaps you could refer to me as another PA, like Sally Parfitt,' she suggested. 'Let me maintain a low profile.'

They halted in front of the café, and Chay's hand closed on her shoulder, turning her slightly so that she could see her reflection in the plate glass window.

He said harshly, 'Take a good look at yourself, Adrien. Look at your hair, your skin, your eyes. You couldn't fade into the background if you tried. And it would fool no one anyway.'

'Why not?'

'Because of this,' he said. And pulled her towards him. The kiss was brief, but searingly, hungrily explicit in its demand. He didn't use any force, but when he let her go

Adrien had the absurd impression that her lips were bruised.

She took a step backwards, fighting the insidious throb of excitement which made her want to go back into his arms. Offer her mouth again. She stared up at him, searching for something to say, trying to read his expression. But the grey eyes were hooded.

He said laconically, 'Now we've given the gossips a field-day, let's have that tea.'

She ought to refuse. She *wanted* to refuse. To make some excuse, find the Jeep and drive somewhere that he'd never find her again.

Yet somehow they were in the café, and Chay was ordering tea and a plate of sandwiches.

'Jean says you don't eat enough,' he remarked, as the young waitress departed.

'I'm perfectly all right,' she retorted. 'Jean fusses too much.'

'I think I'll let you tell her that yourself.'

He sounded coolly friendly, she realised with wonder. As if that sudden blaze of desire had never existed.

She took a deep breath. 'Chay—I need to talk to you about something.'

'Are you quite sure it's necessary?' His gaze met hers levelly.

She swallowed. 'It's important—to me.'

'Are you going to tell me you're pregnant?'

'Of course not. It's far too soon to know.'

'There are tests—aren't there?' The question was casually interested.

'Yes,' she said. 'But I don't need one. There's no baby.'

'How can you be sure?'

Because I'd know, she thought. Because your child would be a beautiful glowing secret to be sheltered inside me. And instead I just feel—empty.

She said shortly, 'Female intuition.'

His mouth curled. 'Not the most reliable monitor.'

She supposed it was a reference to Piers, and bit her lip.

At that point the tea arrived, and setting out the crockery and pouring the tea provided a brief diversion.

As she passed him his cup, she said, 'You're probably right. Mine's been letting me down for years.' She paused. 'Why didn't you tell me that it was Piers who stranded me in the treehouse and not you?'

'Because it was easier that way,' he said after a pause. His hand strayed to the scar on his cheekbone. 'Or it was before you started using me as target practice.'

'But you were sent away,' she said soberly. 'It must have been dreadful for you. And it wrecked your relationship with Angus. You were rarely allowed back to the Grange after that, even in vacations.'

'And when I did return there was more trouble. Is that what you're leading up to?'

She winced. 'I'm trying to understand,' she said. 'I can see how angry you must have been. How bitter.'

And when Angus rejected you again it must have been the last straw, she thought. You wanted to hit out—and there I was—being indulged by Angus and given expensive presents. You wanted to punish me for my part in it all.

'I was exiled to the sixth form in one of the best schools in the country, and then on to university,' Chay told her drily. He offered her the sandwiches and took one himself. 'Hardly penal servitude.'

'Oh,' she said, remembering that overheard conversation between her parents. 'But I thought...'

'I know what you thought,' he said. 'And what you still think, for that matter. What's this all about, Adie?'

Adrien looked down at the tablecloth. 'I thought it was time I apologised for my part in it all.'

'Consider it done.' He sounded indifferent. 'It was all a long time ago.'

'But still having repercussions—in both our lives,' she said in a low voice. 'Isn't that why you bought the Grange?'

'Yes.' His tone was suddenly uncompromising. 'I always intended it to belong to me.'

She swallowed. 'And—was I part of the plan?'

'Yes.' His smile was crooked. 'Which just proves how unwise some ambitions can be.' He paused. 'I've got something to tell you, too, Adrien.'

He was going to confess that he'd stolen the pendant, she thought wretchedly. And she couldn't bear it. Because nothing could excuse the damage he'd done to Angus and to herself, and she couldn't face hearing him admit that he was capable of inflicting that kind of hurt.

She glanced at her watch and manufactured an exclamation. 'I've got an appointment with a client. She's got this very dark dining room... So, I—I'll see you back at the house later.'

She saw his face close, and a sudden bleakness enter the grey eyes. He said quietly, rising to his feet, 'As you wish.'

Adrien sent him a swift, meaningless smile and fled.

She drove out of the village, deliberately choosing a road that would take her in the opposite direction to the Grange. She needed to distance herself so that she could sort out the turmoil in her mind.

She parked in a lay-by and leaned back in her seat, closing her eyes, letting her memory pick its way painfully back across the years.

She'd been touched and surprised when Angus Stretton had said he was giving a party for her at the Grange to celebrate her eighteenth birthday.

'I always wanted a daughter to spoil,' he told her. 'And it's kind of your parents to allow me to share this special time with you all.' He smiled at her kindly. 'And it's time this house was livened up.'

Adrien thought what a shame it was that he didn't have a family living with him at the Grange. Guarded remarks from her parents had told her that Mr Stretton was married, but his wife was an invalid, permanently confined to a nursing home.

But it was good that he had Piers, she told herself. And even better that Piers would be paying one of his periodic visits that weekend of her party. None of her friends had met him, and with his dark good looks he was going to cause a sensation.

But she didn't expect Chay to be there.

It had been two years since she'd seen him. And before that she'd gone out of her way to avoid him, staying away from the Grange altogether during his brief sojourns.

But when he'd smiled at her, and said her name, she'd found it difficult to maintain her hostility.

Besides, that tall, cool-eyed stranger had borne no resemblance to the quiet boy who'd turned from friend to enemy. And who seemed to want to be her friend again.

And when he'd said gently, 'Adie—am I still the monster from your childhood?' she'd forgotten she was sixteen and officially an adult, and had blushed to the roots of her hair, stammering some disclaimer.

Within a day he'd been gone again, but Adrien had found their fleeting encounter impossible to put out of her mind. His image seemed lodged in her head, waking or sleeping.

Looking back, she could see there had hardly been a day when she hadn't thought about him. When she hadn't wondered where he was and what he was doing. And when he would return...

Slowly but surely, the memory of him had become implanted in her heart and mind and started to bloom.

So when she went up to the Grange on her birthday

morning, and found him standing there in the drawing room, she ran to him on a blaze of happiness which took her straight into his arms. And then his mouth touched hers, warm, sensuous and very assured. Making no concessions to her inexperience. Imposing a subtle demand that was totally new to her, and which scared and thrilled her in equal measure.

When at last he lifted his head, he said softly, 'Well, now....'

Then they heard Angus coming, with her father, and fell apart. Angus paused when he saw them, and glanced at Chay, his expression almost wary, and Chay looked back, smiling faintly.

Then they began to discuss the final arrangements for the party, and the odd little moment was forgotten.

'Isn't it wonderful that Chay's home?' she asked her father as they walked home.

'Not particularly,' he said shortly. 'Because it will mean that those never-ending demands for money will start all over again. And Angus deserves some peace.'

The dismissive words shocked her. Was that really why Chay had come back? she thought, feeling sick with disappointment. Because Angus was a rich man and Chay was trying to get a business of his own off the ground?

The question hung over her like a shadow all day, but it couldn't spoil the anticipation of her party. As well as her friends from school, a lot of the local people were going, and Angus had hired a disco and arranged a lavish buffet supper.

Adrien wore a cream silky dress, with the gold watch her parents had given her on her wrist and small gold studs in her ears.

She was desperate to see Chay, to feel his arms around her again and seek the reassurance she needed from his kiss, but he seemed to be keeping his distance. Everyone wanted to dance with the birthday girl, and Chay appeared content with that. Later, she told herself. Later she'd be alone with him and it would all be different.

She could feel the blood move in her veins, thick and sweet as honey. Could feel her skin tingle and warm in expectation of his touch.

He'd come back for her sake, she told herself. That was how it had to be.

Piers was much in evidence, of course, and Adrien told herself she didn't mind too badly, because he was a fantastic dancer and had murmured that she looked beautiful. And it might give Chay something to think about too.

Angus had already given her a collection of classical music on CD, but during the course of the evening he called for silence and presented her with a velvet jewellery box.

He said, 'For my wished-for daughter,' and smiled at her while everyone laughed and applauded.

When Adrien opened it she found a garnet pendant gleaming at her. The stones were set in a delicate oval of gold, and instinct told her that the piece was very old, and probably valuable. She gasped and stammered her thanks, and Chay lifted it gently from its satin bed and fastened it round her throat.

She felt the brush of his fingers on her nape and bent her head to hide the excited flush which warmed her face.

'The clasp doesn't seem terribly reliable,' he commented. 'You'd better be careful, Adie.'

Later those words would come back to haunt her.

Eventually, worried that the clasp might give way while she was dancing, she replaced the lovely thing in its box and put it with the rest of her presents in the library.

But when the party was over, and she went to collect her things, she couldn't resist having another look, and found the box empty.

She stood staring down at it, her brain going numb as

tendrils of fright began to uncurl inside her. Had she only imagined taking it off? she wondered frantically. Was it lying on the floor somewhere, broken?

'What's wrong, sweetheart?' Piers had entered the library behind her, and she mutely held out the empty case, her eyes enormous in her white face.

He said softly, 'So, we have a thief amongst us. My uncle has to know about this.'

He took her arm and marched her back to the drawing room.

'Adrien's pendant has been stolen,' he announced abruptly, indicating the empty case she was holding. 'I say the police should be called.'

I'm dreaming, Adrien thought. This is a nightmare, and soon I'll wake up and it will be over.

There was a brief and terrible silence. She could see her parents looking aghast, and Angus's face, stricken, suddenly old and defeated, as he turned to look at Chay.

He said tiredly, 'You'd better go and get it. I suppose it's in your room.'

And Chay said quietly, the grey eyes defiant, 'You know it is.'

Angus nodded. 'You'll fetch it,' he said. 'And then you'll leave this house and not come back. Or I can't answer for the consequences.'

'And that's it?' Piers demanded angrily. 'He comes back here scrounging, tries to steal from a guest under this roof, and you just let him go? I say he should be arrested.'

'You're not the master here yet, Piers.' Angus's voice was bitterly forceful. 'I will handle this matter as I wish. Chay will return the pendant to me, and then he'll leave.'

It was warm in the room, but Adrien felt cold and dizzy suddenly. She caught at her father's sleeve. 'Can we go— now—please? I can't bear any more.'

'Yes, of course,' he said swiftly. 'I'm sorry, darling.'

Her mother came to her side, putting a sympathetic arm round her, urging her out of the room.

Back at the cottage, she lay on her bed, uncaring of the creases in the cream dress.

She said, 'Why did he do it?'

Her father said quietly, 'Angus refused to give him any more money. That was his revenge. I'm only sorry that he chose to involve you. That was too cruel.' He paused. 'You'll get the pendant back, of course.'

'No.' Adrien began to cry, sobs shaking her body. 'No, I don't want to see it ever again. It's spoiled—all spoiled.'

It would always remind her of Chay, fastening it round her throat. Of his touch on her skin. And she never wanted to remember that—never.

Not just the party had been spoiled, she realised. But her whole life.

Because Chay, whom she loved, was a thief, and therefore lost to her for ever.

Adrien stirred, opening her eyes, forcing herself back to reality. For a moment, as she looked at the windscreen, she thought it was raining again. Until she realised that it was her own eyes that were blurred, her face wet with tears as all the old pain tore into her. As the sheer force of everything she felt for him overwhelmed her.

Her unfulfilled body was starving for him, craving him, but that was only part of it. Her heart and mind wanted him too, she thought, pressing a clenched fist to her trembling mouth. Needed him as fiercely as she needed air to breathe.

Had there ever been a time when she hadn't loved him? she asked herself. All these years she'd fought her longing for him, trying to hide behind barricades of bitterness and contempt. Hoping that if she told herself over and over again that she hated him, that would somehow make it true.

But she knew now that all her denials had been useless.

She thought with desperation, I loved him then, and I love him now. But I can't stay with a man I can't trust. And that's all there is to it.

And until he allows me to leave, I shall simply have to—endure.

And presently, when she had no more tears left, she started the engine and drove back to the Grange, to face the time that was left.

CHAPTER TEN

THANKFULLY, there was no one about when she got back to the Grange, and Adrien was able to whisk her tear-stained face and bedraggled appearance safely to her room.

She took a long shower, using her favourite scented gel, and shampooed her hair rigorously. She felt as if she was shedding the past like a skin. And if she kept her eyes firmly on the future, however bleak it might seem, she'd be able—somehow—to cope with the present. That was the theory, anyway. In practice, living under the same roof with Chay but not living with him, it might not be so easy.

She towelled herself dry and slipped on lacy briefs and a matching bra. Then, wrapped in the old jade robe, she curled up in her armchair and switched on her hairdryer, combing the long auburn strands with her fingers and flicking them into place with the deftness of long practice.

She had almost finished when a peremptory rap at her door cut across the buzz of the drier. She clicked the off switch and went to answer it, tightening the sash of her robe.

Chay was waiting with thinly veiled impatience. 'I thought you'd gone into purdah.' The grey eyes flicked over her. 'Didn't you hear me knocking?'

'I've been drying my hair.' Just the sight of him was enough to start that helpless inner trembling.

'So I see.' He reached out and fingered one silky strand. His mouth twisted slightly. 'You look about sixteen, Adie, do you know that?'

She thought, her face warming, And when you look at me like that, I feel sixteen again.

Aloud, she said with a certain constraint, 'Did you want something? Is there a problem?'

'I came to give you this.' He bent and retrieved a large flat box tied with ribbons that had been propped against the wall, and handed it to her.

'What is it?' Adrien looked at it uncertainly.

'Open it,' he advised, following her into the room.

She untied the ribbons, lifted the lid and parted the folds of tissue paper. The sheen of satin met her eyes. Black, she thought, until the light caught it and she saw a shimmer like deep crimson.

It was a dress, she realised as she lifted it out and held it up. Low-necked and long-sleeved, with a brief swirl of a skirt cut cleverly on the bias.

He said, 'I'd like you to wear it for the drinks party on Saturday.' He paused. 'They call it Venetian red.'

'It—it's beautiful.' Her mouth was dry. 'But you don't have to buy me clothes. That's not part of the deal.'

He shrugged. 'Look on it as a bonus for all the work you've done for this weekend.'

It was as if the deepest, darkest mahogany had suddenly become fluid, she thought, feeling the beguiling slide of the fabric through her fingers.

She said, 'How did you know my size?'

'Would you believe—instinct?'

Her lips trembled into a smile. 'That's probably as dangerous as female intuition.'

'I back my judgement,' he said.

'And the colour,' she went on. 'I—I never wear red.'

The grey eyes met hers. 'Try it on and see.'

He was still formally attired in the dark business suit he'd been wearing earlier. He walked across to the armchair and sat down, loosening the knot of his tie and unbuttoning the close-fitting waistcoat.

Her throat tightened. 'In front of you?'

He nodded. 'Here—and now.' He leaned back in the chair, stretching out long legs. 'I've decided to take you up on your previous offer,' he added softly.

She'd always known she would regret that particular piece of bravado. And he was waiting for her to protest—to remind him that theirs was a business relationship—that he'd promised...

Lifting her chin, Adrien untied the sash of her robe, letting her gaze meet his in direct challenge as she took it off and tossed it to the floor.

One glance at the dress's wide, deeply scooped neckline had already told her that she wouldn't be able to wear a bra under it.

Still watching him, she reached round and unfastened the clip, shrugging the narrow straps from her shoulders. For a moment she held it in front of her, using the lace cups as a shield, her hands deliberately teasing before she removed it altogether, letting it flow down to join her robe on the floor. She no longer felt awkward or shy under his intense scrutiny. She wanted him to look at her. To do more than look. To touch, and to take. As she would take him.

She raised her arms, unhurriedly pushing her hair back from her face, hearing his sudden sharp intake of breath as she held the pose for a count of seconds. Then she picked up the dress and slid it over her head. It felt voluptuously cool against her heated skin, curving into her waist and skimming her slender hips as it drifted into place. There was a sweet ache in her breasts as the satin caressed their hardening peaks, and she knew that his own body would be experiencing a similar response.

She slipped her arms into the long sleeves, then paused, almost startled, as she glimpsed herself suddenly in the long wall mirror. She wouldn't have dared choose it for herself, but now she saw how the deep, dramatic colour heightened the flame in her hair and turned her skin to milk. As he'd known it would.

She felt different—exotic—all inhibitions flown.

She turned gracefully and walked towards him, barefoot, holding the unfastened bodice against her, the skirt whispering about her knees.

She said sedately, 'I need help with the zip, please,' and turned her back to him.

She half-heard, half-sensed that he'd got up from the chair. There was a pause and Adrien tensed, scarcely breathing, waiting...

He sighed, burying his face in her hair, then letting his hands slide under the edges of the dress and close softly on her breasts. She leaned back against him, moving her hips slowly, letting her body brush his with deliberate enticement, blind to everything but the urgent demand of her own sensuality.

His hands skimmed her inflamed nipples, drawing a soft whimper from her throat.

He turned her in his arms, his hand tangling in her hair, quenching the fierceness of his kiss in the moist compliance of her parted lips.

When he lifted his head, she could hear the rasp of his breathing, and reached up to draw him down to her again. But he shook his head, his mouth curling into a crooked smile.

He said quietly, 'It would be so easy, Adrien—and so impossible. Because I need more than you have to give. And I won't settle for less.'

He put her from him, gently but decisively, and walked to the door. She clutched the dress against her, her eyes wide with disbelief as she watched him go. At the door, he turned.

He said, 'As I tried to tell you earlier, I have another guest arriving during the weekend.' He paused, then added with cool finality, 'I've told Jean to put her in the room next to mine.'

And went.

It was a long time before she moved. Before she was capable of a simple action like taking off the dress and hanging it up. Before she could make her arms and legs obey her, and force her dazed mind to come to terms with what had just happened to her.

There was a girl looking back at her from the mirror, a stranger, naked except for a tiny triangle of lace, whose face looked haggard in the growing shadows of the room. Someone who looked solitary, and frighteningly vulnerable.

She stared at this girl, trying to view her dispassionately. To see her as Chay would have seen her only a few minutes before—the small, high breasts, the tapering waist and slender legs. Her eyes shadowy with promise. Her semi-nude body in itself an invitation.

But desirable? She could no longer be sure of anything. Least of all her own untried sexuality.

With a tiny cry, Adrien swooped on her robe and huddled it on, and turned away, as if that, somehow, would obliterate the image from her mind.

So much for all the heart-searching she'd subjected herself to, she thought, her throat closing. At the very moment she'd found the courage to tell Chay she'd been wrong about him he'd been trying to tell her that it no longer mattered.

That he'd found someone else with whom he'd share a future instead of a past. Someone who'd value him for the man he'd become rather than the bitter figure of vengeance she'd created in her mind.

He had wanted her, she thought. There had been moments when she'd been quite certain of that. Because he was subject to temptation like everyone else. And tonight had been, briefly, one of those moments.

But in the end he'd walked away, because he was reinventing his life and she no longer had a place in it. Because it was more important to him to keep faith with the new woman he'd found than give way to some transient physical impulse.

It might even have been her disastrous attempt at surrender to him which had made the final decision for him, she thought, her hands clenching in involuntary pain. Which had convinced him that the bargain he'd forced on her was not what he wanted after all, but just a sterile, soulless diversion.

Perhaps it had made him see how much his new lady meant to him, she thought, swallowing. And that was why he'd returned to London with such haste. To give her the commitment and assurances that she deserved. To put the past, and its questions, behind him once and for all.

And now, when it was too late, she knew with startling clarity that it no longer mattered to her what Chay had done, or what he'd been. That it was meaningless to go on doubting him.

Because she was his, and he was hers, for all eternity, and she hungered for him with every breath she drew.

And no amount of time or distance would ever change that. Nor the cold rationality of accepting that he'd chosen someone else and that she was condemned to a wilderness of loneliness.

She gave a small moan and clamped her hands over her mouth to stifle it.

She was like the boy who'd cried 'wolf'. She'd told herself over and over again that it was just a job, that there was no emotion involved and she could walk away unscathed at the end. And now Chay had taken her at her word. The contract was broken. The link severed. And only she knew that she was bleeding to death.

There would come a time when she could grieve for what she had lost, but now she needed every ounce of resolve to get through this weekend. To smile and entertain Chay's business guests. To earn, with charm and efficiency, the money that had saved her from disaster. And to bow out with grace when the new lady of the house arrived. Pride demanded that much.

She might not be needed at all, she thought bleakly. Perhaps, on balance, Chay might prefer her to leave at once, ridding himself of any lingering temptation and an inconvenient reminder of the past in one fell swoop.

She wrapped the robe round her more securely and went out of her room. At the other end of the corridor she could see that the door of the guest room adjoining the master suite was standing open, and as she stood, hesitating, Mrs Whitley appeared from the linen room, carrying towels.

Adrien imitated a smile. 'I hear we're having an extra guest,' she said brightly.

'Oh, Mr Haddon has told you, madam.' The housekeeper appeared relieved. 'I understand it was rather a last-minute decision, and he was concerned that it might put us out.'

'I'm sure we can cope,' Adrien said quietly, following the older woman along the corridor. 'Is there anything I can do to help?'

'No, thanks, madam.' Mrs Whitley beamed at her. 'I'm used to the way she likes things done by now.'

'I see,' was all Adrien could find to say to that. So this was an established relationship after all, she thought. And perhaps there'd been a slight glitch somewhere along the way which had turned Chay's thoughts briefly towards alternative amusement. Only for him to realise the error of his ways...

All the arrangements seemed perfect, she acknowledged

as she stood rigidly in the doorway. It wasn't the largest of the guest rooms but it was one of her favourites, with its pretty chintzes. There were bowls of flowers everywhere, and the bed looked inviting, with pillows piled high and crisp linen.

Not that the lady concerned would be spending much time there, she thought, wincing. Her nights would undoubtedly be passed with Chay in the big canopied bed next door. She would be the one in his arms, responding rapturously to the caress of his hands on her skin, listening as his voice whispered his love for her.

She cleared her throat. 'I've got a bit of a headache, Mrs Whitley. Do you think I could have dinner on a tray in my room?'

'Of course, Miss Lander.' Was there understanding as well as sympathy in the housekeeper's glance? 'Would you prefer a light supper? Can I get you some paracetamol?'

'I have some.' And what painkiller on earth could relieve the agony that was grinding inside her? Adrien wondered as she turned to retreat. 'Something simple would be fine, if it's no trouble.' She hesitated. 'If you'd just tell Mr Haddon that I won't be coming down…'

'Oh, he's dining out himself, madam,' Mrs Whitley said briskly. 'He told me so just now. It's not a problem.'

How desperate we are to avoid each other, Adrien thought, as she trailed back to her room. But perhaps even that's for the best.

And she wished with all her heart that she could believe it.

She spent the evening in her room. Mrs Whitley brought her supper of mushroom soup and a herb omelette, followed by chocolate mousse, and, taking one look at her white strained face, recommended an early night. Then stood over her while Adrien swallowed the painkillers for the fictional headache which had now become full-blown reality.

It seemed impossible that she should sleep, yet she did. When she woke the sun was streaming through the curtains and for a brief moment the day seemed full of promise. Until she remembered.

But it was only the morning she had to get through, she told herself resolutely, getting out of bed. In the afternoon Chay's visitors would be arriving, and she would have no time to spare for her own thoughts.

She had the dining room to herself when she went downstairs, a used cup and plate indicating that Chay had already breakfasted.

She drank some of the fresh coffee that Mrs Whitley brought her, and crumbled a piece of toast to pieces in lieu of eating.

She cleared the table and put the used dishes on a tray to take to the kitchen. The cleaners had arrived, and were already hard at work, she saw, as she emerged from the dining room.

Adrien thought she had never seen the Grange look more beautiful. In spite of everything that had happened since, it had been a privilege to plan its restoration and watch the house slowly revive.

It was a labour of love, she thought, and sighed.

'There's a fax for you.' Chay was standing in the office doorway, holding a sheet of paper. He was wearing close fitting black trousers and a matching polo shirt open at the neck. He looked heavy-eyed, in need of a shave, and not a little bad-tempered, and Adrien's heart turned over in love and longing at the sight of him.

She said coolly, 'Thank you,' as he dropped the paper on to the tray. The message was brief: 'Come over around coffee time. I have a surprise for you. Zelda.'

'You should have explained to her that I have first call on your time this weekend,' Chay said with equal coldness.

'Everything's ready.' Adrien lifted her chin. 'I think I should be allowed half an hour off for good behaviour.' She hesitated. 'In fact, I was wondering whether you really needed me at all.'

His mouth tightened. 'What the hell does that mean?'

She said quietly, 'Your—other guest. Won't she expect to act as your hostess?'

He shook his head. 'She'd hate it. She tends to be shy,' he added wryly.

Her brows lifted. 'So presumably your future entertaining will be kept to a minimum.'

'You can let me worry about that.' His voice and expression were uncompromising. 'And make sure you're back in good time.'

'Yes.' Adrien bit her lip. 'Yes, of course.'

She went to the utility room and loaded the dirty crockery into the dishwasher. Mrs Whitley was there, taking things out of the tumble dryer.

'Our boss isn't in a very good mood today.' Adrien kept her tone deliberately light.

Mrs Whitley pursed her lips. 'Hangover,' she said succinctly.

'Oh,' said Adrien.

Just before eleven, she took the Jeep to the village. Zelda was waiting for her, the coffee already made.

'So, what's the surprise?'

'I decided the little black dress needed some help.' Zelda handed her a flat package. When Adrien opened it, she found a waistcoat in black and silver brocade.

'When on earth did you make this?' She slipped it on over her workaday cream shirt. 'It's gorgeous.'

'I made it last night. It's furnishing fabric—left over from that little sitting room we did for Lady Gilmour.'

Zelda grinned at her. 'The old bag's not coming to dinner, I hope?'

'No, just to the drinks party tomorrow.' Adrien paused. 'But I may not be going to that.'

'Why not?' Zelda stared at her. 'I thought you were signed up for the duration.'

Adrien shrugged. 'Things keep changing.' She took the waistcoat off and folded it carefully. She said in a low voice, 'Zee—I don't think I can take any more.'

'Oh, dear.' Zelda sighed deeply. 'This is what I was afraid of. You've fallen in love.'

Adrien smoothed the brocade with her fingertip. She said simply, 'I've loved him all my life.'

'Adie,' Zelda said gently, 'a few weeks ago you were planning to marry Piers Mendoza.'

Adrien bent her head wretchedly. 'I was fooling myself,' she said. 'I'd never have gone through with it. I was more in love with the house than I ever was with Piers. But he was there—and he was a link with the past and he seemed to want me,' she added with difficulty. 'Besides, I'd convinced myself that Chay would never come back. And that I hated him. I—needed to hate him because of everything that had gone on in the past. So I built up this whole big illusion about being in love with Piers.'

'My God.' Zelda cast her eyes to heaven. 'And then Chay did come back.'

'Yes.' Adrien gave a brief, unhappy smile. 'And now I've lost him.' She paused. 'He—he has someone else.'

Zelda grimaced. 'It's becoming an epidemic. Who is she?'

'I don't know. But he's invited her down this weekend and put her in the room next to his. And I don't think I can stand it,' she ended wretchedly.

Zelda was silent for a moment. 'You're sure it isn't still the house?' Her tone was dry.

Adrien gasped. 'Of course not.' Her voice shook. 'It's always been Chay. Only I was so muddled...' She tried to smile again. 'It was much easier to hate him.'

'Oh, love.' Zelda put her arms round her and gave her a swift hug. 'Well, I think you have two choices. We can sell up here and move far enough away that you'll never see or hear of him again. And they say, "Out of sight, out of mind."'

'Yes,' Adrien agreed listlessly. 'What's the other choice?'

Zelda shrugged. 'If you want him, fight for him.'

'I don't think I have the right weapons.'

'Oh, come on,' Zelda said bracingly. 'He's male; you're female. That usually works pretty well.' She gave Adrien a measuring look. 'After all, that's what this whole thing is about. I never went for that "just a job" story. You've been lit up like a Christmas tree since that first day. And that certainly never happened with Piers.'

Adrien flushed. 'I didn't realise I was that transparent.'

Zelda smiled at her. 'Babe, you've never admitted your true feelings before—even to yourself. It makes a difference. Now, go into battle—and win.'

As Adrien went into the cottage to collect her mail the phone was ringing. She picked up the handset and gave her name and number, but no one answered and then the caller rang off.

Adrien pulled a face at the phone. 'If it's a wrong number you could at least apologise,' she muttered.

She began to go through her letters, tossing junk mail into the wastebasket and putting bills and personal letters to one side.

She was trying to decipher a message on a postcard from Mykonos, from an old schoolfriend, when someone knocked at the front door. Still frowning over her postcard, she wandered over to the door and turned the handle.

'Hello, beauty.' Piers Mendoza smiled at her. 'Surprised to see me?' And, laughing, he pulled her towards him and kissed her.

CHAPTER ELEVEN

FOR a moment, shock held Adrien still, then she pulled away, furiously scrubbing a hand across her mouth.

'What the hell are you doing here?'

'I was in the area,' he said.

'Was that you on the phone just now?'

'I was checking you were here. After all, I could hardly turn up at the Grange, and I gather that's where you're living these days.' His voice deepened, became almost pleading. 'I had to see you, Adrien. I had to explain. To put things right between us.'

She went on staring at him, her eyes wide with disbelief. 'But you're in Brazil.'

His mouth thinned. 'Don't remind me. But I had some unfinished business in London, so I came back two days ago.'

She said tersely, 'You should have stayed in London. Goodbye, Piers.' She made to close the door, but he slipped past her, shutting it himself and leaning against it.

'You could at least hear me out,' he told her reproachfully.

'There's nothing to hear,' she said coldly. 'You conned me, Piers, and I could have gone bankrupt.'

'I was desperate, Adrien.' His voice was suddenly hoarse. 'You don't understand down in this backwater, but it's a jungle out there. And Chay Haddon's one of the tigers. I had no choice. I had to save my own skin.'

'At the expense of mine.'

'You do what you must in order to survive, Adrien.' He

shrugged slightly. 'As you've doubtless discovered by now. I'm sure Chay charged highly for his rescue package.'

She bit her lip. 'I don't know what you're talking about.'

He laughed. 'Don't lie, darling. I can see in your eyes you're no longer the dizzy little innocent I left behind. I just hope he made your initiation enjoyable,' he added softly. 'He's waited long enough for it.'

She said shortly, 'You're disgusting. And I'd like you to leave.'

He threw up his hands in capitulation. 'Sweetheart, I'm sorry. I'm just jealous, I guess. I always have been.'

She shook her head in bewilderment. 'But why?'

'Because my uncle preferred him.' He spoke with sudden harshness. 'A housekeeper's bastard above his own nephew. Can you believe it? He was at the Grange the whole time, and I only came on visits, so there was always a chance he could cut me out with Old Angus. Steal my inheritance.'

Adrien said gravely, 'So—he had to be taught a lesson? Was that it?'

'Can you blame me?' He sounded almost injured. 'I wanted him out of the reckoning. It never occurred to me that your dreamy bird-watching hero would turn himself into the tycoon of the Millennium.'

'And take your inheritance, anyway.' Her voice bit.

'Yes,' he said. 'But I made him pay for it. And I added a premium for you, my sweet.' He looked at her with narrowed eyes. 'You've always been his one weakness. It's made—negotiations easier.'

'Chay has no weaknesses,' she said. 'Not any more. So don't expect any favours.'

'Ah.' He studied her speculatively. 'So what's happened, Adrien? Did you finally run out of hero-worship? Or did you fail to—er come up to his expectations?' He grinned. 'Well, that was always on the cards. You're a lovely girl,

Adrien, but you're not that special. And Chay Haddon can afford to pay for any woman he wants—and a wide range of services.'

She walked to the door and threw it open, her eyes blazing. 'Get out—now.'

'I seem to have touched a nerve,' he said, unperturbed. 'Well, we're not all as fussy—or as rich as the great Mr Haddon. And I plan to visit London on a regular basis from now on. Why don't you move back there and rent a place? Let me show you how much fun bed can be?'

She said steadily, 'Because you sicken me. You're sleaze on legs, Piers, and I can't believe I ever let you anywhere near me. Don't contact me again.'

'Harsh words,' he said with a shrug. 'Let's test your resolve.' And he pulled her into his arms and put his mouth on hers.

Her impulse was to struggle. To kick and fight, and mark his face with her nails. But a warning voice reminded her that anger made him dangerous, that it might be better to stand passively and suffer the pressure of his lips and the worm of his tongue trying to invade her mouth.

It was soon over. He smiled at her, but the look in his eyes was ugly. 'Don't worry, Adrien. You won't be hearing from me again. Who needs a cold bitch like you anyway?'

He walked to the Mercedes parked at the kerb, blew her an insolent kiss, then drove away with a squeal of tyres.

She thought, shuddering, I need to wash my face.

She turned to go back into the cottage and saw Chay standing a few yards away, his face like stone.

As their eyes met, Adrien felt her heart stop beating. She seemed to be frozen to the spot, watching him walk towards her.

He said, too quietly, 'So that was the surprise your friend was talking about?'

'No.' She shook her head violently. 'No, that was something completely different. She'd no more idea that Piers had come back than I did.'

'You sound as if he wasn't a welcome visitor.' His mouth was grim. 'Unfortunately for you, I witnessed the tender farewell.'

'No,' she said. 'You thought you saw it. Like I thought I saw you at the treehouse.'

'You weren't exactly fighting him off.'

She stared at him, reading the condemnation in his voice, the contempt. And felt her own anger kindle in response.

She said slowly, 'How dare you judge me? And what concern is it of yours, anyway? I'm working my notice at the Grange, Chay Haddon, and you have no right to interfere in my private affairs.'

He said harshly, 'Tell me this isn't happening, Adrien. That you're not contemplating any kind of relationship with that piece of scum.'

'And he speaks so well of you,' she said mockingly. 'My life's my own, Chay, and I make my own decisions. I don't need your approval.'

'Are you going to see him again?' His hand closed on her arm urgently. 'Answer me.'

'He's asked me.' She couldn't believe she was saying these things, but some demon drove her on. The hurt inside her lashed out at him. 'He wants me to meet him in London.'

'And you're considering it? God.' He shook his head, his face suddenly haggard. 'You're a fool, Adrien.'

'And you're a hypocrite,' she bit back recklessly. 'Don't forget that you're the one who put me on the market in the first place. You can hardly complain if there are other buyers.'

'I'm not likely to forget.' He was white. 'It's going to haunt me for the rest of my life. But you can't do this, Adrien. You don't know what he's really like.'

'And you're so much better?' she challenged, and shook her head derisively. 'No, Chay. You have your life and I have mine. I'll make my choices, and you won't stop me.'

'Ultimately, perhaps not.' His tone was hard. 'But while you're working for me you won't chase him back to London. My car's down the road. You're coming with me.'

'I have the Jeep...'

'It can stay here. I'm keeping you chained to my wrist this weekend, Adrien. When it's over you're free to ruin your future in any way that seems good to you. Until then, you still belong to me.'

'Oh?' She lifted her head defiantly. 'How do you plan to explain that to your lady guest?'

'She'll understand,' he said. 'Unlike you, Adrien, she trusts me.'

Her laugh rasped her throat. 'And you call *me* a fool.'

'Piers is a married man,' he said. 'I am not.'

'Not yet, perhaps.' The knife inside her twisted slowly, but she didn't falter. 'But you plan to be. Isn't that right?'

'Yes,' he said. 'But, unlike Piers, when I'm married my wife will never have cause to doubt my fidelity. My woman, her man, until death parts us.' He paused. 'Now, let's go home.'

'I am at home.'

He smiled bleakly. 'Of course you are. I phrased that badly. Is there anything you need before we return to the workplace?'

'My bag and some letters.' She went in and scooped them up from the hall table, then turned to find him standing just behind her.

She said between her teeth, 'The world lost a great policeman when you decided to become a property tycoon.'

He said equably, 'Lack of trust works both ways, darling. Now, is there any possibility of declaring a truce—at least until my guests depart? The continual sniping could be a serious embarrassment—and very boring for the audience.'

'Fine,' she said. 'Truce declared. As long as I can go when the guests go.'

'Agreed,' he said wearily. 'I won't try to stop you again.'

She supposed, in its way, it was a small victory. But as she followed Chay to the car it felt far more like a crushing defeat.

Whatever her personal feelings, Adrien had to admit as they drove home from the Country Club on Saturday that the weekend seemed to be going well.

To her surprise, she had found she genuinely liked the three couples whom Chay had invited, although apart from Madame Byron, who was in her thirties, they were all considerably older than she was.

The oldest of the wives was Arlena Travis, a plump, grey-haired, exquisitely groomed American with a Southern drawl like warm honey.

Barbara James lived in London's Holland Park, but confessed to Adrien that her long-term ambition was to persuade her husband to move back to Suffolk, where she'd been born and raised, because she missed the countryside so much.

Nathalie Byron's English was nowhere near as good as her husband's, and she'd tended to say little at dinner the first evening. When they'd adjourned to the drawing room for coffee, Adrien had dragged up her 'A' level French course from the recesses of her memory and had begun to talk to the elegant Parisienne slowly and carefully, in her own language, with the other two eventually joining in with much laughter and pauses for correction in grammar and pronunciation.

Adrien had wondered how the wives would regard her, even though Chay had introduced her formally as his associate. She certainly doubted her ability to play her part adequately. Yet they seemed to accept her without question.

Even the all-purpose black dress had acquired some belated chic with Zelda's waistcoat.

'Why, that's so lovely,' Mrs Travis had said before they'd gone into dinner. 'Where did you get it?'

'My business partner made it for me,' Adrien said, aware that Chay was standing within earshot. 'It was a surprise.'

Another, less welcome surprise was how devastating Chay looked in formal evening clothes. It was the first time Adrien had ever seen him in a dinner jacket, and she was stunned, her heart beating painfully, her stomach lurching whenever he came into her line of vision.

She was seriously glad when the evening drew to an end, and no one wanted to stay up to the small hours. The day had been a strained one, and she was tired. She was wearing her hair up in a loose knot, and she'd just unfastened it and shaken it loose when she heard a tap at her door.

When she opened it, Chay was standing there. He'd unfastened the top buttons of his shirt, and his black tie was dangling from his fingers.

He said gravely, 'I wanted to thank you for the effort you put in with Nathalie Byron. Henri was very impressed. He worries that she sometimes feels isolated on this sort of occasion.' His smile did not reach his eyes. 'I'm—grateful.'

'It was my pleasure,' Adrien said. 'She's charming.'

'You did well,' he said. 'And you looked very beautiful, very relaxed.' He brushed the shoulder of the waistcoat with the tip of his fingers. 'I like the surprise,' he added. 'Goodnight.'

Her lips framed her own goodnight, but it was a soundless whisper that followed him as he walked away. All evening he'd shown her the same polite friendliness, and it terrified her.

Because it showed her the bleakness of a future where

she would never know what it was to be truly a woman. Because it was Chay, and Chay alone, who could awaken her body's responses. And without him she was condemned to physical and emotional sterility.

She wanted to run after him and throw herself into his arms. She wanted to plead with him to take her and make her complete. To join his nakedness to hers and compel her surrender.

But she didn't dare to do any of those things, because another rejection could destroy her.

Zelda had told her to fight for him, she remembered as she turned slowly away and shut her door. Instead, because of Piers, she'd ended up fighting with him. And now they were strangers, facing each other across some endless abyss.

And today she'd hardly seen him, she thought now, because all the men had gone to play golf. At the Country Club she'd played tennis with Nathalie, and two other women whom the professional had introduced to them. They'd all had a swim in the pool, and a massage, and visited the beauty treatment rooms.

'My stars, but I'm looking forward to my dinner,' Arlena Travis said happily as the car turned into the Grange's drive. 'There's nothing like a day's pampering to give you a healthy appetite.'

Adrien agreed, but her own stomach was suddenly churning nervously. She'd caught sight of a strange car—a red Peugeot—standing outside the house. The other guest had arrived at last, she realised, swallowing.

Perhaps the new formality between Chay and herself might help her get through the next difficult few hours, she told herself, without much hope.

'She's in her room, Miss Lander,' Mrs Whitley returned when Adrien asked, with a certain constraint, where the

newcomer was. 'She's had a trying journey, and she's resting.'

Not only shy, but fragile too, Adrien thought wryly, as
she went up to change for the drinks party. Was that really
what Chay wanted?

She showered, dried her hair, and pinned it into a topknot
again. She applied cosmetics with more than usual care,
blotting out the violet shadows under her eyes and smoothing blusher delicately on to her cheekbones. She needed a
public face to hide behind tonight.

She hesitated for a long time in front of the wardrobe,
then chose a slim-fitting black skirt and a white silk blouse.
She had just finished buttoning the blouse when there was
a peremptory rap at her door and Chay's voice called, 'Adrien—are you ready yet? People will be arriving soon.'

'Almost there,' she returned, slipping her feet into high-
heeled black pumps. 'I'll be down in two minutes.'

She'd expected him to leave it at that, but when she
opened her door he was still standing there, his frowning
gaze sweeping her.

He said abruptly, 'I asked you to wear the dress I brought
you.'

'I'd—rather not.' Her voice sounded stifled.

His voice gentled. 'Adrien—it's your last evening in my
employ. Indulge me—please.' His mouth twisted. 'You can
always look on it as a uniform.'

She looked past him rigidly. 'Just as you wish,' she said
at last, and turned back into the room.

'I'll wait,' he said. 'In case you need help with the zip.'

She shook her head as she closed the door. 'I can manage—really.'

The silken dress slid over her head, clinging to her slender curves as if it loved her. Closing the zip was a struggle,
but she persevered, knowing unhappily that she dared not
risk even the most fleeting intimate contact with Chay.

She turned slowly in front of the mirror, watching the subtle flare of the skirt and the play of the dark crimson sheen that altered her every movement. It was beautiful, she thought, and probably the most sophisticated dress she'd ever worn.

At least, she thought, I'll be bowing out in style. And, sighing, she went downstairs to join the others.

As she hesitated in the drawing room doorway they all turned to look at her, and the involuntary murmur of appreciation brought real colour to her face. Only Chay was silent, his face coolly expressionless as he studied her.

'Honey, you look like a million dollars,' said Mrs Travis, herself resplendent in a silk knit suit in shades of mother of pearl. 'That colour's like something from an old painting.'

'It's called Venetian red.' Adrien came forward, recovering some of her composure now that a lightning glance round the room had revealed only familiar faces.

'Ah, Venice.' The older woman sighed pleasurably. 'One of my all-time favourite cities.' She gave Adrien a slight conspiratorial nudge. 'And heaven for a honeymoon.'

Adrien, burningly aware of Chay's cynical glance, murmured something indistinguishable and escaped to talk to Nathalie Byron instead.

She was standing with her back to the door when she heard Chay's voice, warm with affection, saying, 'So there you are at last, darling. Come and be introduced to everyone.'

For a moment Adrien felt herself freeze, then she mustered a too-bright smile and braced herself to turn and look at the woman framed in the doorway. And halted, her eyes widening incredulously.

The newcomer was tall and slim, dressed elegantly in black. Her silver hair was cut in a sleek bob, and there were pearls at her throat and in her ears.

She said in a quiet, clear voice, 'Not everyone, Chay. I see one old friend, at least.' She walked across the room and took Adrien's nerveless hand in hers. 'How are you, Adrien?'

Adrien said numbly, 'Mrs Haddon? But I don't understand…'

'I'm actually Mrs Stretton now.' Grey eyes just like her son's surveyed her calmly. There was a sadness in their depths, and a network of fine lines on her skin. 'Angus and I were married just after he went to Spain.'

Adrien shook her head, feeling winded. 'I had no idea.' She turned accusingly to Chay. 'You didn't tell me.'

His voice was cool. 'You never asked.'

It was true, Adrien realised to her shame. She'd not even enquired whether his mother was still alive, let alone what had happened to her.

Oh, God, she whispered silently. How could I be so thoughtless—so unthinking?

She said quietly, 'I'm so sorry. It's good to see you again, Mrs Stretton.'

'Do we have to be so formal? I'd much prefer you to call me Margaret.' Her glance appraised Adrien again, and she nodded at Chay. 'You were right about the dress, darling. It's quite perfect for her.' She patted her arm. 'Now, please introduce me to your other guests.'

How many shocks could you absorb in one day before you fell to pieces? Adrien wondered as she dazedly complied.

It was better when other people started arriving and she was fully occupied in making sure everyone had a drink and someone to talk to, ensuring the trays of nibbles were being circulated. Because it gave her no time to think, or weigh up the implications of it all. Or contemplate all the unanswered questions. The time for that was still to come.

She stayed on the move, carefully maintaining the length of the room between Chay and herself.

'Such a lovely party,' she heard on all sides. 'You must come to us for dinner—for drinks—for bridge…' And she smiled and said something grateful and noncommittal, allowing them to think she would still be around to accept those obligations.

'What a wonderful surprise.' Lady Gilmour cornered her. 'I knew Angus Stretton's first wife had died, poor thing, but I had no idea he'd married again.'

'I really don't know anything about the background to it all, Lady Gilmour…'

Lady Gilmour lowered her voice discreetly. 'She was a complete invalid. She lost a baby quite early in the marriage and had a terrible nervous breakdown. She spent several years in a nursing home, and just as she seemed to be better they realised she'd contracted one of those terrible wasting diseases with an impossible name.

'Angus was quite heartbroken, of course. He used to visit her faithfully, and made sure she had the best of care and all the latest treatment.'

She sighed faintly. 'No one blamed him for finding happiness with Margaret, and they were both very circumspect. She pretended to be a widow with a child, and we pretended to believe it. It would have been terrible if Ruth had heard so much as a whisper, but I don't believe she ever did.'

Adrien stared at her. She was remembering Chay, seated at Angus's desk, and the feeling that she was seeing a ghost.

She said, stumbling a little, 'Chay is Angus Stretton's son? Is that what you're saying?'

'Yes, of course, my dear.' Lady Gilmour's face was astonished. 'I thought you of all people would have known.

Your father and Angus were such friends—and you—well, you were almost part of the family.'

She gave Adrien a warm smile. 'And we're all delighted to know that you're at the Grange again. How well everything's turned out, after all. Now, I must have a quick word with Mrs Grimes about the Garden Club. I don't believe the new treasurer will do at all...' And she disappeared purposefully.

Adrien stood clutching her untouched glass, her mind spinning as she tried to assimilate what she'd just been told. Chay was Angus's son, she thought, yet he'd been sent away twice in disgrace and Angus had allowed it to happen. Allowed Piers to remain as his official heir. But why?

Chay said softly, 'People are beginning to leave.'

Her own voice was urgent. 'Chay, I need to talk to you. I've only just realised about you—and Angus...'

'Well?' he said. 'What about it?'

She stared up at him. 'How can you ask? It—it changes everything.'

'No,' he said, quite gently. 'It doesn't change a thing. And I think everything necessary's been said already. Now, help me say goodbye.'

She went with him mutely, wincing from the hurt of his dismissive words. It occurred to her that the door into his life had just been finally closed against her. That she was now doomed to stay outside, cold and alone, for the rest of her days.

And the realisation filled her with terror.

CHAPTER TWELVE

THE success of the drinks party carried over into dinner. Mrs Whitley had excelled herself. An exquisite seafood salad was followed by baby chickens cooked with white wine and grapes, and an amaretto soufflé. Margaret Stretton's arrival had provided a new focus for attention, and, far from seeming shy, she was coping with great charm and aplomb.

The laughter and talk gave Adrien a perfect opportunity to be quiet with her bewildered and unhappy thoughts. It was as if all these years she'd been staring into a distorting mirror. And now for the first time she was free to see things as they really were.

And realise, too, what a culpable fool she'd been, she lashed at herself.

There was sudden quiet round the table, and Adrien looked up with a start to see Chay push back his chair and rise to his feet.

He said, 'I'd like to propose a toast to Adrien—who took a neglected house and turned it back into a home. She's been working as my assistant to make sure everything was ready to welcome you all this weekend, and now it's time for her to move on—return to her own life—her own career.'

He lifted his glass. 'Success and happiness, Adrien.'

As the words echoed round the table, and they drank to her, Adrien saw Arlena Travis's brows lift, and the other women exchanging surprised looks with their husbands. She bent her head, her skin warming with faint colour. She had not expected such a public dismissal.

171

'There's one more thing.' Chay reached into an inside pocket in his dinner jacket and extracted a slim flat box. He walked round the table to Adrien's side.

'I have a farewell present for you,' he said. 'A keepsake to remind you of all the time we've spent together.' He put the box on the table in front of her. His face was still, his eyes unreadable.

Her fingers shook as she removed the lid, because she knew what she was going to see and she didn't know how to deal with it. She made a small choked sound as the dark red stones of the garnet pendant gleamed up at her, and Chay lifted it from its white satin bed and fastened its slender golden chain round her neck.

'The original clasp was faulty,' he said. 'But I've had it fixed.'

She had almost forgotten how beautiful it was. How the stones seemed to possess their own inner flame. She looked down, watching them shimmer against her pale skin, and touched them with one finger delicately, fearfully, as if they might burn.

'Thank you.' Her voice was a stranger's. 'I never expected—anything like this.'

She looked up at him, searching his cool, enigmatic face, begging silently for enlightenment. But he turned away and went back to his seat.

'My stars.' Arlena Travis leaned forward. 'That is one glorious piece of jewellery, honey.' She gave it the shrewd look of a connoisseur, then nodded. 'And very old, as well as valuable. Does it have a history?'

'Oh, yes.' It was Margaret Stretton who spoke, her tone reflective. 'Originally it was bought by a young man as a birthday gift for the girl he wanted to marry. But his parents, rightly or wrongly, felt she was too young to make such a serious commitment, and that any mention of marriage might even scare her away.'

Adrien realised she had almost stopped breathing. She found herself staring at the older woman as if she was mesmerised.

'There were other obstacles, too,' Margaret Stretton went on. 'Quite serious ones. So it was agreed it would be safer to offer the pendant as simply a family gift, without strings, and that the young man should start to woo her gently and without pressure.'

She sighed. 'But unfortunately it all went wrong, and instead they parted in great bitterness.'

She smiled round the table. 'Not a very happy story, but all in the past. It certainly doesn't matter any more. And I'm glad the pendant's found a good home at last.'

And what about me? Adrien wanted to shout aloud, her hands gripping each other in her lap until her fingers ached. Don't I matter any more either?

Well, she had the answer to that round her throat. The pendant was a farewell gift. What was sometimes known as a 'kiss-off'—except that there hadn't been that many kisses...

As a mistress, she'd hardly even registered, she acknowledged with a wry twist of her heart.

She stared across at Chay, willing him to look at her, but he was talking to Nathalie Byron and she could only see his profile, strong but oddly remote.

Unreachable, she thought as pain wrenched at her.

She pushed back her chair and rose, a smile pinned on. 'Ladies, I think our coffee will be in the drawing room by now. Shall we go?'

It was not an easy interlude. No one asked Adrien directly why she was leaving, but she could feel curiosity simmering around her and she poured the coffee and handed the cups, and smiled and chatted as if she didn't have a care in the world.

Barbara James came and sat with her, talking generally and gently about the restoration of the house, and the problems it had thrown up, then asking for advice on the redecoration of a rather cold north-facing bathroom in her London home.

Adrien responded gratefully, thankful for a question she could actually answer.

When Barbara moved on, her place was taken by Arlena Travis.

'I've come for a closer look at that necklace,' she announced, putting on her glasses. 'Antique jewellery is my passion, so I guess my husband is real glad someone beat him to this piece.'

She gave a deep sigh of appreciation. 'That is some love-token, honey. Now, I'd have done the conventional thing and picked emeralds to go with your hair. But these rubies are just so right for you, somehow. And with that dress—magnificent.'

Adrien put down her coffee cup very carefully on the table in front of her.

She said politely, 'I'm sorry, Mrs Travis. I don't quite understand. These are garnets.'

Mrs Travis gave her an old-fashioned look. 'Oh, come on, honey, are you crazy? These are rubies, and particularly fine ones, too.' She patted Adrien's hand. 'But if you won't take my word for it just get them appraised for insurance. You'll find out.'

Adrien's lips felt numb. She managed, 'I'll be sure and do that.' She gave her companion a meaningless smile and got to her feet. 'Would you excuse me, please?'

She walked across the room to Margaret Stretton. She said, 'Would you take over for me, Mrs Stretton? I—I have a splitting headache and I'd like to go to my room.'

She didn't wait for the reply, just murmuring a general goodnight before she fled.

Safety upstairs, she shut her door behind her and leaned against it, gasping for breath.

Rubies, she thought, her mind reeling. When she was eighteen, Chay had bought her rubies. But hadn't told her. Had let her think the pendant was just a semi-precious trinket.

He couldn't steal his own gift, so why had the pendant vanished, to resurface in his room?

It was Piers, she thought, her throat tightening. How couldn't she have seen it before? Piers, who would also have known the real value of the pendant. And Piers, because it had ostensibly come from Angus Stretton, would have regarded it as part of his inheritance. And resented it being given away.

He'd clearly had no idea that Chay was his cousin. He'd been and always would be 'the housekeeper's bastard'.

But stealing the pendant and planting it in Chay's room must have seemed an ideal way of ridding himself permanently of a hated rival. Because of the value of the stones, Chay would be bound to be arrested. That was how Piers would have reasoned.

And, as a bonus, it would drive a permanent wedge between Chay and the girl he loved. Destroy the new understanding that had arisen since his previous attempt to separate them.

And it hadn't been because Piers had ever wanted her for herself, she realised. Right to the end she'd simply been someone he could use. Even when he'd arrived at the cottage the previous day he'd been able to turn it to his advantage.

And I fell for it, she acknowledged miserably. But why, when everyone knew the truth about the pendant, was he allowed to get away with it? It makes no sense.

Why hadn't Angus Stretton challenged him and thrown

him out? And why had Chay been sent away when he was guiltless?

She began to walk up and down the room, her arms wrapped tightly round her body.

She remembered the snatches of conversation between her parents, the harsh, damaging comments that she'd assumed alluded to Chay. But it had been Piers they'd been talking about. Piers who had always been demanding money. Piers who was dangerous.

She thought desolately, How could I have been so wrong—so blind?

There was still so much she didn't know. And now she probably never would discover the whole tangled truth.

She undressed and put on her robe, but she didn't get into bed. She felt too wretched and too restless, and sleep was a million miles away. Instead she curled up on the window seat and stared out into the darkness, unhappy thoughts chasing themselves round in her head.

Eventually she heard the sound of voices as the rest of the party came upstairs to bed. And then, shortly afterwards, there was a quiet tap at the door.

'Adrien?' It was Margaret Stretton's voice. 'Are you all right? May I come in?'

For a moment Adrien was sorely tempted to stay quiet, and pretend she was asleep. Then she realised that the light from her lamp would be visible under the door, so she padded across and turned the handle.

'We were concerned about you.' Mrs Stretton walked into the room. 'I wondered if you'd like some hot chocolate.'

Adrien said stiltedly, 'That's—kind of you. But, no, thanks.'

The grey eyes surveyed her keenly. 'Poor child,' she said gently. 'You've had so many shocks this weekend. I'm not surprised you had to run away.'

'I can't believe I didn't guess.' Adrien's tone was
hushed, as if she was talking to herself. 'That I couldn't
see Angus and Chay were father and son—when I thought
I knew them both so well.'

'You weren't the only one,' Mrs Stretton comforted her.
'And you weren't meant to know—not then. In fact, it was
vitally important that no one did.'

'Especially—Piers Mendoza?'

'Yes,' Mrs Stretton said heavily. 'Him above all.'

'But why?'

'Come and sit with me.' Margaret Stretton took Adrien's
unwilling hand and led her back to the window seat.

'You never knew Angus's sister Helen,' she began. 'But
she was the loveliest girl, and only eighteen when she met
Luiz Mendoza, Piers's father, and married him in spite of
all Angus could do. He disliked him instinctively, you see,
and distrusted him too. He felt that under all the good looks
and charm there was genuine evil. Something he'd rarely
encountered before.

'He made enquiries through some high-powered connections of his and discovered that Luiz was a minor racketeer,
with a finger in all kinds of unsavoury pies in Brazil, and
a heavy gambler, too, who lost more often than he won.

'When Piers was still a baby, Helen died—killed in a
road accident, apparently by a hit-and-run driver. Her life
had been heavily insured the year before by her husband.'

Adrien's hand went to her mouth. 'Oh, God—you
mean…?'

Mrs Stretton nodded. 'There was never any proof, but
Angus knew that Luiz had arranged it. He'd already got
through Helen's own money, and was badly in debt to some
very nasty people.' She grimaced. 'Like father, like son.'

She was silent for a moment. 'Luiz knew that Angus's
wife was in a private hospital, and would never give him
another child, and that Piers was his sole male heir. Angus

was convinced he would allow nothing and no one to stand in Piers's way, and he couldn't risk any further threat to his family. So Chay, for his own safety, had to be—the housekeeper's son.

'When Luiz died, Angus was prepared to give Piers a chance, for Helen's sake, but he soon discovered his mistake.' She shook her head. 'Piers might lack his father's complete ruthlessness, but he's adept at dirty tricks—and blackmail. He didn't guess the truth, but he recognised the affection between the two of them and set out to destroy it. Anyone that Angus loved was seen as a threat to his prospects. That's why he pretended to send both of us away and moved to Spain. To let Piers think he'd won.'

'You mentioned—blackmail…?'

Margaret Stretton nodded. 'Piers guessed about us—Angus and I—and threatened to tell his wife. Ruth was so ill—not just physically, but mentally too. She used to have terrible fits of hysteria and depression, even attempting suicide at one point. Angus paid to protect her. To keep her illusions intact. Because she'd become convinced, you see, that one day there'd be a miracle cure and she'd come back—to her home and her marriage.'

There were sudden tears in her eyes. 'She had to be allowed to go on believing that for the short time she had left.'

'Yes,' Adrien said slowly. 'But—it must have been very hard on Chay—as well as you.'

Margaret Stretton smiled. 'Chay is a realist, like me. And he was always determined to carve out his own path to success. He knew, as well, that Piers would never keep the Grange. That he only had to be patient.'

Adrien bit her lip. 'Yes,' she said. 'He's been very—patient.'

Mrs Stretton rose. 'Try and sleep now.' Her voice was kind. 'And don't worry about getting up tomorrow. I'm taking Arlena and the others to the antiques fair. You don't have to do that.'

'Does that mean I'm free to leave?' Adrien asked woodenly.

At the door, Margaret Stretton turned and smiled at her again. 'Of course,' she said. 'If that's what you really want. And only you know that, Adrien. It's your decision entirely. Goodnight, my dear, and sleep well.'

After she'd gone, Adrien sat where she was for a long time.

Then she went to the chest of drawers in the bedroom and found the empty velvet case that had housed the pendant originally. All these years it had reminded her of heartbreak and betrayal. Now it was time to set the record straight.

And to fight.

She arranged the pendant meticulously on its satin bed, then let herself quietly out into the corridor and went to Chay's room.

She didn't knock. Just turned the handle and walked in.

He was standing by the window, staring out. He'd discarded his dinner jacket and black tie, but apart from that he was still fully dressed.

He turned slowly and surveyed her, his face cool, his mouth set. 'Isn't it rather late for social calls?'

'This is the last one, I promise. I won't trouble you again. I came to give you this.' She held the velvet case out to him. 'I can't take it, Chay.' Her voice trembled a little. 'It's cost too much—in all sorts of ways.'

'My God,' he said. 'Have you kept that box all this time? Why, Adrien? To remind yourself how much you hated me?'

She winced. 'Something like that. But it isn't necessary any longer. So, I'm giving it back, along with the rubies.'

'Consider them a productivity bonus.' He made no attempt to take it from her. His eyes were hard. 'Most people expect some kind of golden handshake at the end of a contract.'

'Well, I'm not most people.' She glared at him. 'And I'm not playing your damned games any longer.'

'Games?' he came back at her savagely. 'Who the hell are you to talk to me about playing games?' He shook his head. 'I really thought you were over Piers—that you'd seen through him at last. But, oh, no. At the first opportunity you're back in his arms.

'Well, go to him, Adrien, if he's want you want. But keep the pendant and lock it up in a bank somewhere. You'll need it when he dumps you again. Or when you have to buy him off.'

His laugh was brief and humourless. 'In ancient times they said rubies were an antidote to poison and a cure for grief. I hope that's true, for your sake. Because you're going to need both of them.'

This was the moment for every scrap of courage she'd ever possessed.

She said, 'I've only ever needed you, Chay. Only ever wanted you.'

His mouth tightened. 'That's not true, and we both know it. You were planning to marry him, for God's sake.'

'I'm not proud of that,' she said. 'I never looked past the charm. Perhaps I didn't want to. I was so alone, Chay. So lonely. In my heart, I was waiting and waiting for you to come back. But you never did. And he was a familiar face. Someone from the time before that loneliness.'

'Was it loneliness that sent you back into his arms yesterday?' His voice was harsh. 'I was there, Adrien. I saw you kissing him.'

'No,' she said. 'You saw him kissing me. That's a different thing entirely. And I believe you were meant to see it. Why else were you there?'

He said slowly, 'There was a phone message. Jean took it.' His brows drew together. 'It said you'd met an old friend and wouldn't be back until late.'

'He called me on his mobile at the cottage to make sure I was there. He must have rung the Grange next.' She shook her head. 'He set the trap, and once again we walked into it.'

'You told me that he wanted you back. You admitted it.' Chay's face was still stony.

'You accused me of meeting him behind your back. I was hurt. I hit back.' She spread her hands. 'I have red hair, Chay. That's something that will never change. Or not until I'm old and grey, anyway.'

'You'll never be that, Adrien,' he said quietly. 'The image I'll always have of you is how you looked tonight—in Venetian red with my rubies round your neck.'

'Chay.' Her voice broke on his name. 'Don't…'

'You were a solitary child,' he went on, as if she hadn't spoken. 'I was isolated too. I told myself I preferred it that way. Yet when you weren't there, I always felt—incomplete. All the time you were growing up I had to accept that we'd become strangers. That I had to stand back—stay aloof.'

There was sadness in his eyes, an odd vulnerability twisting his mouth. 'It was a nightmare—waiting for you to stop hating me. Longing for the moment when you'd look at me and smile again. When it finally happened, I felt reprieved—reborn.'

He sighed. 'I'd just started to make some serious money when I saw the pendant. I knew I had to have it for you. I wanted it to be a talisman, to keep you safe until you were ready to marry me. I was going to ask you that weekend. Tell you I'd wait until you were ready.

'None of us had the least idea that Piers would be arriving for your birthday. He just—turned up. I thought you must have invited him.'

'No,' she said vehemently. 'No—never.'

'So I had to change my plan. I couldn't risk him knowing how I felt about you. How serious it was. Because I knew he'd try to destroy it, or take you from me.

'When he stole the pendant and planted it in my room I knew that Angus was right, that he was capable of anything. That next time it could be drugs.

'I couldn't involve you. You were too young—too vulnerable. I told myself it wasn't our time. That one day I'd return and claim you.

'But when I found you again, you were engaged to him.' His voice was suddenly husky. 'Can you imagine how that made me feel? I could see nothing—think of nothing—except you in his arms—his mouth—his hands—touching you—possessing you.'

He shuddered. 'I went slightly crazy. I told myself that you'd belonged to him, but now you'd belong to me, in every way. I planned how I'd take you to bed—how I'd make love to you so completely that he'd be driven from your mind for ever. That you'd forget he ever existed. Until you could see, taste and breathe nothing but me.

'But instead, by forcing myself on you, I ruined everything for both of us. And I can't forgive myself for that.'

'Is that why you wouldn't make love to me again?' Her eyes widened. 'Out of some conviction that you'd hurt me the first time?'

He said tiredly, 'Adie—you were a virgin. I should have known that and treated you differently—with more consideration.'

Her voice was passionate, 'Chay, my darling fool, I didn't want to be considered. I wanted to be loved. I needed you to kiss the hurt away and show me how it ought to be between us. I thought that I'd disappointed you. That you didn't want me any more.'

'I've wanted you all my life.' There was yearning in his voice, and something deeper, too. Something almost primitive, making Adrien's body stir with sudden excitement. 'Throughout all the anger and the hurt and the partings you were the lodestar of my life. You drew me to you always.' His voice roughened. 'I wanted only to keep you safe, and instead I've driven you away.'

She shook her head, untying the sash of her robe. 'Your mother said the choice was mine,' she told him huskily. 'And I choose to stay. Oh, my love, let's stop punishing each other and be happy. I'm yours—if you want me.'

He was shaking as he lifted her into his arms, his mouth burning against her naked skin. The little velvet case fell unnoticed to the floor as he carried her to the bed and followed her down on to it, his hands tearing at his own clothing with savage energy.

Adrien twined her arms round him—her legs. She cried out in shocked pleasure as his mouth tugged at her nipple. His hands grazed her thighs with trembling urgency and she opened herself to him, arching against him voluptuously, her fingertips seeking him, guiding him.

She moaned as he filled her, the sound hoarse, almost pagan. There was no time for niceties or even lover-words. Their mutual need was too fierce, too consuming. The desire to take and he taken too strong. The time for denial— even for gentleness—was over.

She moved with him, her grace against his power, caught, possessed, by this new and overwhelming rhythm. With each thrust she seemed to draw him deeper and deeper inside her, her body clasping him like dark petals round a stem. She felt herself carried closer and closer to the edge of some whirlpool of emotion, and fear mingled with excitement.

Then, far in the depths of her being, she felt the first tiny pulsations of pleasure, like the flutterings of a wild bird. Sensed them building quietly into sweet ripples of delight that suffused her entire being.

And told her there was more.

Sighing, she lifted herself to him in a demand she barely understood, and heard her falling breath change to a whimper as all control was suddenly ripped away by some blind, atavistic force. She was total animal, drinking savagely from his mouth, her hands raking at him, her voice blurred, unrecognisable, urging him on.

Her body convulsed in sweet agony as she was lost, torn apart, dazed and dazzled by the shattering rapture of her climax.

As he came, he gasped for her, his voice hoarse and breathless, as if he was drowning. And she felt the ultimate scalding heat of his possession.

Some time later, he said, 'Are we still alive?'

'Never more so.' She caressed his lips with hers, her hands stroking his sweat-slicked hair. 'How could you know—so completely—what I wanted?'

'Because you're the other half of me.' He kissed her deeply, his tongue teasing and sensual. 'How could I not know?' He paused. 'Marry me, Adie, my one true love. I can't live without you.'

'And you were sending me away.' She put her palms against his chest, savouring the race of his heart.

'But only so that I could follow. You wouldn't have got far. I was hoping that if I let you go—you might miss me and want to come back.' His smile twisted her heart. 'If all else failed, I thought you might want the house.'

'The house is beautiful.' She put her lips to the pulse in his throat. 'But I'd walk out of it tomorrow to go with you.'

'I think we'll stay. It's time there was happiness here— and new life,' he added softly.

'Yes,' she said. 'Ah, yes.' Then, 'We'll build another treehouse.'

'As many as you want.'

'We'll fight,' she warned.

'How else would we make up?' Chay settled her against the pillows and drew the covers over her.

'Does it have to be marriage?' She curved herself into his arms, smiling wickedly. 'I've just begun to enjoy being your mistress.'

His lips touched her hair. 'Nothing need change. Wife by day,' he whispered, 'mistress by night. That's the deal, my love. And there's no negotiation. This time it's for ever.'

'For ever,' she echoed drowsily, and turned, in tenderness and trust, to sleep at last in her lover's arms.

Although born in England, **Sandra Field** has lived most of her life in Canada; she says the silence and emptiness of the north speaks to her particularly. While she enjoys travelling, and passing on her sense of a new place, she often chooses to write about the city which is now her home. Sandra says, 'I write out of my experience; I have learned that love with its joys and its pains is all-important. I hope this knowledge enriches my writing, and touches a chord in you, the reader.'

THE MISTRESS DEAL

by

Sandra Field

On the other side of that door was the enemy.

Lauren Courtney took a deep breath, smoothing the fabric of her skirt with her palm. The enemy. The man who had evidence—surely fabricated evidence—of a fraud apparently perpetrated by Lauren's beloved stepfather.

CHAPTER ONE

ON THE other side of that door was the enemy.

Lauren Courtney took a deep breath, smoothing the fabric of her skirt with her palm. The enemy. The man who had evidence—entirely fabricated evidence—of a fraud supposedly perpetrated by Lauren's beloved stepfather. Wallace Harvarson a liar? A cheat? Lauren would as soon believe the sun rose in the west.

But Reece Callahan, owner of the huge telecommunications company whose headquarters were in this glittering building in Vancouver, apparently did believe the sun rose in the west. So it was up to Lauren to set him straight. To protect Wallace's reputation now that her stepfather was dead and could no longer speak for himself. That she was gaining entrance to the Callahan stronghold under false pretenses was unfortunate, but necessary; she was under no illusions that a man as ruthless and successful as Reece Callahan would see her otherwise.

Lauren straightened her shoulders, catching a quick glimpse of her reflection in the tall plate-glass windows that overlooked English Bay from the seventh floor. Her chestnut hair was pulled back into a cluster of curls that bared her nape; her suit, a designer label, was severely styled in charcoal-gray, the skirt slit at the back; her blouse was a froth of white ruffles. Italian leather pumps, silver jewelry and dramatic eyeshadow: she'd do. Under normal circumstances she wouldn't be caught dead in charcoal-gray; primary colors were more her forte. But she'd decided back in New York that she needed to look both

5

elegant and composed for this interview. That her heart
was pumping rather too fast under her tailored lapel was
her secret. A secret she intended to keep.

The receptionist opened the paneled oak door and said
politely, "Mr. Callahan, Miss Lauren Courtney is here to
see you."

As Lauren stepped inside and the door closed behind
her, Reece Callahan got to his feet and walked around his
massive mahogany desk, his hand outstretched. "This is
indeed a pleasure, Miss Courtney. At your gallery opening
in Manhattan last year, when I purchased two of your
sculptures, I unfortunately arrived too late to meet you."

While his handclasp was strong, his smile was a mere
movement of his lips; his eyes, ice-blue, didn't melt even
fractionally. His face was strongly hewn, with a hard jawline, a cleft chin and arrogant cheekbones that instantly
Lauren itched to sculpt. His hair, thick with the suggestion
of a curl kept firmly under control, was a darker brown
than hers. The color of his desk, she thought, polished and
sleek.

His body—well, she'd like to sculpt that, too, she realized, her mouth suddenly dry. Beneath his impeccably tailored business suit, she sensed a honed muscularity, a
power all the more effective for being hidden.

A cold man. A hard man. Definitely not a man to respond to an appeal to sentiment. Yet sentiment, she
thought in sudden despair, was the only weapon she had.
He was also several inches taller than her five-foot-nine;
she wasn't used to looking so far up, to feeling small, and
in consequence at a disadvantage. She didn't like it. Not
one bit. Steeling herself, knowing Reece Callahan was indeed the enemy, Lauren detached her fingers from his
clasp and said coolly, "I hope you're still enjoying the
pieces you purchased?"

"They wear well. I've always liked works in bronze, and yours are particularly fine."

Even though she'd fished for the compliment, it pleased her. "Thank you," she said.

"I'm always glad when my investments do well. The prices you're commanding are escalating very nicely."

Her smile was wiped from her face. "Is that why you bought those bronzes? As an investment?"

"Why else?"

"Not because they spoke to your soul?"

His short laugh held nothing of amusement. "You've got the wrong man."

He'd said a mouthful there. On the basis of the past couple of minutes, Reece Callahan didn't have a soul. But wrong man or not, Lauren was stuck with him. Striving to regain her calm, she said politely, "May I sit down?"

"By all means. Can I get you a coffee?"

"No, thanks." She sat down gracefully in a leather chair, crossing her knees in a swish of silk. "I'm afraid I've obtained this meeting under false pretenses, Mr. Callahan. This isn't a social visit to discuss my work."

"You surprise me—I'd been assuming you were here to solicit a commission. Hawking your wares, so to speak."

Her lashes flickered. "I've never done that yet and see no reason why I should start with you."

"How admirably high-minded of you."

It wasn't part of her strategy to lose her temper before she'd even broached the reason for her visit. Lauren said with a smile as detached as his, "You wouldn't have invested in two of my pieces if you hadn't thought me talented. And even in the worst of times, I've never allowed the whims of the rich to dictate my creativity."

"Then why are you here, Miss Courtney? The rich may

be whimsical, but they also have responsibilities. I, in other words, have a great deal to do today and I'd prefer you to come to the point.''

Because he was leaning against the side of his desk, she was forced to look up at him. Her mistake to have sat down, Lauren thought, and said evenly, ''I've picked up a rumor—a very distasteful one. I'm trusting you'll reassure me it's nothing but a rumor. In which case I can be out of here in three seconds flat.''

She had his full attention; he rapped, ''I have much more important things to do with my time than spread rumors. Gossip of any kind has never appealed to me.''

''I've heard you're about to publish evidence of fraud on the part of Wallace Harvarson.''

He raised one brow. ''Ah…now that's no rumor.''

Her nails dug into her leather purse. ''You cannot possibly have such evidence.''

''Why do you say that?''

''He was my stepfather, he would never have been dishonest—I adored him.''

''That says more about your lack of perception than about the morals of Wallace Harvarson…clearly you're a better sculptor than a judge of character.''

''I knew him through and through!''

''You didn't change your last name to his, though.''

''He was my mother's second husband,'' Lauren said tightly. ''My own father died when I was three. Although she divorced Wallace when I was twelve, he and I stayed in touch over the years. As you no doubt know, he died fourteen months ago. Obviously he can't defend himself against this ridiculous charge. So I'm here to do so in his place.''

''And what form does this defense take?''

She leaned forward, speaking with passionate intensity.

"My own knowledge of the kind of man he was. Altogether I knew him for nineteen years, and I can tell you it's impossible he would have lied and cheated and stolen money."

"My dear Miss Courtney, that's a very touching response. Although a few tears might improve it. Tears or no, such a reply is meaningless in a court of law. I plan to publish the legal evidence for Wallace Harvarson's fraud next week, and in so doing clear the name of one of my companies. I will not tolerate being seen in the business world as less than honest. Which was your stepfather's legacy to me."

Appalled, she whispered, "*Publish* it? You can't mean that!"

"I mean every word." Reece Callahan drew back his sleeve, looking at his gold watch. "If that's all you have to say, I think we can profitably terminate this interview."

With swift grace, Lauren got to her feet. "If you publish such outright lies about my stepfather, I'll sue you for defamation of character."

"Please don't—you'd be laughed out of court. Besides, do you have any idea what that would cost you?"

"Does everything come down to money with you?"

"In this case, yes—Wallace Harvarson milked my company of five hundred thousand dollars."

"What's the truth, Mr. Callahan? That you made a bad business decision that cost you half a million and now you're looking for a scapegoat?"

"You go public with a statement like that and I'll be the one suing you," he said in a voice like steel. "My secretary will see you out."

"I'm not leaving until you promise you won't drag my stepfather's name through the mud for your own ends!"

He straightened, taking a step toward her. "You really

do have gall, Miss Courtney. I happen to know you bought
your studio with your inheritance from your stepfather, and
that you're still the owner of a very nice little property on
the coast of Maine that belonged to him.''

Her brain made a lightning-fast leap. ''You've known
all along that I'm Wallace's stepdaughter?''

''I always research the artists I'm investing in—it makes
good business sense.''

''So you've been leading me on ever since I got here—
how despicable!''

''That label belongs to you rather than me. You're the
one who's been living off the proceeds of fraud. I suppose
it beats doing the starving-sculptor-in-a-garret routine.
Even if your artistic integrity is a touch tarnished.''

White with rage, Lauren spat, ''My integrity isn't the
issue here—what about yours? Smearing the reputation of
a dead man in the full knowledge that I can't possibly hire
the kind of lawyers you can afford…doesn't that give your
conscience even the smallest twinge?''

His blue eyes were fastened on her face; he said in a
peculiar voice, ''You really do believe he's innocent, don't
you?''

''Of course I do! Do you think I'd be wasting my time,
let alone yours, if I thought for one moment Wallace could
have done anything so underhanded?''

''Then I'm sorry. Because you're in for a rude awak-
ening. And now I really must ask you to leave—I have an
appointment in ten minutes.''

Hating herself for doing so, knowing she had no other
choice, Lauren swallowed her pride. ''Is there nothing I
can do to make you change your mind?''

''Not a thing.''

''There must be something…''

His eyes like gimlets, he said, "I'm surprised, with your reputation, that you haven't offered the obvious."

Lauren flushed. "My sexual reputation, you mean?"

"Precisely."

Her fists were clenched at her sides so hard the knuckles were white. "So you researched that, too. And along with the rest of the world, you believed every word the gutter press printed about me. Fabrications my mentor Sandor fed his journalist friends. Yet you're the one who says he doesn't believe in gossip?"

"Your mentor's highly respected."

"Whereas I was a mere upstart with the kind of looks the press adores. Do you wonder why I'm begging you not to publish all these lies about Wallace? I know the power of the media to ruin reputations…know it and fear it and have suffered from it."

"When I arrived at your gallery last year, you were leaving by another door. Arm in arm with two men, no less. I doubt that your lack of morals is just gossip invented by a vengeful ex-lover."

Her shoulders sagged. "I didn't come here to defend myself against promiscuity," she said in a low voice. "Neither did I come to say I'd sleep with you if you promised not to publish."

"So why didn't you sue Sandor—your ex-lover, your ex-teacher, your mentor—if he was lying?"

"It was four years ago," she blazed. "At that time I'd sold exactly two pieces in my whole life—I wasn't into selling then, I knew I hadn't reached the point where I wanted my stuff out there in the real world—as it happens, I do have artistic integrity, Mr. Callahan. Short of asking Wallace for money, I didn't have one cent to rub against another. And lawyers come expensive. As you know."

"Indeed." Hands in his pockets, Reece looked her up

and down with a deliberation that made her flinch inwardly; she felt as though his ice-cold eyes were stripping her naked. But Lauren had toughened in the years since Sandor had set out to drag her through the gutter personally and artistically; she raised her chin, breathing hard, and said not one word. He said noncommittally, "You're not dressed cheaply."

"There are some wonderful secondhand places in Greenwich Village. I know them all."

"I see." Casually Reece leaned back against the desk again. "Perhaps I should reconsider."

In a flash of incredulous hope, she said eagerly, "You mean you believe me about Wallace?"

"That's not what I mean at all. But there is something you could do for me. A way in which you could be useful to me."

The light died from her face. "And in return, you wouldn't publish anything about my stepfather?"

"That's correct."

She said in a level voice, "I won't sleep with you, Mr. Callahan."

"I'm not asking you to, Miss Courtney."

"Soiled goods," she said bitterly.

"As you say."

Briefly she closed her eyes. "Then what do you want of me?"

"You could be of use to me for the next week or so—after that I'm off to London and Cairo. But while I'm here, I have a number of engagements that mix business with pleasure, never my favorite way of operating but sometimes it's unavoidable. I'd want you to pose as my companion. My lover, to put it bluntly. I can't imagine you'd find that difficult."

Her response came from a deep place she couldn't have named or ignored. "No! I'm a sculptor—not a call girl."

"Either you want to protect your stepfather, or you don't. Which is it?"

His voice was clipped, utterly emotionless. She flashed, "Why would you want to be seen with someone whose reputation's not much better than a call girl's?"

"Because you interest me."

"Oh, that's just lovely. As if I'm a stock market quote. Or a microchip."

"You're a very talented woman. As well you know. You're also articulate, well-dressed and pretty enough for my purposes. In other words, you'll do. So which is it, Miss Courtney—yes or no?"

Pretty enough, she thought in true fury. She wasn't just pretty, she was beautiful: without a speck of vanity she knew this, for her mirror and the rest of the world had told her so often enough. But to Mr. Ice-Water-In-His-Veins Callahan she was merely pretty.

Not that that was the real issue, Lauren realized hastily.

She dragged her thoughts back to Wallace, his quick-silver smile and ready laughter, the way that his rare and always delightful visits had rescued her from an adolescence that had been rife with real unhappiness. Her mother had resented her burgeoning beauty, while her mother's third husband had despised her budding talent; between them, they had made her teenage years a misery. She'd left home the week she'd graduated from high school; it had been Wallace who'd seen to it that she hadn't starved in a garret during the years when she'd been studying at art school, sculpting all hours of the night, and gradually unearthing her own strengths.

And weaknesses. Of which Sandor was the prime example.

This was no time to think about Sandor. She said carefully, "Let me get this straight. For one week you want me to publicly pretend I'm your mistress." She flicked her eyes up and down his expensive suit, letting them linger on his silk tie, which bore the crest of a very distinguished university. "While you may not be *my* idea of the ideal date, there must be lots of women who'd bypass your personality in favor of your money. Since I can't believe you're offering this out of the kindness of your heart, I wonder why you've chosen me to come to your rescue?"

To her intense fury, he gave a bark of laughter. "Your tongue's got a bite like sulfuric acid."

"All the more reason for you to avoid me."

"Oh, I think I can handle you."

Discovering a profound wish to knock him off balance, she said sweetly, "You're forgetting something. You're a big name, with your mergers and your innovations and your huge profits—don't think I hadn't done *my* research. As for me, I had a major show in London last year, and I have a growing reputation in the States. If you and I pose as lovers, the press will have a field day. There will be gossip, Mr. Callahan. Lots of lovely gossip."

"So your answer's no." He moved toward the door. "Don't forget to buy Wednesday's paper, will you? You'll see a whole new side to your stepfather, and—trust me— it won't be based on gossip."

She couldn't bear that. She couldn't. Her only alternative was to toe the line. Do as Reece Callahan had proposed. Because Lauren was under no illusions; even if she could afford to sue Reece, and even if by some remote chance she won, the damage would have been done. Wallace's name would always be linked with dishonor. She said coldly, "I was merely pointing out the pitfalls of your course of action."

"How altruistic of you."

"If I do this, it would be an act. Only an act. In private I wouldn't allow you to come within ten feet of me."

"You're assuming I'd want to."

Her breath hissed between her teeth. "Tell me precisely what you'd require of me."

"You'd stay in my condo near Stanley Park. On Saturday you'd go with me to a cocktail party and dinner that I'm hosting. One of my CEOs is laboring under the delusion that his daughter would make me a fine wife. Your presence will disabuse him of that notion. Then on Sunday there's a private dinner party at the home of a man I'm thinking of bringing on board. Unfortunately his wife is more interested in me than in her husband's career. You'll give her the message I'm not available. Two days later we'll fly to my house in Whistler—I don't often go there this time of year, I use it mainly for skiing in February. But I'll be doing business with some Japanese software experts—and you'd host their wives. Then we go to a yacht club off the east coast of Vancouver Island, where I'm to meet an associate in the commodity market. After that, it's back here and you can go your own way." He paused. "Eight days, not counting tomorrow."

Lauren's adventurous spirit, never much in abeyance, quickened. She'd heard of Whistler, the luxurious ski resort north of the city; and she'd never been to Vancouver Island, set like a green jewel in the waters of the Pacific Ocean. Keeping her face impassive, she said, "I get the message. Because you're rich, a lot of women are after you."

He raised one brow. "You could call it an occupational hazard."

She almost smiled, feeling the first twinge of liking for him. Shoving it down, she said crisply, "If I choose to do this, I need to make something clear—I'm not after you, no matter how much money you have. In public, I'll do my best to convince the world that you and I are madly in love. In private, I'll require a room of my own and strict boundaries around my privacy."

"I assure you," Reece said silkily, "that will be no problem."

He found her undesirable. A turnoff. That's what he meant. Stifling a surge of rage as fierce as it was irrational, Lauren said, "I'd also require a signed statement from you that you would never, directly or indirectly, damage my stepfather's name."

"Providing you keep to the terms of our agreement."

Her turquoise eyes flung themselves like waves of the sea against the hard planes of his face. "I would. I promise."

"So you're saying you'll do it?"

She bit her lip. "We'd never bring it off—it's so obvious we don't like each other."

"You're being too diplomatic. Mutual antipathy— wouldn't that be a more accurate description?"

"It would, yes," she snapped. "Plus, to put it bluntly, you don't look like you could act your way out of a paper bag."

"You let me worry about that," he retorted. "Yes or no? Eight days of your time or your stepfather's reputation—which is it to be?"

"I'll do it," she said. "You've known all along that I would."

"So you're astute as well as talented."

"You're getting a bargain," she mocked.

"We'll see," he said dryly. "In addition to our basic agreement, I'll require you to sign a statement that you'll never discuss our supposed relationship with the press.

Come to this office at three tomorrow afternoon. I'll have the documents drawn up for us both to sign. You can arrive at my condo at ten tomorrow night—I'm out earlier in the evening.''

''Very well.'' Lauren gave him a derisive smile. ''I do hope all this acting won't be too taxing for you.''

''If you're asking for a demonstration, you're out of luck. I don't believe in wasted action.''

She clenched her fists. ''Your secretary must know we're not lovers—that we just met this morning.''

''My secretary is very well paid to keep her mouth shut.''

''Now why should I be surprised?'' Lauren said cordially. ''Goodbye, Mr. Callahan. I won't say it's been a pleasure.''

''Don't push your luck—the document's not signed yet.''

She said tartly, ''If Wallace is looking down on me from heaven, I hope he appreciates what I'm doing for him.''

''People who cheat and lie don't go to heaven.'' Reece opened the door. ''Goodbye.''

They were in full view of his secretary. ''Then I guess you won't go there, either,'' Lauren said, reaching up and kissing him on both cheeks. ''Goodbye, darling,'' she added in a carrying voice. ''I'll see you tomorrow.''

Pivoting, she smiled at the secretary. ''I'll see myself out,'' she said, and walked toward the elevator. The slit in her skirt, she knew, showed her legs rather admirably. To her great satisfaction she heard Reece Callahan's door snap shut with more force than was required.

At least she'd achieved that much.

Had she ever in her life conceived such an overwhelming dislike for a man? Even Edward, her mother's third husband, liked dogs and rhododendrons, and laughed loudly at his own jokes. Reece Callahan wouldn't know how to laugh.

Cold. Hard. Manipulative.

She was going to read both documents very carefully before she signed anything.

CHAPTER TWO

CHARLOTTE BOND, better known as Charlie, said incredulously, "You agreed to do *what?*"

"You heard," Lauren said. "I agreed to act as Reece Callahan's mistress, in public only, for the space of one week. Well, eight days. That's all. It's no big deal."

"Lauren, I dated Reece. Twice. He plays major league. And he's got a hole where his heart's supposed to be."

"So why did you date him twice?"

A rueful grin lit up Charlie's piquant face. "I couldn't believe that a guy with those rugged, damn-your-eyes kind of good looks could really be as cold as the proverbial glacier."

"You saw him as a challenge."

"I guess so." Charlie gave a snort of self-derision. "What a joke. Although we did have a few things in common."

Charlie was a top-notch tax consultant, whose logical brain was the antithesis of Lauren's: they had a friendship of opposites that had survived Charlie's move from New York to Canada's west coast last summer. "Don't you see?" Lauren said equably. "It's because he's such a cold fish that I feel quite safe taking this on. No risk Reece Callahan's going to lose his head over me. We'll act as lovers in public, go our separate ways in private, and Wallace's good name will be safe. Simple."

Charlie grimaced. "Trouble is, I feel responsible. If I hadn't brought up Wallace's name quite innocently to Reece, in connection with that software company Wallace

19

was involved with, Reece wouldn't have mentioned I should keep my ear to the ground for some very interesting revelations about Wallace. None of which were to Wallace's credit. As soon as he said that, all my alarm bells went off and that's when I phoned you.''

''You and I were due for a visit anyway,'' Lauren said comfortingly. ''And I'm so glad I've finally made it to the west coast. Oh, Charlie, it's wonderful to have a bit of money to spend! To be able to get on a plane and fly here and not have to worry about the cost. For so many years I've been rock-bottom broke, having to count every cent I spent.''

But Charlie was still frowning. ''Just so long as you don't get hurt.''

''By Reece Callahan?'' Lauren made a very rude noise. ''Not a chance. Did I tell you he bought those two bronze pieces as an investment? They're two of my best works, and yet they're owned by a man who doesn't give a damn about what they say—his only concern is that they increase in value. And you're worried I might fall for him? Huh. Pigs might fly.''

Charlie sighed. ''It's an awful waste. He's got a great body.''

''To sculpt, yes. To go to bed with? No, ma'am. Anyway, I'm off sex, have been for years.''

Charlie took a big gulp of her Chardonnay, her face still troubled. ''You're absolutely certain of Wallace's innocence?''

''Of course I am!''

''You did tell me once that your inheritance from him was less than you'd expected.''

''That's true enough. And his mother's jewels that he'd promised me, they never did turn up. But, Charlie, everyone can have setbacks on the financial markets, you know that from your own work. It doesn't mean the person's committed fraud.''

"He never confided in you?"

Lauren's brow crinkled in thought. "We didn't talk about stuff like that. Serious stuff." Her voice wobbled. "He was such fun, always laughing or singing pop songs at the top of his lungs—I miss him so much."

"Mmm…" Charlie ran her fingers through her tousled blond curls. "Just make sure you look after yourself as far as Reece is concerned. And read all the fine print on these documents you're going to sign."

"I will." Lauren grinned at her friend.

"Let's go out for supper, I don't feel like cooking. There's a divine Czech restaurant just down the road."

"And neither of us will mention Reece Callahan's name again. Okay?"

"Okay," said Charlie. Nor did they.

Promptly at three o'clock the next afternoon, Lauren presented herself to Reece's secretary. The October day had turned unexpectedly warm; her dress was a chic linen sheath in deep blue with long sleeves. Gold hoops that Wallace had given her for her eighteenth birthday swung at her lobes, and she'd pulled her hair back with a gold clip. Her makeup was dramatic, that and her dress making her eyes look almost indigo.

The secretary said pleasantly, "Mr. Callahan shouldn't be too long, Miss Courtney—but he is running a little behind schedule."

So she was to be kept waiting like a common supplicant? Like a patient at the dentist's? Which was just how she felt: all her nerves on edge, dread like a lump in the pit of her stomach. Lauren said, "Oh, I'm sure he doesn't mean to keep me waiting, Miss Riley. I'll go straight in."

"I don't think—"

But Lauren was already opening Reece's door. He was seated in front of his computer screen and looked up in annoyance. She said with warm intimacy, "Hello, darling—I knew you wouldn't want me to sit outside…how are you?" Then, as she closed the door, she gave him a wicked grin, her voice going back to normal. "I should tell you that at the age of thirteen I planned to become the second Sarah Bernhardt. I could get to enjoy this."

He said curtly, "The first thing you'd better learn is never to interrupt me when I'm working."

"But, dearest," she cooed, batting her artfully mascaraed lashes, "I'm your heart's delight."

For a split second Lauren thought she caught a flash of emotion deep in Reece's eyes. But then it was gone. If indeed it had existed. He said sharply, "I mean it, Lauren."

"What a dull life you must lead."

He surged to his feet. He'd discarded his jacket and tie; his shirt, open at the throat, revealed a tangle of dark hair. "Let's get something straight," he said with dangerous softness. "I'm the one with the evidence about Wallace. So I get to call the shots."

Her chin lifted mutinously. "I don't like being told what to do."

"Then you'd better learn fast."

"I think you're forgetting something, Reece—this is a reciprocal deal. You've got something I want and I've got something you want. So both of us get to call the shots."

"There can't be two bosses—that's a basic corporate rule."

"We're not talking corporations, we're talking love at first sight. Passion, adoration and lust." She gave him a complacent smile. "The rules are different."

"Certainly that's your area of expertise."

She flushed. "Let's get something else straight. Right now. You can quit throwing my reputation in my face."

"What's that cliché? If the shoe fits…"

So angry she forgot all caution, Lauren blazed, "If you think for one minute that I'm going to let you walk all over me for eight consecutive days, you'd better think again. Because I'm not. No chance."

"You look rather more than pretty when you're angry," he remarked. "How do you look when you're making love?"

"*You'll* never find out!"

"According to the media, you wouldn't know how. To make love, I mean. You use a guy, milk him dry, then go on to the next one. Which can hardly be dignified by the word *love*." He closed the distance between them, taking her by the shoulders with cruel strength, his eyes boring into hers. "What I don't understand is how you can create works of art that breathe truth and morality from such a shoddy little soul. Or why, when you're so extraordinarily talented, you play cheap sexual games to further your career."

She flinched; in attacking her work, he was stabbing her where she was most vulnerable. She said fiercely, "I came here to sign a couple of documents, not to have my character torn to shreds by a man who wouldn't recognize an emotion if it hit him in the face. Especially if that emotion was called love."

As suddenly as he had seized her, Reece let her go. "You don't have an answer for me, do you?"

"My character and my sculptures are entirely congruent."

"Oh, for God's sake."

She said with sudden insight, "You know what your

problem is? You're not used to people contradicting you. Especially a woman. I bet you're surrounded day and night by *yes, sir, no, sir, whatever you say, sir*. Very bad for you.''

"Whereas you're surrounded by men who fall all over you, agreeing with every word you say just so long as they end up in your bed.''

Anger flicked along her nerves. She said amicably, "Reece, I'll spell it out for you again. Please don't spend the whole week harping on my love affairs—I have a low tolerance for boredom.''

"Is that a challenge, Miss Courtney?''

"It's a statement of fact.''

"Frankly, I don't care if you're bored out of your skull the entire eight days. Just as long as you do what I say.'' Reece pulled open a drawer and extracted two sheets of typescript. "Read this. There are two copies, one for each of us. I'll get my secretary to witness our signatures.''

The document, in carefully worded legalese, said that Lauren Courtney would present herself in the public realm as Reece Callahan's lover for a period of eight days, and would preserve total confidentiality about the contents of this agreement in perpetuity. In return, Reece Callahan contracted never to publish anything of any nature about Wallace Harvarson, stepfather of the aforesaid Lauren Courtney.

The language, while cumbersome, was clear. Lauren said steadily, "I'm ready to sign if you are.''

Reece folded the papers to hide the text and pressed a buzzer on his desk. A few moments later the secretary walked in. "I'd like you to witness our signatures, Shirley, please,'' Reece said. "Lauren?''

Once she signed, she was committed. For a few seconds that felt like hours, Lauren stared at him blankly. Was she mad promising to live for over a week with a man who was the antithesis of everything she believed in? What did she really know about him? Maybe the moment she walked in the door of his condo, he'd fall on her. And what recourse would she have? If she didn't stay for the full eight days, he'd publish a bunch of scurrilous lies about Wallace. Charlie had tried to warn her that Reece would be a formidable foe. But had Lauren listened? Oh, no.

"Lauren?" Reece said more sharply. "You have to sign in both places."

Yes, sir, she thought crazily, picked up his platinum pen and signed each copy. Then she watched as Reece added a totally illegible scrawl, and the secretary her ultraneat script. The secretary then left the room, never once having looked Lauren in the eye.

It was done. She was committed.

Reece said irritably, "This is a business deal that will terminate a week from tomorrow. Stop looking at me as though you've just married me for life."

She blurted, "Have you ever been married?"

"Are you kidding?"

"Yes or no will do."

"No."

"Neither have I… Sandor had a soul above such petty, bourgeois standards."

"Lauren," Reece said coldly, "signing those forms wasn't a license for true confessions."

"Wasn't a license for you to behave like a human being, you mean?"

"We're not in public. We don't have to act."

"If I stuck a pin in you, would you bleed?" she demanded in true exasperation. "Or would ice water drip on the carpet?"

"It irks the hell out of you that I'm not bowled over by you, doesn't it?"

Truth. That's what she sought in her work, and that's how she endeavored to live her life. Lauren said concisely, "You insist on seeing me as something I'm not, and you've built such a barrier between yourself and the real world that you treat everything and everyone in terms of either monetary value or functionality. That's what irks the hell out of me."

His mouth hardened. He said brusquely, "Here's my card with my condo address and phone number. I've opened a couple of accounts for you downtown in case you need clothes—the details are on this piece of paper. And this is your copy of our agreement. Ten o'clock tonight, Lauren. Please don't be late."

Automatically she took the papers he was holding out and shoved them in her purse. "I'll be there."

He stepped back, holding her gaze with his own. "One more thing. You're the most beautiful woman I've ever seen."

As her jaw dropped, he opened the door. "See you tonight, darling," he added, giving her a smile of such breathtaking intimacy that her heart lurched in her breast. Speechless, she dragged her eyes away and walked past the secretary like a woman in a dream. The elevator was waiting for her. As the doors slid open, she heard the soft closing of Reece's door behind her.

You're pretty enough.

You're the most beautiful woman I've ever seen.

Which was the truth and which was an act? And if she couldn't tell the difference, what had she let herself in for?

The cab swung into the grounds of Reece's condo at fifteen minutes to ten that evening. Lauren, though she had difficulty admitting this to herself, hadn't wanted to be late. In consequence she'd allowed extra time for traffic. Too much time, she realized, paying the taxi driver, and taking her big suitcase from him. She noticed that the grounds had been designed with a Japanese theme, a harmony of rock, fern and shrub overlaid by the gentle ripple of water. An island of peace, Lauren thought, and wished she felt more peaceful.

She felt anything but peaceful.

If she arrived early, would Reece think she was too eager for his company? She could simply stand here for the next ten minutes and admire the garden.

To heck with that. No games, no pretense. She headed for the lobby, where the uniformed desk attendant recognized her name immediately, and called the elevator for her. "Mr. Callahan is expecting you, madam," he said with a pleasant smile. "The top floor."

She gave him an equally pleasant smile back, wondering why she should feel like a high-class call girl when she was anything but. The elevator smoothly deposited her outside double doors with exquisite wrought-iron handles; Reece's unit was the only one on this floor. Her feet sinking in the thick carpeting, Lauren pushed the bell. Let the adventure begin, she thought, and fixed her smile on her face.

CHAPTER THREE

REECE swung the door open. For the space of five full seconds Lauren stared at him, all her rehearsed greetings fleeing her mind. He was naked to the waist and barefoot, his hair wet and tousled. Detail after detail emblazoned itself on her brain: the pelt of dark hair on his deep chest; his taut, corded belly; the elegant flow of muscle and bone from throat to shoulder. He said flatly, "You're early."

"I allowed too much time for the traffic."

"You'd better come in—I just got out of the shower."

His jeans were low-slung, his jaw shadowed with a day's beard. He looked like a human being, Lauren thought, her mouth dry. He also looked extraordinarily and dangerously sexy. "Here," he said, "let me take your suitcase."

She surrendered it without a murmur, staring at the ripple of muscles above his navel as if she'd never seen a half-naked man before. As Reece turned his back to her, putting the case down, the long curve of his spine made her feel weak at the knees. Only because she was an artist, she thought frantically. Nothing to do with being a woman in the presence of an overpowering masculinity. Yet why hadn't she realized in his office how beautifully he moved, with an utterly male economy and grace?

He said, "I might as well show you your room right away. What's in the other bag?"

In her left hand Lauren was clutching a worn leather briefcase. "My tools...I never travel without them."

"Here, give them to me."

"I'll carry them." She managed a faint smile. "I've had some of them for years."

"You don't trust me, do you?" he rasped. "Not even with something as simple as a bag of tools."

"Reece," she said vigorously, "the agreement is to act like lovers in public. Not to fight cat-and-dog in private."

He looked her up and down, from her ankle-height leather boots and dark brown tights to her matching ribbed turtleneck and faux fur jacket with its leopard pattern of big black spots. "You're obviously the cat. So does that make me the dog?"

"You're no poodle."

"A basset hound?"

She chuckled, entering into the spirit of the game. "You have very nice ears and your legs are too long. Definitely not a basset."

"Do you realize we're actually agreeing about something?"

"And I'm scarcely in the door," she said demurely, wondering with part of her brain how she could have said that about his ears.

"Let me take your coat."

As she put down her tools and slid her jacket from her shoulders, her breasts lifting under her sweater, he said, "I wondered if you'd back out at the last minute."

The smile faded from her face. "So that you could blacken Wallace's name from one end of the country to the other? I don't think so. Which room is mine?"

"At the end of the hall."

For the first time, Lauren took stock of her surroundings. Her initial impression was of space; and of some wonderful oak and leather furniture by a modern Finnish designer whom she'd met once at a showing in Manhattan. Then her gaze took in the collection of art that filled the space with color, movement and excitement. She said dazedly, "That's a Kandinsky. A Picasso. A Chagall. And surely that collage is James Ardmore. Reece, it's a wonderful piece, I know he's not very popular, but I'm convinced he's the real thing. And look, a Pirot, don't you love the way his sculptures catch the light no matter where you stand?"

Her face lit with enthusiasm, she walked over to the gleaming copper coils, caressing them gently with her fingertips. When she looked up, Reece was watching her, his expression inscrutable. She said eagerly, "It begs to be touched, don't you think? I adore his stuff."

"I have another of his works. In my bedroom."

She didn't even stop to think. "Can I see it?"

Reece led the way down a wide hallway, where more paintings danced in front of her dazzled gaze. His bedroom windows overlooked the spangled avenues in Stanley Park; but Lauren had eyes only for the bronze sculpture of a man that stood on a pedestal by the balcony doors. She let her hands rest on the man's bare shoulders, her eyes half shut as she traced the taut tendons. "It's as though Pirot creates something that's already there," she whispered, "just waiting for him."

Reece said harshly, "Is that how you make love?"

Her head jerked 'round. Jamming her hands in her pockets, she said, "What do you mean?"

"Sensual. Rapt. Absorbed."

She'd hated being anywhere near Sandor's bed by the end of the relationship. Not that Reece needed to know that. "How I do or do not make love is none of your concern."

"So what are you doing in my bedroom?"

The bedside lamp cast planes of light and shadow across Reece's bare chest; Lauren was suddenly aware that she was completely alone with him only feet from the wide bed in which he slept. "You think it was a come-on, me asking to see the sculpture?" she cried. "Do you have to cheapen everything?"

As if the words were wrenched from him, he said, "I bought the condo new just ten months ago. You're the only woman to have ever been in this room."

She knew instantly that he was telling the truth; although she couldn't have said where that knowledge came from. Frightened out of all proportion, she took two steps backward. "It doesn't matter if you've had fifty women in your bedroom," she said in a thin voice. "I haven't slept with anyone since Sandor and I'm certainly not going to start with you."

"You expect me to believe that?"

"I don't care if you do or not!"

"But that was four years ago and—"

"Three years and ten months," she interrupted furiously, "and what business is it of yours anyway?"

"None. I'll show you to your room."

If eyes were the windows of the soul, Lauren thought fancifully, then Reece had just closed the shutters. But did he have a soul? He certainly had emotions. She'd learned that much in the last few minutes.

She trailed after him, noticing another Picasso sketch on his bedroom wall, as well as a delightful Degas impression of a dancer. Reece was striding down the hallway as though pursued by a hungry polar bear. About to hurry after him, Lauren suddenly came to a halt. In a lit alcove in the wall stood a small Madonna and child, carved in wood so old its patina was almost black. The figures were simply, rather crudely carved; yet such a radiant tenderness flowed from one to the other that Lauren felt emotion clog her throat.

She wasn't even aware of Reece walking back to where she was standing. He said roughly, "What's the matter?"

"It's so beautiful," she whispered, her eyes filled with wonderment.

"Unknown artist, late fourteenth century. You can pick it up, if you want to."

"But—"

"Lauren, pick it up."

With a kind of reverence she lifted the statue, her hands curling around it with the same tenderness that infused the figures. "Look how her shoulder curves into her arm and then into the child's body," she said. "Whoever carved it must have loved his child...don't you think?" She lifted her face to Reece, a face open and unguarded, totally without guile.

Briefly he rested his hand on her cheek. He said thickly, "You could have been the model. For the mother."

"That's a lovely thing to say..."

The warmth from his touch coursed through her veins; he was standing very close to her. And this was the man she'd thought bore no resemblance to a human being? A man who had no soul? "Wherever did you find it?" she asked, wanting to prolong a moment that felt both fragile and of enormous significance.

"In a little village in Austria—way off the beaten track."

"Would you mind if I made a copy of it? I'd destroy the copy once it was finished." Very gently she put the carving back in its niche.

"I'll be out every day," Reece said. "You can do what you like."

She glanced up. The shutters were back, she thought in true dismay; his face had closed against her. Her question came from nowhere, the words out before she could stop them. "Did your mother love you, Reece?"

He said with deadly quietness, "You have no right to ask that question and I have no intention of answering it."

"I guess I—"

"Your room's at the end of the hall. Do you want anything to eat or drink before you go to bed?"

"I'm not a child to be sent to bed because she's misbehaved!"

"No. You're an intrusive and insensitive young woman."

"If you have problems with my question, then say so. But don't blame me for asking it."

"We have a business arrangement—nothing more. Kindly remember that, will you?"

Lauren said evenly, "Years ago, I allowed Sandor to cower me into submission over and over again...and I almost lost myself in the process. I vowed I'd never let that happen again. So don't try, Reece—it won't wash."

"We're fighting cat-and-dog again. And that's not in the agreement, isn't that what you said?"

He was right; she had. "There's something about you," she said tightly. "You're like a chunk of ironwood. Or a length of steel."

"Just don't think you can shape me to your ends."

"Do you despise all women? Or is it just me?"

"You never let up, do you?" he said unpleasantly.

She paled, suddenly remembering the statue in his bedroom. "Oh. You prefer men."

"I do not prefer men! It's very simple, Lauren. I've got no use for all the posturing and stupidities that masquerade in our society as romance."

"That carving of the Madonna and child—it's not about romance. It's about love."

"Love—what do you know about love? Do you have a husband? Do you have a child?"

She winced, her face suddenly pinched and pale. "You know I don't," she said in a stony voice. "I loved Sandor. But he didn't want marriage or children. Or me. The real me."

"You sure know when to pull out all the stops," Reece said nastily. "You can make tea or coffee in your room. I eat breakfast at six-thirty and I'm gone by seven. I'll be back tomorrow evening at six, cocktails at seven, dinner afterward. Wear something dressy. Did you buy yourself some clothes?"

"Of course not," she said shortly.

"You've got to look the part, Lauren! As well as act it."

She took refuge in a matching anger. "I have my own money, and if I need clothes I'll buy them myself."

"Do you have to argue about everything?" he snarled.

"With you, yes."

"I should have asked for character references before I signed that goddamned agreement."

"Adversity might teach you a thing or two," she retorted. "I'm going to bed. Good night."

"Be ready by quarter to seven tomorrow evening."

"Yes, Reece, I'll be ready." And wearing the most outrageous outfit I own, she thought vengefully. She turned away, marching toward the door at the end of the hall, and heard him say behind her, "I'll bring your case down. And your tools—if you trust me to, that is."

So much for the grand exit, Lauren thought with a quiver of inner laughter; she'd forgotten about her suitcase. "That far I trust you," she said.

Her bedroom was painted terra-cotta, the bedspread and drapes in shades of teal blue, the whole effect confident yet full of welcome. Two exquisite Chinese scrolls hung on either side of the marble fireplace, while the shelves held an enviable collection of Ming pottery. Aware through every nerve of Reece's footsteps as he entered her room, she turned to face him. He said evenly, ''That door leads to the bathroom, and the balcony's over there. I'll see you tomorrow evening around six or six-thirty.''

He didn't want to see her in the morning, that was obvious. She leaned over to switch on a lamp, her hair swinging softly around her face. ''Enjoy your day,'' she said with the merest breath of sarcasm.

For a full five seconds Reece stared at her in silence. She raised her chin, refusing to look away, wishing with all her heart that he'd put a shirt on. Then he said crisply, ''Good night, Lauren,'' and closed the door with a decisive snap.

Lauren sank down on the wide bed, knowing she'd give almost anything to be back in the unpretentious guest bedroom in Charlie's apartment. Anything but Wallace's reputation, she thought unhappily.

Eight days wasn't long. She could manage. Even if Reece Callahan repulsed and attracted her in equal measure.

It would be a great deal safer if she were indifferent to him.

Lauren woke early the next morning. The sun was streaming through the French doors that led onto the balcony and she knew exactly what she was going to do all day. But she'd need a key to Reece's condo.

Quickly she dressed in her leggings and sweater. In her bare feet, her hair loose around her face, she hurried down the hall, not even glancing at the statue of the Madonna:

she'd have lots of time for that. In the spacious living room, she called, "Reece? Are you up?"

"In the kitchen."

He didn't sound exactly welcoming. Pasting a smile on her face, she walked into an ultramodern kitchen equipped with what seemed like acres of stainless steel. Reece was, thank goodness, wearing a shirt. He was munching on a piece of toast, gazing at the papers strewn over one of the counters. She said, "You start early."

"So, apparently, do you. What do you want?"

"A key—I need to go out this morning."

"The doorman has an extra, I've told him to give it to you." He shifted one of the papers, making a note with the pen in his free hand.

"That toast smells good," she said provocatively. "I think I'll have some."

"Can't you wait until I've gone?"

"Are you always cranky in the morning?"

"Not with people I like."

"Try harder," Lauren said, glaring at him as she headed for the coffee machine.

His voice like a whiplash, he said, "Sandor's beginning to have all my sympathy."

The mug she was filling almost slipped from her grasp; scalding liquid splashed the back of her hand. With a gasp of pain, she banged the mug down on the counter and ran for the sink, where she turned on the cold tap and thrust her hand under it. Then Reece was at her side. "Here," he ordered, "let me see."

"It's nothing!"

He took her by the wrist, putting the plug in the sink with his free hand. "You haven't broken the skin—you're better off immersing it in cold water."

The cold water did relieve the pain. Biting her lip, Lauren said, "There's a moral here—I shouldn't start fights before I've had my caffeine fix."

"You're still in love with Sandor."

Her wrist jerked in his hold like a trapped bird. "It was over years ago, Reece."

"Which isn't an answer—as you well know."

"You're not getting any other."

He moved closer to her, his eyes roaming her face. "No makeup," he said. "The real Lauren Courtney."

"You're unshaven," she responded in a flash, "but do you ever show the real Reece Callahan?"

With sudden deep bitterness he said, "Is there a real Reece Callahan?"

Shocked, she whispered, "If you have to ask the question, then of course there is."

"Oh, sure," he said, moving away from her and drying his hands. "Let's scrap this conversation. Did you say you wanted some toast?"

"Yes, please." Only wanting to lighten the atmosphere, she added, "This is a very intimidating kitchen—I'm what you might call an erratic cook."

He didn't smile. "Pull up a stool and I'll bring you a coffee. Cream and sugar?"

"No cream. Three spoonfuls of sugar."

"To sweeten you?"

"To kickstart the day. Creativity is enhanced by glucose—at least, that's my theory."

He gave his papers a disparaging glance. "With the negotiations I've got the next few days, maybe I should try it."

"Honey's better than sugar, and maple syrup's best of all."

"So you're a connoisseur of the creative process. You

should write a book," he said dryly, putting her coffee in front of her.

"No time... Do you know what, Reece? We've just had a real conversation. Our first."

"Don't push your luck," he rasped, "and don't see me as a challenge."

She flushed. "A useless venture?"

"Right on."

She said deliberately, "I don't believe you bought every one of the paintings and sculptures in this condo strictly as an investment."

"You can't take a hint, can you?" Reece said unpleasantly, taking the bread out of the toaster.

"The Madonna and child? An investment? You bought that statue because in some way it spoke to your heart."

His back was turned to her; briefly, his body shuddered as though she'd physically struck him. Then he pivoted, closing the distance between them in two quick strides. Towering over her, he dug his fingers into her shoulders. "Stay out of my private life, Lauren. I mean that!"

His eyes were blazing with emotion, a deep, vibrant blue; his face was so close to hers that she could see a small white scar on one eyelid. She'd hit home; she knew it. And found herself longing to take his face between her palms and comfort him.

He'd make burnt toast out of her if she tried. Swallowing hard, Lauren said with total truth, "I'm sorry—I didn't mean to hurt you."

He said harshly, "I'm going to be late for work. If your hand needs attention, the first-aid kit's in my bathroom cabinet. I'll see you this evening." Gathering all his papers in a bundle, he left the kitchen.

Thoughtfully Lauren started to eat her toast. The ice in his eyes had melted with a vengeance. And he'd bought the Madonna and child for intensely personal reasons that she was quite sure he had no intention of divulging.

One thing she knew. She wasn't going to be bored during the next few days.

CHAPTER FOUR

"LAUREN, what in hell are you doing?"

The chisel slipped, gouging into the wood. With an exclamation of chagrin, Lauren whirled around. "Don't ever creep up on me again when I'm working, Reece—look what you made me do! And what are you doing home anyway? You said six o'clock this evening."

Reece hauled his tie from around his throat. "It's six thirty-five and we're supposed to leave in twenty minutes."

Lauren's jaw dropped. "It can't be. I stopped for lunch no time ago."

"Six thirty-six," he said, ostentatiously looking at his gold watch.

"Oh, no," she wailed, "I promised I'd be ready."

"You did."

"Reece, I'm sorry. You'd better get out of here so I can change. I swear I won't be more than ten minutes late."

"What did you do to your finger?"

She glanced down at two Band-Aids adorning her index finger. "I cut it. No big deal."

"You're a mess," he said.

She looked down at herself, laughter flickering across her features. She was wearing her oldest leggings and a T-shirt embellished with several holes from her welding torch; her hair was pulled back into an untidy bundle on her neck. "You mean you won't take me to the cocktail party like this? Where's your sense of adventure?"

40

"I'm starting to wonder," Reece said with a note in his voice that brought her head up fast.

The words came from nowhere. "Don't you go seeing me as a challenge, either," she said.

"I'm beginning to think Wallace Harvarson has a lot more to answer for than a mere five hundred thousand dollars," he said tightly. "Go get ready, Lauren. Pin your hair up. Pile on the red nail polish. But for Pete's sake, hurry."

She started to laugh. "It'll take more than a few pins to make me presentable," she said, and stood up, moving away from the table and stretching her muscles with unselfconscious grace.

The answering laughter vanished from Reece's face. He said sharply, "You did that today?" She nodded, watching him walk closer to the rough carving she'd been working on for the last few hours. He said, as though the words were being dragged from him, "I can see where you're headed—and already it's a thing of beauty."

"I thought I could just make a copy," Lauren said ruefully, pulling the ribbon from her hair and shaking it in a cloud around her head. "But it got away from me."

The lines of the emerging sculpture of a mother and child were utterly modernistic, yet imbued with an ancient and ageless tenderness. Reece said in a hard voice, "I'm going to have a shower. I'll wait for you in the living room. I'm the host of this shindig this evening and I want to arrive on time."

"Yes, sir," she retorted, and watched him march across the dark-stained floors and out of the door. She put her chisel down on the table. Had she ever met a man who was such a mass of contradictions? He'd seen instantly what she was striving to create from the block of wood;

and run from it as though all the demons in hell were after him.

But she mustn't see him as a challenge.

The challenge, she thought wryly, looking down at herself, was to transform herself from a frump to a fashion model in less than twenty minutes. Move it, Lauren. You've got all week to figure out Reece Callahan.

It might take a lifetime. A thought she hastily subdued.

Seven o'clock. Lauren was late. Scowling, Reece switched to the news channel, and not for the first time wondered what in God's name had possessed him to suggest that Lauren Courtney pose as his lover. As a result, Wallace Harvarson was getting off scot-free and he, Reece, was saddled with an argumentative and thoroughly irritating woman who didn't count punctuality among her talents. Because she had talents. That bloody statue had got him by the throat the minute he'd seen it; which she, of course, had noticed right away.

The new federal budget was due to be tabled; he tried to pay attention. Then, behind him, overriding the newscaster's voice, he heard Lauren say, "Will I do?"

He flicked the remote control and stood up, turning to face her. She had draped herself against the door frame, her eyelids lowered demurely. Her dress was black, a full-length sheath slit to mid-thigh. A vivid scarlet-and-blue scarf swathed her throat and fell provocatively over one breast; her thin-strapped sandals had stiletto heels and her earrings dangled almost to her shoulders, little enameled discs of blue and red that moved with her breathing.

He said ironically, "You'll be noticed."

She smiled; her lips were also scarlet, he noticed, dry-mouthed. "Isn't that the whole aim?"

"I guess so." He walked closer, noticing her incredibly

long lashes. "How do you keep your hair up? It's contradicting all the laws of gravity."

It was piled in a mass of curls, making her neck look impossibly long and slender. "Pins and prayer," said Lauren.

"Let me see your hands."

"You would ask that," she said, and held them out, palms down. The hot coffee had left red blotches on the back of her left hand; she had two clean Band-Aids wrapped around her index finger.

"Do you often cut yourself?" he rapped.

"It's an occupational hazard," she said limpidly. "To quote you."

"Is the cut deep?"

"Nope. But I'm human. I bleed."

"In contrast to me."

"You said it. I didn't."

"You don't have to." He didn't know which he hated more, the way the black fabric clung to her breasts, or the mockery in her turquoise eyes. In a hard voice he added, "This is all very amusing and I'm sure we could stand here trading insults for the next hour. But my car's waiting downstairs. Let's go...and Lauren, don't forget what this is all about, will you? Wallace—remember him?"

"Are you telling me to behave myself?"

"Yeah. That's exactly what I'm doing."

"You don't have a worry in the world," she snapped. "I promise I'll be the perfect mistress."

She looked as though she'd rather take a chisel to him. A blunt chisel. He checked that he had his keys in the pocket of his tuxedo and said with a mockery equal to hers, "Shall we go, darling?"

Her nostrils flared. "If you think I'm going to start this charade one minute before I have to, you're out to lunch."

The sudden mad urge to take her in his arms and kiss her into submission surged through Reece's body with all the force and inevitability of an ocean wave. Oh, no, he thought, I'm not going there. Not with Lauren Courtney. Sure recipe for disaster. He said coldly, "I don't give a damn what you do when we're alone. But you'd better stick to the bargain in public. Or else the deal's off."

"Fine," she said. "Let's go."

She stalked to the elevator ahead of him, and stared at the control panel all the way down. His car was a black Porsche; he held the door while she folded herself into the passenger seat, revealing rather a lot of leg as she did so. Her silk stockings were black, her legs long and slender; his hormones in an uproar, Reece got into the driver's seat and slammed the door. Once this week was over, he'd find himself a woman. An agreeable woman without an artistic bone in her body. He'd been too long without one, that was his problem.

Nothing to do with Lauren.

In a silence that seethed with things unsaid, they drove to the city's most luxurious hotel. Reece pulled up in front of it. "Okay," he said, "we're on. You'd better act your little head off, sweetheart, or I'll pull the plug on your precious stepfather so fast you won't know what hit you."

"How nice," Lauren said, "an ultimatum. Guaranteed to make me feel as though we've been making mad, passionate love the whole day long."

Very deliberately he put his arm around her shoulders, caressing her bare flesh and dropping his head to run his lips along her throat. "We made mad, passionate love the minute I came home from work, that's why we're late…and we're going to do the same as soon as we get rid of all these people. Right, my darling?"

He felt her swallow against his cheek. "Right," she cooed and delicately nibbled at his ear with her teeth.

Sensation scorched along every nerve he possessed. The soft weight of her breast was pressed against his sleeve; her perfume, as sensual and complex as the woman herself, drifted to his nostrils. His body's response was instant and unequivocal. He wanted her. Wanted her in his bed. Now. Naked, beautiful and willing.

Then Lauren murmured against his earlobe, "You'd better not kiss me, not unless you want scarlet lipstick all over your face when we walk through the door. We don't have to be quite that convincing, do we?"

She was totally in control. That was the message. She didn't want him, Reece thought grimly. She was only toying with him, playing a role, the very role he'd insisted on.

He was an idiot. A prize jerk.

With a superhuman effort, he managed to say lazily, "I'm sure we can convince them we're mad for each other without the benefit of Revlon. Perhaps you'd better wipe my ear."

Her fingers were warm, brushing against his hair as they smoothed his flesh. He fought down a tide of sensation that would drown him if he let it and said, "The valet'll park the car. Let's go, Lauren."

She took his face between her palms, looked straight into his eyes and whispered with passionate intensity, "I'm crazy about you, honey. You know that, don't you?"

For a split second he found himself believing her, so convincing was the blaze of emotion in her eyes. But she was acting. Only acting. Feeling a rage as fierce as it was irrational clamp itself around his throat, he said, "Haven't I believed every word you've said from the moment we met?"

Her lashes flickered. Gotcha, he thought. "And don't call me honey. Even in jest." Then he climbed out of his car, passing the keys to the uniformed valet. "Callahan's the name," he told him easily.

"Thank you, sir."

Reece walked to Lauren's door, opened it, and took her hand, raising it to his lips. "Have I told you yet how beautiful you look?"

She swayed toward him, her lips in a provocative pout. "A hundred times and never enough."

A man's voice said loudly, "Reece—good to see you."

Reece turned. "Marcus, I'm glad you could make it. And Tiffany, how nice to see you. May I introduce Lauren Courtney? Dearest, this is Marcus Wheelwright, CEO of the European branch of my company…and his daughter Tiffany."

Marcus was fiftyish, heavy-set and jovial. Tiffany, Reece noticed, was her usual ice-maiden self, wearing a white satin gown with diamonds glittering around her throat, her blond hair sleekly perfect. He wouldn't be surprised if Lauren's hairdo fell down before the night was over; but Tiffany's would never do that. And Tiffany was probably never late for anything. Hurriedly he brought his attention back as Marcus shook Lauren's hand. "Not the sculptor?" Marcus asked. "I didn't know you two knew each other."

"We met recently," Reece said. "Love at first sight, wasn't it, darling?"

Lauren laughed up at him, lacing her arm through his. "Absolutely…I'm still in a state of shock. Are you based in Paris, Marcus?"

"Paris. Hamburg. Oslo. You name it," Marcus said; he had the look of a man recovering from a disagreeable revelation. Whereas Tiffany, Reece noticed, looked coldly furious.

Lauren started to discuss the art market in Paris, skillfully including Tiffany and Reece in the conversation, every movement of her body giving out the message that she was a satiated woman who'd been equally generous in return. It was a masterful performance, Reece thought savagely, and struggled to play his part. Then Marcus drew him aside with a question about their French office; answering automatically, all his senses keyed to Lauren, Reece heard Tiffany say, "So you're Reece's latest plaything."

"That's not what I would have called myself," Lauren replied.

"Don't fool yourself on that count—I'm the one who'll last. I have breeding, all the right connections." Tiffany gave Lauren's earrings a scornful glance. "And taste."

"Whereas I'm merely talented, intelligent and beautiful," Lauren said.

"Also incredibly conceited!"

"Merely realistic."

Reece smothered the urge to laugh out loud and tried to pay attention to Marcus, who wanted to fire his office manager; deflecting him from the topic, Reece said heartily, "I should go inside, Marcus. I'm glad you and Tiffany have had the chance to meet Lauren—I'm a very lucky guy."

"You certainly are," Lauren said, laughing as she briefly laid her head on his shoulder; several of her curls, he noticed, were already tumbling from their pins. He let his palm rest warm on her nape, feeling the contact scour his nerves in a way that had nothing to do with deception and everything to do with his hormones. He didn't need to act. He lusted after Lauren Courtney like a tomcat in springtime.

Did he want her to know that?

He did not.

"I'll talk to you later," he said to Marcus and Tiffany. "Come along, darling, let's get a drink."

As he and Lauren walked arm in arm into the glittering ballroom, decorated with tall standards of lilies and thousands of tiny gold lights, she said sweetly, "I don't know why you want to discourage Tiffany. She's perfect for you—there's ice in her veins, too."

"You wouldn't by any chance be daring me to prove otherwise?"

"No! I'm simply making an observation."

"I'm not so sure about that. Are you forgetting that once midnight rolls around, you and I will be alone in my condo?"

Her arm tensed under his. "But you promised—"

"Ah…there's Cindy," he said casually. "If you can get past her, you can deceive anyone."

Cindy Lothan, the wife of another of his CEO's, had a brain like a steel trap; she and her husband made a formidable pair. Swiftly Reece made the introductions. But Lauren was relaxed and charming, drawing Cindy out with a skill Reece had to admire. As Lauren discussed the latest upsets in the stock market with every air of knowing what she was talking about, he put his arm around her waist, caressing the swell of her hip. She quivered in response like a high-strung racehorse. Reece's thrill of primitive triumph just as quickly turned to ashes in his mouth. She was acting. Only acting. And he'd damn well better remember it.

Lauren always at his side, Reece played the room, making the contacts he needed to make, saying what he needed to say. The dinner was delicious, his speech went extremely well, and he danced almost exclusively with Lauren, fighting with all his willpower to control his body's response to her closeness. By the time midnight rolled around, he felt as though the evening had lasted for three days. He looped his arm around Lauren's shoulders and said with intimate ease, "Sweetheart, I think we should head home—are you ready?"

Her lips curved in a smile laced with sexual complicity. "I thought you'd never ask."

To hell with this, Reece decided, and for a moment allowed his very real desire to blaze from his eyes; and watched her own eyes widen and color rise in her cheeks. The room fell away. She can't be acting now, he thought. No one could make herself blush to order. Not even Lauren.

He said huskily, "I want to be alone with you."

Her tongue traced the softness of her lower lip. "And I with you."

What he really wanted was to tear her dress from her body and make love to her on the hotel carpet. Forcing himself to smother the image of her naked limbs sprawled in graceful abandon at his feet, he said roughly, "Let's go, then."

However, everyone they passed wanted to say goodnight and thank him for a great party, conversations from which Reece extricated himself with rather less than his usual expertise. But finally they made it to the lobby and the valet disappeared to get his car. Lauren slipped into the passenger seat, Reece put his foot to the accelerator and they surged away from the hotel.

Lauren said flatly, "Thank God that's over. I don't think I've ever worked so hard in all my life."

It was as though she'd flung cold water in his face. So

she'd been acting all along, he thought furiously. Right down to the blush. He said in a voice from which he removed any trace of emotion, "You did a fine job. Deception comes easy to you."

She shot him an unfriendly look. "You're no slouch in that department yourself."

"Isn't corporate ethics considered a contradiction in terms? As opposed to artistic integrity, that is?"

"You're spoiling for a fight, aren't you?" she fumed. "I'm only too happy to oblige. Every person in that hotel ballroom thinks you and I are having a scorcher of an affair. And when I disappear from your life next week, they'll assume you dumped me. Because, of course, no woman in her right mind would give up the opportunity to get her greedy little paws on your millions."

"On day eight," Reece snarled, "we'll stage the granddaddy of all rows plunk in the middle of the Vancouver airport, and you can tell me to go to hell. You can shout it from the bloody rooftops as far as I care. The fight at least won't be acting and the press can have a field day with me being the dumpee rather than the dumper."

He pulled up with a jerk at a red light. Lauren said in an odd voice, "But you hate gossip."

"Not as much as I hate acting," Reece declared, and wondered what on earth had possessed him to say that.

He glanced over at her. She no longer looked angry. Instead she was staring down at her hands, which were linked in her lap. In a small voice she said, "You weren't acting some of the time. Are you going to leap on me as soon as we get to your place? Because if so, I'll get out now and go to a hotel."

Rather a lot of her hair had tumbled down her neck; she looked tired and unhappy. He quelled an uprush of compassion, saying coldly, "You dress in slinky black crepe, fall all over me and expect me to behave like that chunk of wood you're carving? I'm a normal red-blooded male, for Pete's sake.''

"And I'm passably pretty.''

So she'd noticed that particular deception. "I take that back. You really are the most beautiful woman I've ever seen.''

"Oh, sure.''

"It's the truth!''

Her head jerked up; he noticed with another of those disconcerting surges of emotion that she'd chewed some of the lipstick from her bottom lip. "You know what?'' she declaimed. "I don't have a clue when you're telling the truth and when you're lying yourself blue in the face.''

The lights changed. He drove across the junction and said impatiently, "You think I've got you all figured out?''

She sighed. "I suppose it doesn't really matter, does it? This is only about acting, and there's only a week to go. But you haven't answered the question. Are you going to leap on me, Reece?''

"No.''

Her fingers were still twisting in her lap. "Can I trust you?''

He said with cold fury, "I'm not into rape.''

"At least admit that I'm smart to be asking the question.''

His own anger died. "I'm six inches taller than you and eighty pounds heavier. Yeah, you're right.''

A faint smile lit up her face. "Thanks.''

It wasn't part of the next seven days for him to start liking her. "Ten minutes and we'll be home,'' he said repressively.

"You'll be home—I won't.''

"Give it a rest, Lauren.''

Conspicuously she said not one more word, gazing out of the window as they drove toward the park. As Reece pulled up outside his condo, he said, "Try not to look as though you hate my guts in front of the doorman, okay?"

Her eyes glittering, she said, "But, honeybunch, your body drives me mad. Surely that includes your guts."

He wanted to laugh at her audacity; he wanted to kiss her senseless. He did neither. Rather, he walked around the hood of his car, helped Lauren out with the air of a man who had seduction on his mind, and, his arm snug around her waist, said good-night to the doorman. The elevator door opened and closed behind them. Reece dropped his arm, moved away from her and said in a clipped voice, "Tomorrow night is a private dinner party in Shaughnessy Heights. Three other couples. I'm wearing a business suit. Be ready by seven."

"I'll set the beeper on my watch to go off at six," Lauren said with equal crispness. "That way I won't forget."

He was easily forgettable. That was the message. Swiftly Reece unlocked the door of his condo and stood back for her to precede him. She said, her back to him, "I'll see you tomorrow."

"Sweet dreams," he said ironically, and watched her hurry across the living room with none of her usual grace. He then stripped off his tie, poured himself a stiff whiskey and flipped on the television movie channel. Comedy. Drama. Violence. It didn't matter. Anything to distract him from Lauren's body and his ferocious need to possess that body.

What he mustn't forget was what a consummate actress she was.

CHAPTER FIVE

THE following evening Lauren marched into the living room of Reece's condo at ten to seven. Tonight it was Reece who was going to be late, she thought irritably, and tried to focus on a delightful Chardin oil painting hanging beside a Stieglitz photograph.

The key clicked in the lock and Reece walked in, hauling at his tie and flinging his jacket on the nearest chair. Then he saw her and for a moment stopped dead. "You're on time."

"I'm not always late."

"But you're always argumentative… I'm going to have a shower. Ten minutes. Help yourself to a drink."

She didn't need a drink. She needed to stay stone cold sober the entire evening. She picked up the small sketch pad she'd brought from her room and started copying a Picasso stroke for stroke. Reece Callahan was nothing to her. Nothing.

If Wallace were alive, he should be down on his knees to her in gratitude.

If Wallace were alive, she wouldn't be here.

Her sketch was a disaster and her fingers were cold. She tossed the pad on a wing chair and went to stand by the window, blind to the panoramic view of Stanley Park and the snowcapped Rockies. Then Reece came back in the room. He was fiddling with a gold cuff link, his shoulders very broad in his pristine white shirt, his damp hair curling over his ears.

"My turn to be late tomorrow night," Lauren said.

53

"You've got the night off tomorrow—I fly to Seattle for meetings and won't be home until nine or so."

She didn't try to mask her relief. Reece said curtly, "The following morning we leave for Whistler. Don't wear an outfit like that for the Japanese delegation."

Don't tell me what to do, she thought. "You don't like what I'm wearing?" she purred, fluttering her lashes at him. "But you bought it for me, remember? You said you couldn't wait to get me home and tear it from my body."

"If the market ever dries up for bronze sculptures, you could make B-grade movies," Reece jeered. "Let's go. Our host's name is Brian, his wife's Bianca, and she's the one who's out to get me."

"No accounting for taste," Lauren remarked, and picked up her black wool shawl from the chair, throwing it around her shoulders.

"Smart move, wearing that shawl," Reece said, ushering her out the door. "So you won't catch pneumonia."

Her jade-green top did show rather a lot of cleavage. Her wide-legged silk pants swishing softly as she walked toward the elevator, Lauren said amiably, "If you've got it, flaunt it, and the level of this conversation is definitely B-grade."

He pushed the button for the ground floor; then his gaze wandered to the creamy curves of her collarbone, and the shadow between her breasts. "Oh, you've got it."

Color crept up Lauren's cheeks. She'd worn this outfit before and thought nothing of it. Why should Reece Callahan make her feel as shy and uncertain as an adolescent? She found herself longing for the evening to be over before it had even begun; to be alone in her bedroom, away from a man who unsettled and infuriated her. Then Reece took her by the shoulders, his lips drifting down her throat to the hollow at its base. Her pulse leaped, then began to race with frantic speed. The elevator doors opened.

She said in a venomous whisper, "The doorman's nowhere in sight. You can quit right away."

Against her skin he murmured, "Security cameras—this is for their benefit."

The waft of his breath jangled every nerve she possessed. She lifted her fingers to stroke his thick dark hair, discovering it to be unexpectedly silky to the touch, and said shakily, "Darling, we're already late."

As he moved away from her, his arm brushed the fullness of her breast; her indrawn breath was no act, Lauren realized with a lurch of her heart, and felt her nipples harden. Hurriedly she drew the shawl around her body and almost ran outside to Reece's car. How could her body betray her by responding to a man she both disliked and feared?

Frigid was a word Sandor had thrown at her more than once during their stormy relationship; in the ensuing months and years, not one of the men she'd dated had tempted her to have an affair. Her conclusion had been inevitable: sex wasn't for her.

Not that she was contemplating having sex with Reece. That was out of the question.

"You're very quiet," Reece said, starting the car.

She shivered. "There's no audience."

"Are you cold?"

She huddled into her shawl. "No. Thanks."

"Sometimes you behave like a Victorian virgin," he said, whipping out into the traffic. "And how's that for a laugh?"

Ridiculously, Lauren felt tears prickle at the backs of her eyes. But she never cried, and she wasn't going to start with Reece Callahan. She said with sudden fierce honesty,

"I'm so tired of all the innuendoes and sneers from men who believed Sandor's version of events without even asking me if I had a different version. You're just like them, Reece—I'm condemned before I even walk in the room. Not that I give a hoot in hell what you think about me...and that's the last word you're getting out of me until we arrive." Ostentatiously turning her face to the window, she closed her eyes.

She didn't fall asleep, she was too riled up for that. But she didn't cry, either. When eventually they pulled into a long curve of driveway, Reece said evenly, "We're here."

Lauren sat up, opened her purse and checked her lipstick. "I'll do the best I can this evening because of Wallace. Just don't forget it's an act, will you?"

He said with dangerous softness, "Lauren, when I kissed your throat, I felt your pulse race. That wasn't an act."

"More proof that I'm easy—that Sandor's right," she said bitterly, and climbed out of the car. A Tudor mansion loomed in the darkness; she disliked it on sight, and stalked toward the huge oak door with its insets of mullioned glass. Fake beams, fake glass and fake woman, she thought, and rounded on Reece, her eyes glittering. "You know what? I hate the sight of you."

His answer was to bury his hands in her tumble of loose curls and kiss her hard on the mouth. As the front door opened, Reece released her so quickly that she staggered, turning a stunned face to her host. She said weakly, "You must be Brian," and held out her hand. It was, she noticed, trembling slightly.

With a courtesy she had to admire, Brian ignored her confusion. "Hello, Lauren, welcome to Stratford House...Reece, come in. Oh, here's Bianca. Darling, this is Reece's friend, Lauren Courtney. You're from Manhattan, am I right, Lauren?''

Bianca was a voluptuous brunette who looked ready to throttle her, Lauren thought with distant humor. Bianca must have seen that kiss on the front step: a kiss from which Lauren was still inwardly reeling. It had been so sudden and so shocking that she'd had no time to react. Wasn't this even more proof that all those horrible accusations Sandor had hurled at her were still true? Frigid. Ungenerous. Heartless. On and on they'd gone, and she in her vulnerability had believed him.

Desperately she tried to pull herself together, praying Reece was in ignorance of her response. Or rather, her lack of it. Because, of course, he'd kissed her hoping Bianca would see. All part of the act.

With a superhuman effort Lauren managed to sound relaxed. "I'm so pleased to meet you, Bianca."

"Do come in," Bianca said with minimal warmth. Then, her voice changing, she added, "How are you, Reece? Lovely to see you. Let me get you a drink while Brian introduces Lauren to our other guests."

Divide and conquer, Lauren thought shrewdly, and tucked her arm into Reece's. "I'm actually rather thirsty, Bianca. We had to rush around so we wouldn't be late, didn't we, darling?" she said, smiling besottedly up at Reece.

There were sparks of blue fire in his eyes as he lifted her fingers to his lips, kissing her knuckles with lingering pleasure. "Until I met you, I was known as Mr. Punctuality," he said. "Right, Brian? Lead the way, Bianca. I'll introduce Lauren to the rest in a few minutes."

Lauren knew she was blushing. All the better, she thought wildly. It adds veracity. And I'll make darn sure Bianca doesn't put arsenic in my wine.

As they followed Bianca into a paneled library where
an imposing oak bar and a great many horse brasses took
precedence over the books, Reece winked at her.
Impulsively she winked back, bumping him gently with
her hip and watching his irises darken. His strongly carved
lips curled in a smile; his eyes weren't at all like ice. Was
it act or reality? Desire or deception?

Did she really want the answers?

With all the social ease and charm she was capable of,
she engaged Bianca in conversation. When they went into
a living room dominated by overstuffed furniture, she kept
her arm tucked into Reece's and interspersed her remarks
with adoring looks and endearments. What did it matter
that the other guests would label her a clinging vine? That
was the deal she'd struck.

The food was excellent, the wine flowed freely, and the
conversation sparkled. Lauren was seated across from
Reece. As she took the last spoonful of raspberry torte, she
glanced over at him. He was laughing at something Brian
had said, and as though she'd never seen him before, his
image imprinted itself on her mind: his white teeth and
tanned face, alive with strength and intelligence; the lock
of dark hair falling on his forehead; the entirely masculine
vitality that infused every one of his movements.
Handsome, sexy, and utterly male. How could she ever
have thought him a cold fish?

He spells danger, she thought blankly. Maybe the reason
she hadn't really looked at him before had been pure self-
protection. Because if she'd looked, she'd never have embarked on this crazy scheme.

Six more days. She'd be all right. Of course she would.

The party broke up at one a.m., Reece and Lauren being
the last to leave. Again Lauren did her imitation of a clinging vine, neatly foiling Bianca's attempt to corral Reece

and show him the new solarium. As soon as they were in his car with the doors shut, she announced, "You owe me, buddy. Big time."

He laughed, putting the key in the ignition. "Did you ever play interference in football? You'd be a natural."

"You're the one built like a football player," she said incautiously.

"Don't tell me that's a compliment?"

She'd drunk rather too much Cabernet Sauvignon and in the semidarkness she didn't feel the slightest bit frigid. "I believe it is," she said. "Imagine that."

"Seriously, Lauren, you did wonders this evening. You kept Bianca from eating me alive and no one else even realized what was going on. Thanks."

"Beyond the call of duty?" she said with a cheeky grin, and slid her feet out of her elegant pumps with a sigh of relief. "That's better—my feet are killing me. I've been scared to take my shoes off at dinner parties ever since someone swiped my shoes during the speeches at a reception I once went to. I had to walk out in my stockinged feet with my nose in the air, as though it was the latest fashion to go unshod to fancy parties."

Reece threw back his head, laughing all the way from his belly. "I promise I'll always protect you from shoe thieves, my darling Lauren."

My darling Lauren... Lauren said primly, "That's very nice of you, Reece."

Still chuckling, he began asking her about the reception. From there they moved to a Broadway play they'd both seen, and before she knew it, they were back at the condo. Reece opened the car door on her side. Then he leaned over and picked her up, straightening and heading for the lobby. "Put me down," Lauren croaked.

"Your feet are hurting. It's the least I can do after

Bianca," he said, and smiled at the doorman. The elevator doors opened and shut. In its gleaming gold walls, Lauren gazed at the outline of a tall dark-clad man holding a woman whose hair rippled over his sleeve, and felt herself tremble with what was surely desire.

Desire? Her?

I don't desire him, she thought frantically. I can't! This is a business arrangement, it's only going to last a few more days. I mustn't get involved. Anyway, I hate sex. Sandor saw to that.

She wriggled in Reece's arms. "You can put me down now. No one's watching."

He tightened his hold. "This is nothing to do with the doorman," he said, carrying her out of the elevator and along the thick carpet. Stooping slightly, he inserted the key in the lock and then kicked the door shut behind him. "Stop squirming," he said thickly, "it's driving me nuts."

She squirmed all the harder. "Reece, put me down!"

Swiftly he lowered her to the floor, put his arms around her and kissed her with a fierce possessiveness.

Lauren stood stiff as a china doll in his arms. For the second time Reece was kissing her. But this time there was no Bianca to impress; only the two of them in an empty apartment. This time he wasn't acting. Fear flicked her nerves sharp as a whip, memories surging back of what it had been like with Sandor, that long-ago sensation of being smothered by his weight, by the power he had wielded over her.

But then, as though a pendulum had swung from one extreme to the other, fear was usurped by a flood of other sensations. The warmth of Reece's lips, so confident of their welcome. The slide of his palms down her back to her waist, the hard wall of his chest pressing against her breasts. Her blood started thrumming in her veins and an ache of desire—unquestionably it was desire—blossomed in her belly. In sheer surprise her body sagged in Reece's embrace. Without even considering what she was doing, Lauren clutched the sleeves of his jacket and kissed him back; and wondered if she could faint from sheer pleasure.

His lips teased hers apart. She felt the first thrust of his tongue and welcomed it with all her heart, her hands moving to his shoulders, then linking themselves at his nape, where his hair brushed her skin with tantalizing softness.

His kiss deepened, an intimacy she was more than ready for, her body melting into his. His arms tightened around her waist, his fingers digging into the curve of her hip. With one hand he found the swell of her breast, caressing its firm rise with lingering sensitivity. Lauren gave a tiny, spontaneous cry of delight. He said huskily, against her mouth, ''My beautiful Lauren...'' Then, again, he swept her up into his arms.

Through eyes dazzled with longing, she realized he was carrying her across the room, past the Picasso and the Chardin to the doorway of his bedroom. He pushed the door open with his foot, and once again she saw the wonderful bronze sculpture against the forest-green wall, and the shimmering lights of the park beyond the balcony. The bed looked huge, and it was this that finally made Lauren find her voice. ''Reece, what's going on? I—''

He lowered her to the floor so that she was enclosed in his embrace, and said hoarsely, ''You're where you belong.''

''But we—''

He closed her mouth with his own, and in a surge of sweetness she forgot about Sandor's cruelty. Had she ever in her life felt so encompassed by a man's embrace? So certain that it was here in Reece's bedroom that she did indeed belong? Knowing she was taking a huge step into the unknown, Lauren wrapped her arms around his waist, her palms seeking the warmth of his skin beneath his shirt. His muscles were tense, the hard curves of his rib cage exciting her beyond measure. Of their own volition her hands smoothed his chest and the taut, rippled belly, and all the while his tongue played with hers in a heated kiss she wanted to last forever.

Against her mouth, he muttered, "I wanted you the first moment I saw you walk into my office—why else did I suggest this crazy arrangement of ours?"

Her body froze, desire obliterated with horrifying suddenness. Wrenching her head back, Lauren gasped, "But you believed Sandor then, you said so."

He nibbled at her lips, saying thickly, "This is no time for talking. I want to see you naked, I want to—"

"And now I'm proving you right, aren't I?" she gabbled. "I'm easy, I'm promiscuous, I've only known you for four days and I'm about to fall into your bed."

"For God's sake—you've had other lovers since Sandor, you must have."

"I haven't! I told you I hadn't."

"What does it matter?" Reece said impatiently, clasping her by the shoulders. "We're meant to be together, I know we are. Anything else is irrelevant."

Her heart now felt as though it was encased in ice. "You think it's irrelevant whether or not you believe me about something as basic as promiscuity?"

"If you've had other lovers, Lauren, that doesn't mean you're promiscuous."

"You don't believe one word I've said, do you?" she cried, pulling away from him. "How can that be irrelevant?"

He said harshly, "We're not marrying each other."

"No. Just having a one-night stand. Or a one-week

stand.'' She struggled to get her breath through the pain in her chest. ''I must be mad to have kissed you—why did I do that?''

''Because you wanted to.''

He was right. For the first time in many years, she'd craved a man's body, opened herself to his kisses and his touch without a thought for the consequences or the context: behavior so totally out of character that in the last few minutes she'd become a stranger to herself. And it was Reece who had done that to her. A man she scarcely knew, rich, ruthless, and full of secrets. Reece with his beautiful body and his implacable will.

He said grimly, ''At least you're not bothering to deny it.''

Swallowing hard, Lauren fought to find the words that might bring her back from the chasm into which she had so nearly tumbled. The simplest thing would be to turn tail and run for home as fast as she could; but if she did so, Wallace's good name would be ruined. She said with icy precision, ''I'll function as a hostess for the Japanese wives—not as your mistress. The same goes for your contact at the yacht club. In other words, for the rest of our time together we can stop acting. And then I'm out of here. So fast you won't see me for the dust.''

His eyes like shards of glass, Reece said, ''You're burning your bridges, Lauren—I could be useful to you. I know a lot of people with the kind of money to afford your sculptures.''

''As investments,'' she said bitterly. ''No, thanks. I've made my own way in the world so far, and I'll continue to do so.''

''With help from Sandor. And Wallace.''

''That's right,'' she said furiously, ''rub my nose in my mistakes. Of course, you never make them, do you?

You're not a fallible human being like the rest of us—I bet you've never done a single thing you've regretted with all your heart.''

His fingers bit into her flesh with cruel strength. ''I told you to stay out of my personal life,'' he blazed. ''But do you listen? You—''

''So you have made mistakes...big ones, by the look of you,'' she said in a dazed voice.

''I—''

''Won't you tell me about them?'' she begged. ''Please?''

''I will not—they're none of your goddamned business,'' he grated, pushing her away as though he couldn't bear to touch her, then wiping his palms down the sides of his trousers.

Cut to the quick, Lauren cried, ''Thank God, I didn't get into your bed. The only thing you're willing to share is your body, isn't it, Reece? Go ahead and do that with other women if that's what turns you on. But I deserve more than that. I want a man who'll share himself body and soul.'' She bit her lip, wondering where her words had come from, certain in her heart they were true. ''I'll be ready Tuesday morning to go to Whistler. In the meantime, I don't want to lay eyes on you.''

''You'll stay here tonight and tomorrow night,'' he said in an ugly voice. ''Or the deal's off.''

''You're just like Sandor—in love with power,'' she retorted, too angry to care what she said. ''So how could you ever fall in love with an ordinary person? A woman with feelings and integrity? I wouldn't make love with you if you were the last man on earth.''

''Yes, you would,'' he sneered. ''If I'd kept my mouth shut about wanting you in my office, you'd be in my bed right now. Because you were willing, Lauren—that was no act.''

She'd been more than willing: against all her experience and expectations, she'd been enraptured. Her shoulders slumping, she said wearily, ''So you get the last word— good for you.''

As she turned away, Reece made no move to stop her. Feeling as though she'd been run over by a truck, Lauren trailed to her bedroom and shut the door, leaning back against the frame. All this luxury and elegance, yet she might as well be in prison.

There were only six more days left in her sentence. Six days and six nights.

It was the nights she had to worry about. Because Reece had been right: she would have made love with him. Just as if Sandor hadn't time and time again convinced her she was a wipeout in bed, a failure as a woman.

But she'd learned her lesson. She wouldn't lay as much as a finger on Reece from now on.

She couldn't afford to. Not when acting could so easily turn into reality.

CHAPTER SIX

LAUREN worked like a woman possessed all the next day, and by seven that evening knew she had to stop. The carving of mother and child was as complete as she could make it; now she had to put it away for a month and then look at it afresh to see if it had accomplished what she'd hoped for.

She was almost sure it had: that it was both powerful and true. Carefully she draped it in one of the towels from the bathroom. As always when she'd finished a piece, she felt drained yet restless, too wound up to settle to anything, too wired to sleep. One thing she knew: she'd prefer not to be in the condo when Reece returned from Seattle.

On impulse she phoned Charlie. "It's Lauren. Any chance you're free for a visit?"

"I'd love to see you. I haven't eaten yet—feel like Szechuan food?"

That's just what Lauren needed: a crowded restaurant and some good food. "Great idea!" They agreed to meet in Chinatown, and Lauren went to have a shower. An hour later, she and Charlie were seated across from each other in a dimly lit restaurant decorated with red dragons and tasseled lights, sipping Chinese tea and eating meat dumplings in a ferociously spicy sauce.

Charlie said briskly, "Okay, Lauren, come clean. What's it like being the mistress of the richest man in town?"

"I'm not!"

"So you've come close," Charlie said shrewdly. "I'm not surprised—I figured there was dynamite somewhere in

Reece Callahan. You don't get where he is without having all kinds of drive and a killer instinct.''

"He's an arrogant, hard-nosed tyrant who doesn't know the difference between the truth and a lie. Especially if a woman's doing the talking.''

Charlie grimaced. "So he believes Sandor's version of your past and he's blind to what's under his nose?''

"Precisely." Lauren swallowed too much sauce and nearly choked. Hastily she gulped some tea. "But it really doesn't matter. Five more days and I'm home free.''

"It matters. By the look of you.''

Charlie was an old and trusted friend. Lauren said flatly, "Can you believe he turns me on? What's *wrong* with me?''

"I told you he was a hunk.''

"I get the occasional glimpse that there's a real human being buried inside him—and then he does something that makes me so angry I could spit.''

Heartlessly Charlie began to laugh. "About time you paid some attention to the opposite sex.''

"I've never stopped dating," Lauren said indignantly.

"Safe men. Predictable men. How long since you've been with a man who infuriates you and yet you want to jump his bones?''

Lauren said in a staccato voice, "I will not jump Reece Callahan's bones or any other part of his anatomy.''

"What would be the harm if you did?''

"I might find out I liked it," Lauren blurted, then pulled a face of sheer horror. "Can you believe I just said that?''

"I can and you did.''

"And where would it get me, to have an affair with Reece? After next Saturday we go our separate ways.''

Her expression suddenly serious, Charlie rested a hand on Lauren's wrist. "Maybe you should go for it anyway.

It's time you got out of the prison Sandor built for you…you've let him run your life far too long. Sandor was a handsome, charming manipulator with an ego as big as an oil tanker and not a shred of human kindness…you deserve better than to trail in his wake for the rest of your life.''

"Your description of Sandor would apply equally well to Reece Callahan," Lauren said tartly.

"They're as different as night and day—and you know it."

"So Reece is better looking."

"Sandor was hollow inside," Charlie announced. "Reece isn't. That's the difference."

"Huh," Lauren said, unconvinced. "The fact remains, I was taken in by Sandor, and I'm in no hurry to repeat my mistake."

"Of course you were taken in by him. He was your instructor, he was talented, sexy and charismatic. And you were very young when you first met him. Why wouldn't you be taken in?"

Lauren gave a deep sigh. "I'm afraid to trust my instincts anymore," she said unhappily. "Basically, I'm afraid to trust men. In case I get hurt again."

"But you take so many risks in your work. Couldn't you spread them out to include the men in your life?"

"Once I get back to New York, I might."

"You could start right here in Vancouver."

"Charlie, are you serious? Are you really advising me to have an affair with Reece?"

"Yep."

"Surefire recipe for disaster."

"You might indeed find out you like it."

It wasn't an opportune moment for Lauren to remember how her body had melted into Reece's, her lips parting to the thrust of his tongue. She took another gulp of tea, hoping her flushed cheeks could be attributed to the sauce. Charlie said smugly, "I rest my case."

"You don't miss a trick, do you? But how can a man I totally dislike have my hormones doing the hiphop?"

"Good question. By the time I've eaten my curried duck, maybe I can come up with an answer."

"I shouldn't have dumped all that garbage about Reece on you, Charlie—"

"It wasn't garbage and I think you should hang in there with him. I do trust my instincts, and they're telling me he's a very different ball game from Sandor."

"Maybe I'll try not to lose my temper so often," Lauren said thoughtfully, "that'd be a start." Then, reaching for the bill, she glanced down at her watch. "Eleven-ten?" she exclaimed. "It can't be!"

So it was nearly quarter to twelve by the time Lauren inserted her key into the lock of Reece's condo. Before she could fully turn it, the door was wrenched open. Reece said furiously, "Where the *hell* have you been?"

He was wearing jeans and an open-necked shirt; his hair was tousled and his eyes blazed blue. He was also, Lauren saw, white about the mouth. "Out with a friend," she said, puzzled. "What's the matter?"

He grabbed her by one arm and hauled her into the room. "For God's sake, are you okay? And where the devil *were* you?"

She didn't like being manhandled; never had since her days with Sandor. But remembering her resolve, Lauren said as calmly as she could, "I was having dinner in Chinatown."

"Why didn't you leave me a note telling me where you were?"

"Because it didn't occur to me," she said truthfully. "Let go of my arm."

"I didn't have a clue what you were up to!"

"Reece, I'm twenty-seven years old and you're not my keeper!"

"And who's this friend? What's *his* name?"

"It was a woman and what's it to you?"

"We're yelling at each other again," he said flatly. "Lauren, I genuinely thought you were in some kind of trouble."

His jawline was tight, and his shoulders still rigid with tension. "Trouble?" she repeated, frowning. "What kind of trouble?"

"This is a big city. Any number of things could have happened. So next time just leave me a note, will you?"

"I live in Manhattan—I'm streetwise. You don't have to worry about me."

"You're an extremely attractive woman who's carrying a purse with a wallet in it, and while this may not be New York, Vancouver's got its own share of criminals."

"So you can fly to Seattle but I'm supposed to sit home in your condo and wait for you to get back? You've got the wrong woman!"

"You think I don't know that?"

"Not for much longer, though. Whistler and the yacht club—then you can kiss me goodbye." Her sense of humor getting the better of her, she added, "Metaphorically, that is."

"Keep your metaphors," Reece said violently. "I want to kiss you right now and I mean that literally."

"Because I'm easy," she flashed.

"Because you make me say things I have no intention of saying. Because the sheen of your hair, the curve of your lips are driving me out of my mind. Because you've ambushed my orderly, very-much-under-my-control life. How's that for starters?''

"Oh," said Lauren.

He ran his fingers through his already disordered hair. "I was pretty sure you wouldn't abandon our agreement without letting me know—so I decided you were in some kind of trouble. But I had no idea where to start looking for you."

Something shifted deep within her. "You're saying you trust me? About the agreement?"

"You might drop it in the middle of one of our yelling matches," he said wryly. "But you wouldn't sneak off when I'm not here. Not your style."

"I would have been home earlier, but my friend and I got talking." Lauren added generously, "I'm sorry I worried you, Reece—that wasn't my intention."

He turned away, heading for the living room. "I need a drink," he said. "Want anything?"

"Sure, I'll have a glass of wine." Running her fingers absently over the copper sculpture, she said, "I still don't understand why you were so upset. It wasn't for the sake of my big blue eyes—so what else was going on?"

He passed her a crystal glass of Chardonnay, and took a healthy swallow from his whiskey. "Leave it, will you?"

"You sure know how to shut doors in people's faces."

"Talking of shut doors, I went into your room. Looking for you. The sculpture's beautiful, Lauren."

She didn't like the thought of him in her bedroom. But she'd already lost her temper once in the last five minutes and she wasn't going to do it again. "That was the main reason I had to go out...I'm always at a loose end when I finish a piece."

"So," said Reece, his eyes suddenly as intent as a hunter's, "where do we go from here?"

Her fingers tightened around her glass. "Whistler," she said fliply. "Where else?"

"I'm not talking geography."

"In that case, nowhere."

"We could go to bed. Now. Together."

Her heart gave an uncomfortable lurch. "No, Reece, I won't do that. We agreed to be lovers in public, not in private and we went through all this last night."

"You want to make love with me."

Only when you touch me. "It's been nearly four years, why wouldn't I?"

"You keep saying you haven't been to bed with anyone for four years—you really expect me to believe that?"

"Yes," she said, her chin raised, "I do."

He swished the amber liquid in his glass, his eyes never leaving her face. "In which case, the way you respond to me—I shouldn't take it personally. Anyone would do."

"*I* don't know," she cried. "I've dated men in the last four years and not one of them has tempted me to abandon celibacy. Not like you." She tossed back some wine. "And why am I telling you all this? The bottom line is that I'm not going to bed with you. And that's that."

He said disagreeably, "What are you holding out for?"

"You would think that!"

"Let's quit the playacting, okay? I want you in my bed. But I'm damned if I'll dress it up into something it's not."

"With adoring looks and endearments? The way we've been behaving in public?"

"Precisely."

"Reece," she said, "have you ever been in love?"

He scowled at her. "Not since I was sixteen and crazy about the girl next door."

"So as an adult you've never given yourself to a woman body and soul?"

"No. Of course I haven't."

Delicately she raised her brows. "Of course you haven't? Maybe you should try it sometime. It'd turn your controlled life upside down—I guarantee it."

Very deliberately, he ran his finger down the curve of her cheek to the corner of her mouth, watching her eyes dilate. "Sex between you and me would be passionate, inventive and powerful. But I'm not going to call it romance, and I'm not going to call it love."

"You're not going to call it anything. Because it isn't going to happen."

"I could persuade you."

She took an involuntary step backward. "How long since a woman said no to you? Too long. Obviously."

"If you think I'm going to beg, you've got it wrong."

Suddenly exhausted, her voice thin with strain, Lauren said, "I've had enough of this—this stalemate. What time do we leave in the morning?"

"Be ready by ten," he said curtly.

"Fine. I'll see you then." She put her glass down beside the sculpture and turned to leave.

"Stalemate or no, we're not finished with each other."

She looked back over her shoulder. He was standing very still, the lamp beside the leather couch throwing planes of light and shadow over his strongly carved features; the force of his willpower struck her like a blow. She said, "Until you make it clear you believe me—that I've never been promiscuous, that I haven't slept with anyone in four years—I'm keeping my distance. If we add Wallace to that equation, what have we got? Two people who shouldn't be sharing a drink, let alone a bed." She pushed a strand of hair back from her face. "Don't you see? Truth is what I strive for in my work. So this is desperately important to me…and if I sound preachy and self-righteous, I'm sorry."

He was gazing at her in a silence that screamed along her nerves and which she had to end. "Although please don't assume if you do believe me that I'll fall into your arms like a damson from a tree. I just plain don't want to get involved with you."

"Now you really are lying."

The more quietly he spoke, the more he scared her. "We struck a bargain," she said, "and we're damn well going to stick to it."

"You don't back down, do you?"

"You'd prefer me to grovel?"

He suddenly laughed outright, his teeth very white against his tanned skin. "I have difficulty imagining it."

"If I can act like I'm in love with you, a little groveling shouldn't be a problem," she said irritably. "Ten o'clock. I'll be ready."

"Lauren, it's not all acting. With either one of us."

She wasn't going to touch that one. "Good night," she said coldly, and swept out of the room as best she could when wearing tights and granny boots. As she got undressed in the bathroom, all her movements jerky and uncoordinated, her thoughts went 'round and 'round like hamsters on a wheel. I can't stand him. I want him. I can't wait until I see the last of him. How will it feel to say goodbye to him? I will not go to bed with him. But I want to. I want to.

She tossed her underwear on the nearest chair and reached for her nightgown; and as she did so, caught sight of herself in the long mirror on the wall. Slowly she straightened. Sculpture of an enraged woman, she thought dryly. Or, to be more accurate, of a frustrated woman. Didn't she, in her heart of hearts, crave for Reece to be here now, beside her, his gaze drinking in her creamy limbs and full breasts? His hands around her waist, pulling her back against his body? So that, once and for all, she could lay Sandor to rest? Or did Sandor have absolutely nothing to do with all this?

Her pulses racing, Lauren yanked on her nightgown and scrubbed her teeth with vicious energy. Then she jumped into bed and pulled the covers over her head.

She wasn't going to think about Reece. In bed or out.

Only five more days.

CHAPTER SEVEN

To say that Lauren was awestruck by Reece's house in Whistler was an understatement. With Reece piloting his own helicopter, they'd flown up Howe Sound past a long range of snowcapped mountains, following the winding highway to the resort with its chalets and elegant ski lodges at the base of Blackcomb and Whistler mountains. The golf course was a swath of vivid green amid the tall evergreens; tourists were strolling along the walkways around the village shops.

The helicopter swung toward the lower slopes, then gently dipped down to land behind a house built of richly stained cedar and slabs of stone. The rotors stilled. They climbed out, and in the ringing silence, Reece said in a matter-of-fact voice, "Maureen and Graham look after the place. I have meetings all afternoon, and I've arranged a tour of the village for the wives. So you're free until seven-thirty. And tonight, please wear something that keeps you decently covered."

"What a concept," Lauren said.

His lips narrowed. "Tomorrow I'll be working in my office here, I've got some catching up to do. We'll leave for Vancouver Island the next morning."

The air smelled sweetly of pine and moss, and she had always loved being near mountains. Besides, she'd told Charlie she wouldn't lose her temper so often. Lauren said sincerely, "This is a beautiful place, Reece. I'm glad I'm here."

He looked her up and down, from her bulky wool

sweater to her slim-fitting jeans and polished loafers. "The sun's caught in your hair," he said huskily, "it's like a mixture of copper and bronze."

"There's no audience…you don't have to say things like that."

"I said it because I wanted to. Because it's true."

She flashed, "Do you believe it's true that there's been no one for me since Sandor?"

He hesitated. "I'm starting to, yes."

"Until you stop hedging your bets, you can keep your compliments."

"You're utterly different from anyone else I've ever met," Reece said with sudden explosive force. "I move with the jet set, where women trade lovers faster than stocks at the New York exchange. Where fidelity's considered old-fashioned and affairs are part of the entertainment."

She was seared by a jealousy all the more horrible for being so unexpected. "And where do you fit in that picture?"

Something changed in his face. "For the last few years, I haven't. I got tired of all the games. But I'd learned my lesson—wave your fortune in front of a woman and she's after you. Spend money on her and she's yours."

"Let me tell you the first lesson I learned in art school, Reece Callahan. Money can't buy talent—it's a gift. So your money's of absolutely no use to me."

"I've been getting that message all along." Again Reece hesitated, looking uncharacteristically unsure of himself. "If we leave Sandor out of the equation, there's still Wallace. Wallace did commit fraud, Lauren. The evidence is indisputable. I don't want you thinking I made it all up out of thin air."

She took a step backward. "He couldn't have! I just can't believe that of him."

"So you don't believe me—and I'm not ready to believe you."

The sun glittered on the needles of the pines, a bird squawked in the undergrowth, and through the trees she could see the mountain's stark outline, black and white against a blue sky. "I'm tired of fighting with you all the time," she said unhappily, "because it doesn't get us anywhere. Can't we just fulfill our bargain and leave it at that?"

"I don't know—can we?"

"Of course we can," she said shortly. "I'll see you at seven-thirty and I'll be a model of decorum."

"Decorum," he repeated ironically. "Well, that'll be a change."

"Hey, I've been adoring, brash and charming. Decorum's no sweat."

"The ABCs of our agreement? What about assertive, beautiful and confident?" He grinned at her, his teeth as white as the snow on the mountains. "Not that we should omit delectable, erotic and fiery."

"Or aggravating, bossy and controlling. Referring to you, of course."

He laughed. "And then there's deprived and extraordinarily frustrated."

"Tell me about it," she grimaced.

Reece shoved his hands in his pockets. "You know what?" he said. "I like you."

The breeze was playing with his hair; his smile was far too infectious. Hardening her heart, Lauren said, "You can't like someone who's a promiscuous liar."

"So I'm supposed to believe I'm the first man in four

years to turn you on?'' he retorted. ''When most of the time you hate my guts?''

Put like that, it did sound unbelievable. Lauren said crossly, ''Look at yourself in the mirror sometime. You're gorgeous. You've got a great body, and you breathe power and confidence. I'd have to be a chunk of marble not to respond to you.''

He said with matching irritation, ''Why do I feel like I've just been compared to a centerfold? Mr. Hunk-of-the-Month, guaranteed to turn you on, and all for five ninety-five.''

''It's your personality I have the problem with,'' she cried. ''Wallace couldn't have stolen from you, I'll never accept that—so how can I go to bed with someone who believes that the only man who ever treated me with anything like kindness was a common thief?''

''Maybe he was both,'' Reece said heavily. ''Kind to you and deceitful to me.''

''We're going around in circles,'' she said helplessly. ''And I'm sure you have more important things to do than stand here arguing with me.''

''I do. You're right. Seven-thirty sharp, Lauren.'' Then Reece turned on his heel and vanished through the trees, leaving Lauren with a sweet-scented breeze and an oddly hollow heart.

If she'd been completely truthful with Reece, she'd have put a stranglehold around his neck and kissed him senseless. And how was that for inconsistency?

Prompt at seven-thirty Reece discovered Lauren in the huge living room, with its vista of mountains and sky, augmented by an expanse of glass, a granite fireplace and a massive Haida carving of a killer whale. Lauren, not to his surprise, was standing in front of the whale, her head to one side. He said, suppressing a surge of pleasure that she should be here in a house that he loved, "A young carver from the Queen Charlotte Islands did that. What do you think?"

"It's wonderful," she said softly. "So obviously symbolic, yet so fully alive."

It was exactly what he'd thought when he'd first seen it. Disliking an intimacy of thought that could, perhaps, be as strong a tie as any bodily intimacy, he ordered, "Let me look at you."

She turned around, her eyes demurely downcast. Her black satin pants were topped with a tangerine embroidered jacket, high-collared and long-sleeved. Her hair was smoothed into a long plait down her back, and her makeup minimal. He said, trying to subdue the laughter that wanted to escape his chest, "How did you get rid of your curls?"

"Gloop," she said.

With a touch of grimness, he added, "You have a persona for every occasion."

"That's the deal."

"I rue the day you walked into my office—I haven't had a moment's peace since."

"I hear the doorbell," she responded, and laid her hand lightly on his sleeve. "Shall we greet our guests, dear?"

He was almost taken in, so soft was the curve of her lips, so sweet her smile. Keep your head, Reece, and don't give her the satisfaction of knowing you want to undo every single button on that embroidered thing she's wearing and caress her breasts until she begs on bended knee to be in your bed.

After that, the evening seemed to go on forever, weighted by a formality that normally Reece enjoyed. The food was delicious, from sushi to tempura; from his position cross-legged on the floor, he watched Lauren charm the guests in her vicinity. She was being a perfect hostess. His mother would have approved of her, and suggested in her well-bred voice that he marry her; Clea, his sister, would have adored her. And Lauren, unless he was very much mistaken, would have liked Clea. More than she liked him, for sure.

Clea, younger than he by seven years, dead these five years...

As always, his thoughts slammed to a stop. After all this time, he still couldn't bring himself to remember the last day they'd spent together, the casualness with which he'd left her on the sidewalk outside the bank in Chicago, without the slightest premonition that he would never see her alive again. His fingers tightened around the stem of his glass. Stop it, he thought savagely. There's no point in thinking about it. It's over. Over and done with.

Then he suddenly found himself looking up, aware almost instinctually of being watched. Lauren's turquoise eyes jolted into his; she was gazing straight at him, such compassion on her face that for a moment he longed simply to take her in his arms, put his cheek to her hair and pour out to her everything that had happened that fateful afternoon. An afternoon that had marked him forever.

Oh, sure, he thought caustically, what would you do that for? You've never told anyone how you feel about Clea's death, so why would you start with Lauren Courtney? With a deliberation he knew would wound her, he hardened his features against her, shutting her out as effectively as if he'd turned his back on her; and watched her eyes darken with pain. Then her gaze dropped to her plate. Her neighbor on her right asked her a question. She fumbled for an answer, her cheeks as pale as the delicate porcelain plates they were eating from.

Clea wouldn't have approved of the way he'd behaved. But Clea was dead.

Clea was the reason he'd bought the statue of the Madonna and child; somehow it symbolized all that she'd lost.

Longing to be alone, Reece smiled at the elderly gentleman across from him, and asked about a temple he'd visited on one of the northern islands; minute by minute the time went by, until eventually he and Lauren were standing in the wide front door saying the last of their goodbyes. He raised his hand in a salute as the final car vanished down the driveway and closed the door on the cool, pine-scented darkness. "That went very well," he said.

Lauren didn't even bother to respond. Resting her hand on his sleeve, she asked with the directness he'd come to expect from her, "What were you thinking about at the dinner table, Reece? You looked devastated."

His earlier brief impulse to confide in her had buried itself under the layers of reserve that had been his only defense all those years ago. He said bitingly, "The lousy stock market index? The fact I'm going to have to fire my Thailand CEO? You're the one who keeps insisting we stick to our bargain, so why don't you keep your curiosity to yourself?"

"Can't you admit you're human like the rest of us?" she implored. "Do you think the world would come to an end if you said that sometimes you hurt?"

"Shut up," Reece grated.

Her fingers tightened on his sleeve. Biting her lip, she said, "I saw your face...you looked haunted. Whatever happened, or whatever you did—it couldn't be so bad that you can't tell me about it."

He stared down at her hand as though he'd never seen

it before. No rings. Tangerine polish on her nails. Unhealed cuts on two of her fingers. These were the fingers that had carved the statue in her bedroom, so pervaded with ageless emotion that his throat had closed when he'd seen it. These same fingers two nights ago had stroked his belly and lain against his rib cage, warm and strong, filling him with a primitive desire more intense than any he'd ever known.

She wanted his body, yes. But she wanted his soul, too. And that she couldn't have. It wasn't up for grabs.

He picked up her hand, lifted it from his sleeve and let it drop. Then he said coldly, "Your imagination's functioning overtime and your pushiness turns me off. Go to bed, Lauren."

Her lashes flickered under the dark wings of her brows. Then, with a courage he had to admire, she raised her chin. Her voice perfectly level, she said, "You may have lots of money, Reece. But you're poor in the things that matter. Like intimacy. And sharing."

"Keep your pop psychology—I don't need it."

"You don't need anything. Or anyone. Least of all me," she said very quietly. Then she turned on her heel and walked away from him.

Her hips swayed in her satin trousers; her back was very straight. He fought down the crazy urge to call her back, to hold her to his heart and describe that sunny afternoon in Chicago, the blood on the sidewalk, the crowds, the police and the sirens. The guilt that had seized him by the throat and never let him go.

No, he thought. No way. You're a loner, Reece Callahan. And you'd damn well better stay that way. Just because a woman with eyes like a tropical sea and hair like burnished teak thinks you should bare your soul is no reason to do so.

She'd disappeared down the hallway that led to her bedroom. But she'd disappeared from more than his sight, he knew that in his bones. Lauren Courtney was a proud woman. She wouldn't beg him for anything.

She'd stick to the terms of their bargain because she was also an honorable woman; but on Saturday night she'd vanish from his life just as she'd vanished to her room.

Game over.

Cursing under his breath, Reece headed for his own bedroom; and seven hours later got up after a sleep broken by nightmares in which Clea and Lauren were screaming for help and he was unable to reach either one of them. Feeling as though he'd been beaten over the head with a baseball bat, he staggered to the shower. Half an hour later, clean-shaven, dressed in a navy-blue suit and looking, he hoped, minimally better, he strode into the breakfast room. But Lauren wasn't alone. There were two people in the room.

Sam Lewis, his protégé and at one time Clea's boyfriend, was standing at the window looking out. Lauren was at his side, laughing at something Sam had just said; they looked at ease with each other, young and carefree. Reece said sharply, "Sam—what are you doing here?"

Sam turned, a grin still on his narrow, pleasant face which was topped with black curls. "Hi, there, Reece. I was in Vancouver on business, and found out from Maureen that you were here. So I came up to say hello."

Lauren had also turned. She was wearing tailored cargo pants with a crisp white shirt, her braided hair gleaming in the sun. She said coolly, "Good morning, Reece. Sam and I were just discussing hiking in the mountains for the day."

Subduing an emotion he refused to label jealousy, Reece said, "Check the grizzly sightings before you go. And take bear spray, Sam.'' He sounded like an elderly uncle, he thought irritably, and with a sudden fierce intensity knew he was the one who should be going hiking with Lauren. Not Sam.

He couldn't go hiking with Lauren. For one thing he had to work all day. For another Lauren wouldn't go with him. Not after last night. Scowling, he poured himself a cup of coffee and stirred in more cream than was good for him. Sam said easily, ''I'll check with the warden station before we leave. We'll probably take one of the lifts and hike in the alpine meadows—the view's incredible up there.''

''Fine,'' Reece said briefly. They all sat down at the breakfast table, where Reece ate melon and strawberries that tasted like sawdust and listened as Sam described Whistler's ski slopes. Lauren looked heartbreakingly beautiful, he thought. With her hair swept back, the purity of her cheekbones and the arch of her brows had the elegant restraint of a medieval portrait.

She hadn't once met his gaze since he'd sat down. He said flatly, ''Lauren, there's been a change of plan. I'd like you to go with the wives of the Japanese delegation to Pemberton tomorrow morning—they'll be having brunch at the golf club there. The bus will get back here about three and we'll leave at five in the 'copter.''

She raised her brows. ''Whatever you say. I should explain, Sam, that I've been acting as a hostess for Reece the last few days—I'm heading back to Manhattan early next week.''

''I see,'' said Sam in the kind of voice that meant he didn't see at all but was too polite to ask for details.

''If I'm on duty tomorrow,'' Lauren went on, ''I'd better enjoy my day off today,'' and gave Sam the full benefit of her generous smile.

Sam, Reece noticed with a flare of pure rage, looked dazzled. "Maybe I could have a word with you after breakfast, Sam," he said in a tone of voice that was an order, not a request. "How long are you staying?"

"Tomorrow morning, if that's okay. I'm flying back to Boston midafternoon to work on the Altech proposal. Which I presume is what you want to talk to me about."

It wasn't. Ten minutes later, when Reece had ushered Sam into his office and closed the door, he said abruptly, "I want to make something clear. Under no circumstances are you to tell Lauren about Clea."

Sam stood a little taller, a new maturity in his thin face. "Clea and I were in love," he said, "she was one of the most important people in my life. And she's been dead for five years. Why can't I tell Lauren about her if I want to?"

"Lauren and I have a business arrangement," Reece said. "Clea's death has nothing to do with her."

"Maybe you should tell her about Clea yourself," Sam said stringently.

Reece held on hard to his temper. "There's no need. You heard what she said—she's going back to Manhattan very soon. And my private life is precisely that—private. So please don't mention Clea's name."

"All right," Sam said. "Although I think you're wrong."

"You've changed in the last while," Reece said slowly.

"Yeah…finally growing up." Sam grinned. "These negotiations you've been having me do…it's a sink or swim process. So I've been studying some Olympic-class types, watching how they manage. You among them."

Reluctantly Reece smiled; he'd always liked Sam, and with an inner wince of pain remembered how happy he'd been all those years ago with Clea's choice of partner. Quickly he shifted the conversation to business matters, and twenty minutes later watched through his study window as Sam and Lauren climbed into Sam's rented car to drive to the ski lift on Blackcomb. What if Lauren fell in love with Sam? How would he feel about that?

Lauren in love with Sam—what difference would it make? He himself had no intention of ever falling in love, certainly not with a woman as contrary and elusive as Lauren Courtney.

Get to work, Reece. You know where you are in the world of business. You're in control in that world.

So what did that imply? That he was out of control where Lauren was concerned? That he was running away from something?

Swearing under his breath, Reece turned on his computer and took some papers out of his briefcase.

CHAPTER EIGHT

LAUREN enjoyed Sam's brief visit. After Reece's inexplicable mood changes, Sam's straightforward pleasure in her company was a relief. Besides, he had the tact not to ask any questions about herself and Reece, questions she would have found difficult to answer. All the more difficult because as she hiked the high alpine meadows that day, part of her was wishing it was Reece who was with her. Reece, rather than Sam.

Who in the world would choose Reece's arrogance and emotional coldness over Sam's sunny nature? No woman in her right mind.

But when Sam took her hand to help her up a ridge, or when he brushed a mosquito from her arm, she felt absolutely nothing. Not the slightest twinge of desire. It had been the same with all the men she'd dated in the months since Sandor. In no way could she compare this with the fire in her blood whenever Reece touched her.

It'd be safe to go to the yacht club with Sam, she thought as she followed him to his car the next morning to say goodbye. Safe, sensible and prudent. Like her life the last four years.

Hugging Sam, she lifted her face as he kissed her on both cheeks. "It was lovely to meet you," she said sincerely. "Get in touch the next time you're in New York, won't you?"

"I will—I spend a fair bit of time there. Be sure you go kayaking while you're at the yacht club. 'Bye, Lauren."

Smiling, she waved as he drove away, then turned back

to the house. Three more days were left in the bargain she'd struck with Reece. Then she could head home. Back to her normal life, with its hard work, its routines and pleasures. Back where she belonged.

Didn't she?

She opened the door and stepped inside. Reece was standing so close she could have reached out and touched him. He snarled, "On Saturday do you plan to embrace me with the same enthusiasm?"

She said incredulously, "You're jealous!"

"Don't make me laugh."

"I don't plan to hug you at all."

"Did you keep to the terms of our bargain, Lauren? Or did you tell him all about Wallace and what a son of a bitch I am?"

"Difficult though it may be for you to believe, we didn't talk about you at all."

"So did you kiss him—up there in the mountains when the two of you were alone together?"

Her shoulders sagged, anger deserting her to be replaced by a despair that frightened her with its intensity. "You still think I'm up for grabs by the first man that comes along, don't you, Reece? You'd rather believe Sandor, a man you've never met, than the woman who's standing right in front of you... You don't know how I'm longing for the weekend—it can't come too soon."

"That's entirely mutual," he grated. "The bus will pick you up here in an hour. Be ready at five to leave for the island." Then he strode away from her down the hall.

Lauren watched him go. The only thing Reece could give her was orders, she thought painfully. It didn't seem like much.

*   *   *

The last of the tankers traveling through the wide strait between the mainland and Vancouver Island fell behind as the helicopter swept toward a cluster of small islands set like unpolished emeralds in a turquoise sea. A yacht in full sail looked the size of a child's toy; a group of kayaks floated like matchsticks on the tide. Then Reece began the descent, and through the rounded window Lauren sighted the peaks of the yacht club roof nestled in the trees.

She couldn't imagine a more exquisite location. If only she were here alone, free to roam to her heart's content. Making no attempt to hide the defiance in her tone, she spoke into the headset. "Tomorrow morning I'm going kayaking."

"Not alone, you're not."

"Then I'll just have to find someone to go with me, won't I? With my reputation, that shouldn't be difficult."

"Lay off, Lauren. Unless you want me to land in the woods."

She bit her lip, unwillingly admiring the interplay of feet and hands as Reece brought the helicopter to the very center of the landing pad. When the rotors had stilled, an attendant came for their luggage and the manager ushered them to the east wing of a building that fitted the landscape seamlessly. He opened a door at the very end of the wing. "The bedroom's through there, the bathroom's to your right, and the living room's set up with a bar and all the amenities. Your client will meet you at the main bar at seven, Mr. Callahan, and dinner's at eight."

Lauren scarcely heard the last part of his speech. Bedroom. Wasn't that what he'd said? Bedroom. In the singular. As he left the room, she marched across the living area, yanked open the two doors and discovered that the first led into a palatial bathroom and the second into a bedroom, furnished with a vast king-size bed. Bedroom and bed, both in the singular. She said furiously, "This isn't in the bargain, Reece—that we share a bed. How *dare* you do this to me?"

He said impatiently, "I made the arrangements weeks ago, before I knew you existed. Anyway, that bed's big enough that we never need come within three feet of each other."

"I will not sleep with you!"

"Then you can sleep on the sofa."

He'd gone too far. On top of last week, it was one thing too many. Her fury evaporated and to her utter consternation Lauren, who never cried, burst into tears, noisy and copious tears that wouldn't stop no matter how hard she tried. Burying her face in her hands, she stumbled toward the bathroom, desperate for privacy. Then Reece took her by the shoulders, guiding her toward the bed. Striking out at him, she sobbed, "Leave me alone—I can't bear you to touch me. Oh, God, why did I ever *do* this?"

Reece thrust her down on the bed, put his arm around her and said in a voice she hadn't heard him use before, "Don't cry, Lauren. Please don't cry."

"I'll cry if I want to," she wept, her breath hiccuping in her throat. "I just can't take this anymore."

He pulled her to his chest so that her sobs were muffled against his shirt, his hands rubbing her back and her shoulders, his cheek resting on her hair in a way that, at some far remove, felt altogether perfect; and perhaps it was this that finally brought Lauren's breathing under control. "I never cry," she snuffled, "never. Not even Sandor made me cry, or all those horrible newspaper articles. What's *wrong* with me?"

"Why don't you ever cry, Lauren?"

The tears seemed to have unlocked her tongue. "I learned not to. Years ago when Wallace left, my mother wouldn't allow me to cry for him. And then the older I got, and the more obviously attractive, the more she resented me and wanted me out of the house. Which hurt. A lot. But I was too proud to cry in front of her and somehow I guess I lost the knack.''

"Do you ever see your mother?"

"Oh, sometimes. We're excruciatingly polite, just as though nothing's wrong, and it's so false I hate it. My second stepfather's very conservative and very dull—just for the record, he believes Sandor, too. Which doesn't exactly make me warm to him.''

"Any more than you've warmed to me."

"Do you blame me?" she said with a spark of her normal spirit.

"So let me get this straight…you're sleeping on the sofa tonight," Reece went on in an odd voice.

"You're darn right I am. Since you're not being chivalrous and offering me the bed.''

"I'm not the one with the problem," Reece said. "Why won't you share the bed with me?"

She rolled her eyes. "Do I have to spell it out? You know what happened when I kissed you that time—and you think I'm going to sleep within fifteen feet of you? Give me a break.''

"So you want me."

"I've been celibate for four years and you're not normally this dull-witted.''

"You want me, yet you're going to spend the night on a sofa that was chosen more for elegance than comfort because you won't risk us making love. That doesn't spell promiscuity to me.''

"Wow," she said. "Imagine that."

With sudden intensity he took her by the shoulders. "I want to trust you, don't you see? By God, I want to.''

"Then do it," she said in exasperation.

"Yeah...just like that." He hesitated. "Do you really hate my guts?"

"How would I know?"

"There's no one else to ask," Reece said dryly.

"I need to blow my nose," she announced, then tugged free of him and marched to the bathroom. In the gold-edged mirrors she scowled at her reflection, transferring the scowl to Reece as he came to stand beside her. "I look a fright."

"You do."

A reluctant smile tipped her mouth. "If I'm to resemble even remotely the seductive hostess of a very rich man, I've got some serious work to do on my face. Out, Reece."

His eyes were smiling into hers in the mirror; his height, the breadth of his shoulders, the strong line of his jaw all entranced her, with an attraction so strong that Lauren was suddenly frightened out of her wits. What would happen if she gave in to it? Wouldn't she regret it for the rest of her life? She forced herself to look away, leaning into the mirror to wipe a tearstain from her cheek. "Cocktails in twenty minutes," she said. "We'd better hurry."

"Do you plan to keep in touch with Sam?"

Her head snapped up. "Yes."

"But not with me."

"No."

The jaw she'd been admiring tightened ominously. "So what's the difference?"

"Sam's a goldfish, you're a shark."

"You sure know how to make a man feel good," Reece rasped. Swinging her around to face him, he planted a very angry kiss full on her mouth, then let her go so abruptly that she had to clutch the edge of the polished granite counter for support.

Her fingers gripping the cold stone, she erupted, "You seem to think you can kiss me any time you feel like it, then push me away as if I was nothing but a chunk of wood."

"You look even more beautiful when you're angry," he said with as much emotion as if he really were discussing a chunk of wood. "I'll go and arrange for a kayak for you tomorrow morning—you're to be back in time for lunch."

"I can arrange my own kayak!"

"And you'll go with a guide—that's an order."

Another order. As he strode out of the bathroom, Lauren pulled a hideous face in the mirror. She then got dressed in an orange silk pantsuit and slathered on makeup to hide the marks of her crying jag. So Reece was beginning to trust her. This should have made her happy; and instead only deepened her fear. Why could she take risks with bronze and wood and not with a living, red-blooded man?

If she had the answer to that question, she'd probably be sharing the king-size bed with Reece.

Lauren didn't share the bed with Reece. After an evening during which she smiled until her jaw ached, she spent a night twisting and turning on the sofa, by four a.m. convinced it had been upholstered by a sadist. It was a relief to get up at six-thirty and head for the dining room for an early breakfast before she went kayaking; but ten minutes later, Reece joined her at her table.

"I decided to go with you," he said.

She'd been longing for a few hours away from him; as the end of their bargain came nearer, her whole nervous system was winding itself tighter and tighter. Her dismay must have shown in her face. Reece said tersely, "Hating my guts is beginning to seem like a very mild term for the way you feel about me."

"I was brought up to be polite."

"Then smile at me, darling," he said in a silky under-tone, "the waitress is coming." Lifting her hand to his lips, he nibbled at her fingertips.

As heat coursed through Lauren's veins, she swayed to-ward him. The waitress said formally, "Have you had the chance to look at the menu, madam?"

A blush stained Lauren's cheeks. "Fruit salad, toast and coffee, please," she babbled. Surely those were common enough items to be on any menu?

"And you, sir?"

Reece ordered, the waitress left and Reece said in a harsh whisper, "Every other woman I've ever had any-thing to do with has been an open book to me. But not you. You say you hate me and then you gaze at me as though you'd like to eat me for breakfast."

That was exactly the way she'd felt. For a wild moment Lauren was tempted to tell him they should skip the kay-aking, go back to the bedroom and truly share the king-size bed. But what if Reece were then to give her the same message as Sandor: that she was a failure in bed, awkward and unresponsive, her beauty useless to her and to anyone else? She couldn't bear that. It had been too humiliating, too shameful.

She was afraid to go to bed with Reece. She'd rather face New York's toughest art critics than the blue-eyed man sitting across from her at the table.

"Lauren, what's wrong? You look so unhappy."

The concern in his voice almost undid her. "Nothing that tomorrow won't fix," she mumbled, digging the tines of her fork into the linen cloth.

He said tautly, "Let's strike a deal. Let's forget about Wallace and our bargain and that goddamned king-size bed and go out kayaking. Sunshine, tides and the sound of water...and maybe some killer whales. How about it?"

The fork blurred in her vision; she was on the verge of crying again. Oh, God, what was the matter with her? "Sounds like a plan," she faltered.

"Good. I'm familiar with the area where they've been sighting the whales, so we'll head straight there...the salmon migrations were late this year, that's why they're still around."

Lauren managed something like a smile. "Instead of a shark, I should have compared you to a killer whale."

"Not likely—they live in family groups," he said, then added abruptly, "Good, here comes the coffee. Only way to start the day, wouldn't you agree?"

He hadn't meant to say anything about families, Lauren thought, stirring cream into her coffee and gazing at her attractively arranged plate of fruit. As the waitress moved away, she said, "I've never asked you about your family."

"Nothing to tell...my parents are dead."

"No brothers or sisters?"

After a fractional pause, he said, "No."

He was lying; she was almost certain of it. She speared a ripe strawberry with her fork, saying, "I was an only child. Every Christmas from age five to eight I wrote an impassioned letter to Santa Claus asking for a little sister to be left under the tree. Then one of my friends told me Santa didn't exist." Her smile was rueful. "The pains of growing up. Did you ever want a brother or sister?"

"I had a sister. She died."

There was a small, dreadful silence. Lauren put her fork down. "Reece, I'm so sorry."

"It was a long time ago. Closed book. You should take sunscreen this morning—the light reflecting off the water can give you a bad burn."

The skin was taut over Reece's knuckles; his eyes were hooded. He hadn't meant to tell her about his sister, that was obvious. However she'd died, and however long ago, the pain of her death was still very much alive.

Lauren longed to comfort him. Yet tomorrow afternoon when they arrived back in Vancouver, she was planning to turn her back on him. *No,* she'd said, *I won't keep in touch with you.*

Did she mean that? Could she simply turn her back on a man who made her angrier than she'd ever been in her life, whose body entranced her, whose character baffled and fascinated her in equal measure? What if she never saw him again? Was that what she wanted?

She took a mouthful of raspberries and ate them as though they were made of Styrofoam. When in the last four years had she felt as alive, as vital as she had in Reece's company? As frustrated, as happy and as furious? After Sandor, she'd buried herself in her work and neglected her sexuality, her very ordinary needs for intimacy. Her career had benefited. But what about the rest of her?

"Did you hear what I said?" Reece demanded.

"S-sorry?"

"I asked how much kayaking experience you'd had."

She struggled to gather her thoughts. "Oh, quite a lot. With friends in Maine."

"Will you give me your home phone number?"

She blinked. "I—yes. If you'll do the same."

"I have a number where I can always be reached, I'll give you that."

"Why, Reece?" she said faintly.

"God knows," he said in a raw voice. "I just can't stand to say goodbye tomorrow and never see you again."

"I feel the same way." She produced the ghost of a smile. "But—like you—don't ask me to explain."

He said flatly, "I don't believe Sandor anymore. I'm sorry I ever did."

A sliver of melon fell back on her plate. Feeling as though the earth had shifted beneath her feet, she whispered, "If I start to cry again, then you won't believe me that I never cry."

"You've never used your sexuality to further your career, have you?"

"Not unless you count Sandor in that category."

"I don't. You were young. You were no doubt starry-eyed about being in Manhattan. And he was your mentor."

"I was in love with him. At least, I thought I was. Until one day he stole a design of mine and then denied it—and that was the end of that."

With sudden vigor Reece said, "Let's go kayaking, Lauren. Now. I've had enough of the past and the fact that you and I lose our tempers with each other five times a day."

"Ten times."

"I refuse to argue about it," he laughed, pushing back his chair. "How's that for restraint?"

It was she who was exercising restraint, Lauren thought. When he laughed like that he looked so carefree, so vital, so overwhelmingly male that it was as much as she could do to keep her hands off him.

He believed her about Sandor. And he wanted her phone number. A big grin on her face, she followed him out of the dining room.

CHAPTER NINE

THE waters of the strait were jade-green, thick strands of bull kelp aligned with the tide that surged between the islands. An eagle watched from a tall hemlock as the two kayaks passed; a seal slipped from the granite into the water. An hour after they'd set out, Reece said in a low voice, "Whales have been seen in this area. The tide's just right, let's hang around for a while."

"It's so beautiful," Lauren sighed.

For once Reece was blind to the scenery; he had eyes only for Lauren. His mouth dry, he watched the sun on her profile as she drank in the graceful sweep of cedars and the dazzling white gulls that soared so effortlessly through the channels. She was totally unlike any other woman he'd ever wanted; he'd been a fool to judge her by stereotypes and secondhand reports.

He had to bed her. Soon.

Before they went their separate ways tomorrow? Was that what he wanted? To put some sort of claim on her, to say in the most primitive way possible to her and to the rest of the world that she was his? And his alone?

She'd been happy that he'd asked for her phone number.

"Reece," Lauren said in an urgent whisper, "what's that?"

A dark snout had lifted itself from the water. Then the body followed in a sleek curve, the stark pattern of black and white dramatic and unmistakable. In a swoosh the whale blew, the mist hanging in the air as the tail vanished beneath the sea, leaving only ripples on the water. Then three more whales surfaced, one much smaller than the other two. Their bodies arched with infinite grace, then they too were gone. The water rocked and was still.

The first whale reemerged, twisting higher in the air, its flippers gleaming in the sun; it slapped down on the water, spray flying in all directions. A few moments later, the waves lifted the hull of Reece's kayak. He spared a glance for Lauren. Her face was entranced. Would she look like that when he made love to her?

How long was he willing to wait?

The whales reappeared twice more. Then the water became once again an unbroken swath of dark green silk. Lauren said softly, "That was wonderful…thanks so much for bringing me here, Reece."

"A pleasure," he said with a crooked grin. "Want to see some Kwakiutl rock carvings?"

She smiled back, an uncomplicated smile of pure delight. "What do you think?"

"Oh, I'm censoring my thoughts," he said lightly.

"Maybe it's just as well we're in separate kayaks."

"You could try sharing the bed tonight."

"On the strength of exchanging our phone numbers? I don't think so."

She sounded very adamant. Too adamant? He said casually, "We'll paddle between those two islands, the carvings are only ten minutes away."

She shot him a fulminating look. "Why do you want to make love to me, Reece? So tomorrow you can kiss me goodbye and go on to your next woman?"

"I've never operated that way!"

"You've never been in love, either. Never let a woman close to you. Are you going to tell me how your sister died?"

Bloodstains on a city sidewalk… His paddle hit the water at the wrong angle and his boat slewed sideways. "No."

"You're only interested in one kind of intimacy, that's your problem."

"We're arguing again, Lauren."

"The alternative seems to be for me to do exactly as you please."

Throwing her weight into her stroke, she dug her paddle into the water. Reece said innocently, "Want some chocolate-coated almonds?"

"You drive me crazy," she exclaimed, braking with one of her blades. "Yes, I do."

He brought his kayak closer to hers, reached in the pocket on his lifejacket and took out the package of almonds. But as she reached out her hand, Reece took her by the wrist, pulled her even closer and kissed her with lingering pleasure full on the mouth. His boat tipped dangerously. Releasing her with something less than finesse, he said, "You taste better than chocolate."

"Nicest compliment I've had all day. Well, the only one, actually."

He started to laugh, tipping some almonds into her palm. "You're as graceful as a killer whale, how about that?"

"You're like a chunk of granite. Unmovable."

"You're as beautiful as a sea cucumber," Reece said solemnly.

Earlier he'd pointed out some of the slimy, olive-green sea cucumbers that were draped over the rocks, their bulbous bodies adorned with livid red spots. "Yuk," said Lauren. "I know what you're like—the tides. Deep and dangerous."

"Dangerous?"

"Oh, yes," Lauren said, "very dangerous. I want some more almonds, then I want to see the rock carvings."

If only he didn't like her so much. If only he weren't convinced his money meant less than nothing to her. If only she wasn't so heartstoppingly beautiful…if none of these were true, would he be able to turn his back on her tomorrow? And what if he did seduce her? Would that bind her to him even more tenaciously?

Permanence wasn't in his plans. The one thing he'd learned from Clea's death was that there was no permanence. He tipped more of the almonds into her hand and said easily, "There's some incredible driftwood along the shoreline near the yacht club. I'll show you on the way back."

Lauren loved the rock carvings; but the driftwood induced in her a silence that Reece already recognized as her creativity going into high gear. As she wandered among the huge tangled roots and twisted branches, which were polished by the sea and bleached by the sun, he realized something else. The driftwood was free. He couldn't buy it for her. And he'd be willing to bet that given a choice of a fifty-carat diamond and a stump rounded like an ancient turtle, she'd take the stump.

He wasn't falling in love with her. Of course he wasn't. Falling in love, like permanence, wasn't on his list.

Lauren wandered back to him, her face abstracted. "I'm so glad you showed this to me."

Add generosity to her list of virtues, he thought, and fought against the temptation to strip her naked and bed her on the pale sand, where hemlocks whispered in the breeze and the driftwood would be their only witness. "I'll tow your kayak back, if you want to stay for a while," he offered. "You can walk back to the club from here."

Her smile was blinding. "Would you? That'd be wonderful."

As he paddled away from the beach, Reece was willing

to bet she'd already forgotten all about him. He wasn't sure whether to be angry or amused that she could so cavalierly dismiss him: that she was happy to be abandoned on a deserted beach in the wilderness. New experiences were supposed to stretch your character, he thought wryly. His must be way out of shape after a week in Lauren's company.

Not that that was permanent, either.

Lauren stayed on the beach for almost two hours. In the end, she lugged a relatively small piece of driftwood back to the club, its branches curved like waves rising from the sea. She knew exactly what she was going to do with it. Walking to the deck that wrapped around Reece's suite, she shrugged off her lifejacket, went inside and got right to work. Reece didn't come back for lunch; at four in the afternoon, she realized she was extremely hungry. She'd have a quick shower and get something to eat from room service.

Bundling her hair under a plastic cap, Lauren let the water beat on her shoulders and arms. The work she'd done in the last few hours had been deeply satisfying; but she was honest enough to realize she was also using it as escapism. In twenty-four hours, she and Reece would go their separate ways, he to London, she back to Charlie's, and thence to her studio in Manhattan. Worlds apart.

She was dreading the moment when they'd actually say goodbye; dreading it with a poignancy that had her nervous system on red alert. As the water streamed down her breasts and thighs, she wondered with an inner shiver of desire what it would be like to have Reece's hands roam her body. If she made love with him, what barriers between them would fall? What would she learn about this man of contradictions, so complex and private, so forceful and intense? And what would she learn about herself? That she wasn't the failure Sandor had labeled her?

She mustn't even think this way. Because once Reece returned to his true milieu, he'd forget all about her and their ridiculous bargain.

She closed her eyes, letting the water lave her face. She'd called him dangerous. But her own thoughts were even more dangerous. Jerkily Lauren turned off the gold taps and stepped onto the mat, wrapping herself in a luxuriously soft towel. Pulling off her shower cap, she shook out her hair and walked out to the bedroom to get clean clothes. With her free hand, she picked out a long skirt of fine wool and an embroidered shirt, tossed them on the chair and rummaged in the drawer for underwear.

A man strode into the bedroom, flipping through a sheaf of papers. Reece.

As Lauren gave an exclamation of dismay, her hand slipped, the towel exposing the creamy slopes of her breasts. Reece stopped dead in his tracks. His papers dropped to the floor. He said hoarsely, "Oh, God, Lauren, you're exquisite…"

And then she was in his arms, and he was kissing her as though she was the only woman in the world and he the only man. As though she was his heart's desire, she thought dizzily, and felt the first imperious thrust of his tongue. The towel slipped further. As she made a frantic grab for it, he stayed her hand. "I want to see you," he said thickly. "All of you."

"But—"

He drew the folds of the towel away from her body, his eyes drinking in her full breasts, the sweet curves from waist to hip, the nest of dark hair at the juncture of her thighs. Then he dropped the towel to the floor to join his papers. With one hand he ripped at the buttons of his shirt, with the other traced the swell of her breast to its tip.

Fire streaked her flesh. She gasped with mingled shock and pleasure, in a wild surge of hope wondering if she might not, with Reece, enter a country she'd never traveled before. One from which Sandor had barred her. She swayed toward Reece as he tossed his shirt on the foot of the bed, her nipples rasped by his body hair, her flesh pierced again by that elusive streak of fire.

He took her face in his hands, kissing her with such passionate intensity that Lauren forgot all the reasons why she shouldn't be doing this. Forgot everything but the heat of his skin and her longing to be released from all her old fears and inadequacies. Dimly she sensed him fumbling with his belt; then he pushed her back on the bed, falling on top of her.

He was naked, fully aroused, his weight pinioning her. She made a tiny sound in her throat, for this was going too fast and beneath it all she realized she was still afraid. He muttered, ''Dearest Lauren,'' and kissed her again, his tongue seeking hers, his hands roaming her body just as she'd fantasized in the shower. His palms clasped her waist, lifting her and arching her body to his, his mouth sliding down her throat to her breasts. As he took one rosy tip and teased it between his teeth, she gasped with delight.

''Reece, oh, please, yes…''

But before the fire could encompass her, he had moved from there like a man driven, assailing her with a host of sensations too sudden and too shattering to assimilate. She sought for words, and in a frightening flashback remembered how often with Sandor she'd tried to explain what she wanted, only to end up feeling that somehow she'd failed him.

She didn't want to fail Reece. But neither did she want

to fail herself. As Reece's fingers sought for and found the soft, wet cleft between her thighs, she said urgently, "Reece, I—"

"Yes," he muttered huskily, "you want me as much as I want you, don't you, my darling?" and thrust deep within her.

Again fear was eclipsed by wonderment. She clutched him by the shoulders, glorying in his strength and fierce impulsions, and cried out his name in a broken voice that she scarcely recognized as her own. As though it was all the signal he needed, his mouth plummeted to hers. As she opened to him, she brought his hand to her breast, aching for that streak of fire; but before it could reach her, she felt him break within her, a deep throbbing that both excluded her yet was so intensely intimate that she wanted to weep.

His heart was pounding against her ribs, his quickened breathing stirred her hair. He said thickly, "Lauren, beautiful Lauren...oh, God, that was much too fast, but I've desired you for so long. Too long. Let's spend the rest of the day in bed, so we can—" His eyes fell on his watch, still on his wrist. In utter consternation, he said, "I left the meeting to get those papers...they'll be wondering where I am." Sudden laughter gleamed in his eyes. "I don't think I'll tell them. What do you think?"

Through a haze of frustration and despair, Lauren managed to find her voice. "None of their business," she said raggedly. Yet her heart was tripping in her breast, for surely that was tenderness shining from his eyes and warming his smile. Tenderness and concern.

"Sweetheart," he said, "I've got to go, but I'll be back as soon as I can—give me two hours. Why don't you stay just where you are, and we'll pick this up where we left off? Because this is only the beginning, you know that, don't you?''

She didn't. But she produced a creditable smile of her own, saying almost too casually, "I'll tidy your papers while you get dressed."

But the first thing she did was find the towel and knot it firmly above her breasts, knowing she didn't want to be naked in front of him anymore. The papers were still in order; she aligned them carefully and passed them to him as he finished doing up his shirt, her eyes somewhere at the level of the top button. He said urgently, "Lauren, I shouldn't have fallen on you like that, it all happened too quickly. But when I saw you, I—"

"You'd better hurry," she said with another of those meaningless smiles, smoothing his shirtfront so she wouldn't have to look at him.

"Yeah…" He gave her a quick, fierce kiss. "We've got the whole night," he said huskily. "A whole night for me to show you how much I want you."

He jammed his feet in his loafers and turned away. A moment later Lauren heard the outer door close behind him. She flung open the closet, grabbing a pair of bush pants and a shirt. She had to get out of here. Out of the bedroom. Out of the club. Go somewhere where she could think.

The beach, she thought. The beach with the driftwood. That's where she'd go. Maybe there she could make some sense out of a lovemaking that had tantalized her with what might have been, yet had withheld true fulfillment.

Hadn't it simply proved Sandor right? That she was a cold woman, whose creativity and imagination stopped short of the bed? Pain flooded her heart. Reece had had no problem unleashing his passion. So what was wrong with her?

Desperate to be outdoors, she went through the patio doors to the deck, going down the steps and crossing in front of the club. There was an attractive wild garden flanking the dining room; as she ducked beneath a dogwood tree, a voice said cheerily, "Hi, there, Lauren. What are you up to?"

She gave a nervous start. "Oh, Ray," she said. "I—I was just out for a walk."

She'd met Ray Hardy and his wife Diane last night at dinner, and had warmed to them both. They'd won a lottery four years ago, and now were taking a great deal of pleasure in spending their gains. Their enormous power-boat, *Winner,* was moored in the bay.

"Another nice day," Ray said contentedly. "We plan to leave shortly—Diane's got a hankering to do some shopping in Vancouver, and I've had enough of hanging around these financial types. Don't get me wrong, your Reece is a fine fella, just a touch too high-powered for me."

For me, too, Lauren thought unhappily. "You seemed to be holding your own at dinner last night."

"Decided when I won all that money I should learn a bit about looking after it. A couple of financiers took me for a ride before I smartened up—that's why I pay attention to a guy like Reece, you can see he's honest as the day's long."

It was an interesting perspective on Reece. Even though part of her was desperate to be alone, Lauren was reluctant to hurt Ray's feelings by hurrying off. "I'm sorry you got cheated out of some of your money."

"I said to the second one, 'Wallace,' I said, 'you're the real loser here because you get to live with yourself.' Not that that recovered any of my losses, mind you—but I felt a whole lot better for saying it."

Lauren's brain had stopped dead. Wallace meant one person to her—one person only. It couldn't be the same man. *"Wallace?"* she repeated faintly.

"That's right. Wallace Harvarson. Charming fella, all the right connections, but crooked as the branches on this tree."

Lauren clutched the trunk of the tree, her head whirling. "You're saying Wallace Harvarson cheated you out of a lot of money?" she said incredulously. "Are you sure?"

"Sure as I'm standing here... Hey, what's up? You don't look so good."

She said weakly, "Wallace was my stepfather. Wallace is the reason I'm with Reece."

Ray took her by the elbow and steered her toward a cedar bench tucked in the shade. "Now you sit right down and tell me what's the matter," he ordered. "I feel real bad that I've upset you like this."

His plump face was full of genuine concern. As briefly as she could, Lauren described the bargain between her and Reece. "I didn't believe a word Reece said—I couldn't imagine that Wallace, whom I adored, had been responsible for fraud. But he must have been. If he cheated you, he cheated Reece, too. Oh, God, I've been such a fool. Such a blind, stupid fool."

She pressed her palms to her cheeks. The evidence Reece had spoken of at their first meeting had been real, not fabricated; how he must have laughed at her impassioned defense of a man whose true character had been unknown to her. She'd been oblivious. She'd seen the man she'd wanted to see.

Ray said comfortingly, "Now then, you did what you thought best. This bargain to protect your stepfather's name—you did it in good faith, and that's what counts."

She said with true desperation, "I can't face Reece after this. I couldn't stand to see him again."

"Well, now, he did kind of take advantage of you."

In the most basic way possible, she thought miserably. Less than an hour ago in the big bed that overlooked the ocean. "Ray," she said urgently, "would you and Diane take me to Vancouver with you? Then I could get the first flight to New York—I really need to go home."

"Sure thing. Why don't you get your bags, and I'll bring the dinghy to meet you? That way they won't see you from the main desk... I kind of like to read spy stories," he explained apologetically.

"Give me five minutes," she said, and ran back to the wing where she and Reece were staying. It no longer mattered that she would be breaking the bargain. When Reece published the story of Wallace's fraud—because he would publish it, there'd be nothing stopping him—he'd be telling the truth. The stepfather she'd loved had been a figment of her imagination.

As pain engulfed her, she stumbled on the rough ground, throwing out a hand to keep her balance. A lovemaking that had confirmed all her fears, a revelation that had destroyed her beloved stepfather...how could she bear it?

She'd bear it because she had to. What she couldn't bear was to see Reece again. Because the worst thing of all was that she couldn't trust her own judgment. Wallace's many kindnesses had blinded her to his duplicity. Then she'd fallen under the spell of Sandor's charisma, only gradually realizing that his outward charm masked cruelty and a need to dominate.

What of Reece? What was he really like?

Drawing a long, jagged breath, she climbed up the slope to the deck and slipped through the door. Four minutes later she left by the same door, her suitcase in her hand, her driftwood sculpture in a plastic bag. She'd left the briefest of notes on the bed, its gist that she'd found out the truth about Wallace, that she was going home, and that she never wanted to see Reece again.

Ray had pushed the dinghy against the bank. She clambered in, positioning her case amidships and sitting where it would be hidden should anyone be watching from the club. They boarded *Winner* from the far side, and the crew started the engines. The wind blowing her hair around her face, Lauren watched the yacht club grow smaller, then vanish from sight as they rounded a pine-clad peninsula.

It wasn't Wallace she was thinking of. It was Reece. With every moment, as the wake spread behind them, she was being carried further and further from him; her whole body felt as if it, too, were being stretched, clinging to him in desperation.

She wasn't in love with him. She couldn't be: she'd told him she never wanted to see him again. So why did her heart feel as though it was being torn in two?

CHAPTER TEN

AT FIVE minutes after midnight, Lauren unlocked the door of her Manhattan studio. She was exhausted from jet lag and emotional stress; yet she was also wide awake, every nerve jangling. She put down her case and saw that the light on her telephone was flashing. Messages, waiting for her. Was there one from Reece?

Would he come after her?

A plan which had been playing in the back of her mind sprang fully-fledged into existence. She'd go to Maine. Now. She'd sell the house by the sea that Wallace had left her and she'd send the proceeds to Reece. She wouldn't get five hundred thousand for it, the full amount of Wallace's fraud; but she might get three. That would be a start.

It was the only way she knew to make reparation for the wrong Wallace had done.

Ignoring the telephone, she put on a pot of coffee in the kitchen, then found the key to the Maine property. Tossing the clothes she'd had at the yacht club on her bed, she quickly packed an overnight bag. She loved to drive. She'd take her time, stay at a couple of bed-and-breakfasts, try and sort out her life and get it back on track after an interlude that would surely, very soon, be relegated to the realm of temporary madness. The sooner forgotten, the better.

Once Lauren got out of the city, she drove steadily through the night; midmorning, she booked into a pleasant country inn, phoned Charlie to let her know where she was, then fell asleep like one stunned. When she woke up, she got in touch with a real estate agency in Maine that was near her house in Fox Cove. She then traveled along the coast the rest of the day. To her dismay, it was Reece who persisted in usurping her thoughts, rather than Wallace. Reece, whose hurried lovemaking had left her bereft.

She stayed the next night near the New Hampshire border, rather enjoying the sense of being in limbo, of no one knowing where she was. About noon the following day, she pulled up outside the house that Wallace had bequeathed her.

It was a restored saltbox house with white trim, set on an acre of prime property; in summer, roses and honeysuckle filled the air with their rich perfume, overlying the salt tang of the sea. Lauren had always planned to live in the house when she tired of New York. But how could she, now that she knew the property had come to her under false pretenses? From a man who'd been a liar and a cheat?

As she stood there, feeling the first deep ache of loss for a landscape she'd always loved, a silver Mercedes drew up behind her. The large voluble woman who climbed out was named Marjorie; she was the real estate agent and had already found a buyer. "He went 'round it yesterday, and he's submitted an offer, along with a postdated cheque," she said. "Rather irregular, but he's had his eye on it for months, so he was delighted to hear it was for sale and didn't want anyone else beating him to it. This can all be cleared up in no time, Ms. Courtney."

That was what she wanted, wasn't it? Better a quick, clean break than protracted negotiations. Lauren looked over the offer, skimming through the fine print. The man's price was more than fair, and his conditions minimal. As she took out her pen and signed the document, Marjorie heaved a big sigh. "I wish all my sales were that easy. You wouldn't believe how fussy people can be." She checked the date on the offer. "You can move out that quickly?"

"I want this over and done with," Lauren said. "I'll call the removal firm in a few minutes. Thanks so much, Marjorie, and I'll talk to you later this afternoon."

Marjorie took the hint and drove away. Lauren unlocked the front door and walked in. The rooms were awash in sunlight that had an added clarity from the ocean's near-ness. Normally the pine floors, pastel walls, and carefully garnered antiques welcomed Lauren back; but not today. Wallace's past and her own decisive actions had exiled her from a house that had always been a refuge and a place of renewal.

Tears streaking her cheeks, she slowly walked from room to room, occasionally picking up a knickknack or running her fingers along a picture frame, saying her pri-vate farewells. She was so immersed in this ritual that the scrunch of tires in the gravel driveway and the slam of a car door came like a physical intrusion. Then the doorbell rang.

She could ignore it. But perhaps it was the purchaser, come to discuss some further details. She swiped at her cheeks and walked downstairs, her dark green skirt sway-ing around her knees.

As the door swung open and Reece saw Lauren standing in the sunlight, his heart gave a great thud in his chest. He hadn't been at all convinced she'd be here. She looked very unhappy; then in swift succession shocked, frightened and aghast. He said, "You sure took off from the yacht club in a hurry."

He'd planned to sound conciliatory; but the total lack

of welcome in her face infuriated him. Part of his anger, he knew, arose from sheer relief that she was safe. But not all of it.

The color had drained from her cheeks. "Reece?" she whispered, gripping the door frame as though it were all that was holding her up. "What are you doing here? How did you know where to find me?"

"Oh, it wasn't easy. I had all the Vancouver hotels checked, then your studio—no sign of you anywhere. So I thought you might come here, and flew in an hour ago."

"I thought you had to go to London."

"Haven't you heard about delegating?"

"Am I supposed to feel flattered?"

"You've been crying," he said abruptly.

"If I've just had hysterics, it's nothing to do with you."

"It's everything to do with me," he retorted; and listened to the words replay in his head.

"Oh, no, it's not. So why don't you fly right back where you came from and leave me alone?"

"We've got some unfinished business."

"I absolve you—you can publish anything you like about Wallace. What a fool you must have thought me! *But I adore Wallace. I knew him through and through, he'd never do anything dishonest*...well, I've learned my lesson. I couldn't trust Sandor and I shouldn't have trusted Wallace and as for you, you can't get out of my life too soon."

Reece planted one foot firmly on the step so she couldn't slam the door in his face. "The unfinished business has nothing to do with Wallace."

She ignored him, her cheeks now bright as red flags. "As you're here, you can take this. It's a start, at least." And she thrust a piece of paper at him.

He unfolded it. It was a postdated cheque for three hundred thousand dollars, made out to Lauren. "What's this all about?"

"I've just sold the place. Those are the proceeds. I now owe you two hundred thousand, which you'll get as soon as I can sell my studio."

"Are you out of your mind?" he asked in a cracked voice.

"You think I can live with myself knowing my stepfather cheated you out of half a million dollars?"

"You didn't cheat me! He did."

"For years he was the only real family I had. I feel responsible. Or is that a concept you don't understand?"

"Lauren," Reece said strongly, "I don't like standing on the doorstep like an insurance salesman. Let's continue this indoors."

"There's nothing to continue."

She looked as though she meant it. He tugged her fingers free of the door frame, and stepped up so he was level with her, his body very close to hers. The result was entirely predictable: he wanted to take her in his arms and kiss her until she melted in his embrace.

Right. Just like the last time.

Which was, of course, the unfinished business he'd mentioned. However, if he had any sense, he'd wait a few minutes before broaching the subject of sex. She didn't exactly look receptive.

Pushing past her, he looked around in genuine appreciation, feeling the old house welcome him, hearing through an open window the soft rhythms of the sea. "Have you spent a lot of time here over the years?"

She was backed against the wall, her eyes inimical. "When are you going to publish the evidence against Wallace?"

"What makes you think I will?"

"I broke the terms of our agreement."

"So did I. We said no sex."

Her lips tightened. "I'm glad you're not laboring under the delusion that we made love."

"Low blow, Lauren."

"It's the only language you understand."

"Why don't you just come right out and tell me what a rotten bastard I am?" he said pleasantly.

She straightened, jamming her fists in the pockets of her skirt, which swirled around her hips. "You're a destroyer," she said bitterly. "I loved Wallace. I loved this house. If my mother cared about me when I was little, she certainly gave no evidence of doing so as I got older. I don't remember my real father, and my second stepfather couldn't wait for me to leave town. So I put my need for a loving parent onto Wallace, and my search for security into this house. And now you've smashed both of them. Do you destroy everything you touch?"

A bloodstained sidewalk in Chicago... Reece said evenly, "I'll offer the purchaser twice what he paid, and give you the house back."

"Money can't fix everything, Reece." Her voice broke. "Don't you see? I *loved* Wallace. And now I'm left with nothing. With less than nothing, because what I thought I had was false."

The words, unplanned, came from deep within him. "Tell me what you loved about Wallace."

"He was kind, he was fun, he made me laugh. He used to sing old Broadway hits at the top of his lungs and teach me all the lyrics. He did crazy things, like going swimming in April and riding a bicycle in the snow...and he listened to me. Listened and was smart enough not to give advice."

Tears were trickling down her cheeks; she ignored them with total disdain. Knowing better than to touch her, Reece said, "And you think that his dishonest financial dealings have erased all that? People aren't single-faceted, Lauren. Yes, he committed fraud—although like Robin Hood, he only took from the rich. And yes, he was a wonderful stepfather who spent a lot of time with you. One side of his personality doesn't negate the other. You're in danger of throwing out the baby with the bathwater."

She was frowning at him. "I am?"

"Sounds to me as though he gave you much more than he took away from me. Because he gave you what money can't buy. Love and security when you desperately needed both."

"You're right," she said slowly, "he did."

"He was an imperfect human being. Just like the rest of us."

Even more slowly, she said, "When I called you a destroyer, you looked—well, shattered would be one word. What were you thinking about, Reece?"

His throat closed. He couldn't tell her, he'd never talked to anyone about the nightmare scene that had greeted him when he'd come back from the bank machine. His mother, the day before her death eight years ago, had asked him to look after Clea. But Reece had failed and Clea had died.

He came back to himself to realize that Lauren had stepped closer, her hand resting on his sleeve, her face gentled by compassion. "Please tell me."

"I can't," he said in a raw voice.

"You can trust me."

Her eyes, turquoise as the sea that glimmered through the window, were full of pleading. He'd never trusted anyone but Clea with his emotions, he realized with a shock of surprise. And then she'd died and he'd closed down.

Now Lauren was asking him to extend that same trust

to her. "How can I trust you? We've known each other less than two weeks."

"We did go to bed together yesterday."

Feeling obscurely angry, he retorted, "It's one thing to strip my body. Another to strip my soul."

"For me, the two go together."

"For you, maybe."

Compassion, he noticed, had been replaced with what could only be called distance. She said flatly, "Then we have nothing more to say to each other. When I've cashed that cheque, I'll send you another for the full amount. And when I've sold the studio, I'll do the same thing."

"If you put your studio on the market, I'll buy it and deed it back to you."

"You wouldn't dare!"

"Try me. Nor will I accept any money from this house."

"Reece, I'm trying my best to make amends."

"You don't have to—don't you get it?"

"You just can't accept money from a woman."

"And where will you work if you sell your studio? On the street? Show a little common sense, for God's sake."

"I'll rent a space. I'll manage, I always have."

"And what if you're pregnant?" Reece said nastily. "Have you thought of that?"

She paled. "No…"

"Are you on the Pill?"

"Of course not. I told you I hadn't slept with anyone since Sandor." Distraught, she added, "It all happened so fast, I didn't even think about protection."

"Nor did I. For which I take full responsibility. Don't you see, Lauren, we're tied together, we can't just go our separate ways. I want to make love to you again, so that—"

"No!"

She'd taken a step backward into a pool of sunlight, her hand warding him off; predominant among the emotions churning in his chest was hurt. He said, "I know I—"

"The bargain's over, I'll send you a cheque and you can give it to a home for stray cats for all I care."

She meant it, he thought sickly. She really didn't want anything more to do with him. Feeling as though he'd been knifed in the ribs, determined not to show he was bleeding, he allowed anger to overwhelm the pain. He was damned if he was going to beg. He'd never had to before, and he wasn't going to start now. Kiss her into submission? No, thanks. If she wasn't willing, to hell with her. He said harshly, "I'll call you in a month or so to find out if you're pregnant. You'd better hope you're not—I'd hate for you to have someone you despise as the father of your child."

The light was shining mercilessly on her face; beneath her anger, she looked strained and stubborn. She couldn't wait to get him out of her life, he thought savagely. But what did he care? He'd never gone where he wasn't wanted, and he wasn't going to change that for a sculptor with enormous talent, tangled hair and a body that obsessed him. "Goodbye, Lauren," he said with formal precision, and without waiting for her to reply, turned and left the house.

This was going to be the shortest car rental in history, he thought, climbing in and driving away. But maybe he'd needed to see Lauren to realize there was nothing there for him. The only connection left between them was a cheque he neither needed nor wanted; and a possible pregnancy whose ramifications he couldn't even begin to contemplate.

Not much for the week they'd spent together.

Painfully little.

But why would he want more?

CHAPTER ELEVEN

LAUREN turned the music up another notch. The studio was crowded, the wine and beer were flowing, and everyone seemed to be having a wonderful time. Except for her.

It was just under a week since Reece had visited her in the house she'd inherited from Wallace. The sale had gone through without a hitch, and yesterday she'd mailed a cheque for three hundred thousand dollars to Reece's London headquarters. She'd sounded out a real estate agent about selling her studio, although something had stopped her from actually putting it on the market. The certainty that Reece would indeed buy it?

The buzzer sounded again; a few moments later Sam walked in the door. He was carrying a bouquet of Calla lilies that he presented to her with a flourish, and a bottle of very good wine. Above the noise, she teased, "Maybe we should hide that in the cupboard, most of this crew have passed the stage where they'd appreciate it. Lovely flowers, thanks."

"They reminded me of miniature sculptures," he said, and kissed her cheek. "Sorry I'm late, I got held up in a meeting. You're looking altogether ravishing."

She was wearing a pencil-slim long skirt with a glittering gilt top that hugged her breasts; her hair was a mass of curls around her face. She was giving the party for two reasons: to celebrate the sale of a major work, and to cheer herself up. She felt far from ravishing; but no one need guess that. "Thank you," she said. "Come along and I'll introduce you to some of my friends."

"How about I dance with you first?" Sam said, dumping the lilies and the wine on the counter and steering her toward the expanse of hardwood floor under the high rafters of her studio. Edging his way through the crowd, he took her in his arms. "Nice to see you...is your stint as Reece's hostess done with?"

Lauren missed a step. "Yes."

Sam looked at her quizzically. "Are you going to tell me what that was all about?"

"I am not."

"He dropped in on our meeting tonight—that's why I was late. He looked like hell."

"You mean he's in the city?" she squawked. "Did you tell him you were coming here?"

"Nope."

"Good," she said with heartfelt gratitude.

"Lauren, Reece is a thoroughly decent guy—even if he does come across as a bit autocratic."

"A bit? He invented the word. Besides, he's completely out of touch with his emotions."

It was Sam's turn to miss a step. "If he is, there are good reasons."

"So tell me what they are."

"He's the only one who can do that."

"I'll be a cranky old woman of ninety-nine before it happens."

"Why don't you just ask him?"

"I have. No dice."

"Try again."

"As I told him I never want to see him again, that might be a little difficult."

"Two autocrats," Sam said dryly.

"I am not!"

"Could have fooled me. By the way, a guy wearing a

purple sarong is letting in more people—that okay with you?''

''My parties always seem to get a bit out of hand…too many starving artists, I guess.''

''Hey,'' said Sam, ''guess who's just come in the door?''

Alerted by something in his voice, Lauren jerked her head around. Across the width of the crowded, noisy studio, her eyes met Reece's. Met and clashed, his a blaze of blue. His formal business suit was an interesting contrast to the sarong, she thought faintly, and tried without success to pull her gaze away.

''He looks a touch out of sorts,'' Sam said cheerfully. ''Why don't we go over and say hello?''

Lauren clutched his sleeve. ''No way!''

''Lauren, you can have a scene with him in the middle of the dance floor, or you can have it over by the door. Your choice.''

''I am not having a scene with Reece Callahan anywhere. Least of all at my party.''

''Tell him that.''

''Anyway, you don't have to sound so delighted at the prospect of the two of us going at each other tooth and nail.''

With sudden seriousness, Sam went on, ''You and Reece are made for each other. Although by the looks of it, neither one of you wants to admit it.''

''That's the most ridiculous thing I've ever heard.''

Sam eased her past a couple so blatantly and blissfully entwined that Lauren averted her eyes, aware of a stab of pure envy. ''You're just the woman Reece needs,'' Sam persisted. ''And you're not exactly indifferent to him.''

''I'm not indifferent to tarantulas.''

Sam laughed, shoving through the melee around the bar.

"Nearly there. I noticed a gorgeous blonde over by the window, I'm going to check her out. But holler if you need me."

"Gee, thanks a lot," Lauren said, and found herself planted in front of Reece. He looked no more pleased to see her than she him. Sam said with infuriating calmness, "Nice to see you, Reece. Women like it when you smile at them, ever notice that?"

"Keep your advice to yourself and why didn't you tell me you were coming here?" Reece said with dangerous softness.

"You didn't ask. See you, Lauren."

Determined to seize the initiative, Lauren said, "Reece, if you came here hoping for a major row or a cozy twosome, you've got the wrong night and the wrong woman."

"Why did Sam bring you over here?"

"Oh, he thinks you and I are made for each other."

A muscle tightened in Reece's jaw. "It's time he took a vacation—his brain's addled."

"So if you don't think we're made for each other, why are you here?"

"Are you pregnant?"

Her lashes flickered. "It's too soon to tell and I don't think you came here to ask that," she retorted. Someone had turned her CD player to top volume; as the party eddied and swirled throughout the studio, she and Reece could have been isolated on a desert island for all the attention they were getting.

Reece shoved his hands in his pockets and said in a raw voice, "I came because I want to make love to you again, Lauren. I'm sorry about the last time—I should never have gone near you at the yacht club knowing my colleagues were waiting in the other room, I must have been out of my mind. But when I saw you with that towel slipping from your breasts, I just plain lost it.'' He raked his fingers through his hair. ''I don't know if any of that makes sense to you, and I don't really expect you to forgive me.''

Her temper died. She knew in her bones Reece was being as honest as he knew how; and responded with a matching honesty. ''Reece, for my own reasons, I don't want to make love to you again. But thank you for apologizing, I needed that.''

''Why don't you want to?'' he said hoarsely. ''I swear it would be different this time.''

She crossed her arms over her chest, her gilt top shimmering in the dim light. She might as well tell him the whole truth; he'd probably guessed it anyway. ''I hated sex with Sandor—he called me frigid, and he was right. So the other day in bed with you was simply a confirmation of everything he'd ever told me.'' She bit her lip. ''I couldn't bear to make love with you again—don't you see? I couldn't bear to.''

''My God,'' Reece said softly. ''So he did that to you, too?''

''He didn't do it—I was the one with the problem.''

''He was totally wrong for you.''

''It's so ridiculous that he accused me of promiscuity,'' she burst out. ''Why would I go to bed with other men when everything I'd learned from him told me to steer clear of sex?''

Very gently Reece rested his hands on her shoulders. She flinched from his touch, unable to help herself, and saw his face contract. ''Listen to me,'' he said forcefully. ''Remember that kiss in Vancouver? Remember the night I carried you into my bedroom? I know you desired me that night, I saw it, I felt it. We can do that again, we can prove Sandor wrong. Provided you'll trust me.''

She shook her head, her eyes downcast. ''I'm afraid to.''

"I swear I'll be as good to you as I know how. And if at anytime you want to stop, you have only to say so."

Ducking her head, she mumbled, "I'm crying again. I don't know what it is about you, but I'm like a leaky watering can." In sudden defiance she looked up, tears clinging to her lashes. "Anyway, why would you want to do that? Go to bed with a woman who doesn't enjoy sex? Sounds like masochism to me."

"Because I'm ninety-nine percent sure you'll enjoy it with me," he said with a crooked smile that made one tear plop to her cheek. "And if that makes me sound conceited as hell, so be it."

"And what if I do like it?" she cried. "You kiss me goodbye and take off for Cairo on the first flight?"

"Now that I've started delegating, I might just continue."

Panic closed her throat. "I don't know which scares me more—that I'll hate it or I'll love it."

"You've got to trust me, Lauren—that's partly what this is about. The other person you've got to trust is yourself."

The heat from his fingers seeped through the flimsy gilt fabric; the force of his personality beat against her defenses. "Trust goes both ways," she said slowly. "How did your sister die, Reece?"

Involuntarily his nails dug into her shoulders. Then, with a complete absence of emotion, he said, "I left her on the sidewalk in Chicago while I went to a bank machine. She was shot down and robbed. The last thing my mother asked me to do before she died was to look after Clea."

A series of nightmare images flickered through Lauren's brain, vivid, terrible and ineradicable. Instinctively she put her arms around Reece's waist and held him as tightly as she could. "I'm so sorry," she whispered.

"It's five years ago now."

"But you never talk about it."

"What's the point?"

She said intuitively, "Sam knows...doesn't he?"

"Sam was Clea's boyfriend."

So that was why Sam had come so quickly to Reece's defense. "He never told me."

"I asked him not to."

Suddenly exhausted, letting her hands drop to her sides, she said helplessly, "No wonder you shut down your emotions."

He said flatly, "You see why I don't tell people—look how it's upset you."

"That's no reason not to tell me," she flashed.

"It's every reason, I would have thought."

She stated the obvious. "You loved her."

"Oh, for God's sake, Lauren—drop it, will you?"

His eyes were hooded; she knew she'd get nothing more from him about Clea. "So where do we go from here?" she asked with careful restraint.

"Start hiding all the beer in the hopes everyone'll go home," he said promptly. "So we can go to bed with each other."

She gazed up at him. He'd loved Clea and Clea had died. More as a statement than a question, Lauren said, "But you don't love me."

"I want to undo the harm I did at the yacht club—especially now I know the circumstances."

Her decision would change her whole life, Lauren was under no illusions about that. Change it for better or for worse. "I—I've got to pay some attention to this party," she muttered. "Put some food out. Make the coffee."

"So what's your answer?"

He'd removed his hands from her shoulders, as though he scorned to use touch as a weapon to plead his cause.

And he was giving her the chance—as Charlie had said—to rid herself of Sandor once and for all.

But only a chance. Not a certainty.

Under the cover of some astonishingly raucous rap music, Lauren mumbled, "Yes."

"What did you say?"

"Yes—I will," she yelled just as someone turned the music off.

Her words rang under the rafters. Heads turned, a ripple of laughter ran through her guests, and the man in the purple sarong, whose name Lauren had never caught, waved a beer bottle over his head and yelled back, "I've been waiting all evening for you to say that, my darlin'."

The beer bottle arched spray through the air. Purple-sarong gave her a blissful smile, Reece looked murderous, and Lauren swallowed the urge to dissolve into hysterical giggles. Then her friend Daly, a painter of some renown, grabbed her by the waist, perhaps taking pity on her. "I knew you wanted to dance with me," he said, and whirled her onto the dance floor.

"There isn't any music," she muttered.

"We make up our own," Daly said. "Who's the irate gentleman in the Wall Street suit?"

"I couldn't possibly begin to explain," Lauren said. "Daly, have you ever been in love?"

"Dozens of times. Trouble is, I bed 'em and I move on."

"You men are all alike."

"Some of us are worse than others. Sandor was a creep, Lauren. One hundred percent sleaze. Kindly don't put me in the same category as him."

She'd always liked Daly. Wondering with one part of her brain whatever had possessed her to give this party,

Lauren said, "You've been in lust. Not in love. That's what you're saying."

"Yep. I don't know who the guy in the suit is, but he looks about as different from Sandor as you could get. Glad you said yes to him, Lauren—yes to what, by the way?"

"None of your business," she said fractiously. "Do you think if I produced a big pot of very strong coffee my guests would take the hint?"

Daly laughed. "You can try. Want a hand with the grub?"

She gave him something like a genuine smile. "Thanks—you're a real pal."

"Time you came out of that icebox you've been living in," Daly said lightly. "Let's see if I can steer you in the direction of the kitchen."

For the next hour Lauren kept herself extremely busy serving curried meat balls, broiled shrimp and cheese straws, as well as tactfully suggesting coffee to as many of her guests as she could. Reece, to her infinite gratitude, was keeping his distance; although every now and then she'd find him watching her with an intensity that made a shiver race along her spine.

The party started to break up around two in the morning, and by three the last of the stragglers—among them the man in the purple sarong—had gone through the door. Lauren closed it behind him, shoved the bolt across and put the chain in its slot. Was she locking purple-sarong out or herself in? she wondered crazily, and said in a voice that sounded almost normal, "What a mess this place is. But people had a good time, didn't they?"

"Except for you and me," Reece said wryly.

He'd turned the music off. The studio echoed with silence and emptiness. Feeling horribly at sea, she said,

"Half the time I was praying for them to leave and the rest of the time I wanted them to stay all night."

"Let's go to bed, Lauren."

"Shouldn't we clean—"

"I'll help you in the morning."

"It is the morning."

His features a hard mask, Reece rasped, "You're really dreading this, aren't you?"

"Do you want to back out?" she said with a flash of hope.

"No, I don't want to. I'm not going to ask you the same question because I'm pretty sure you'd say yes...let's go upstairs."

Her bedroom and bathroom were in a loft over the studio. "What if Sandor's right?" she said in sudden anguish. "What then?"

"Trust me, Lauren," Reece said forcibly. "That's all you've got to do—trust me."

"That's one heck of a lot," she said with something of her normal spirit.

He laughed. "It sure is. You go first."

The stairway was steep, and her skirt rather tight. Conscious in every nerve of her body of Reece on her heels, Lauren slipped off her shoes and climbed the stairs. Turning at the top, she said, "I need a shower, I won't be—"

"Let's have one together."

"No! No, I won't be long," she said frantically, scuttled to the bathroom and locked the door.

Sanctuary, she thought, gazing at her face in the mirror. She looked scared to death. Petrified. Terrified. Cornered.

Trust me, Reece had said. Trust me and trust yourself.

Which was precisely what she wasn't doing. She wasn't giving herself a chance. Taking a deep breath, Lauren lifted her chin and gazed deep into her own eyes. To the best of her ability, she was going to trust Reece. Trust that he had her best interests at heart.

Because, of course, she had no idea why he was really here. To make amends? Intuitively she knew there was more going on than that. To get in touch with his own emotions, buried with his dead sister? Perhaps that was closer to the truth. Perhaps Reece had his own healing to do. And perhaps she could help him in that.

Somewhat heartened, she stripped off her clothes and showered. Her nightgown was hanging on the hook on the door. It was full-length, made of delicately embossed cotton; she hauled it over her head, dragged a brush through her hair and opened the door.

Reece was sitting on her bed, taking off his socks. His shirt was already slung over the back of her Windsor chair; it shone very white against the taupe walls. He smiled at her. "I'll have a shower, too. Any clean towels?"

"In the cupboard," she said, and watched the muscles ripple across his chest as he stood up. The door closed behind him; her newfound courage seemed to have deserted her. She sat down hard on the other side of the bed, her fingers clasped in her lap, and wondered what Wallace would think were he to see her now. If it hadn't been for his duplicity, she wouldn't be here, waiting for a man who felt like a stranger to make love to her.

All too soon, Reece came back into the bedroom, a towel wrapped around his waist. In a strangled voice, Lauren said, "Put out the light...please?"

As he flicked the switch, the dim glow of the city filtered through the skylight over the bed. Then Reece sat down beside her, taking her hands and chafing them gently between his own. The warmth of his shoulder seeped through the thin cotton of her gown.

She had to go through with it. She had to.

CHAPTER TWELVE

LAUREN'S fingers were ice-cold. And it was up to him to warm them, Reece thought. Warm her fingers and warm her heart. Undo the damage that bastard Sandor had caused her, and free the woman of passion he was convinced lay behind her panic-stricken eyes.

Free her, and what then?

One thing at a time, Reece, he told himself, and brought her hand up to his lips, dropping small kisses along her thumb and the back of her hand, then turning it to bury his face in her palm. Her wrists were as stiff as boards; her rapid, shallow breathing smote him to the heart. Raising his head, he cupped her face and, with infinite gentleness, kissed her on the lips.

Her jaw was rigid, her mouth unresponding, so much so that he wondered if his confidence had been misplaced. Had the damage gone too deep? Or was he quite simply the wrong man for her? Both thoughts filled him with a hollow ache of emptiness he didn't want to analyze.

With exquisite control, he moved his mouth over hers; and felt the first tentative softening of her lips. He said softly, "Lauren, my beautiful Lauren...I'm so happy to be here with you," and with a small shock of surprise knew his words to be the truth. He wanted her body, no question of that. But more than that, he wanted her presence.

He took her lower lip between his teeth, nibbling its soft curve, letting his tongue brush her mouth with tantalizing brevity. As she made a tiny sound deep in her throat, he put his arms around her, stroking the taut line of her shoulders with repetitive smoothness. His own body was in no doubt of what it wanted. *Slow down, Reece. This is for Lauren. Not for you.*

Then her hands slid up his torso and linked themselves behind his neck. Her breath wafted his cheek in a small sigh. "Reece, I…"

"Tell me what you want, sweetheart. I'll do anything I can for you."

Briefly she burrowed her face into his bare shoulder, her sweetly scented hair falling to his chest; then she looked right at him. "I don't know what I want…show me what I want, Reece. Please?"

His heart pounding like a triphammer, he bent to kiss her again, this time unleashing some of his desire; after a fractional hesitation, he felt her match him kiss for kiss, her lips parting to the dart of his tongue, her own tongue playing with his. Wondering if his heart could burst in his chest, Reece fought for control. He mustn't rush her. He'd done that once. Never again.

He kissed her lips, the hollow of her cheekbone, the sweep of her forehead; then let his mouth drift down her throat to the pulse where the beat of her blood told its own story. He fumbled for the buttons on her gown, saying with a thread of laughter, "These things weren't invented with me in mind."

She said shyly, "I could take it off."

Shaken to the core, he said, "You're so full of courage."

"I want you to make love to me," she whispered.

His hands unsteady, he helped her lift the soft folds of cotton over her head. Her creamy skin gleamed in the soft light; her full breasts, her curve of waist and hip, struck him dumb. He felt as though he'd never made love to a woman before. He felt as though he'd been given an immeasurable gift that he in no way deserved.

Teasing her nipples to hardness, he watched her eyes darken, heard her breathing quicken in her throat. Suddenly she took his face between her hands, kissing him with an unbridled fierceness that took his breath away. He drew her down beside him on the bed, feeling the towel slip from his waist; and again had to draw on all his willpower to subdue his body's tumultuous response.

Wanting only to give her pleasure, he caressed her breasts until she whimpered with need, her body arching so that the softness of her skin rubbed against his body hair. Her eyes were dazed with wonderment; very slowly, he drew one hand down her belly, seeking out the soft, damp crevice between her thighs. She gave a single, sharp cry, moving her hips against his with an unpracticed seductiveness that told Reece more than he needed to know about Sandor's selfishness and her essential innocence. He dropped his face to her belly, rejoicing in the smoothness of her skin, then moved downward, parting her thighs, his tongue plummeting to give her the pleasure she'd been denied; yet stopping before she could topple over the edge.

In a broken voice he'd never heard before, she gasped, "Reece, oh, Reece...I've never felt like this in my life. So overcome, so frantic."

He touched her where she was most sensitive, watching her features convulse. As she cried out his name, he hurriedly reached for the little package by the bed; then he slid into her, moving as slowly as he could, until he thought he'd die from the pain of holding back. Not until she was begging him for more did he plunge into her. Thrusting in and out, he waited until she was shuddering with the inexorable rhythms of surrender before allowing himself to meet her in that place where he was most alive and most intimately joined to her.

A new place, Reece thought dazedly. Depths he'd never plumbed. A union unlike any other.

Very slowly, he lowered his body to hers, feeling against his ribs the frantic racing of her heart, her dazzled face only inches from his. "Lauren," he muttered, "are you all right?"

She opened her eyes. Brilliantly turquoise, they smiled up at him. "All right? I'm overwhelmed, I've come home, I—I just never knew…" Then suddenly she clutched him to her and began to weep, her face buried against his throat.

He held her hard, rolling over on his side so his weight wouldn't crush her, feeling her sobs shaking her frame. "Was I too fast for you? I didn't—"

She looked right at him, her breath still heaving in her chest. "You were perfect—I wanted you so badly. But I must have been clumsy, I'm sorry if—"

He began to laugh, hugging her to him and inhaling the lilac scent of her hair; and knowing he'd never felt as close to a woman as he did to Lauren now. "No more apologies. I think we both did just fine, how about that?"

Her cheeks pink, she said, "We did, didn't we?"

"Next time," he said deliberately, "we'll do even better."

"How long do I have to wait?" she asked saucily.

"Not as long as you might think."

As she blushed entrancingly, he drew one hand down the length of her body. He was exactly where he'd wanted to be ever since she'd walked into his Vancouver office that day in her severe gray suit: in Lauren's bed. Learning about her. Discovering her vulnerabilities and her incredible courage, her laughter and her newly released passion.

Passion whose subtleties they'd only just begun to explore. He thrust his hands into the soft weight of her hair, drawing her face to his and kissing her as though they'd never made love, as though she were utterly new to him and all the more needing to be wooed.

"You're my heart's desire," he said roughly, and heard the words echo in his mind. He wasn't in love with her. Of course not. He wanted her, that was all. Wanted her more than he'd ever wanted anyone or anything in his life.

With all his powers of imagination and empathy, Reece set about showing Lauren just how much he wanted her; he was rewarded, as the first light of dawn streaked the sky, by a mutual release that overpowered him in its intensity. He lay on top of her, sweat filming his forehead, his heartbeat like a drumroll in his chest, and wondered how he was ever going to say goodbye to her.

He had to go to London the day after tomorrow. No choice.

Two more days, he thought, letting his cheek rest on her hair, feeling through every nerve ending the sweet clasp of her arms around his ribs. That'll be enough. We're both adults, with full lives, and this is a temporary madness. We'll be fine. Of course we will be.

The shrilling of the telephone woke Lauren from a deep sleep. With a jolt she realized a man's body was curled around her, one arm heavy over her hips, one thigh pinioning her to the mattress. Reece. With whom she'd made love twice through the night, discovering within herself a woman she hadn't known existed.

She rolled over, grabbed the receiver and mumbled, "Hello," only to be greeted by the dial tone and the continued peal of a telephone bell.

Reece sat up beside her. "It's my cell phone," he muttered. "Where did I put my jacket?"

He scrambled out of bed, lunged for his jacket and took the phone from the pocket. "Hello," he barked. Then he said nothing for several minutes.

His body, so lean and strongly muscled, was utterly beautiful, Lauren thought. She wouldn't sculpt him, though. Not yet. Not until he was so much a part of her that she wouldn't even need to see him for her hands to trace his outlines.

She wanted him again. Wanted him fiercely and now. Half appalled, half amused by her own reactions, so delicious and so surprising, she realized Reece was now talking. Abruptly her heart grew cold, as she heard him say, "Gary, I can't believe this has happened. So much for thinking we were on top of it. Okay, I'll leave as soon as I can. But I can't possibly arrive before midafternoon—at least the jet's at Kennedy, so there won't be a holdup there. You'll meet me at Heathrow? Fine, I'll get the pilot to radio ahead. 'Bye."

Without even looking at Lauren, he quickly entered some numbers. "Randolph? I'll need the limo in fifteen minutes." Giving Lauren's address, he went on, "Kennedy Airport, yeah. You'll call Tom and alert the crew we'll need to head for London as soon as possible? Thanks." Then he jammed the phone back in his pocket and turned to face Lauren.

"You must have heard that. I've got to go to London, pronto. A major deal could fall apart unless I get over there and do some damage control—it's something we've been working on the last four months. And I'm the only one to handle it."

Her smile had congealed; aware that she was cold, she

grabbed at the sheet, pulling it up to hide her nakedness. In a stony voice, she said, "Go ahead."

"I'd never have anticipated this," he exploded, "I thought Gary and I had covered all the angles—but I was wrong. I'm not going to London because I want to—I'm going because I have to. I want to be here with you, surely you know that?"

"Of course," she said politely.

He pulled her to her feet, his hands clasping her shoulders. The sheet slipped down her body; she clutched at it, feeling exposed and vulnerable. He said urgently, "Lauren, last night was—I can't begin to tell you how wonderful it was. Listen to me, will you? This business shouldn't take more than a week maximum, then I'll come right back here. Before I go to Cairo."

"You'd better get dressed," she said. "Your driver will be here in a few minutes."

"You're not listening to me! I know the timing's lousy. But it's not the end of the world...I'll be back, do you hear me?"

"If I want you back," Lauren said.

"Oh, you want me," he said furiously, pulling her toward him and kissing her with such passionate hunger that her body ached with desire even as her soul was filled with a fierce resentment that he should leave so precipitously. Although why should she be surprised? He'd never married, he must be an expert at extricating himself from women's beds.

She pulled her head free. "Don't, Reece! You don't have to pretend. Or lie. I'm sure I'm an amateur compared to your other lovers, so why would you want to stay?"

His breath hissed between his teeth. "Are you accusing me of setting this up? As a way—an extraordinarily graceless way—of dumping you?"

"Why wouldn't I? I'm no sexual gymnast, no sophisticated jet-setter who's read all the manuals. I behaved like a virgin. Not your type."

"Why don't you let me decide who's my type—as you so cold-bloodedly put it? Are you also saying if I come back here in a week, you won't let me in?"

"It's all happened too fast," she cried, pressing her palms to her cheeks in unconscious drama. "Last night I—I was transported. And now you're leaving. Going four thousand miles away. How am I supposed to behave? Wave my handkerchief at the window and shed a few decorative tears?"

His crooked grin relieving some of the tension in his face, Reece said, "I have difficulty with that picture—you're more likely to take a sledgehammer to my forehead. Don't you see, Lauren? This is about trust, too. I wouldn't leave here for anything less than a real emergency—you've got to believe me. Because it's true."

She twisted a fold of the sheet between her fingers. "I—I guess I'll let you in," she muttered. "If you come back."

"I've said I will...I'll call you in a couple of days and let you know how things are going. Now I'd better get in the shower and get out of here."

Grabbing his clothes, he headed for the bathroom. Lauren quickly dressed in black pants and a loose mohair sweater, needing the protection that clothing offered. Could she trust Reece? Or was she being an utter fool? Once he'd left, wouldn't he realize he'd had enough of her? After all, he'd more than made amends for events at the yacht club. He'd given her pleasure and fulfillment beyond her wildest imaginings, and hadn't that been his aim?

Why would he bother to come back? He certainly wasn't in love with her, that wasn't part of his life plan.

She brushed her hair, put on earrings and lipstick and went downstairs. The studio looked even messier than it had before she had gone to bed. She ground some coffee and plugged in her espresso machine, trying to keep her mind on what she was doing. Someone had spilled red wine over the counter, and someone else had trodden two shrimps into the hardwood floor. Although Sam's bottle of wine had been drained, the Calla lilies had been stuck in water in a biscuit jar. She found a vase in the cupboard, sliced their stems and was arranging them when Reece came running down the stairs, doing up his cuff links on the way. He said, "I didn't set up that phone call to get out of helping you clean up this mess, either. Those are nice flowers," he added.

"Sam gave them to me."

His lips narrowed. "You planning on falling in love with Sam?"

"I'm not planning on falling in love with anyone," she said sharply. "What about you?"

"Same. Tell me what your favorite flowers are."

"Lilacs. The purple ones with the gorgeous smell."

"Randolph's outside, I've got to go. Look at me, Lauren."

Reluctantly she raised her eyes to his face. His hair was still damp, his eyes very blue. He said strongly, "When I said how wonderful last night was, I was telling the exact truth. And no, it's not my standard line when I say good-bye. *You* were wonderful…so passionate, you took my breath away. In an ideal world, I'd be staying right here and making love to you the whole day through."

Trust me. That's what he was saying. "I—it was wonderful for me, too, Reece." Impetuously she stood on tiptoe and kissed him on the mouth, feeling the contact rip through all her defenses. "Have a safe journey," she quavered.

Cupping her chin, he kissed her thoroughly and at length; her cheeks were as red as her sweater when he stepped back. "Talk to you soon," he said, unlatched her door and was gone.

Lauren stood very still. The studio was distressingly, horribly empty. Why hadn't she hugged him? Why hadn't she told him he'd been incredibly generous last night? That she'd loved his body and everything he'd done upstairs in her bed?

It was too late now. He'd gone.

But she'd see him again soon, she thought stoutly, reaching in the cupboard for a coffee mug and discovering they were all dirty. Of course she would.

He'd said so.

CHAPTER THIRTEEN

THE day Reece left passed fairly quickly, because Lauren was busy washing dishes, lugging down the garbage, and scrubbing the floor. She went to bed very tired, certain that she'd sleep; and as soon as her head touched the pillow was achingly aware of the elusive scent of Reece's body, and of the empty expanse of sheets. She was alone in her bed; except for last night, she'd been alone in her bed for years. But last night had changed everything.

She tried recounting the names of all the people at the party, those she'd invited and those she hadn't; she composed a mental letter to her gallery about her next show; she stared at the rectangle of clouds through the skylight. She felt as though she'd been invaded, as though Reece had flowed through her veins, and was now a denizen of her heart. She was no longer complete, she thought miserably. In just a few hours in her bed, Reece had stolen her hard-earned peace and security.

Why had she ever opened her body to a man who had a business empire that spanned the globe and a heart guarded against both vulnerability and love? She was entirely capable of reading between the lines: the tragic death of his sister had killed something in Reece. He might desire Lauren, but he wouldn't fall in love with her.

She should have sent him away the moment he had walked in her door.

Eventually she did fall asleep. The next day she focused on business matters, visiting her gallery, paying bills and doing some shopping. When she went to bed at eleven, she fell asleep right away; then woke at three in the morning longing for Reece to be beside her.

He should phone today. Who knows, maybe he'd be knocking at her door by nightfall, she thought.

Somewhat comforted, she drifted off to sleep again. The next morning she found out she wasn't pregnant, a bittersweet discovery even though reason told her the last thing in the world she needed was to bear Reece's child. The hours of the day dragged by, her back ached, and by five that afternoon she was battling true panic because she couldn't concentrate on her work, so anxious was she for the phone to ring. Work had always been her refuge; what if she lost even that?

Then the phone did ring, three times in succession: Sam inviting her to a movie, purple-sarong inviting her to go camping, a research company inviting her to answer a survey. She declined them all with varying degrees of politeness, and was alternately enraged and despairing that her peace of mind could be so dependent upon a phone call.

At seven-ten, when she'd almost given up hope, the telephone shrilled. She grabbed the receiver and said breathlessly, "Hello?"

"Lauren? Is that you?"

"Reece—where are you?"

"Heathrow. Again." As her heart leaped with joy that he was on his way to New York, he went on, "Did you listen to the news tonight?"

She hadn't. She'd been too preoccupied with cramps, the clumsiness of her fingers and the recalcitrance of the sheet metal she was working with. "Why? What's up?"

"I've got to go to Ecuador. Three of my staff were taken hostage last night. I've hired some professional negotiators to deal with the ransom, but I have to be there, too. Partly for moral support for the three guys that are prisoners, partly to do my own share of the negotiations.''

His voice was clipped and emotionless. ''How long do you think it'll take?'' she asked, trying to sound just as composed.

''I've no idea. Sometimes these things are settled right away, sometimes they drag on for weeks...I'd have phoned you sooner, but Gary and I have been working around the clock on that deal that nearly fell through. Lauren, I'm sorry, I know this isn't what I promised, but I couldn't live with myself if I didn't go down there and see for myself what's going on.''

''You'll be careful, Reece?''

''Of course I will,'' he said impatiently.

He was a very rich man; he'd be a prime candidate for being held to ransom himself. All the horror stories she'd ever read in the news flooded her mind; her heart felt like a lump of ice in her breast. ''Please look after yourself,'' she begged.

There was a small silence. ''You really care?''

This time it was she who was silent. ''I—of course I care what happens to you, I wouldn't want anyone to fall in the hands of kidnappers.''

''I see,'' he said with a trace of grimness. ''I can't promise how often I'll be in touch, as I'm not sure what conditions will be like down there. But I'll come back as soon as I can, that I do promise. Do you know yet whether you're pregnant?''

''I'm not.''

''Good,'' Reece said. ''Neither of us needs that complication.''

Suddenly furious, she retorted, ''Heavens, no. A baby? In your perfectly controlled life? Way too messy.''

''Give it a rest, Lauren.''

"Oh, pardon me," she snapped. Her fingers tightened around the receiver: a piece of plastic that was her only connection to Reece before he disappeared into dangers all the more threatening for being unknown. Appalled, she said raggedly, "Reece, I'm sorry. My back hurts, I haven't been able to settle down and work since you left, I'm hardly sleeping—I don't want you to go to Ecuador thinking I'm angry with you."

"If it's any help, I'm not sleeping, either." His voice deepened. "All I can think of is the softness of your skin, your beauty, the way you responded to me...I'll be back as soon as I can, I swear."

"I'll look forward to seeing you," she said. It was the truth, wasn't it? Although the words seemed hopelessly inadequate to express the storm of emotion in her breast.

"I've got to go—the jet's waiting. Take care of yourself, and if I can't phone you myself, I'll get someone in my London office to keep in touch."

"Thank you...'bye," she whispered.

The connection was cut. Slowly Lauren put down the phone and looked around the studio as though she'd never seen it before. A man with piercing blue eyes had severed her from a life she'd painstakingly rebuilt in the years after Sandor. A life in which she'd been more than content.

She couldn't go back. The past was just that: the past. And the future was so clouded with uncertainties that there was no refuge for her there, either.

Work, she thought. I'll work until I drop and I'll sleep the rest of the time. And who knows, Reece may be back in only a few days.

The days dragged by, and turned into weeks. November became December. Punctiliously every third day a man called Ross phoned Lauren from London to report on the negotiations, at first on their total lack of progress because of the outrageous demands of the hostage takers, and later on the inch-by-inch concessions being made by both sides. This was normal, he assured Lauren. She shouldn't worry, every precaution was being taken to insure the safety of the negotiating team.

Reece himself phoned four times, the connections so bad that Lauren could scarcely hear him. He sounded tired and frustrated, deeply worried about the safety of his employees, yet unable to accede to the demands of the kidnappers because to do so would have endangered the lives of local inhabitants. Lauren had never felt so helpless in her life; helpless and horribly lonely. As a result she threw herself into her work, staying up half the night for two weeks in a row, and producing a massive sculpture in steel and wood that far surpassed anything she'd ever done and that left her exhausted.

Besides talking long-distance to Charlie every week, the other thing she did was see a lot of Sam. He was involved in a project in New York, and was more than happy to drop in for coffee or go to a movie with her. Over a leisurely meal in a little bistro in Greenwich Village, he started talking about Clea, painting a picture of an intelligent, high-spirited young woman whom Sam had adored, and who had loved her brother Reece deeply. "Reece was devastated by her death...I don't think he's ever got over it. I'd never known him to be in love with any of the women he dated, but after Clea, he was like a block of ice." Sam buttered a slice of baguette, his thin face abstracted. "Part of me will always love Clea, and I know in my bones we'd have been happy together. But she's dead, Lauren. She won't be back...and now I've met someone else, in Boston."

"Someone nice?" Lauren ventured.

Sam grinned. "Bright and gorgeous and plays a mean game of tennis." Abruptly he sobered. "I haven't dared tell Reece. I'm afraid he'll think I've abandoned Clea. I'll never abandon her in one sense. But life moves on, and I want a wife and children and a house in the suburbs, all the normal stuff for a guy my age."

"I think you should tell him. When he comes back."

"And who knows when that'll be."

"It's got to be soon," Lauren cried.

"For someone who swears she's not in love, you're sure behaving like you are."

"I'm not! I won't let myself be. Because you're right, Reece took his heart and put it in the deep freeze and it'd take more than me to haul it out of there. So why would I be so stupid as to fall in love with him?"

"Then you both miss out."

"You're a born romantic, Sam."

"Guess you're right." He twirled his linguine around his fork. "Did I ever tell you about Reece's country place in Provence?"

Lauren settled back to listen; she loved hearing stories about Reece, about a younger, happier Reece; it all added to the emerging portrait of a complex man who'd loved his family and was now driven by demons she'd do anything to exorcise. As she went to bed that night, she added to the puzzle the fact that Reece had returned the cheque she'd sent him; nor had he published one word about Wallace.

The next day she went to the library, and on microfiche read the newspaper accounts about Clea's murder on a sidewalk in Chicago one hot summer day. There were photographs, all too graphic, engraving themselves on Lauren's brain. The ones of Reece made her flinch, so

haggard, so ravaged did he look; so utterly alone, no matter
that he was surrounded by people.

She didn't take any notes; she didn't need to. Her spirit
heavy, she left the library and walked home. For ten days
she worked, like a woman driven, on a small bronze of
two figures, a Pietà in reverse, for the man was holding
the woman's body. Then, after a certain amount of research, she mailed a cheque for the exact amount of the
sale of her house to an organization in Chicago that
worked with street kids. If—when—she saw Reece again,
she'd tell him what she'd done.

Of course she'd see him. He'd promised she would.

But there were times, especially in the middle of the
night when she woke to an unshared bed, that Lauren
doubted this. She lost weight, her eyes looked shadowed,
and the next piece she embarked on carried her to even
darker territory in her unconscious, places she'd never
been before. Charlie told her to throw the key to her studio
in the Hudson River. Sam lectured her about vitamins and
taking a holiday. Even purple-sarong, when she met him
one day on Forty-second Street wearing a pair of perfectly
respectable jeans, told her to book a flight to a beach in
Baja.

She couldn't. She had to be home to get the snippets of
information that were all that connected her to Reece; she
needed the security of friends and familiar surroundings.
And then one day in mid-December, when the shops were
full of Christmas decorations that seemed to mock her unhappiness, the telephone rang.

She was expecting a call from her agent. "Lauren
Courtney," she said crisply.

"I'm back in London."

She would have known that voice anywhere. She sat

down hard on the nearest chair. "Reece?" she faltered. "You're home? You're safe?"

"Yes, yes, and yes." His voice altered. "You okay?"

"I never c-cry," she gulped, swiping at the tears that were streaming down her cheeks.

"I thought you'd be happy."

"I am—oh, I am."

"We got in a couple of hours ago. The families of the three guys who were released were all at the airport...the men'll need psychiatric assessments, but I think they'll be fine now that they're home."

"So they were all released?"

He gave her some of the details, none of which she remembered afterward because she was too busy trying to overcome a maelstrom of emotion. Reece was safe. In London. Safe.

"You still there?" he said finally; she could almost see his crooked grin.

"Yes."

"You're being awfully quiet." She didn't know what to say; that was one reason. He went on, "I've got a ton of stuff to catch up on over here. I wondered...would you consider coming over for Christmas? Spending it with me in Surrey? I have a place there that I think you'd like."

"Just you and me?"

"Along with the housekeeper and the groundsman."

"I—I don't know that I'd get a flight this late."

"I'll look after that, I've got connections. Are you saying you don't want to come?" His voice was unreadable.

"You really want me there?"

"I wouldn't be asking you if I didn't."

"All right," she said in a rush. "I'll come."

"How about the twenty-third? We can drive down to Surrey that afternoon."

Ten more days, she thought. How will I last that long? "That sounds fine," she said. "Although there's one condition, Reece."

"Yes?" he said guardedly.

"We give each other one gift only, costing under twenty-five dollars and handmade."

He began to laugh. "That's fine for you. I'm the original clown when it comes to making anything other than hard cash."

"It doesn't have to be fancy."

"This some kind of test?"

"Sometimes money makes things too easy."

"You're so different from anyone else I know," Reece said vigorously. "But if this is what it takes to get you here, then I agree." He hesitated. "How are you, Lauren?"

He didn't mean that in the usual way; he really wanted to know. She said with careful accuracy, "Tired. Confused. So happy you're safe." Taking her courage in her hands, she added shyly, "Wanting very much to go to bed with you again."

"I can't tell you how I'm longing to hold you in my arms."

She gave a breathless laugh. "Ten days isn't long."

"Ten days sounds like forever."

Her whole body felt as though it were on fire. "I think we'll have a very happy Christmas," she said.

"I think you may be right. Lauren, I should go, I've got a million things to see to. I'll call you in a couple of days with all the arrangements. Take care, won't you?"

"You, too," she said. "'Bye, Reece."

As she put down the receiver, she was smiling. Impulsively she turned on the radio and to the strains of Bing Crosby began to dance around her studio floor, imagining that Reece was with her, holding her in his arms just as he'd said he longed to do.

Heaven, she thought. Sheer heaven.

Christmas with Reece. What other gift could she possibly want?

CHAPTER FOURTEEN

REECE was half an hour early at the airport on the twenty-third. He was never early for appointments, his time was too valuable for that. So why was he standing in the crowded arrivals area watching a clock change its digital numbers with agonizing slowness? Not, as Lauren would have said, his style.

Lauren. Would they recapture the passion, the intimacy they'd shared in her loft bedroom? Or was that a once-in-a-lifetime closeness, destined never to be repeated? And why did he care so much about the answer to his own questions?

What was she to him, this woman with hair like sunlight on copper, and a body that lacerated all his senses? She was as far from complaisant as a woman could be; she'd challenged his ingenuity for her Christmas present; and he was desperate to possess her again.

He hadn't allowed himself to feel remotely like this in the last five years. Not even before that, if he were honest. He'd never permitted a woman to arouse him to such extremities of emotion; hadn't wanted to. Which had had nothing at all to do with Clea and everything to do with a growing cynicism about the power of his own fortune.

He took out a financial magazine and tried to concentrate. Slowly the red numbers on the clock changed, until, over the heads of the crowd, he saw a tall woman with turquoise eyes hesitating at the barrier. He lifted the bouquet he'd been clutching, waving the great sheaf of lilacs over his head; and watched her face break into laughter.

She edged her way through the crowd toward him. She was wearing a dramatic long cape of loden green; as she finally reached him, he said, "This isn't your Christmas present. It's a welcome-to-England present."

Her eyes dancing, she said, "Where on earth did you get lilacs at this time of year?"

"It wasn't easy...hello, Lauren."

Her cheeks were flushed; she looked uncertain, happy and shy all at the same time. He leaned over and kissed her on the lips, and as his heart rocketed in his chest, murmured against her mouth, "Do you have any idea how much I want you?"

"I'm not sure this is the place for me to find out."

"You're probably right. Let's go find your luggage."

He tucked her arm in his, covering her fingers with his own, and realized with a jolt of surprise how happy he was. The same kind of feeling he'd had as a little boy, waking up one Christmas morning and finding Santa had brought him the model yacht he'd craved.

He was a big boy now and this was certainly the woman he craved. Should he be reminding himself that he'd outgrown the model by the following Christmas?

To hell with it, thought Reece, and said deliberately, "I thought of taking you to a hotel in the city. First. Then driving to Surrey afterward."

Her blush deepened. "So why aren't you?"

"I guess I'd like us to settle in. In the country."

"I'd like the same. I love Manhattan, but trees and fields sound really good to me right now."

He let his eyes roam her face, simultaneously so familiar and so unknown. "You look tired," he said slowly.

"You mean all that very expensive makeup I splurged on two days ago hasn't done its job?"

"Why so tired, Lauren?"

She hesitated. "If I said the Christmas rush or jet lag, it would be only partly true. Basically, I found the time you were in Ecuador so long that I worked like a madwoman the whole time. Night and day. If it's any consolation, I did three pieces that are probably the best I've ever done. My agent was really bugging me before I left— she's got potential buyers lined up already, but I couldn't deal with the commercial end of it yet. Wasn't ready."

As always, Reece found himself oddly exhilarated by her honesty. Later, when they were alone, he'd ask her more about the three works she'd produced; and knew he'd like to see them. To buy them? He said impulsively, "I didn't really buy those bronze pieces of yours as an investment. There was something about them—I can't explain, but it was as though you knew me. Knew something very important about me…I certainly wasn't going to tell you that on the first day we met."

Someone jostled her, thrusting her against Reece's chest. As his arms automatically went around her, the lilacs sprinkled her cape with tiny mauve blossoms. "Thank you for telling me now," she said softly.

The feel of her body so close to his was driving him out of his mind. "Let's get out of here. I want to be alone with you."

"You really are glad to see me?"

Surprised that she should have to ask, he said, "Of course, isn't it obvious?"

"I don't take anything for granted where you're concerned."

"That, darling Lauren, you can take for granted," he said, and watched her smile glimmer in her eyes. As they claimed her luggage, inched their way out of the city and drove steadily nearer his country estate, Reece found they had plenty to talk about. He described the excruciating weeks he'd spent in Ecuador, she told him about a play she'd seen, they discussed movies and books; as always, he was intrigued by her often unique way of looking at things, and by the play of expression on her face.

Finally they turned into the driveway of his estate. Dusk was falling; as the huge Queen Anne house loomed into view, he saw Lauren's eyes widen. He said awkwardly, "We could stay in the big house, if you'd like. But I thought you might prefer the lodge, it's more comfortable."

He turned down the lane, which was overhung with the bare branches of beech and ash; the lodge, made of stone with a slate roof, had a wreath hanging beside the oak door, and golden light streaming a welcome from the lead-paned windows. Lauren let out her breath in a small sigh. "I like this much better."

"I thought you would. The big house is fine for impressing all the right people—but not for day-to-day living. Hazel, the housekeeper, said she'd leave dinner ready for us. You must be hungry...I'll get your suitcase, if you'll take the lilacs."

He was talking too much. Because he was as excited as a child at Christmas? Because he very much wanted her to like the house that of all the properties he owned was his favorite? He took out the key and unlocked the front door, catching a tang of pine from the wreath along with the subtle, delicate scent Lauren was using. What he mustn't do was fall on her as if he was the one who'd just been released by kidnappers.

The hallway was decorated with holly and mistletoe, its burnished oak paneling reflecting the light from an intricate pewter chandelier. Reece led the way into the living room, where a fire was laid in the hearth. A fir tree was standing in the corner, with a cardboard box beside it; what had seemed a fine idea yesterday now seemed merely sentimental. He said clumsily, "I'm hoping you'll help me decorate the tree tomorrow, that's why I asked Hazel to leave it."

She clasped her hands in delight, like a child. "I'd love to! What a welcoming room, Reece."

He'd always loved its crowded bookshelves and old-fashioned chintz-covered furniture. "The windows overlook the garden. The Christmas roses are in bloom," he said. "Here, let me take your cape and hang it up. And I'd better find some water for those lilacs, they're dropping blossom all over the carpet."

She said suddenly, "If I didn't know better, I'd say you were nervous."

She'd hit altogether too close to home. "I'll put some soup on, too," he said. "What is it, ten-thirty at night to you?"

Lauren lifted her chin. "I don't want any soup. Let's put the lilacs in water and go to bed."

For all her brave talk, her hands were clasped so tightly around the woody stems that her knuckles were white. Flooded by an emotion he couldn't have named, an emotion totally new to him, Reece said huskily, "You're a beautiful woman in all senses of the word. And I agree, bed is where we need to be. Here, give me the lilacs."

But she held on to them. "I'll come with you."

In the kitchen, Reece shoved the flowers in a silver bucket, added water and dumped them on the counter. Lauren said stubbornly, "I want them in the bedroom, they're such a lovely present."

So he lugged the bucket up the narrow staircase and across the hall. The master bedroom also overlooked the garden and the magnificent oaks that sheltered the lodge from the main house. The fireplace was a Victorian addition with a charming metal grate; the bed, canopied, seemed to his overactive imagination to dominate the room. He put the lilacs in the corner. "Would you like me to light the fire?"

"Yes, please…and I'd like a hot bath. Travel always makes me feel scruffy."

"The bathroom's through that door," he said, kneeling to touch a match to the twisted papers in the grate.

By the time flames were leaping up the chimney and he'd lit some candles, he could hear water running in the bathroom. He hung up his coat and suit jacket. Lauren was here, he thought. Here with him for at least a week, just the two of them. No CEOs, no partygoers in purple sarongs, no kidnappers. And, despite his raging hunger for her, no need to rush.

He sat down on the bed, unlacing his shoes and pulling off his socks. "Want me to scrub your back?" he called, tossing his tie over the nearest chair.

Above the splash of water, he heard her laugh. "Sure," she said, "just as long as you're wearing the same amount of clothing as I am."

Grinning to himself, Reece stripped off the rest of his clothes and walked into the bathroom, a room he had insisted be thoroughly modernized. Lauren smiled up at him; although she'd been generous with the water, her breasts were fully exposed, gleaming wetly in the flickering light. His response was instant and unmistakable. She said wickedly, "Guess I shouldn't linger."

He knelt by the tub. She'd piled her hair on her head, exposing the fragile line of her nape. Taking her face in his hands, Reece kissed her with all the pent-up hunger of the weeks they'd been apart. As she kissed him back with an abandon that set his pulses racing, he ran his hands over her body, rediscovering the gentle jut of her bones, rejoicing in her slippery skin. "Come to bed with me, Lauren—now," he said, grasping her wrists and pulling her upright.

She stepped, dripping, onto the mat. He took a towel from the heated rack and wrapped it around her, smoothing it over her curves. Had he ever felt so alive, so certain he was exactly where he needed to be? Then Lauren lifted her face to his, a face blind with hunger. He kissed her, thrusting with his tongue. The towel dropped to the floor.

He was never quite sure how they got from the bathroom to the bedroom, where flames danced on the ceiling and the bed was waiting for them. But somehow she was lying under him, the softness of her breasts and her fierce kisses inflaming his senses until he wondered how his heart could be confined in his chest, so loudly was it pounding. Her hands were everywhere, her breathing as rapid as a bird's, her small, broken cries of rapture like music to his ears. He did his best to hold back, to give her all the pleasure he was capable of, tangling his hands in her hair, laving her nipples, stroking the wet petals between her thighs as she writhed beneath him, her every movement driving him closer and closer to the brink.

And then she toppled, crying out his name in a climactic blend of pain and pleasure that carried him with her. He fell on top of her, throbbing deep inside her, his breath rasping her skin. He was both drained and filled, he thought dazedly, both prisoner and freed. Burying his face in her hair, Reece closed his eyes.

Her arms were wrapped around him, her heart rate gradually slowing. She smelled delicious. He said huskily, "Happy Christmas, Lauren."

She chuckled. "So was that my present?"

"Nope. You don't get that until the twenty-fifth."

"It felt like a present." She stretched luxuriously, her

eyes like deep pools of light. "A wonderful present. Not sure you can surpass it."

"Wait ten minutes," he said, lazily drawing one finger along the rise of her breast.

Her nipple hardened. Trying to look severe, she said, "Ten minutes is a very long time."

"We can always improvise in the meantime," he drawled, leaning over to lick her creamy skin.

"Oh, Reece, I'm so happy to be with you!"

She looked happy. She also looked fulfilled, sensuous, and so beautiful that he had difficulty getting the words out. "I'm happy to be with you, too," he muttered, and knew he'd had enough of words. He began kissing her, taking his time, exploring the planes of her face and the long column of her throat before moving lower, always giving her time for her own responses, which were, he realized with a catch in his throat, growing bolder and more confident every time they made love.

Perhaps that was the real gift he'd given her, Reece thought with a humility new to him. And then stopped thinking altogether as he was caught up in a storm of passion, its rhythms as old as time. Losing himself, drowning in her heat and urgency, he let go of the last vestige of his control and heard his own hoarse cry of satiation echo in his ears.

Panting, he lowered his body to lie beside her, holding her close, never wanting to let her go. Because how would he ever have enough of her? How could he? She completed him as he'd never before been completed.

Was that love?

How would he know? As an adult, he'd never been in love.

Finding he didn't want to follow these thoughts, Reece murmured, "In New York, it's well past your bedtime."

"Even in Surrey," she whispered. "Reece, how can I thank you? Do you see what you've done? You've healed me. Made me whole again. I want you so much, my body adores you, I feel so free with you...so wanton."

Emotion slammed through his chest like an ambush; she'd always had this knack of slicing through his defenses as though they were nothing but thin air. "The pleasure's all mine," he said gruffly; and knew that at some deep level he was evading her. "Maybe we should try and get some sleep—you've got a tree to decorate tomorrow."

"So I have," she said contentedly. "Are we having turkey on Christmas Day?"

"It's thawing in the refrigerator and Hazel's left at least ten pages of instructions."

"I cook a mean turkey," Lauren murmured. "Good night, Reece."

Her gaze was clear and guileless. She'd said nothing about love, he thought. He'd freed her body. But her soul was still in her own keeping. And wasn't that the way he wanted it? "I'll blow out the candles," he said, and climbed out of bed. One by one the soft points of light vanished, leaving only the dull glow of coals in the grate. Then, in the velvet darkness of a country night, Reece climbed into bed beside Lauren, put his arms around her and fell asleep.

On Christmas morning, Lauren woke late. She lay still for a few moments, hearing the small sounds of Reece moving around downstairs. They'd made love in the middle of the night in total silence, each anticipating the other's needs in a way that might not have been possible a couple of days ago. He was a wonderful lover, she thought, generous, ardent and sensitive. And wasn't that enough? Of course it was.

There was no reason whatsoever for her to feel this tiny edge of anxiety, this ripple of uneasiness.

Yesterday, they'd decorated the tree with ornaments that had been in Reece's family since he was a child; they'd made mince pies and a delicious curry. At midnight, they'd walked to a carol service in the nearby Norman church whose walls were over a foot thick and whose air breathed of all the men and women who'd found solace within those walls.

Reece was climbing the stairs; the fourth step always creaked. Then he came in, wearing jeans and nothing else, carrying a tray. "Breakfast," he said, laughter lines crinkling around his eyes. "Not sure it'd pass Hazel's eagle eye."

Mugs of coffee topped with whipped cream, fresh strawberries and peaches, and croissants hot from the oven. "Hey," Lauren said, "a man who can cook. I'd better hold on to you."

The words replayed themselves in her head. Hoping Reece wouldn't read anything into them, she sat upright, adjusting the pillows. Hold on to him? Her return flight was booked for just after New Year, and beyond that she had no idea what would happen. Reece wasn't saying. And she wasn't asking.

"I took the croissants out of the freezer and put them in the oven," Reece said. "Not rocket science."

They ate a leisurely breakfast. Then Lauren dressed in a cream silk shirt and wool skirt, and they went downstairs to put the turkey in the oven. Afterward, Reece plugged in the lights on the tree in the living room, lit the fire and turned on some music. Passing her a flat, rectangular package, he said, "Merry Christmas, Lauren."

She'd put her own package on the antique milking bench that served as a coffee table. Fumbling with the ribbon and paper, she drew out a wooden-framed photograph of a rocky beach edged with graceful cedars. The woman standing above the tideline beside a tumble of bleached driftwood looked lost in contemplation.

"But that's me," Lauren said.

"I took it after I left you there when we were kayaking, remember?"

"It's a lovely photo…is the frame homemade?"

"I took woodwork way back in public school. That's a piece of oak from an old shipwreck off the coast of Maine. I thought you might like it."

"I love it," she said and kissed him. "Thank you for not buying me something terribly expensive, somehow that wouldn't have felt right." Then she added eagerly, "You must open mine, you'll see why."

Hers was in a box, carefully wedged with tissue. He drew it out, removing the paper, to reveal a small wooden sculpture, a curve of driftwood shaped like a wave of the sea, from which emerged the sleek bodies of three killer whales. Gazing at it for a long minute, he said huskily, "We were thinking alike."

"I wasn't going to give you a sculpture, it seemed like cheating. But somehow I knew this one belonged to you." She added impetuously, "You see, what happened at the yacht club is forgotten. Behind us. You've more than made amends."

For a moment the leaping whales blurred in his vision. The words forced from him, he muttered, "You've forgiven me."

"Of course I have."

"I only wish I could forgive myself as easily—for Clea, I mean."

"Oh, Reece…" Lauren put her arms around him in a whisper of silk, feeling the tension knotting his shoulder muscles. "I went to the library and read about it in the newspapers...it was such a terrible tragedy. But it wasn't your fault. It could just as easily have been you who died, or anyone else. There's no defense against that kind of random violence."

He let out his breath in a long sigh. "You're right, I know. Or at least, my head knows. But if only I hadn't left her alone on the sidewalk."

In a sudden flash of insight, Lauren said, "That's why you had to go to Ecuador, wasn't it? To be as close as you could to the men who'd been kidnapped because you felt responsible for them. You were trying to make reparation for Clea."

"I suppose you're right—I hadn't thought of it that way. I did feel responsible for them, yes."

She said unsteadily, "You're a good man, Reece." And for once saw that she'd rendered him speechless. If only she could heal him as simply as he had healed her. But his wounds were deeper, she thought with painful accuracy. Deeper and more lasting.

He said roughly, "I'll always cherish your present, Lauren, it's beautiful."

"We were on the same wavelength—or rather, the same beach," she teased, wanting only to erase the strain from his face.

He got to his feet. "How about some champagne, along with smoked trout?"

"Just as long as we go for a walk before dinner."

"I'll drag you up hill and down dale and across a couple of English stiles."

So there was to be no more talk of Clea. "I saw some gloriously mouldy Stilton in the door of the fridge," she added. "The kind with big globs of green all through it."

He laughed. ''I'll eat some, too. That way we can still kiss each other.''

They kissed each other a great many times over the next three days. Kissed, made love, laughed, washed dishes, walked and talked. Twice they wandered over to the Queen Anne house, where Lauren was transported by Reece's collection of art; and where she met the housekeeper, Hazel, whose initial scrutiny of her amused her and whose subsequent friendliness was, she realized, in some way earned.

Lauren didn't think she'd ever felt so carefree, so happy and cherished. She loved being with Reece. And he, unless she was badly mistaken, felt the same way about her. He even looked younger, lighthearted in a way that touched her.

Except every now and then, when she'd catch him simply staring at her, his face unreadable, his eyes shuttered in a way she remembered all too well and thoroughly disliked. The next time she saw him doing that, she must ask him what he was thinking about. Even though she was afraid she wouldn't like the reply.

It couldn't be anything serious, she thought in a rush of confidence. Nothing could disrupt the wondrous happiness that enveloped her, day and night.

Enveloped her like Reece's embrace.

CHAPTER FIFTEEN

THREE days after Christmas, a driving rain kept Reece and Lauren indoors in front of the fire. Lauren was reading a novel she'd chosen from the eclectic array on the bookshelves, while Reece was trying to catch up on the newspapers that had been accumulating since they'd arrived. Turning a page of the financial section, he said lazily, "Have you invested the money from the house in Maine, Lauren? There are some good tips here."

She hesitated briefly. Then she said in a level voice, "I sent the entire amount to an organization in Chicago that looks after street kids."

He lowered the paper, his face inimical. "You *what?*"

"You heard. I did a lot of research first, and picked a very reputable group."

"You just couldn't accept that money from me, could you?"

"I couldn't keep money that had been stolen—tainted with fraud. It was really nothing to do with you."

"You're splitting hairs."

"Reece, we're arguing again. Let's not, please—not over money."

"You're so—"

The telephone rang in the hallway. He surged to his feet, the newspaper sliding to the carpet. "I'll get it."

Heartsick, she watched him leave the room. They hadn't had a single disagreement since she'd arrived; in fact, they'd been so perfectly attuned to each other that she'd let down all her guards.

She couldn't have kept Wallace's money. She couldn't.

Reece came back in, his face still closed against her. "It's for you. Your agent."

"Beth? I didn't give her your number, how did she track me down?" Quickly Lauren went out into the hall. "Hello?"

"Hi, Lauren, thank goodness I've reached you. I got your number from your landlord after swearing on a stack of Bibles that you wouldn't mind. Listen, the curator of the new art museum—you know who I mean, the one and only Maxwell Galway—is very interested in your latest sculpture, the one you finished just before you left. Unfortunately, he's leaving for Japan the day after tomorrow. Can you fly home? Right away?"

Her brain whirling, Lauren stared at the delicate grain in the oak paneling. This was the breakthrough that could launch her career; it was a huge honor to have one of her works even considered by the museum, let alone purchased. But how could she leave here? Leave Reece?

"Lauren? Are you there?"

"Yes…you've taken me by surprise, that's all."

"This is a chance in a lifetime, I don't need to tell you that. I'm sure you can get a flight tonight. Or tomorrow morning."

A sale like this would be a huge feather in Beth's cap, too, of course. "Can I call you back? In half an hour?"

"You're not thinking of turning this down? Maxwell Galway could make or break your career."

Suddenly angry, Lauren said, "Beth, I'm staying here with a friend, so there's that to consider, and I have no idea about seat availability. I'll call you back."

"Fine," said Beth, not sounding as though it was fine at all. "You know my number."

Lauren plunked the receiver down and stood very still

in the pine-fragrant hallway. Beth was right. She, Lauren, couldn't afford to turn this down. She really had no choice; she had to go back to New York.

Maybe Reece would go with her.

She hurried back into the living room and quickly explained the gist of the conversation. "I have to go. Maxwell Galway is one of the biggest names in Manhattan, I'd be a fool to pass this up no matter how it turns out. But I don't—"

"So you want me to pull strings for your flight?"

Reece looked frankly hostile. Lauren said strongly, "The last thing I want to do is leave here. But I can't afford not to go, don't you see?"

"I see that your art comes first. That's what I see."

In a flare of temper, she said, "So you can leave me to go to Ecuador but I can't leave you to go to New York?"

"Ecuador was a one-off thing. But you'll always be an artist, Lauren. And I'll always be second to that, won't I?"

"Always?" she repeated uncertainly.

Ignoring her question, Reece said in a hard voice, "I don't like coming second."

"Why does it have to be a choice? I'm a woman and a sculptor, both at the same time. You can't have one without the other, they come as a package."

"I'll call up and get you a flight."

Jettisoning any thoughts she might have had about inviting him to come with her, Lauren said, "So men can have a relationship and a career but women can't? I thought you and I were past that stage."

"I don't like being dropped the minute someone in the art world beckons."

"But this is important!"

"And I'm not."

"You're twisting everything I say. I really hate this," she said wildly and watched him stride out of the room.

From the hall she could pick up snatches of conversation interspersed with long pauses; ten minutes later, Reece walked back in the living room. "The only seat I could get you is tomorrow morning at eight-thirty. We're booked into a hotel near the airport for the night, so we'd better leave within the hour."

She looked around at the peaceful, firelit room where she'd spent so many happy hours. "I don't want to leave."

Reece said flatly, "I want you here for the next five days—not in Manhattan."

"Then come with me," she begged.

"I've got some clout—but I can't manufacture extra seats on a jet. Unfortunately, both my company planes are out of the country so that employees of mine could go home for Christmas. Besides, if I go anywhere, I should go to Cairo."

Her disappointment was so bitter that she felt a stab of terror. The one word that hadn't been mentioned in the last few days was love. Reece didn't love her and was completely averse to falling in love; so she'd better not get too dependent on him. Yet at some level wasn't she craving him to tell her he loved her? She heard herself whisper, "I'll miss you."

"We can keep in touch by phone. And we've got tonight. We should leave, Lauren, it's pouring rain and it'll be a slow drive into the city."

She said defiantly, "I want a kiss first."

"Do you?" he said softly, padding over to her.

His kiss was voracious, a blend of fury and desire that left her weak-kneed and trembling. Determined to hide this, she said lightly, "I'll go and pack. Or else we'll be making love on the carpet."

It took her less than ten minutes to throw everything into her suitcase; she wrapped Reece's gift separately, to carry onto the plane. Then she gave one last glance around the bedroom in which she'd found such felicity. Would she ever be back? Or was this the end?

Feeling as though her heart was being torn in two, she walked downstairs and found her cape and boots in the hall cupboard. Reece was talking to Hazel on the phone, explaining the change of plan. Then he ran upstairs, coming down a few minutes later in a business suit, carrying a leather overnight bag. He looked like a stranger, Lauren thought, a formidable stranger; and for the first time in her life wished she earned her living in some more ordinary way.

He took a black umbrella from the stand by the door. "Ready? We'll have to run for it."

"Reece—"

Something in her voice made him stop in his tracks. He said roughly, "Don't look like that, Lauren—"

"We'll see each other again, won't we?"

"Of course. We're not through with each other yet, you know that as well as I do."

It wasn't the answer she'd hoped for; but it was all she was going to get. "Let's go," she said with assumed calm, and reached for the door handle.

Although Reece was an excellent driver, the heavy rain took his total attention. Lauren sat quietly all the way to the hotel, trying to sort out the jumble of emotions that seethed in her chest. *Always,* Reece had said. And then, later, *We're not through with each other yet.* Yet. A small word with ugly implications. What exactly had he meant? Was she to become a long-term part of his future? Or was she to be discarded when he grew tired of her?

Had these few days of happiness been simply an inter-

lude for him, rather than a building block to something
more lasting?

There was another question, one her brain shied away
from and to which she had no reply. Was she in love with
him? Perhaps, she thought, gazing down at her linked
hands in her lap, she was afraid of the answer.

The hotel enveloped her in the kind of luxury she'd read
about but never experienced. Reece disappeared into the
bathroom to have a shower before dinner; he didn't invite
her to join him. She hung up her cream silk shirt, then
discovered she must have left her toothbrush at the lodge.
Grabbing her raincoat and purse, she wrote a quick note
for Reece and took the elevator downstairs; she'd noticed
a drugstore just down the road.

Somehow Lauren was glad to get outdoors and be alone,
even if only for a few minutes. She hurried along the sidewalk, putting up Reece's umbrella, the raindrops rattling
against the fabric like fire from a machine gun. The drugstore was almost empty. She chose a toothbrush, paid for
it and pushed open the glass door. Absorbed in her own
thoughts, she didn't even notice the young man who followed her into the rainswept darkness.

She and Reece would make love tonight, she thought,
smiling to herself; they'd heal this rift that had opened so
suddenly and unexpectedly. She couldn't bear to leave tomorrow with even a shadow of dissension between them.
And she was being silly to doubt that she had a future with
him; surely his sensitivity and care of her the last few days
made that a certainty.

Out of the darkness a numbing blow struck her right
arm. Lauren gave a startled cry, her purse dropping from
her fingers to the ground. As she staggered, another blow
grazed her cheek, landing on her shoulder, so that she was
thrust against the wall that edged the pavement. The ribs

of the umbrella scraped along the brick. For the moment there was absolutely no pain; as though it were all happening to someone else, she watched a thin young man with his hood pulled over his face grab her purse, run across the road, and vanish into the curtain of rain.

Her knees didn't want to hold her up. She found herself crumpled on the sidewalk, the skirt of her raincoat soaking up a puddle. Then, slowly at first, pain blossomed in her forearm and spread into her shoulder, throbbing with an insistence that made her grit her teeth. She lifted her other hand to her cheek, and saw with horror that there was blood on her fingers.

"Miss? What happened? You okay?"

The next few minutes were always confused in her mind when she looked back. Her rescuer, a brawny man in an old leather jacket, sheltered her from the rain and took a quick look at her cheek. "Nothin' to worry about," he said in rough comfort. "My buddy'll stay with you while I go call the police, won't take a minute."

Her weak, "Oh, please, no police," was lost in the beat of rain. His buddy, as skinny as he was brawny, said, "Lost yer purse, eh? Happens all the time, just be glad he didn't have a gun."

A gun. Clea. With sick horror, Lauren tried to gather her wits. She couldn't go back to Reece with blood all over her face, she must wipe it off. As she tried to reach in her pocket for a tissue, the pain in her arm made her whimper, and her hand wouldn't obey her. The skinny man said, "Here's the police. Don't you fuss now, they'll look after you."

In a blur of flashing lights, a police car drew up to the curb. A uniformed officer knelt beside her, rapping out a series of questions she did her best to answer; after which he helped her to her feet. And then a man in a raincoat, a man she recognized all too well, thrust himself through the small crowd of onlookers. "*Lauren*—what in God's name happened? Are you all right?"

"Do you know the young woman, sir?" the policeman asked.

"Lauren, answer me!"

She said weakly, "I'm fine. I was m-mugged, that's all."

Reece said rapidly to the policeman, "I'll get a doctor to take a look at her at the hotel. Do you have all the information you need?"

"Give me the name of your hotel, please, sir. Although I have to tell you there's not much chance we'll get our hands on the thief."

Reece rattled off his own name and the hotel's; then he put his arm around Lauren. "Let's go."

She said to her two rescuers, "Thanks so much for your help, it was very kind of you... Reece, you'll have to go on my other side, this one's sore."

As he took her left arm, she leaned on him heavily and walked the short distance back to the hotel. Their passage across the lobby was highly embarrassing: she did her best to ignore the discreet stares and whispered comments. Finally they reached Reece's suite. He closed the door and went straight to the phone. She said forcefully, "I don't need a doctor. I need to wash my face and lie down with two ice packs."

"You're going to see a doctor."

She bit back her retort and slid out of her wet raincoat. As Reece put down the receiver, she said, "The toothbrush is in my pocket, can you take it out?"

He bent to pick up her coat, taking out the small plastic bag. "The hotel would have given you ten toothbrushes—didn't that occur to you?"

So this was all her fault? "I didn't think of asking them."

"You didn't think at all."

"If we're going to have a fight, I have to sit down," she said, and lowered herself gingerly onto the king-size bed. "I'm truly sorry you had to see me with blood all over my—"

"How do you think I felt when I came out of the bathroom and saw your note, and then you didn't come back?" he said in a voice like ice. "The five minutes I waited felt like forever. And then when I went outside and saw the lights on the police car, I thought it was game over."

Her shoulder felt as though it was on fire and all she wanted to do was lie down and close her eyes; but she was too proud to plead weakness. "Well, it wasn't."

"No thanks to you. Why in hell didn't you wait for me if you had to go tearing around the streets at night?"

Lauren said overloudly, "I know this must be reminding you of Clea and that's why you're so angry. But give me a break, Reece—I didn't do it on purpose. I have no idea what the odds are of being mugged on a London street, but it was just plain bad luck, okay?"

"Yeah," Reece said in a staccato voice, "it reminds me of Clea. It reminds me of everything I learned that day on that sidewalk in Chicago. Not to let anyone else close to me ever again. Because it hurts too much when things go wrong. I was in danger of forgetting that. But not anymore. It's just as well you're going back to New York tomorrow—past time."

If her shoulder was on fire, her heart now felt as if it were encased in ice. "You don't mean that."

"I damn well do."

Her pride in shreds around her feet, she faltered, "You mean we won't see each other again?"

"There's no point. I shouldn't have forgotten the lessons I learned that day—and for that I'm sorry. This has been wonderful while it lasted, Lauren. But it's over now. Before either of us gets hurt."

A tap came at the door. Reece strode across the carpet, ushering in a gray-haired man in a wet raincoat who said briskly, "Dr. Huskins. A mugging? Atrocious that the streets are so unsafe—where did he hit you, madam?"

She'd never been called madam by a doctor before. As he examined her shoulder and washed her cheek, Lauren realized with an ugly shock that she hated Reece seeing her in her bra, her upper body bare. Hated being exposed to him and consequently vulnerable. Only this morning such a consideration would have been unthinkable.

The doctor recommended bed rest, ice packs and pain-killers, all of which she could have thought of herself. She thanked him politely, and as soon as he was gone, said, "I'm going to take a shower and go to bed."

"I'll order room service for you."

"I'm not hungry. I'll get a cab to the airport tomorrow, would you arrange that?"

"I'll take you to the airport," Reece said through gritted teeth.

"I don't want you to! You've made it horribly clear you can't wait to see the last of me. So order me a cab."

"I don't take orders and I'll drive you in the morning."

"Everything's got to be your way, hasn't it?" Lauren flared. "You can go to Ecuador and Cairo, you can tell me what to do with my own money, you can get rid of me when and how you please. Fine. Do what you like. But don't expect to ever hear from me again."

By a superhuman effort she managed not to wince as she got to her feet, and to walk to the bathroom in a straight line. For the first time in many days, she locked the door. Then she stripped off her clothes and looked at herself in the mirror. Dried blood had crusted under her chin, while her cheeks were as white as the sheets on the bed.

The last bed that she and Reece would ever share.

Her shoulder was a dull red; it was her eyes that looked bruised, she thought clinically. And why not? The world she'd shared with Reece all Christmas, a world she would have said was both drenched in ecstasy and utterly dependable, had fallen apart. In her heart of hearts, hadn't she believed that the intimacy between her and Reece could only grow deeper and stronger, binding them closer and closer as the days—and nights—went by?

But she'd been wrong. He'd opposed her flying to New York for the most important commission in her life, and then an act of violence in the rain had done the rest.

I'll cry tomorrow evening, she thought. Not tonight. Not tomorrow morning at the airport. And not in front of Maxwell Galway or Beth.

Or maybe I won't cry at all. Maybe instead I'll give thanks for a narrow escape from a man who's locked in the past.

Her mouth twisted. Who was she kidding? She'd cry her eyes out once she had time and privacy. But no one else had to know that. Least of all Reece.

CHAPTER SIXTEEN

IT WAS five o'clock in the morning. With a groan of dismay, Lauren punched down her pillow and pulled up the covers. She had a headache because for the seventh night in a row she'd cried herself to sleep; she was also suffering from heartache. She felt wretched. Rotten. Lousy. And, she thought miserably, sexually deprived into the bargain.

Not to mention lonely.

How could she, in so short a time, have grown so accustomed to Reece's body beside her, to the rhythm of his breathing in the dark? To his laughter, his incisive intelligence, his rapier wit? Not that he'd been laughing the morning he'd put her on the plane to New York. Far from it. He'd looked as though he couldn't wait to be rid of her.

She hadn't heard from him in the last week. Surprise, surprise, she thought ironically, burrowing her head into the pillow. For him it was over, and she'd be willing to bet he wasn't lying awake thinking about her. He'd probably already moved on to someone else. As an antidote to too much emotion.

The only comfort she could take was that she couldn't have done anything differently. She'd been herself with Reece. And he hadn't wanted her.

Her thoughts went 'round and 'round, in a way she deplored but was unable to halt. Finally, at half past five she got up, put on a pot of coffee and got dressed in tights and a sweater. As she poked around the scraps of metal and wooden blocks in one corner of her studio, desperate for an outlet for her emotions, she suddenly remembered the clay she'd bought the week before Christmas. Shaping clay had always given her pleasure. She grabbed an old cotton smock, pulled it over her head, and sat down at her table, a mug of coffee nearby.

Three hours later, Lauren pushed back her chair. The bust on the table in front of her had more or less made itself: she'd scarcely had anything to do with it. It was a portrait of Reece, infused with all his energy and decisiveness, faithful to the jut of his cheekbones and the strong line of his jaw. His eyes seemed to look right through her, discerning her most intimate concerns. I'm in love with you, she thought, and in utter astonishment repeated the words in her head. I'm in love with Reece Callahan.

Of course she was. Why else had she cried herself silly the very day she'd found out that Maxwell Galway was going to purchase one of her works? Six months ago she'd have been delirious with joy. But not now. Not when she couldn't share the news with Reece. Not when she was totally estranged from him, missing him achingly and unremittingly, in bed and out.

He didn't love her. He wouldn't allow himself to. But, frowning, she found herself wondering for the first time if he'd been afraid he might fall in love with her. Why else had he picked that ridiculous fight about her flying to New York, if at some level their intimacy hadn't scared him to death? And why else, in the cold flash of lights from the police car, had he looked at her with hatred in his eyes? His hands, she remembered suddenly, had been unsteady; he'd jammed them in his pockets when he'd caught her noticing them.

Could it be true? Had Reece sent her away so he wouldn't fall in love with her? Or was she building castles in the air because she couldn't bear the hard truth?

Her heart was fluttering in her breast like that of a trapped bird, and she found it hard to breathe. There was one way to find out. Ask him. Or tell him she'd fallen in love with him, and see what he said.

Lauren began pacing up and down her studio, her brain racing and her emotions in a tumult. She was being a total idiot to even think this way; wasn't it enough to have been so thoroughly rejected once without courting a second rejection?

Impulsively she picked up the phone and called Sam at his office in Boston. "Sam," she said without preamble, "do you think there's any chance Reece could be falling in love with me?"

"Happy New Year to you, too," Sam said. "Yes, I do."

"You *do?*"

"He certainly isn't indifferent to you. I was talking to him a couple of days ago and asked how you were—you'd think I'd asked about the wicked witch of the west… what's up?"

Briefly she described the events of the last week. "Where is he now, do you know?"

"In England. Staying in Surrey until he goes to Hong Kong later in the week. Why don't you phone him and find out if he's in love with you?"

"I have to see his face when I ask," she said edgily.

"I was supposed to fly to London around noon today. But the meeting was postponed and I haven't gotten around to canceling my ticket. You can have my seat."

"Oh, God," said Lauren, "I'm out of my mind to even think of seeing him again."

"We only go this way once."

Clea. Again. "All right," Lauren said, "I will."

"I'll square it with the airlines, luckily I do have some influence there—not as much as Reece, but enough. You'll pick up the ticket at the counter, okay?'' Quickly he gave her the details. ''Do you want me to phone him? Let him know you're coming? I could try and talk some sense into him.''

''No! No, I have to take him by surprise—that way maybe I'll find out what's really going on...wish me luck, Sam.''

''Right on. Let me know what happens, either way. Or if there's anything else I can do to help.''

''You've already done a lot, thanks so much. 'Bye for now.''

Lauren put down the phone. Absently she ran her finger down the throat of the clay sculpture to the curve of collarbone. What use was clay? It was the real man she wanted. The real man she was going to fight for. And hadn't she, unconsciously, infused his features with all the intensity he'd shown in their lovemaking? All the tenderness that she'd put her trust in? A film of tears distorting her vision, she realized she'd modeled the face of a man in love.

She'd take it with her; maybe it would speak to Reece in a way that she couldn't.

But if it didn't, at least she'd know she'd tried.

Many long hours later, Lauren stepped out of a taxi at the gateway to Reece's property. It was well past sunset, the trees barely discernible against the blackness of sky. ''Sure you want to get out here, miss?'' the cabbie said doubtfully.

She wasn't quite as sure as she had been. ''Yes,'' she said, smiling at him as she hefted the box with the sculpture under one arm and picked up her overnight bag. ''I'll be fine.''

He tipped his cap and drove off. Lauren walked through

the gate and along the driveway to the lodge, her eyes slowly becoming accustomed to the darkness. In the grove of oaks, a branch rubbed against another, squealing like an animal in pain; an owl hooted in the distance. Then she saw the lights of the lodge gleam through the trees.

So Reece was here. Although her relief, she noticed, was almost instantly eclipsed by an equally strong sense of dread. She had no idea what she was going to say to him. Or would she simply thrust the box at him and see what happened?

Steadfastly she walked on, the lights growing brighter. Not stopping to think, because if she did there was a fair likelihood she'd turn tail and run, Lauren marched up the steps and pushed the doorbell. Distantly, over the pounding of her heart, she heard it chime inside, followed by the sound of footsteps.

The door swung open. "Why, Miss Courtney," Hazel said, "what a nice surprise."

Swallowing a crushing disappointment, Lauren said, "Reece—he's here, isn't he?"

"Come in, come in, it's turned chilly, hasn't it?" Hazel said, and took Lauren's bag from her unresisting fingers. "Did you walk all by yourself up the lane? Now I've lived here all my life and that's more than I'd do. Mr. Reece? No, he left for London early yesterday morning. To fly to the States, he said."

"Yesterday?" Lauren repeated numbly.

"I believe so. Some emergency or other, he didn't say what. Or when he'd be home…are you all right, dear?"

Lauren put the box down on the nearest chair. So Reece had been on her side of the Atlantic yesterday and hadn't got in touch with her.

She had her answer. The one she'd come all this way

to find. As the heat of the hallway enveloped her, she said vaguely, "I'm fine, thank you."

Hazel pulled out another chair and eased Lauren into it. "You don't look well, if I may say so," she said. "You'll stay overnight, and I'll call Mr. Reece's office and find out—"

Roused from her lethargy, Lauren spluttered, "No, you mustn't do that."

Hazel's shrewd gray eyes sharpened. "Very well. But I'm going to get you a nice bite to eat and make sure you're settled in before I go back to the big house. Tom, my husband, will come by in the morning. You'll be comfortable here, by yourself?"

"Oh, yes." Lauren was craving privacy; and despite Hazel's genuine kindness was relieved when a couple of hours later she had the house to herself. Hazel had put her in the guest room; she didn't think she could have borne sleeping in the bed she and Reece had shared.

Restlessly she prowled through the house, picking things up, putting them down, feeling Reece's presence in every corner. She'd leave first thing in the morning. Go back to London and get the first flight home and do her best to forget a man who'd turned her life upside down, teaching her the joy and utter misery that was called love.

She found herself taking the clay bust out of its box and staring at it as though it could give her some answers. Carrying it downstairs and putting it on the coffee table, she sat down on the sofa. She'd deluded herself when she'd modeled the face of a man in love. Reece wasn't in love with her. He never had been.

Dazed with unhappiness, she burrowed her face in the soft velvet cushions. Half asleep, half awake, quite unable to gather the energy to go back upstairs, Lauren heard the antique clock chime each passing hour: ten, eleven, twelve, one. Then suddenly she jerked upright on the sofa, her heart leaping in her breast. Someone was turning a key in the lock.

The front door opened with the faintest squeal of hinges, slammed shut, and then footsteps marched along the hall. "Lauren?" Reece called. "Where are you?"

How did he know she was here? She faltered, "In the living room," and, as though it were all happening to another woman, watched his big body fill the doorway, his blazingly blue eyes trained on her face. She grabbed the bust, trying to thrust it between the table and the sofa, and said rapidly, "I shouldn't have come, I'm sorry, I'll never do this again and I'm going to leave first thing in the morning—"

"What's that you're trying to hide?"

His appearance in the middle of the night, so unexpected, so disconcerting, seemed to have loosed all the holds on her tongue. "I made it. I came here yesterday to tell you I love you, but I shouldn't have, you were in the States the day before and you didn't even call me, so I've made a complete fool of myself." Resorting to anger for a situation she had no idea how to cope with, she finished, "Why don't you just go to bed and forget I'm here? You're good at forgetting me, and I'll be gone by the time you wake up. Gone for good, this time."

He walked over to her. He was wearing a charcoal-gray suit with a blue shirt and silk tie; he looked exhausted. "Don't come near me!" she exclaimed, and clutched the bust all the tighter.

For a moment Reece froze in his tracks. "But you said you love me."

She thrust the clay bust at him. "When I made this, that's what I found out. But I have this stupid habit of acting before I think. Really stupid, under the circumstances, and not a mistake I'll make again.''

He took the clay piece from her, setting it down on the table and gazing at it. ''When did you see my face like that?''

''Whenever we made love,'' she said defiantly.

''You saw what I've been blind to.''

''I don't know what you mean…''

''I went to Cairo right after you left. Thought about you the whole time I was there. Came back. Couldn't stand being here on my own. Went to London—when the devil was it, the day before yesterday? I'm so jet-lagged I don't even know what day of the week it is.''

He ran his fingers through his hair, his eyes glued to her face. ''I stayed in the same hotel where you and I stayed, thought about you every minute of the day and night. So yesterday morning I got on a jet to New York. You weren't at your studio, your landlord didn't know where you were, nor did your neighbors. So I phoned Sam, who told me you were here, and told me—fairly forcefully—to smarten up.''

Lauren said faintly, ''Hazel told me you'd flown to the States the day before yesterday—that's why I was so upset.''

''I was half crazy when I left here—didn't know what I was going to do.'' He glanced at the bust on the table. ''The truth's been staring me in the face. But did I see it? No, sir. I was too busy protecting myself from feeling what the whole world feels—joy and pain. The happiness and vulnerability that comes from loving someone.'' He hesitated. ''Do you know what suddenly hit me in the hotel in the middle of the night?''

She shook her head, suspense clamping her by the throat. ''What?'' she said baldly.

"That Clea was the last woman in the world who would have wanted me to shut myself off from loving you. She was very much alive in her short life—and she would have liked you so much, Lauren, I know she would have."

"I'm crying again," Lauren muttered. "I've got to stop this."

"I've been a fool, that's what I'm saying. I acted like a prize idiot about that cheque and about Maxwell Galway, because I knew I was in deep with you and it was time I put on the brakes. The mugging gave me a perfect excuse. End it. Send you home and go back to my nice, safe life."

So she'd been right, Lauren thought dazedly; Reece had been afraid of falling in love with her. Trying to get her facts straight through a surge of hope that felt like sunlight after rain, she said, "So you arrived in New York about the time I was leaving?"

"Yeah…if we'd met at the airport, we could have saved ourselves a lot of time."

"Time, money and grief. When I heard your key in the lock, I thought I was going to get mugged for the second time."

Making no attempt to touch her, Reece said hoarsely, "Lauren, I love you. That's what I'm trying to say."

She bit her lip. "I'm not dreaming, am I? Please tell me I'm not going to wake up in my studio to an empty bed—and an empty heart."

"I'm only sorry it's taken me this long to come to my senses," Reece said violently. "That I caused you pain when you're the last person in the world I want to hurt."

"You really do love me?"

Something like a smile lifted the harsh lines on his face. "Lauren, I really do love you."

She got up and walked right into his arms. "Oh,

Reece,'' she quavered, ''I love you so much. It's been so awful without you—hold on to me and never let me go.''

''I never want to let you go,'' he said fiercely, pressing her so close to his body that she could hear the pounding of his heart. ''You're all I ever wanted and ever will…and you even came looking for me after all I'd done to you.''

''You're worth it,'' she said with a radiant smile. ''Anyway, you came looking for me, as well.''

''We'll invite Sam—and his new girlfriend, he told me all about her—to the wedding.''

''Wedding?'' Lauren said. ''Aren't you getting ahead of yourself?''

He grinned. ''If you want me to go down on my bended knee, I will. Marry me, Lauren? Please?''

''Yes. Oh, yes,'' she said with a ripple of joyous laughter. ''You don't have to get down on your knees. But you could take me to bed. If you want to, that is.''

''Want to?'' he said huskily. ''You don't ever have to doubt that.'' He bent his head to kiss her, a deep kiss of passionate commitment. ''I'm yours, body and soul… you've made me whole again.''

''I love you so much,'' Lauren said, her eyes clear as rainwater, her face alive with happiness.

''Let's go to bed,'' he said. Picking her up in his arms, he carried her up the stairs into his room, where, in the big canopied bed, he pledged his heart to her in a love-making that carried Lauren to a place she'd never been before. A place they'd reached by literally making love, she thought; a place beyond words.

As she snuggled into his chest, her pulses slowing, she gave him a bemused smile. ''Do you have to tear off to Tonga or Tasmania first thing tomorrow?''

''I do not. Do you have to be on the doorstep of a

museum?'' He stroked a strand of hair back from her face. ''I didn't even ask you about Maxwell Galway.''

''He bought one of my works and I don't have to be anywhere else but here.''

''So Galway's smart enough to recognize real talent when he sees it—congratulations.'' Reece gave her a lingering kiss. ''As neither of us has to go anywhere, we could spend the day in bed. Planning our wedding, among other things.''

''What about Hazel and Tom? They're supposed to look in on me in the morning.''

''Hazel likes you. She'll be a model of tact and leave us strictly alone,'' Reece said, kissing Lauren with lazy sensuality.

And indeed, when Hazel unlocked the front door the next morning and saw Reece's suitcase standing in the hall, she backed up immediately, a big smile on her face. Then she hurried home to tell Tom to stay away from the lodge all day.

Susan Napier was born on St Valentine's Day, so it's not surprising she has developed an enduring love of romantic stories. She started her writing career as a journalist in Auckland, New Zealand, trying her hand at romantic fiction only after she had married her handsome boss! Numerous books later she still lives with her most enduring hero, two future heroes – her sons! – two cats and a computer. When she's not writing she likes to read and cook, often simultaneously!

A PASSIONATE PROPOSITION

by

Susan Napier

CHAPTER ONE

To the nervous girl hovering in the darkened doorway, the woman sitting at the long, scuffed dining table looked discouragingly absorbed, her slender body propped over a lecture pad as her pen danced across the ruled page. An untidy array of loose-leaf pages and open books fanned across the table-top in front of her and a half-drunk cup of tea sat forgotten at her elbow. The standard lamp which she had dragged over from the corner of the room to supplement the feeble naked bulb dangling from the ceiling poured yellow light down onto her bent head, refining the neat knot of fine, straight hair at the nape of her neck from its usual dishwater-blonde to burnished gold. Even in a boxy white shirt and fawn cargo pants she still managed to look enviously feminine.

Miss Adams had always seemed kind and approachable; she'd never shouted, or played favourites or picked on kids for things about themselves that they couldn't help, as some of the other teachers at Eastbrook did. Right now, however, her delicately etched features looked aloof in their intentness and the girl's misgivings overwhelmed her dwindling store of courage.

After all, Miss Adams was no longer teaching at Eastbrook Academy for Girls. She had left at the end of the previous year and moved out to the sticks to teach history at Hunua College, the local state high school. The fact that she was helping out on this special fifth-formers' camp during the holiday break between the first and second terms didn't mean she was ever coming back to Eastbrook. She was only here because Old Bag Carmichael had got sick and none of the

5

other teachers from school were available to come and take her place. Miss Marshall would have had to cancel the rest of the camp if she hadn't remembered that her friend and former colleague lived in the nearby town of Riverview. Luckily Miss Adams had been free to donate a few days of her time, but she certainly wasn't going to be around to help cope with any fallout from tonight's escapade—and there was bound to be *heaps* of aggro back at school if the other girls found out who had tattled, no matter that it had been out of worry rather than malice.

Clutching her loose pyjamas against her hollow stomach, the girl began to edge backwards into the gloom of the hall-way, but it was too late.

As Anya turned her head to look up another reference she caught sight of a pale flutter out of the corner of her eye and was wrenched from her absorption, her heart pumping in alarm at the prospect of an intruder.

She didn't usually jump at shadows, but Anya was conscious that the regional park's accommodation was sited in a relatively isolated part of the shoreline reserve, and that she was currently the sole protector of four teenage girls. Cathy Marshall, the camp's supervising teacher, had taken the rest of the girls out with the park ranger to count and record the number of nocturnal bird-calls in the surrounding bush, part of an ongoing park survey on behalf of the Conservation Department.

Her pulse slowed in relief as she recognised the tall, gawky figure of one of her temporary charges.

'Hello, Jessica, what are you doing up?'

Glancing at her slim gold watch, Anya saw that it was well past midnight. She had been taking advantage of the quiet to catch up on some of the research which she had planned to do during these holidays and the time had passed more swiftly than she had realised.

'I...uh...' Jessica swallowed audibly, shifting her weight from one pyjama-clad leg to the other.

'Can't you sleep?' Anya asked, pitching her cool, clear voice low in deference to the night. 'Is your stomach hurting again?'

Jessica and her bunkmate had suffered a mild case of the collywobbles after gorging themselves on guava berries which they had picked off a bush hanging over a roadside fence.

Jessica blinked rapidly. 'No...uh...I just came down to...to...' She trailed off, gnawing her lower lip as her dark eyes skated around the room, searching for inspiration, '...to get a drink of water,' she finished lamely.

Anya decided to overlook the rather obvious invention.

'I see. Well, what are you waiting for?' She tilted her head towards the open kitchen door behind her. 'Help yourself.'

Returning her attention to her books, she listened as the kitchen light clicked on, and after an extended pause there came the squeak of a cupboard door, a clink of china and a gush of water. There was another long silence before the light snapped off and Jessica trailed slowly back, to linger once more in the doorway.

Anya raised her eyebrows above abstracted grey eyes, set wide apart in her delicate face. 'Was there something else?' she murmured, her mind still half on the open page in front of her.

Her impatience caused an agonised pinkening of Jessica's freckled complexion as she hurriedly shook her curly head, but her fingers continued to anxiously twist and tug at the hem of her pyjama jacket.

Anya suppressed an inward sigh and put her pen down.

'Are you sure?' she coaxed, her mouth curving in a sympathetic smile that banished the former impression of cool reserve. 'If you can't sleep, maybe you'd like to stay down here and chat for a while?' she probed gently.

An expression of yearning flitted across Jessica's uncertain face. 'Well…'

'Is there a problem with some of the other girls?'

'*No!*' Her guess had Jessica almost tripping over her tongue with an over-hasty denial. 'I mean, n-no, thanks—it's OK…really! I—I feel quite sleepy now…' She punctuated her stammered words with an unconvincing yawn. 'Uh—goodnight, Miss Adams…' She turned tail and scampered up the stairs.

Anya took up her pen again and tried to return to her research, but the memory of Jessica's anxious expression nagged at her conscience. She regretted the initial dismissiveness which had cost her the girl's confidence. Anya's ability to gain and hold the trust of her students was mentioned in her reference as one of her major strengths as a teacher. It was largely thanks to that glowing reference from Eastbrook's headmistress that she had gained her challenging new post and, after allowing herself to be persuaded to sacrifice a few days of her precious holiday to help run this camp, the least she owed her former school was to fulfil her responsibilities with good grace.

Anya had been a boarding pupil herself at Eastbrook, and was aware of the bitter feuds, petty cruelties and reckless dares that were carried out behind the house mistresses' backs. Remembering some of those escapades, she felt her guilt deepen to active unease and she pushed back her chair, gathering her books and papers up into a neat pile which she stowed in her zipped backpack. It was past time she packed up anyway. Tomorrow was the final day of the camp and the schedule was crammed full of activities, right up until the time that the bus was due to ferry the girls back to school. Then Anya would be at liberty to return to the peace and quiet of her cosy cottage. After years of sharing various accommodations she was revelling in the freedom of total independence, and these past few days of communal living had reconfirmed her belief that she had done the right thing in finally striking out on her own.

Friends and family had thought her crazy for moving to rural South Auckland and taking on a hefty mortgage at the same time as a new job, but at twenty-six Anya had felt it was time for her to take control of her life. It had been a childhood dream to live here in the countryside, and as an adult she now had the power to turn her dream into a permanent reality.

She carried her bag up to the cramped cubicle in which she and Cathy were quartered before walking quietly down the gloomy corridor towards the twin rooms the girls were sharing. She paused outside the first door, eyeing the square of pasteboard slotted into the metal holder which announced the room assignment.

Cheryl and Emma.

Her intuition hummed.

Cheryl Marko and Emma Johnson were a tiresome duo of spoiled little madams who had made it starkly plain that they were only here because the conservation camp was a compulsory part of the syllabus for boarding pupils. They had been due to go out on tonight's bird survey with the others, but Cathy had allowed them to stay behind when, coincidentally, both had complained at the last minute of severe period cramps.

Rather *too* coincidentally, Anya had thought, doling out mild analgesics to the pair as they had languished smugly in their sleeping bags while the rest of the girls clattered out on their mission.

She eased the door ajar and ducked her head inside the darkened room. A full moon pierced the gaps in the uneven curtains, casting pale bars of light over the narrow bunk beds, striping two motionless lumps in the bunched sleeping bags.

Reassured, Anya was about to withdraw when she hesitated, her grey eyes narrowing. For a couple of fashion-obsessed teenagers who constantly preened over their rake-thin bodies, they were displaying suspiciously voluptuous outlines!

Darting inside, she stripped back the hood of the first sleeping bag and stared in dismay at the untidy sausage of towels and designer-label clothes which had been used to pad out the empty interior. A quick check of the second bag yielded the same result.

Her stomach clenched in apprehension. Of course, it was quite possible that Cheryl and Emma were off on some innocent teenage escapade, but she had the sinking feeling that their sophisticated tastes wouldn't be satisfied by a common-or-garden midnight feast or giggling dorm raid.

A quick search of the rest of the empty rooms revealed no sign of the missing pair and, clinging to the slim hope that her instincts were wrong, Anya opened one final door and flicked on the overhead light.

'Girls?'

Jessica jerked bolt upright in her sleeping bag, her spectacles still perched on her nose, while in the next bed a chubby redhead rolled over onto her back, blinking blearily into the glare as she struggled into wakefulness.

'Cheryl and Emma seem to have disappeared,' said Anya crisply. 'Do either of you know where they've gone?'

She fixed her eyes on the redhead's sleep-creased face.

'Kristin? You're friends with both of them—did they say anything to you about what they were planning to do?'

'I was feeling so rotten earlier, Miss Adams, that I didn't really pay attention to what anyone was saying,' she replied plaintively.

Anya wasn't fooled by the self-pitying evasion, nor was she in any mood for a drawn-out question and answer session.

'What a pity,' she sighed. 'I was hoping to handle this on my own, but I guess I don't really have a choice. You girls should get dressed—the police will probably want a word with you—'

'The *police*?' Jessica gasped.

'B-but—shouldn't you wait a bit longer before you do anything?' gulped Kristin. 'That's what Miss Marshall would do if she was here. I mean—they'll probably turn up soon, anyway…'

'I can't take the risk—not with a beach and river nearby,' Anya said firmly. 'If I was still on staff it would be different, but I'm just an unofficial helper on this trip. I can't simply do nothing—that decision isn't mine to take. Fortunately we have their parents' phone numbers—'

It was the master stroke.

'Their *parents*?' Kristin's flush of horror almost matched her vivid hair. 'You can't call Cheryl's Dad—he'd go ballistic! They only went to a party!'

'A *party*?' Anya's heart sank even further. 'What party? Where?'

The facts that reluctantly emerged were hardly reassuring. A group of local boys who had been tossing a rugby ball around on the sand that afternoon while the girls were playing a game of beach-volleyball had extended the invitation to a party at one of their homes. Cheryl and Emma, the only ones daring enough to accept, had arranged to be picked up outside the gates of the regional park at ten o'clock by one of the boys in his car. They had been promised a ride back any time they wanted to leave the party.

Anya hid her horror. 'You mean they agreed to go off in a car with total strangers?' She racked her brains to remember exactly who she had seen on the beach. She had noticed several familiar faces from her new school, and had been able to reassure Cathy that the boys weren't a roaming gang of thugs.

'No, of course not!' Even Kristin knew the difference between reckless defiance and outright stupidity. 'It's OK, Miss

Adams—because Emma knew a couple of them from one of the bands who played at our school ball!'

Anya rolled her eyes. Oh, great…raging hormones *and* delusions of rock star grandeur!

The last straw was finding out that one of the big attractions of the party was the lack of any supervising adults.

'Emma said that this really cute guy—the one whose party it is—told her that it would be a real rave because he had the house to himself for the whole weekend,' added Jessica.

When pressed, Kristin was vague on the exact location of the party. 'The boys said it would only take about ten minutes to drive there. Some big, two-storeyed place on the other side of Riverview…'

'A white house on a hill, with a bridge at the gate and a stand of Norfolk pine trees,' added Jessica, whose memory was as sharp as her intellect.

Anya's mouth went suddenly dry and prickles of alarm feathered the back of her skull.

'The Pines?' she asked, her voice sounding shrill to her own ears. 'Was the house called The Pines?'

Kristin had turned sulky again. 'Yeah, that's it…'

'And you're *sure* about there being no adults there?'

Kristin nodded and was even more disgruntled ten minutes later as she clambered into the back seat of Anya's small car.

'I don't see why *we* have to go,' she grumbled. '*We're* not the ones in trouble.'

'Because no one's answering the phone at The Pines and I'm not leaving you two here alone while I go and get Cheryl and Emma,' said Anya as she fumbled in the glove-compartment for the wire-rimmed spectacles she used when driving and reversed the car out of the parking area. She'd left an explanatory note for Cathy, although she expected to be back well before the group returned from their survey.

Her hands tightened on the wheel as she turned from the bumpy track onto the narrow sealed road which was the main route from the coast to the suburbs of South Auckland and tried to soothe her taut nerves. She was probably overreacting. It wasn't as if she herself hadn't sneaked out to an illicit party or two during her school days—it was more or less *de rigueur* for senior boarders, and even an otherwise goody-two-shoes like Anya had been obliged to break a few rules in order to assure a peaceful life in the dorm.

The trouble was that in the four months since she had left Eastbrook she had got used to not concerning herself with after-hours student high jinks. One of the things she enjoyed about teaching at Hunua College was the separation between work and leisure. When she left school each afternoon she shrugged off her responsibilities at the gate. Oh, she took home lesson plans and piles of work to mark, but she wasn't personally responsible for the welfare of the kids themselves until the start of the next school day.

'What if they've already gone when we get there?' Jessica asked suddenly. 'What if they come back another way and we miss them?'

'This is the only road from Riverview to the regional park,' Anya told her, 'and there's very little traffic along it at this time of night, so we should notice if they pass us. Besides, Cheryl and Emma told Kristin they would be back around two, so they shouldn't have left yet—'

'Unless the party's a bust and they've gone on somewhere else,' came the sly comment from the back seat.

Anya gritted her teeth. As if she didn't have enough worries to contend with! 'Let's cross that bridge when we come to it, shall we?'

She continued to drive in tense silence. Fortunately it was a beautifully clear night, with only the suicidal dance of nocturnal insects in the high beam of her headlights to distract her from the road. The fields on either side of the unwinding ribbon of tarseal were bathed in monochromatic moonbeams and every now and then a glow of warm yellow light pinpointed a farmhouse tucked amongst a wind belt of trees, or perched on the grassy slopes of the foothills which folded themselves up against the towering shelter of the Hunua Ranges.

Ten minutes had been a macho exaggeration on the boys' part, for it was a full fifteen minutes at strictly legal speed before Anya reached the cluster of shops, houses and agri-businesses that made up the small township of Riverview.

She eased up on her speed, not even glancing in the direction of her darkened cottage, set back from the road in the large, overgrown garden which had become her personal challenge and private pleasure. Before she had gone away to school she had spent most of her childhood in a succession of inner-city hotels and apartments where the closest thing to a garden had been a potted palm.

They passed the community's one and only petrol station at the far end of the shops, its neon sign switched off and forecourt pumps locked. As buildings gave way to wire fences and trimmed hedgerows again Anya planted her foot back down on the accelerator, eager to get the coming ordeal over. She hoped that Cheryl and Emma would have the good sense to be co-operative when she fetched them away. She wanted the rescue operation to go as smoothly as possible, preferably without any dramatic scenes that might stir up more trouble than she could handle.

She didn't fancy having to deal with two recalcitrant, and quite possibly drunken, teenagers on her own, let alone a whole partyful. Although she was fit, and considered herself reasonably strong for her build, at little over five feet three inches in height she was often dwarfed by her senior students and relied on intelligence, compassion and humour to command their respect, rather than a dominating physical presence.

Her tension tightened another notch as they came over a curving rise in the road and a row of trees loomed up suddenly on the left, towering triangles of stiffly outflung branches etched darkly against the night sky in the classic Christmas tree shape. Even expecting the familiar sight, Anya felt an unwelcome leap of her pulse.

'Is this it?' Jessica's excited query was redundant as Anya braked sharply and turned off the road, the little car vibrating as its tyres rumbled over the wooden planks which bridged the deep, open drainage ditch running along the grassy verge.

At the end of a long, steeply rising sealed driveway lined with overlacing trees, they could see the big, white weatherboard house, multi-coloured lights glowing dimly behind the drawn curtains of the downstairs windows. Even with the car windows closed they could hear the heavy, rhythmic throb of a bass-beat reverberating through the walls of the house.

'No wonder they didn't hear the phone ring,' murmured Anya, pulling up behind the haphazard scatter of cars parked on the paved turning circle in front of the house.

After a brief hesitation she removed the keys from the ignition and stepped out of the car, bending down to speak through the open door. 'You two stay where you are. Lock the doors and don't open them for anyone else but me…or Cheryl and Emma. I'll be back as soon as I can. Don't get impatient if you have to wait a while, and don't get out of the car!'

Having made her point as forcefully as she could, Anya slammed the door and locked it, dropping the key into the hip pocket of her cargo pants and slipping her folded glasses into the breast pocket of her shirt as she hurried towards the sheltering portico that framed the front door.

Pushing on the doorbell brought no response. Frustrated, she tried knocking, then twisted at the ornate brass doorknob and found that it opened easily. A tentative push allowed her to step inside, where the muffled pounding which had filtered through the exterior walls escalated into an ear-crashing assault that made Anya wince.

There was little doubt she had come to the right place. There was one hell of a party going on!

Lithe young bodies were everywhere—gyrating to the music, propped against walls, sprawled over the furniture and floors; some were entwined in eye-popping embraces, others conducted point-blank conversations at shriek-level in competition with the musical cacophony. Bottles, cans, glasses and the remains of snack packets and pizza crusts seemed to litter every available flat surface. The atmosphere was hazy with cigarette smoke and thick with an aromatic combination of perfume, warm beer and sweat.

Anya threaded her way from room to room, searching for Cheryl's golden-blonde mane and the iridescent black tanktop that Kristin had said Emma was wearing, her task made more difficult by the red- and purple-coloured light-bulbs which had been screwed into the lamps, casting a murky glow over the seething figures, blending the youthful faces into an amorphous mass.

At last she spotted a familiar figure scrunched in the corner of a couch, being leered at by a lanky youth who looked unattractively worse for wear. She was grimly satisfied to note that Emma didn't appear to be enjoying herself very much.

The girl looked up as Anya approached, her pale face registering shock, disbelief and fleeting panic, swiftly superseded by an unmistakable flicker of relief.

'Come on,' Anya mouthed against the music, taking hold of her unresisting wrist and tugging her off the couch, ignoring the boy's slurred protest as she dragged his hapless companion off through the crowd.

'Where's Cheryl?' asked Anya, when she had steered her to the front door, where the noise level was slightly less brain-crushing.

Emma bit her lip, her frightened gaze darting nervously over Anya's shoulder. 'She went upstairs—a-about ten minutes ago... She said we weren't going to separate...but—but then she went up there with one of the boys who asked us to the party—Sean, he said his name was...'

A chill went down Anya's spine and a cold weight coalesced in her stomach. 'Jessica and Kristin are outside in my car. Go and get into it. Do it *now!*'

She paused only long enough to make sure the girl headed out of the door before she turned and raced up the staircase, which was clogged with people sitting on the narrow rises.

Once at the top she sped along the central hall rattling doors. Some of the rooms were locked, and in one that wasn't she flushed out false game: a giggling pair whom she sent smartly on their way. When she tried the next door it was flung open by a lone young girl with brutally short black hair bleached at the tips and a prominent nosering. Padded headphones hung around her slender neck, the wire trailing down to her bare feet.

'*What!*' she barked, hands planted on the skinny hips encased in scruffy denim jeans, her black-glossed lips peeled back in a ferocious snarl.

Anya's single-minded focus momentarily slipped at the startling image of bristling hostility.

'Ah...I'm looking for Sean,' she faltered, and was rewarded by a contemptuous narrowing of cobalt-blue eyes.

'A bit old for him, aren't you?' was the insulting response, followed by an uninterested jerk of the head. 'His bedroom's down at the far end—but the idiot's probably too trashed by now to do you any good!'

The door was slammed in her face just as suddenly as it had been whipped open, and Anya shook her head over the odd encounter as she raced down to the end of the hall.

Charging through the unlocked door, she pulled up short at the sight of the rumpled single bed where Cheryl knelt, her mouth betrayingly swollen, her clothing disarranged but thankfully still in place. Beside her on the edge of the bed sat a shirtless male in unsnapped jeans, listing heavily to one side as he drained the dregs of a small bottle of vodka and lemon mix.

Sean Monroe was one of the stars of Hunua College's first XV rugby team and had the build to prove it. Even though he was still only seventeen, his broad shoulders and thick muscles were more suggestive of a man than a boy, but the sulky defiance that appeared on his handsome face when he saw Anya confirmed he still had a lot of maturing to do.

They knew each other by sight only, since history wasn't one of his subjects, but Anya could have done without this kind of introduction. He would never forgive her for ruining his fun.

'Cheryl, are you all right?' For the second time that night Anya observed an unexpected spark of relief in the humiliated gaze of her quarry.

The girl nodded jerkily as she scrambled awkwardly off the bed, raking her tangled hair back from her face.

'He tried to make me share his drink but I didn't like the taste,' she said in a rather wobbly voice. She gave her companion a nervous look as he flopped back on the bed with a groan. 'I don't think Sean's feeling very well, Miss Adams.'

'I wonder why?' said Anya with crisp sarcasm, devoid of any shred of sympathy.

Her gaze shifted to a beer can which was doubling as an ashtray and she took a closer look at what she had assumed was a relatively innocent cigarette.

'I suppose he tried to make you share that with him, too,' she said, her voice tight with anger as she pointed at the smouldering joint.

'I only had a couple of puffs,' Cheryl defended herself. 'It just made me feel dizzy and sick to my stomach.'

Much as she longed to rail at the trembling girl for her

stupidity, Anya forced herself to swallow her blistering words. Her first priority was to get them all back to camp as quickly and quietly as possible.

She ordered Cheryl down to the car and watched cynically as the girl grabbed up her shoes and bag and scampered out, unable to believe her luck in getting away without an on-the-spot lecture. Just you wait, young lady, thought Anya grimly. Cathy was going to be furious when she was told. A lecture would be the least of Cheryl's worries!

She turned to the young man lying on the bed, intending to vent her repressed anger with a pithy few words on the subject of loutish behaviour. 'Do you realise what you were risking? That girl is under age—' she began heatedly.

Sean swore thickly and catapulted suddenly to his feet, almost knocking Anya over as he dived for the adjoining door. Incensed by his rudeness, Anya dashed after him, realising too late that she had followed him into the bathroom.

When he fell on his knees and vomited noisily into the toilet bowl she felt the first pangs of compassion, and filled a glass of water at the hand-basin to hand to him when he finished. However, when he finally staggered to his feet and took a few sips from the proffered glass he was promptly sick again, and Anya wasn't quite quick enough on her feet to prevent the front of her shirt and one leg of her trousers from being splashed.

Cursing under her breath, she grabbed a towel from the rack and scrubbed at the stains while Sean rinsed out his mouth and stumbled drunkenly back into the bedroom. Her mouth compressed as she used a second towel to quickly clean up the mess on the tiled floor, annoyed at herself for the compulsive act of neatness.

Anya's own gorge rose as she plucked at her soiled garments, her delicate nose wrinkling in fastidious horror. She couldn't sit in a small car with this sickening stench clinging to her clothes—both she and her passengers would likely be ill themselves!

Glancing out to see that Sean was slumped back on the bed, Anya bolted the bathroom door and swiftly stripped off her outer clothes. She flushed the stains in cold water, rubbing some pine-scented soap into the affected patches for good measure. The soaking pieces of fabric would be uncomfortably clammy against her skin but it was better than the noxious alternative!

She was about to wring out the excess water when she heard a crash and muffled moans on the other side of the door. Afraid that Sean had been sick again and was choking as a result, she snatched the nearest dry covering—a man's shirt that had been tossed on top of the laundry basket—and shrugged it on as she shot back into the bedroom.

She was disgusted to see Sean pawing at the rumpled covers of the bed, scrabbling for the smouldering joint which he had somehow knocked off the bedside table.

'Ah-ha!' he said, rolling over with his trophy held high, his glazed eyes barely focussing as Anya marched over, shirt flapping, and snatched the burning brand out of his clumsy fingers.

'Here, I'll take that,' she said sternly, intending to flush it down the toilet.

'Hey, no way, bitch!' He reared up and tried to grab it back. Anya jerked her arm away—he lunged, she twisted— and for a few seconds they were locked in a bizarre kind of dance at the edge of the bed, brought to an abrupt end by a deep voice, taut with outrage.

'Dammit, Sean, I thought we agreed no parties while I was— *What in the hell is going on here?*'

Anya spun around and the man who had appeared in the doorway stiffened incredulously, his cobalt-blue eyes widening in shock.

'*You!*'

The stunned monosyllable dripped with nameless accusation and Anya froze, her whole life flashing before her eyes.

She clutched at the gaping shirt and stared at Sean Monroe's supposed-to-be-away-for-the-weekend uncle.

Scott Tyler. Her personal demon. The man who had strongly opposed Anya's application to join the staff at Hunua College.

The legal adviser to the school board who thought that she wasn't competent to do the job she loved. The man who had admitted that he was just waiting for her to make a mistake that would prove him right!

CHAPTER TWO

IN A distant, still functioning corner of her brain Anya became aware that the music had stopped and there were sounds of high-pitched voices, car doors slamming and engines revving outside.

The party was definitely over and the reason was standing in front of them, storming mad.

She had heard via staffroom gossip that Scott Tyler had been unexpectedly landed with his sister's children while she and her husband were overseas and guessed that a thirty-two-year-old workaholic bachelor would find living with two teenagers caused a severe disruption to his formerly smoothly-running life.

Fifteen-year-old Samantha, who was in Anya's fifth-form class, was a good student but chocolate-box pretty and wildly popular with the boys, and as for Sean…well—if he had been expressly ordered not to do something then naturally he would have disobeyed, simply on principle!

Anya cleared her paralysed throat. She had no intention of being made a scapegoat for a bunch of irresponsible kids. Or shielding Sean, who had sunk back to the bed, gaping stupidly at his uncle's thunderous face.

'I can explain—' she said, gesturing vaguely in the direction of the hapless youth.

The piercing blue eyes shifted from Anya's face to the sweeping movement of her hand and she was horrified to realise that it was the one in which she held the smoking cannabis joint. She hastily whipped it behind her back.

'Don't bother. I think I get the picture—unpleasantly graphic as it is,' he said. 'How unfortunate for you that I

22

worked double-time to complete my business early and managed to get on the last flight back from Wellington. If I'd returned tomorrow as planned you might actually have got away with it.'

The tight drawl did nothing to conceal Scott Tyler's controlled fury and Anya fought not to feel threatened by the daunting combination of his forceful personality and dominating physique.

He seemed impossibly tall from her perspective—big-boned and thick-muscled, his double-breasted grey suit accentuating his powerful build, his loosened tie hanging from the unbuttoned collar of his starched linen shirt. His sheer presence made the spacious cream-painted room feel suddenly claustrophobically small. His dark brown hair was thick and unruly, spiking over his wide forehead, his face an aggressive congregation of hard angles, with broad, high cheekbones surmounted by deep-set eyes and a handsome Roman nose that had been broken at some stage of his life. Not surprisingly, Anya thought. She had been tempted to take a punch at that arrogant nose a time or two herself…if she had been able to reach it!

He had intimidated her from their very first meeting at her personal interview with the Hunua College Board of Trustees six months ago, and in retrospect she could see that he had deliberately set out to undermine her composure. He had lounged in his seat at the end of the table, arms folded, staring at her with an unsettling intensity all through the initial part of the session, interrupting with a series of probing questions about her lack of co-educational experience just when she had begun to feel confident that she was making a good impression on the rest of the interviewing panel.

His obvious disapproval and sharply critical comments had caught her off guard and Anya had found herself floundering on the defensive. Then he had smiled—a cruelly self-satisfied curve of his hard mouth—and her innate stubbornness had kicked in. Her slender spine had stiffened as she revealed her grace under fire, retaliating with a calm, level-headed self-assurance combined with a dry sense of humour which had clawed back the lost ground. For a while, though, she had felt like a prisoner in the dock, and she hadn't been surprised to later find out that Scott Tyler was one of South Auckland's leading barristers, with a reputation for winning difficult cases on the strength of his ruthless cross-examinations.

From the brief research she had done after applying for the job, she knew that, although he wasn't a voting member of the board, his role as legal consultant and a personal friendship with the Chairman gave him a considerable amount of influence.

Fortunately, the headmaster, Mark Ransom, had firmly thrown his support behind Anya as the best of the three other candidates already interviewed, and a majority of the board must have concurred, for several days later Anya had been overjoyed to receive the job offer that had precipitated her move to Riverview.

To her dismay, accepting defeat graciously was evidently not one of Scott Tyler's famed accomplishments, and at each successive encounter, despite her strenuous efforts to be pleasant, they'd seemed to end up on opposite sides of an argument.

Which made it even more important that this silly incident not be blown out of proportion.

'I know what it looks like, Mr Tyler, but you're jumping to the wrong conclusions—' she protested as he turned his attention back to his slack-jawed nephew, grimly assessing the extent of his intoxication.

'I've had a hellish twenty-four hours with some very stroppy clients and I'm not in the mood to handle any more nonsense right now. So I suggest you put your clothes back on and get out,' he tossed harshly over his shoulder, using the same menacing tone which had cleared out the rowdy party-goers below in record time. 'I want to talk to my nephew—*alone*. I'll deal with *you* later!'

Anya would have been delighted to escape, but she wasn't going to leave with that ominous threat hanging over her head.

'Look, I understand that you're pretty annoyed about Sean throwing a party without your permission—'

He jerked around, snarling like a wounded bear. 'How perceptive of you!'

'—but I only found out about it myself about half an hour ago,' she finished stoutly, bracing herself as he prowled back to where she stood. She dug her toes into the carpet, determined not to give ground.

'So you immediately rushed over to strip and join in the fun?' he savaged with brutal sarcasm. 'I had no idea that history teachers were so *progressive*...'

His raking look of contempt made her clear, honey-gold skin bloom with unwelcome fire. Her grey eyes darkened with reproach, which only seemed to feed his smouldering fury.

'Is this one of the methods of "inspiring young minds" that you talked of bringing to the college?' Up close she could see the small scar on the left corner of his narrow upper lip, the one that gave him such an impressive sneer. 'How long have you been offering private lessons in practical sex education as a part of your curriculum?'

'Don't be ridiculous!' she cried, struggling to remain reasonable in the face of his flagrant provocation. There was no point in both of them losing their tempers. She had noticed it was a popular tactic of his—playing devil's advocate, needling people until they became too annoyed to think straight, let alone consider the wisdom of their words. Maintaining control was the key to surviving a verbal encounter with Scott Tyler.

'This is just a set of unfortunate circumstances—' she

stated clearly, tilting her head up in the unconsciously haughty gesture that she had inherited from her flamboyant mother.

'That's what they all say.' His cynical laugh was gritty with scorn. 'The "unfortunate circumstances" usually involve getting caught red-handed at the scene of the crime. I'm a criminal lawyer, remember—I've heard every excuse in the book.'

'And who better than a lawyer to know that appearances can be deceptive?' she snapped back.

'In your case I'd agree…very deceptive. Who'd have thought that the quiet and refined Miss Adams, with her modest hemlines and sensible shoes, would have a penchant for see-through underwear and seducing her students…'

'I was *not* seducing anyone!' spluttered Anya, unable to refute the underwear allegation. For the most part her clothes were classically simple and tasteful, as required of a role-model for impressionable teenagers, but since her slender figure required only the bare minimum of support she didn't have to be practical when it came to buying lingerie. She was free to indulge her secret passion for gossamer-thin lace and frivolous frippery. As long as she was well covered up she considered it no one's business but her own what she chose to wear under her clothes.

Only right now she was feeling very much undercovered and a trifle cool, despite the heat in her cheeks. Glancing down, she saw that the oversized white shirt she was trying to anchor one-handed across her scantily clad body was made of slippery, ultra-fine silk through which it was possible to see the sheer lace of her low-cut emerald bra and matching panties.

'Really…so you just like to prance around half-naked at parties for your own entertainment? You obviously find it sexually arousing to be the focus of male attention,' he taunted, his sardonic stare making her supremely conscious of the way her nipples had tingled to hardness against the twin layers of flimsy fabric. 'That's tantamount to seduction in my book.'

'Then your book would be wrong!' She might have known that he would draw attention to something any real gentleman would have politely ignored. How dared he imply that she found *him* attractive? 'There's a cool breeze coming through the window behind me, in case you haven't noticed!' she pointed out obliquely.

His blue eyes glinted with malice and she hurried on before he could make another devastating comment.

'For goodness' sake, you can't think I took my clothes off because I *wanted* to—'

His face hardened, his whole body contracting with a dangerous tension. 'Are you claiming that Sean tried to rape you?' he ground out.

'No, of *course* I'm not!' she cried, frankly appalled at the direction of his thoughts. One side of the shirt slipped from her distracted fingers and she frantically brought up her other hand to try and overwrap the fabric into more concealing folds.

His hostile preparedness had eased at her shocked exclamation but now his hand shot out and enveloped her fragile wrist in a steely grip.

'Watch what you're doing, woman! For God's sake, give that to me before you singe a hole in one of my best shirts.' He extracted the stubby remains of the mangled joint and let her go, crushing out the still-burning tip with his bare fingers.

'*Your* shirt?' She rubbed her buzzing wrist, goose-pimples breaking out over every centimetre of bare skin being caressed by the borrowed silk. 'I— it was in the bathroom—I assumed it was Sean's...' she stammered.

A vein pulsed in his temple and a possessive growl sounded at the back of his throat. 'What—it's not enough that you play lord of the manor to your friends when I'm away, you have to dress the part, too?' He sent his nephew, who was just getting unsteadily to his feet, a wrathful look that had him plopping heavily back down on his backside. 'When I said I was happy to look after you and Sam for a few weeks, I didn't envisage it meant opening up my wardrobe to you, as well!'

He screwed up the final shreds of cannabis cigarette in his contemptuous fist and scattered the dusty debris out of the open window.

'Is there any more where that came from?' he demanded of Anya.

'I have no idea,' she said succinctly, still grappling with the knowledge that she was wearing his shirt. It made her feel strangely shivery, uncomfortably vulnerable to him in a way that it was difficult to define. 'It wasn't mine. I've never smoked marijuana in my life.'

A tug of his scar hitched his lip into a disbelieving curl. 'You're telling me you never ran across any illicit weed when you were a pupil at that exclusive upper-crust school of yours? Places like Eastbrook are a hotbed of experimentation—WASPy little rich girls doing the rebellion thing, or getting high as a way of punishing mummy and daddy for being too busy with their own lives to pay them enough attention; bored young things always on the lookout for kicks, with easy access to money and no one to really care how they spend it—'

'There's that kind of element in every school, no matter what social strata it serves,' Anya said, stung by the sneering accuracy of his thumbnail sketch. 'And I never said I hadn't come across it, only that I hadn't used it.'

'Come to think of it, cannabis is probably a little low rent for the privileged elite,' he jeered. 'Maybe the junior jet-set prefer designer drugs to go with their designer clothes.'

Now he was going too far! Anya's quiet temper bubbled

to the surface. His entire attitude was in need of serious re-adjustment!

'You have a real chip on your shoulder, don't you?' she burst out. 'Let me guess: your parents couldn't afford to send you to a private school, so you resent anyone who was given the educational and social advantages that you weren't. Well, most young kids don't have any more choice about where they go to school than you did—I certainly didn't!

'And, contrary to your obvious prejudice, Mr Tyler, private school pupils aren't all elitist snobs who take their privileges for granted and look down their noses at the rest of the world. A lot of them are the children of ordinary, egalitarian, hard-working New Zealanders who believe in the kind of discipline, or moral and religious values that aren't offered at a state school.'

She unthinkingly punctuated her lecture with a teacher's wagging finger, and Scott Tyler reacted with the insulting slyness of a naughty schoolboy.

'Careful, Miss Adams, your slip is showing,' he mocked, his gaze dipping down to where her emerald bra-strap peeked from under the sliding collar of his shirt.

She hitched it impatiently back into place with a baleful look, refusing to be diverted. 'My qualifications are rock-solid—it's because of your own reverse snobbery that you didn't want me getting the teaching position at the college. You did everything you could to cast me into a bad light at my interview, and it sticks in your craw that they gave me the job anyway!'

The glow of smug triumph on her delicate face was like a red rag to a bull.

'I didn't want you in the job because I didn't think you were physically or mentally tough enough to cope with the pressures and problems of teaching in a big unisex school which draws a large number of its students from a lower socio-economic group,' he grated, planting his hands on his hips, his open jacket revealing the flatness of his tailored waistcoat against his hard stomach. 'And I still don't!'

Anya bristled. 'There are plenty of other female teachers on the staff—' she said pugnaciously.

'—who've got previous experience in a variety of large unisex schools, whereas you've been insulated in your cushy little Academy for Young Ladies ever since you graduated from training college.'

She lifted her silky-fine eyebrows, echoing his taunting mockery from a few moments ago. 'Careful, Mr Tyler, your inferiority complex is showing.'

He bared even white teeth in the opposite of a smile. 'So the butterfly can bite? Insulting me won't change the facts.'

He saw her as a butterfly? She pictured herself as a small but determined terrier.

'The facts being that so far I've been managing my classes just fine!' Apart from a few natural hiccups she'd rather not mention.

'It won't last,' he predicted bluntly.

'Are you threatening me?'

'Do I have to? If tonight is an example of how you "manage" your students I think the major threat is your own behaviour.'

She compressed her lips, controlling the surge of indignant words that welled hotly in her throat. After his disparaging comments about her former school her explanation wasn't going to go down too well, so she delivered it in edited highlights.

'Look, this really doesn't have to go any further,' she said, adopting her most reasonable tone. 'I'm helping supervise a holiday camp out at the regional reserve, and a couple of the girls came to the party without permission, so I drove over to pick them up. I tracked them down but then Sean was sick all over my clothes. I was cleaning up in the bathroom when

I heard him knock something over and ran back in to check...'

She looked over at the culprit, meeting his bloodshot brown eyes behind his uncle's back. She had half expected him to try and bluster his way out of trouble, but perhaps he was too intoxicated to put together a coherent sentence. Or maybe he was just hoping that by keeping silent he could avoid incriminating himself

'Is that what happened, Sean?' Scott Tyler rapped out, inclining his head but not taking his sceptical gaze off Anya.

The boy shrugged, but he wasn't too strung out to miss that the cynical edge in the gravelly voice wasn't directed his way.

'How should I know why she invited herself?' he mumbled quickly, his sluggish tongue tangling in the consonants. 'It was a party, man...chicks have been coming and going all night.'

A cold trickle of dismay ran down Anya's spine when she saw him leaning back out of his uncle's peripheral sight, smirking maliciously at her.

'All I know is, she followed me into my room and wouldn't leave me alone. Who'da known she was so hot? Ever made it with a history teacher, Unc'l Scott?'

The grubby insinuation with its macho, man-to-man overtones had Anya's eyes snapping back to Scott Tyler's face, which was suddenly rigidly impassive, wiped clean of all emotion. She guessed it was the expressionless mask he wore into the courtroom, when he didn't want anyone to know what he was thinking.

'Whatever he's implying didn't happen,' she said tartly. 'You know very well he's just telling you what he thinks you want to hear...'

One thick, dark eyebrow shot up. 'Is he?'

He was just playing devil's advocate, she told herself.

'You know he is. Look out the window if you don't believe me. The girls I came here to find are down there waiting for me in my car—'

He sent a fleeting, almost uninterested, glance down towards the turning circle. 'There's no smoke without fire,' he murmured with infuriating blandness.

'What are you—a fireman now?' she flung at him witheringly, her slender body vibrating with fury. 'I thought you were supposed to be a hot-shot lawyer. Why don't you act like one and make Sean tell you the *real* truth!'

'His version, or yours? When there's two witnesses, the truth is often a matter of perspective.'

It was on the tip of Anya's tongue to tell him that she had another witness, but she didn't want to involve Cheryl, and thus Eastbrook, unless she could help it.

'Are you saying that you actually *believe* him!'

'You must admit I've ample reason to be suspicious. Don't tell me you aren't aware that there's something inherently erotic about a woman wearing a man's shirt,' he said, his eyes sliding down over her silk-wrapped body in a speculative way that made her blood boil, and not entirely with fury. 'And the little white socks add just the right provocative touch of pseudo-innocence.'

'Oh, for goodness' sake, don't be ridiculous!' A piercing thrill of guilty pleasure made Anya lash out, trying to douse the treacherous feelings aroused by his words with a drenching of pure scorn. 'I suppose you're going to accuse me of trying to seduce *you* next!'

There was a short, electric silence as they stared at each other, and Anya noticed all the things about him she had always tried very hard *not* to notice: the smooth grain of his olive skin as it stretched over the strong bones of his face; the almost feminine lushness of the thick dark lashes which framed his compelling blue eyes, and the strikingly masculine contrast of that thin, yet sensual mouth, and harshly chiselled jaw.

The stubbly regrowth of his beard and faint purplish tinge under his sunken eyes—signs of his 'hellish' day—made him look rakish rather than merely weary.

When he spoke again his voice was deeper, softer, and more dangerous than she had ever heard it. Too soft for the boy behind him to hear. And he allowed a flare of male hunger to show in the deep blue gaze.

'You're welcome to try, but I should point out that I'm a great deal more discerning—and considerably more demanding—than your average randy teenager…'

The sheer wickedness of the barbed challenge sucked the breath out of her lungs, and Anya opened and closed her mouth several times before she summoned the words to prove that she was wasn't totally vanquished.

'Oh, you're impossible! It's easy to see you're related—you're both as bad as each other. Believe what you damned well like; *I* don't care!'

And on that resounding lie Anya swung on her heel and stormed into the bathroom, slamming the door violently enough to cause the mirror to shiver on the wall above the basin and several toiletries to fall over on the vanity top.

Muttering to herself to bolster her sense of outrage, she ripped off the silk shirt and pulled on her wrinkled clothes, the damp patches practically sizzling as they hit her burning skin. She finished zipping up her ankle boots with a vicious tug that jammed a piece of her sock in the meshing teeth and swore through tight lips as she tried to work it free.

She had always thought of cotton ankle socks as utilitarian rather than sexy, but now that serene unawareness was gone for ever. She would never be able to put on a pair of white socks again without thinking of *him*.

He had viewed them as *provocative*, for God's sake! A pair of simple, inexpensive white socks! The man was plainly in need of therapy, she thought as she checked herself out in the mirror, looking in vain for the cool, capable, down-to-earth Miss Adams she was used to recognising in her reflection.

With her glittering, storm-darkened eyes, flushed cheeks, and the baby-fine wisps of hair escaping from the pins at her nape and drifting forward to curve around her smooth oval jaw, she looked disturbingly young and flustered. Not in control.

And she had no make-up to repair the damage to her self-image. She did what she could, smoothing back the strands of hair from her glowing forehead and tucking them firmly into place with tremulous fingers. Had her small mouth always looked that rosy and full? She pressed her lips together in a stern line and willed her colour to fade back to normal. She could do nothing about the way her clothes clung where they were wet, but at least they were clingy in fairly non-strategic areas.

She could hear a low murmur coming from the bedroom and she hesitated for a moment before she squared her shoulders, gathered up her ragged dignity, and reached for the door.

She was going to walk back out there with her head held high, and if fault should be admitted she was prepared to be graciously forgiving, as befitted her normally kind and compassionate nature.

But the sight that met her eyes wasn't promising. Scott Tyler stood beside his seated nephew, his hand resting on Sean's brawny bare shoulder, whether for reassurance or restraint, she wasn't sure.

'Well, has he told you what happened?' she challenged.

Scott Tyler's unreadable mask was firmly back in place

'That could take some time in his present condition,' he said uninformatively, acknowledging the condition of her clothes with barely a flicker of his eyes. His voice flattened into resolute finality. 'As I said before, it's late, and if there are issues to be settled they can wait until a more civilised hour...'

He dropped his hand and moved towards her, obscuring her vision of the boy, imposing himself squarely in the centre of her attention. He was definitely in full protective mode, she decided, and in the split second before his broad chest blocked out her view her heart sank to see that the smirk had returned to the teenager's face. The obnoxious weasel wasn't going to accept responsibility for his actions until he was sober enough to appreciate the true consequences of his lies.

'Well, here's one issue that can be settled right now,' she announced, pulling at a clammy spot on her cotton shirt where it had moulded transparently to her skin. 'As you can see for yourself, I'm going to have to get my clothes cleaned. I'll be sure and send you the bill.'

His thick lashes veiled his expression as he studied the effect of her makeshift laundering.

'By all means. But don't expect me to pay it if there's contributory negligence involved,' he told her in that same flat, non-negotiable tone. 'For all I know you could have dunked them just now in the bathroom, to give credence to your story.'

Anya forgot about being kind and compassionate.

'I suppose being exposed to the seamy underbelly of society all the time has given you a very nasty and obsessively suspicious mind, and distorted your view of the way normal, *innocent*, people behave,' she said, with a cutting disdain that was designed to make him cringe.

He didn't cringe, but he did back off slightly, leaning a broad shoulder against the painted frame of the casement window in concession to his weariness. 'I prefer to think of it as trusting to the wisdom of experience. As a history teacher you must believe in using the lessons of the past to avoid repeating future mistakes.'

Her mouth primmed in frustration, for she hated to admit

he was right, and for the first time he showed a glimmer of untainted amusement, a faint kick of his mouth which delivered a corresponding kick to Anya's pulse. His next words were also guaranteed to raise her blood pressure.

'So be careful you're not making a mistake, Miss Adams, by riling me when I've already told you I'm in a *very* bad mood. Your position at the moment is rather untenable. It could be construed as contributing to the delinquency of a minor, for example…'

She was quick to scorn his bluff. 'Apart from the fact that the whole accusation is nonsense—he isn't a minor.'

He was about to offer a caustic reply when something outside the window snagged his attention. 'Are you sure you want to argue the point now? Because the natives down there seem to be getting restless…'

She frowned at him, suspecting a trick. 'What?'

'There are two girls getting out of a yellow hatchback I presume is yours,' he said, looking out the window. 'They seem to be debating whether to approach the house—'

Anya yelped and flew over to see that he was right. Oh, God, she had been so distracted by his presence that she had completely forgotten about the girls! Supposedly her prime consideration on this mission.

She clutched the windowsill, gazing down in dismay as Jessica and Kristin milled uncertainly around the side of the car. Hadn't she *told* them not to get out?—but of course by now they must be starting to panic at her extended absence.

'Perhaps you'd like me to invite them up to join us while we finish the discussion you seem so keen on prolonging…' came a silky purr.

'*No!*' Anya was too busy castigating herself to notice his openly baiting tone. She could just imagine what four gossipy girls would make of the pernicious scene. She looked at her watch, her thoughts fixated on damage control. If she didn't get back to camp before Cathy read her note, all hell was likely to break loose. Or, should she say, *further* hell?

She glared at the cause of her appalling lapse in judgement. 'I have to go—'

'Oh, what a pity,' he said, his voice dripping with sarcasm. 'Just when I was about to offer you a cup of tea.'

She scowled. Naturally he would see her strategic retreat as his victory. 'When you get *him* sober enough to tell you that my presence here was entirely innocent—' she said, nodding in Sean's direction as she hurried towards the door '—I'll expect to receive a sincere apology. From *both* of you! And we'll consider that an end to the matter.'

She thought that she had succeeded in having the last word, but a surly remark referring to frigid temperatures and the devil's abode floated downstairs in her wake, making her itch to turn around and hit back with an equally vulgar blow. She managed to cling to her decorum but only by locking up her jaw. For a non-violent person she was beginning to have some very disturbing thoughts. All to do with *That Man*.

'Where were you, Miss Adams? We were getting worried,' said Jessica, as Anya herded the girls back into the car and burnt rubber down the drive in her anxiety to escape the invisible laser-beam eyes she was sure she could feel drilling into her back.

'We saw that big guy go in and break up the party but you didn't come out with the others. He looked pretty mad when he drove up and saw all the cars. I bet he went totally psycho at his kid for having a party,' said Kristin in suppressed excitement. 'I bet there was a big fight. Is that what took you so long, Miss Adams?'

'You don't—want—to—know,' Anya ground out through her still-clenched teeth, her usually gentle voice so awe-

inspiringly crabby that there was dead silence all the rest of
the way back to the camp, apart from the occasional frightened sniffle from Emma and Cheryl in the back seat as they
contemplated their uneasy future.

CHAPTER THREE

ANYA had a mildly thumping head when she arrived back at the regional reserve, and by the time she drove home the next afternoon it had developed into a full-blown tension headache.

She was just grateful that the decision of what to do with the chastened pair of miscreants had not fallen on her own shoulders. The two girls had produced copious amounts of penitent tears for a livid Cathy Marshall, who had raked them severely over the coals and segregated them out to do all the most boring, arduous and least-liked of the clean-up jobs rostered for the last day.

Seeing Cheryl scraping out the burnt-on muck of ten days of inexpert cooking from the camp oven and Emma mopping floors and grimacing over the application of a toilet brush had given Anya hope that their too-ready expressions of remorse might actually turn into a genuinely felt regret for their misdeeds.

But executing summary punishment hadn't solved Cathy's basic dilemma of whether to consider the offence a trivial one satisfactorily dealt with on-the-spot, as was her first impulse, or to put the girls on report to the headmistress when they returned to school, in recognition of the potential danger they had posed to themselves and to the Academy's reputation.

Anya couldn't blame her friend for wanting to avoid any official black mark against the camp, but did point out that once their initial fright wore off the girls were unlikely to refrain from boasting about their adventure. If it became common knowledge at the school, it would inevitably reach Miss

39

Brinkman's ears and she would want to know why she hadn't been kept fully informed.

When she got on the bus back to Eastbrook, Cathy was still worrying about what to gloss over and what to emphasise in her written report, having reluctantly come to the conclusion that she couldn't entirely leave it out.

'I could probably get away with just using my discretionary judgement if it wasn't for the fact that you found Cheryl with the boy, and you think there might have been some marijuana around,' she sighed. 'But don't worry, nothing I say is going to reflect badly on you, Anya,' she hastened to add. 'You did the school a huge favour by helping out these last few days. It was just bad luck that those wretched girls took off when you were there by yourself. I'm going to tell Miss Brinkman you did exactly what I would have done in the same circumstances…'

Not quite. For Anya hadn't gone into the full, gory details of her humiliating encounter with Scott Tyler. She had merely said that he had arrived after she had sent the girls out to the car, and that he had been angry and rude. She hadn't wanted to add to Cathy's anxieties by telling her of the personal hostility that had flared out of control during the confrontation, especially when her friend had instantly recognised the name of her protagonist.

'Scott Tyler—the lawyer? The one who got that body-in-the-bag murderer—sorry, *alleged* murderer—off?' Cathy was impressed enough to be momentarily diverted from her troubles. 'Wow, I've seen him on the TV news—he's one tough-looking dude. According to the papers he made absolute mincemeat of a watertight case to get that verdict. You definitely wouldn't want to get on the wrong side of an argument with *him*!'

Tell me about it! Anya had thought. When they had finally got to bed she had tossed and turned sleeplessly for what had remained of the night, running and rerunning her mental videotape of the experience, thinking of how differently the scenario would have played if she hadn't let herself be sidetracked by his angry assumptions, and inventing pithy replies to his insults that she wished she had been able to think of at the time.

In the cold light of day she could almost convince herself that it had been a simple case of overreaction on both sides. Once Scott Tyler's temper had cooled and he was no longer hampered by fatigue he was bound to take a more reasonable view. Surely the cynical lawyer in him would soon conclude that Sean's spiteful words had simply been a drunken attempt to save his own skin?

He might even be content to act as if the whole unfortunate incident had never occurred. Anya certainly would. In spite of her defiant departing words she would prefer not to have to raise the subject with him ever again.

It would be hard enough having to face him next time they met. Scott Tyler had seen her *underwear*, for God's sake! The last time that had happened was on her twenty-first birthday, and the man involved had gone on to break her heart. *Not* a very happy precedent!

Her nervous brooding made the last few hours of the camp stretch and sag like tired elastic and she was glad to finally be able to wave the air-conditioned bus onto the road back to Auckland and hop into her little car.

The hot bands of iron tension compressing her temples began to ease as she pulled into her crushed gravel driveway and parked in the small garage attached to the side of the weatherboard cottage.

She had bought the two-bedroomed house a few weeks after she'd signed her employment contract with Hunua College, rationalising that even if the job didn't work out as she expected there were plenty of other secondary schools scattered around South Auckland that were within reasonable commuting distance of Riverview. As it was, the college was only half an hour's drive along the winding rural roads to the sprawling outskirts of suburban south Auckland.

The house had been an early Christmas present for herself, and although it had put her deeply in debt to the bank she relished the long-term commitment the monthly payments represented. People—her cosmopolitan parents included—had told her that buying property in a small rural town was a poor investment, but they didn't seem to appreciate that to her this wasn't an investment, it was her *home*, a place for her to put down roots and flourish, emotionally as well as physically. Even several months after she had moved in she still felt a sharp thrill of joy each time she came home, to know that she was the proud owner of her own little quarter-acre of paradise.

'Hello, George. Have you come to welcome me home?' She bent to stroke the lean ginger cat which appeared from nowhere to wind around her ankles as she unloaded her bags from the boot. The ginger tom was actually a stray who considered the whole neighbourhood his personal territory, granting his fickle attentions to whomever was likely to provide him with the choicest titbits at any given time.

Anya scratched his bent ear and smiled at his motoring purr, her face lighting up from within, the spontaneous warmth lending her quiet features a glowing enchantment.

Now that she was feeling thoroughly settled in she had been thinking she might get herself a cat of her own. Or even a dog. Thanks to her childhood asthma and her opera singer mother's horror of anything that might compromise her respiratory tract and thus her peerless voice, she had never been allowed to have a pet. The frequent international travelling associated with her mother's career had precluded even a goldfish, and only during her precious holiday visits to her aunt and uncle's dairy farm at Riverview had Anya been able to indulge her interest in animals—with nary a sneeze or wheeze in sight!

'Let's see if I can't find a nice can of tuna for us to share,' said Anya, following George up the narrow brick path that she had laid herself, bordered by the flower beds already dug over in preparation for planting out. Although it was still unseasonably warm for mid-April, the clouds were gathering over the Hunua Ranges and she could scent a hint of rain in the sultry air.

Once inside she kicked off her shoes with a sigh of relief and went around opening the windows to air out the stuffy rooms. It was too early for her evening meal but she carefully divided up a tin of tuna and set down a saucerful on the kitchen floor for George while she tossed the rest with the salad ingredients she had picked up from a roadside stall on the way home and put it in the fridge for when she got out of the bath.

She intended to have a glorious, long, hot, mindless soak in lavender-scented water to steam out all the weary kinks in her body and the nagging worries in her brain. Then she would have her solitary salad with a glass of crisp white wine and relax amongst her books, with perhaps a delicate piece of Bach on the stereo. Oh, the bliss of being free of rules and regulations, and the obligation to be considerate of the rights of others. She didn't even have to worry about how deep to fill the old-fashioned bath, for there was no one to moan if she selfishly used up all the hot water.

Leaving George licking his chops over the empty saucer and eyeing the rush mat by the back door where he invariably liked to curl up and digest her largesse, Anya ran her bath and sank into it with a groan of sybaritic pleasure.

But the bath wasn't the total escape from reality she had expected it to be, for as the enervating heat sank into her tired bones and the fragrant steam wreathed her face in dew, Anya's drifting thoughts circled relentlessly back to the annoying subject of Scott Tyler.

How was it he always managed to get her in tongue-tied knots?

When they had first been introduced she had had fond hopes of their establishing a friendly connection.

She had been welcomed to her afternoon interview in the college boardroom by the chairman of the board, a grizzled man in his sixties, and they had still been shaking hands when he'd suddenly beamed over her shoulder.

'Oh, good, there you are, Scott! I wondered if you were going to make it back in time to sit in on this last one. Come and meet our final candidate—the lass from Eastbrook. We've already talked over her credentials…' He performed a rather perfunctory introduction, distracted from his task by the throaty laugh from the tall, svelte brunette attached to Scott Tyler's arm.

'Sorry, Daddy,' said the woman, giving him an unrepentant buss on the cheek. 'I'd just finished a case in the district court so I buzzed Scott on his cell-phone and took him out to lunch. He and I got to talking shop and the time just slipped away from us.'

'Heather works for a big law firm in the city,' Hugh Morgan explained to Anya with fatherly pride, giving her the excuse to turn away from the jolting connection with a pair of unusual, electric-blue eyes. 'Does heaps of Crown prosecutions. Very clever girl. Came top of her year at law school.'

'Oh, Daddy, that was a little while ago now,' Heather Morgan fluttered with a coy modesty that didn't quite gel with her seriously elegant suit and ambitious air of self-importance. Anya estimated the 'girl' to be somewhere in her early thirties. That coy 'little while' was likely to be more than a decade ago, she thought with uncharacteristic bitchiness.

'You know I don't like to rest on my laurels,' she continued, casting a teasing sideways glance out of her dark almond eyes at the imposing man at her side. 'Especially with Scott around to keep me on my toes.'

She finally directed a condescending smile at Anya in belated acknowledgement of her reason for being there. 'So you're a schoolteacher?' Her bored inflection made it sound like the most dreary and uninspiring job on earth.

Anya inclined her head politely, keeping her tongue behind her teeth as she was wished an insipid good luck. She was amused rather than offended by the woman's arrogant assumption of superiority. The fact that she had graduated her history degree with first-class honours and won a scholarship to Cambridge which she had waived in order to train as a teacher, would doubtless cut no ice with Miss Morgan. Like Anya's parents she would probably just consider it a pathetic waste of potential; because there was no serious money to be made in teaching, no important status to claim, no high-profile perks and rewards for a job well done. Just a quiet satisfaction at having helped guide and expand the minds of future generations of lawyers and teachers.

Anya stood quietly by as the other three continued to exchange personal pleasantries, trying not to let her nerves show, only stirring when she heard a passing reference to Scott Tyler's home.

'You live at a property called The Pines?' she was startled into saying. 'Not the house that's on the road out to Riverview?'

'Yes, that's it.' Scott Tyler looked down at her, the clipped wariness of his words emphasised by a hint of cool reserve in his eyes.

'Have you driven past it? Charming, isn't it? He bought it about…five years ago, didn't you say it was, darling?' Heather Morgan was more forthcoming, deftly making it clear that their relationship was not only professional. 'Mind you, he says it was in a pretty run-down state at the time—the absentee landlord hadn't bothered with anything but basic maintenance for years—so Scott's had it completely redecorated inside and out since then.'

'If it was five years ago then you must have bought it from a close relative of mine,' Anya told Scott Tyler eagerly, delighted at the prospect of a common point of interest that might help individualise her in his eyes during the next hour of question-and-answer. 'Kate Carlyle. She was over here from London to accept an offer on the house. I'm sure you'd remember if you had met her. She's an extremely striking woman—rather famous in America and Europe as a concert pianist...'

He had stiffened slightly. Did he suspect her of being a shameless name-dropper? Well, perhaps so on this occasion—but she was also genuinely proud of Kate's brilliant achievements.

'Oh, yes, I remember Kate Carlyle,' he said, his deep, harsh voice banked with unidentifiable emotion. No doubt, then, that the meeting had been memorable. Even when she wasn't trying, Kate always had a big impact on men. 'Exactly how closely are you related?'

'She's my cousin on my mother's side,' she said happily, tilting her small face to meet his demanding gaze.

His expression tightened in what she took to be suppressed scepticism. 'And how much—or how little—do you have in common with your famous *cousin*?'

Her rueful smile forgave him for having doubts. He was obviously too polite to wonder out loud how such a beautiful, glamorous and talented creature as Kate could be related to plain, unremarkable Anya Adams, who didn't have an artistic bone in her body—much to her parents' enduring disappointment!

'Well, since we're both living on opposite sides of the world we very rarely see each other any more,' she admitted, 'and Kate does a lot of travelling, but we're still family so we naturally try to keep in touch.' At least Anya did. She supposed the occasional rushed few lines of e-mail from Kate in belated response to a long, newsy, handwritten letter from herself could be considered an effort, however feeble, to keep in touch.

'That doesn't really answer my question, does it?' he drawled, with a sardonic twist of his mouth. 'Perhaps I should have phrased it differently…asked if you share similar character traits, and perhaps her personal philosophy of life…?'

Anya was bewildered. She wasn't sure quite where his question was supposed to be leading, and it was obvious from his mocking expression that he was ready to pounce on any response.

What on earth did he want her to say? As far as she was aware Kate wasn't of any particular philosophical bent—unless you counted her dictum of 'music first'. Whatever else Kate might be, she was a consummate professional.

'Well, considering our shared background I guess a certain similarity is inevitable,' she ventured cautiously. 'When Kate was orphaned she came to live with my parents and me. For a while we were brought up together, just like sisters.' With Kate being the senior by four years, and very much the dominant one, already obsessed by music and not at all patient with the childish preoccupations of her eight-year-old cousin.

'So, you're sisters under the skin?' he confirmed with a hint of contempt, paraphrasing her words in a way that gave them a whole different meaning.

For some reason, the closer the kinship she claimed with Kate, the less Scott Tyler seemed to be impressed. Did he think she was exaggerating her own importance in order to curry favour? Did he perceive it as an indication of a sense of personal inadequacy on her part—one that might affect her authority of her students?

Disconcerted by his rising antipathy, Anya let her nerves run away with her tongue.

'I suppose you were told when you bought it that the original part of your house is over eighty years old…and that it was built by John Carlyle—Uncle Fred's father.' History being her professional forte and personal interest, it was a natural subject for Anya to fall back on in moments of uncertainty. 'Did Kate mention that she inherited The Pines after her parents were killed when she was only twelve? Of course, it was a working farm back then and it was leased as a share-milking operation by the estate until Kate was old enough to decide what she wanted to do with it. She sold off most of the grazing land when she turned eighteen, but she held onto the house and the surrounding few hectares as a piece of family history, even though she was already planning to live and work permanently in Europe or the States… In fact the last time she was in New Zealand was when she had finally decided it was time to sell The Pines. What a coincidence that you should turn out to be the buyer, Mr Tyler!'

Oh, God, she was babbling. She never babbled! She could see the glazed look of boredom on Heather Morgan's face and her father's impatient glance at his wristwatch. Meanwhile, the object of her gushing lecture stood like a towering totem pole…rigid, aloof and aggressively unyielding, his rough-hewn face carved into blunt lines of cynical rejection.

It had been more or less from that point on that she had given up expecting any positive support from Scott Tyler. The best she had hoped for was that his professionalism would compel him to at least give her a fair hearing. The trouble was that she had found herself picking up his tension like a tuning fork. He only had to be in the same room and she could feel herself vibrate with awareness, and even when she wasn't looking directly at him he loomed larger than life in her mind, confusing her and making her say or do foolish things. But that didn't mean she was going to lie down and let him walk all over her. It only made her more determined to fight back.

Anya slid down into the bath until the fragrant waves lapped the point of her chin, soaking the tendrils of hair that had steamed free of the knot on the top of her head.

Scott Tyler was a menace. Now he had even followed her into the sanctuary of sanctuaries, her bath. Looking down through the misty water, she could see her small bobbing breasts and boyish hips, so different from the statuesque curves that Heather Morgan flaunted around society on the arm of her rugged consort. Of course, Tank Tyler would probably need a well-built, boldly aggressive man-eater to slake his vile lust upon, she brooded darkly, for he would squash any woman of a more delicate and petite construction.

How had he put it last night?

I'm...considerably more demanding than your average randy teenager.

She could just imagine what kind of demands he had been talking about...

A tiny shiver rippled across the surface of the water and she sank a little deeper, letting it creep as far as her lower lip.

He was probably an arrogant, clumsy oaf in bed, she ordered herself to believe, with no appreciation of the finer nuances of making love. Quantity rather than quality. Dominating and selfish. Impatient.

She closed her eyes, trying to mine her imagination for more scathing criticisms, but instead her treacherous mind presented her with a vivid picture of Scott Tyler in the process of proving his oafishness, his glossy olive skin glistening with a bloom of moisture, his hard muscles flexing and rippling as he moved over the woman pinned beneath his pistoning hips, his blue eyes burning down into hers with reckless desire. He had dark hair on his wrists and a heavy beard growth so her inspired imagination painted a thick pelt of soft hair on his sleek and shining chest, that teased at her breasts with each thrust of his—

Aaaarghh! Anya sat up choking and spluttering, groping for the towel at the side of the bath, coughing up the water that had rushed up her nose as her boneless body had slipped beneath the sensuously rocking surface.

Anya scrubbed at her blotchy face, horrified at the dangerous byway down which her thoughts had drifted. The last thing she wanted to do was start having hot and heavy fantasies about Scott Tyler. As if she wasn't self-conscious enough around him already! She looked down in dismay at her peaked breasts, knowing that this time she didn't have the excuse of a cold draught to explain her body's aching arousal.

Dammit!

She snatched up her loofah and soap and began scrubbing mercilessly at her skin, trying to scour away her sins. So much for her nice, soothing, revitalising bath. She was revitalized, all right, but in a most unwelcome way.

She ducked back under the water to rinse off the soap, deciding to follow up with a brisk, cool shower to wash her hair. As she resurfaced, the water in her ears hummed, and she groaned as she realised that it was the telephone ringing in the kitchen. She debated leaving it, but then considered that in view of the upheavals that had occurred it might be wise to answer it.

Her damp body wrapped in the plush white towelling designer robe that had been a birthday present from her luxury-loving parents in New York, Anya padded into the kitchen, releasing her waist-length hair from its top-knot and blotting at the dripping mass with a towel, half hoping the electronic burr would stop before she got there, but the caller was persistent—rather ominously so, she feared.

Taking a deep breath, she picked up the receiver in a tense grip.

'Anya? For God's sake, what took you so long to answer? How far away could you be in that tiny little shoebox you call a house? Why on earth don't you get a cell-phone like mine, or at least a cordless that you can carry around with you?'

Anya's fingers relaxed at the sound of the irritated greeting. 'Kate? Good heavens, I was just thinking about you,' she said, sternly censoring the last few minutes of her bath.

'Were you, sweetie? I hope that means that you've got some good news for me at long last.'

She might have known that her cousin wouldn't ring for just a chat. 'Well, uh—'

But Kate hadn't finished. 'You know, I wouldn't have to phone if you would just use your computer more often—you know I'm constantly bouncing all over the place and sometimes don't pick up my snail mail for weeks. Didn't you read the e-mail I sent you last week?'

Typical of Kate to expect a rapid reply when she herself was notorious for her time-lagged answers.

'Actually, I've been away—'

'Just a moment!' Anya heard a hand cover the mouthpiece at the other end and quietly resumed mopping her hair, squeezing out the shaped layers which framed her face before rolling up the sodden length in the towel and securing it round her head. She could hear echoing noises and a muffled conversation in French being carried on at the other end, with a good peppering of Gallic expletives.

'Sorry, Annie,' Kate came back on, 'but I'm at Charles de Gaulle on my way to New York and some petty tyrant is trying to tell me that one of my bags is overweight for the baggage handlers. If the hotel chauffeur could handle it why not them? Are they all wimps? Why do I fly business class if not to avoid stupid hassles like this?'

Anya waited patiently, knowing it was pointless to offer either advice or sympathy, for it would undoubtedly be taken as criticism or unwelcome interference. Just as pointless to remind Kate how much she disliked being called 'Annie'.

She stretched the telephone cord to enable her to reach the fridge and take out the bottle of white wine lying on the bottom shelf. She had the feeling she might need a glass before the conversation was through.

'So, have you managed to get yourself invited over to the old homestead, yet?' Kate returned abruptly to the purpose of her call when she had vented enough of her spleen.

'Well, no, not really—' Anya didn't think she could count last night's gate-crashing episode.

'Why not, for God's sake? You've been in Riverview for four months; you must be part of the local scenery by now. Can't you casually wander over and say you want to look around the place you used to visit as a kid...maybe spin a sob story about a pilgrimage to The Pines in memory of your dear, departed Aunty Mary and Uncle Fred?'

'No, I couldn't,' said Anya, irritated by the flippancy of the last remark. She couldn't imagine any sufficiently *casual* way to go knocking on Scott Tyler's door. Especially now!

She extracted the cork from the bottle with a sharp tug. 'It isn't that simple. I told you—Mr Tyler and I don't get on very well...'

That had to be the most masterly understatement of all time.

'I know you did.' Kate had been oddly complacent about the fact, emboldened rather than discouraged. 'He's too rough around the edges for someone like you. He'd eat you up in a minute. But you're doing this for me, not for him. It's not as if I ask you for many favours, sweetie...'

Nor I of you, thought Anya with a rare stab of bitterness, pouring a healthy slug of wine into her glass.

Kate had been disparaging when a pained Martha and Charles Adams had passed on the news that their daughter had taken the backward career-step of moving to a 'down-market' school and had bought some kind of 'tumbledown' cottage in Riverview. But a month ago she had rung up out of the blue, telling Anya that since she was conveniently to hand, perhaps she wouldn't mind acting for her on a matter of great personal delicacy.

Anya's extreme reluctance on learning what the favour entailed had been tantamount to an outright refusal, but Kate had never been one to let such trifles get in her way.

Kate had been staying at The Pines while the sale was being finalised and when she had left for the last time—in a mad rush because of an unexpected offer of a series of concerts in eastern Europe, she'd said, to excuse her forgetfulness—she had overlooked the bundle of personal belongings and keepsakes which she had temporarily moved up to a corner of the attic, out of the way of the commercial cleaners who had been buffing up the house for its new owner. Now a New Zealand magazine writer had begun work on an indepth cover article about Kate and was sniffing around for interesting revelations, and Kate wanted to retrieve the journals and papers she had left behind, preferably without alerting anyone to the fact that they existed.

'Anyway, even if I *did* manage to get myself invited for a look around the house—I'd be unlikely to be allowed to poke around on my own, would I?' Anya protested.

'You're a history freak—attics are history. There was loads of other boring old junk up there. You could ask to see it because you're writing something about the early inhabitants of the area—appeal to his civic pride. Or, better still, do it when there are too many other people around for anyone to notice what you're up to,' advised Kate. 'Doesn't Scott Tyler ever throw parties?'

Anya shuddered and took a hasty sip of wine. 'Of course he does—but I'm not on his guest list. We don't move in the same social circles, Kate—'

'You make it sound like the Royal Enclosure at Ascot.'

Kate said scathingly. 'He's a *lawyer*, not the Prince of Wales. Stop being so defeatist. Try dating someone who *is* on his guest list. I'm not asking you to *steal* anything from him, you know. Just retrieve a few measly papers. Those journals and letters are *mine*—they're in my handwriting, for goodness' sake—'

'So why don't you simply call him yourself and explain you want your trunk back, instead of dragging me into it?' snapped Anya.

She had to wait while another bout of muffled French fisticuffs was exchanged.

'Do we have to go through this all over again?' Kate came back in an emphatically lowered voice. 'You *know* why—because there's some compromising stuff in there that I don't want to entrust to a—to a stranger. Very, *very* personal information that I really, *really* don't want anyone to see.'

Anya had never heard her cousin sounding so near to desperate.

'If I asked Tyler to send me the trunk he's not just going to take my word for it that it's mine, after all this time. He's going to want to go through everything with a fine-tooth comb to make sure that he's not sending me anything that he can legally assert ownership to as part of the goods and chattels of the house. He'll assume I'm trying to rip him off. You should have seen the way he went over the contract the real estate agent drew up. Believe me, he's the paranoid, suspicious type…'

Didn't Anya know it! Unfortunately she also knew exactly how desperate one could feel at the thought of Scott Tyler possessing compromising information about you in his hands.

'What makes you think everything is still where you left it?' she asked weakly.

'Because if he'd already come across it I would have heard about it, believe me,' came the grim reply. 'He would have taken great delight in letting me know…'

That struck a sour note and Anya frowned. 'Kate?'

'Anya, stop arguing about it and have a go, will you? For me? If I hadn't let slip to that wretched journalist that I didn't have any photos of myself as a kid because I'd left Mum's old collection of family photos and my school certificates and workbooks at The Pines, I might let sleeping dogs lie. But I just *know* he's going to go there and ask Tyler about it, then the fat will really be in the fire!'

'Why don't you ask him not to, then?'

'Because he's a journalist, stupid—that would be like a red rag to a bull. He could make a mint on some of the things in my old diaries. I have met a lot of famous people, you know, through your parents and when I was at Juilliard, and on tours...'

Anya had hair-raising visions of what Kate might have got up to with said famous people. She knew her cousin had been sexually active from a young age and saw nothing wrong with indulging her strong sensual appetites.

'I can't promise anything,' Anya said stubbornly, pursuing a rising suspicion of her own. 'And I'm not going to try until you tell me the *real* reason why you won't approach Mr Tyler yourself.'

'Oh, for God's sake!' Kate's stentorian breathing crackled into the phone. 'OK, OK. If you must know, he told me he didn't like classical music and I called him an ignorant, un-cultured barbarian...amongst a lot of other things. You know what I'm like when I'm in a temper. Fortunately, this was *after* we had both signed on the dotted line and I had his cash in the bank. Oh, and maybe after I'd gone he might have discovered that there were a few icky little drainage problems that I never got round to mentioning...'

'Oh, *Kate*!' She had ever been one to ignore life's 'icky' problems in favour of her own comfort.

'*Caveat emptor*, sweetie. I was dead keen on a quick sale and he knew he was buying an old house. So you see, the man would leap at the chance to do me a bad turn on his doorstep. That's why I know he hasn't found anything—yet. He'd love to see me strung up in the press. He'd consider it rough justice, the perfect revenge for my tromping all over his precious ego…'

That explained a lot. Almost everything, in fact. Now Anya knew what had triggered his inexplicable prejudice at their first meeting. It had been the thought of Kate herself, not Anya's feeble attempt to scrape an acquaintance, which had been the cause of his jaundiced reaction. She wished that she had pinned her elusive cousin down sooner; it might have saved Anya a lot of soul-searching.

'Look, I have to go,' Kate agitated, the broadcast chatter in the background almost drowning out her voice. 'This, this—cochon!—is insisting I repack my case and my flight's almost due to go. E-mail me and let me know how you get on. And do it soon, there's a sweetie…'

'But—'

Anya found herself protesting to empty air. Fretting over the call, she didn't linger in the shower, blow-drying her fine hair until the pale strands fanned like polished silk over her shoulders before drinking more of the wine than the tuna salad could soak up. After putting George out to prowl his nocturnal haunts, she sludged in front of a television reality show busting people in the process of committing shameful acts instead of stimulating her intellect with Bach and books, and ended up going to bed in a mood of belligerent depression.

It rained overnight, but by mid-morning the sky was clear again and the sun beamed down on the refreshed countryside. Kate had planned a leisurely lie-in to make up for all the early starts at camp, but her eyes snapped open not long after dawn and she found it impossible to wallow in her inactivity for long. She bounced out of bed, brimming with restless energy, and had done all her catch-up housework by breakfast. After her cup of tea and boiled egg she had intended to work off enough of her tension in the garden to enable her to settle down to the essay she was writing for her post-graduate history paper.

Instead she found herself striding across rain-dewed fields in the direction of The Pines, fuming over the flat battery which had trapped her car in the garage. The local mechanic was out fixing a tractor and wouldn't be able to fetch her a new one until some time that afternoon. Anya couldn't wait that long.

At least the fifteen-minute short-cut across the fenced paddocks would get her to her destination more quickly than trudging along the uneven verge of the winding road. And she didn't want to risk meeting Mark if he was driving out to meet her.

Thank goodness Liz Crawford had rung with a sympathetic warning. Mark Ransom's secretary was the first real friend that Anya had made at the college, and as the headmaster's assistant she had been well-placed to offer helpful tips on how the various school systems worked, and who to seek out for advice and who to avoid amongst the other staff. The two women often lunched together at the shopping mall across the road from the school and Liz had been the first to know, and cheerfully approve, when Anya and Mark had started tentatively dating.

'Anya? I thought I should warn you—Mark apparently received a phone call at home last night...' Liz had paused with rather ominous nervousness '...from Scott Tyler.'

'Oh, no!' Anya closed her stricken eyes. She couldn't believe he had done this to her. And now she had to wonder whether he had an ulterior motive for his vindictiveness. Was he punishing her for something she couldn't help—being Kate's cousin? Why did she feel such a terrible sense of betrayal?

'Do you know what it's all about?' Liz asked delicately.

'I can guess,' groaned Anya.

'Mark didn't go into details, but it's something to do with you and Sean Monroe at a party at Scott's on Saturday night—'

'Let me guess—I "contributed to the delinquency of a minor",' Anya quoted with crisp sarcasm.

'What? No, there was no mention of *that*—besides, Sean's seventeen, isn't he?' puzzled Liz. 'I think it was more of a general concern about the goings-on and what you were doing there. Unfortunately Mark says he can't *not* officially act on information like that once it's brought to his attention— even though it was done outside official channels. You know how stuffy he can be about rules and regs…'

'It's all rubbish, Liz—' said Anya, and poured out the farcical chain of events into her friendly ear.

'I'm sure you'll get it all sorted out,' Liz chuckled, reacting to the story with a reassuring hilarity.

Why couldn't Scott Tyler have seen the funny side of it instead of going off the deep end? Maybe farces were no more to his taste than classical music.

'What I really rang to tell you was that Mark was all het up about it when he came in this morning—' The school office was kept open during the holiday break to carry on the administrative tasks. '—he said he was coming over to talk to you about it before deciding what action to take. He *was* going to ring, but then he thought it was better to raise the matter face-to-face—you know, to try and keep it informal— so he cancelled his appointments—and I can just see him leaving now from the car park.' Her voice rose and Anya could picture her going on tiptoe in her office to improve her sight line to the school gates.

'Oh, God…' Interview by ambush. Anya could think of nothing worse—except perhaps sitting passively around while waiting for the axe to fall.

'I offered to call to check if you were in, but Mark said

he knew you'd be home because you were planning on working on your university assignment today. He obviously wants to keep this quiet for now, but he didn't specifically tell me *not* to call you, so please act surprised when he knocks on your door…'

'Thanks, Liz, but I may not be here.' Anya scooped her car keys off the hook by the phone.

'Why? What are you going to do?'

'Get Scott Tyler to retract!'

As soon as she disconnected the call she flipped through the telephone book and found the number for S.J. Tyler at The Pines which she had dialled from the camp. A brief talk with the housekeeper ascertained that Mr Tyler was working from home today, rather than at his office, and Anya silently punched the air. She hadn't looked forward to driving all the way to the Manukau City Centre in central South Auckland, where he based his large practice, and then having to run the gauntlet of curious and obstructive staff to get to the Big Man himself without an appointment.

The flat battery temporarily checked Anya's momentum, but not for long. She had already changed out of her jeans and T-shirt into a morale-boosting suit, but she quickly swapped it for a cotton-knit top and beige riding pants tucked into supple calf-length leather boots that weren't afraid of meeting a few cow-pats.

In one way the strenuous walk was doing her good, she thought breathlessly now, as she ploughed doggedly through the lush emerald-green grass, ignoring the bovine curiosity of the herd of black and white Friesians that grazed across some of the fields, occasionally ambling across her path. It was taking the edge off her temper as well as giving her time to rehearse her opening speech out loud.

It was a pity she didn't get the chance to deliver it.

The short-cut brought her out at the back of The Pines and she climbed through the last wire fence into the huge yard dotted with citrus and fruit trees, wincing when her shoulder brushed the top strand of barbed wire and a tiny loop of woven cotton sprouted beside the seam. Weaving her way through the low-hanging trees, Anya was trying to push the stubborn loop back to the underside of the loose weave with her fingernail as she skirted the side of the house and didn't at first notice the black-clad figure clinging to the lacy creeper just beneath the top floor dormer window.

When the dry crack of a breaking twig made her look up, Anya's first foolish thought was that someone *else* was trying to sneak a peek into Scott Tyler's house and had elected to take the direct route. She felt a split-second of envy for their boldness before her social conscience reasserted itself, along with her common sense. A cat-burglar in broad daylight? Then she realised that the figure was moving *away* from the open window, not towards it, down rather than up, trying to crab over towards the narrow drainpipe that ran the down the side of the house. She also saw that the figure was too small to be that of an adult, but unfortunately the sparse upper tendrils of the creeper weren't strong enough to support even the slight weight that was being tested upon them and were sagging dangerously away from the white-painted wall.

Anya's heart leapt into her throat and she opened her mouth to cry out a warning but then realised that a shout might be counter-productive. She saw that the climber had already realised what was happening and was frantically trying to scrabble within reach of the downpipe before the fragile framework collapsed completely.

Anya began running towards the place on the paved pathway that she judged was directly beneath the dangling figure and as she did so there was the flash of a pale face and she recognised the rude young girl with the nosering whom she had encountered on Saturday night. She was looking down over her straining shoulder at the six-metre drop, her mouth and eyes wide with fright.

Anya produced a final burst of speed just as there was a tearing, hissing sound and flimsy creeper gave way at both hand and foot. The girl made a final wild swipe at the drain-pipe, her fingernails screeching uselessly across the painted copper, and then she was falling backwards, arms flailing, legs bicycling as she tried to twist her body round and grab at handfuls of the vine to slow herself down. But her momentum was too great and the leaves shredded between her fingers.

'Don't worry, I'll catch you!' cried Anya, her voice dry with fear as she bent her knees and arched her spine, throwing her head back and flinging her arms wide to try and turn herself into a human safety net.

In the last split-second everything seemed to be happening in ultra-slow motion and Anya thought she might actually be able to live up to her words, so it was a brutal shock when the moment of impact exploded on her with stunning force, a sharp knee cannoning into her chest and driving her flat to the ground, and the whole world turning to suffocating black velvet.

CHAPTER FOUR

'OH, HELL, are you all right?'

Anya stirred, realising that the smothering blackness which had enveloped her wasn't unconsciousness, but the black-clad chest of the girl who had landed squarely on top of her and smashed her backwards onto the unyielding ground. Anya spat out a mouthful of acrylic cardigan as the girl scrambled off her in a flurry of curses and knelt anxiously at her heaving sides. 'God, I'm sorry—are you badly hurt?' she asked, her voice thin with fear.

The overhead sun dazzled Anya's eyes, white spots dancing mockingly in her vision as she tried to suck in the breath to answer, but there seemed to be no power in her deflated lungs and she took great, dry, whistling gulps to try and equalise the pressure in her burning chest. Her neck was cricked sideways under the overhanging corner of a low step, the back of her ringing head resting on the damp grass beside the path. As she lay there staring up at the jutting brick she was lucid enough to be thankful that her head had not cracked down on that sharp edge as she fell. It would have been lights out permanently!

'Oh, no—do you think you've broken something?' The girl sprang to her feet, shaken but clearly unhurt, her bright, kohl-lined blue eyes looking huge in her ashen face, and Anya finally managed to pump some air into her abused lungs.

'No—I—don't—think—so,' she managed to croak, mentally blessing the fact that the lawn hadn't been recently mown and the grass beneath her head was thick and springy.

She started to squirm away from that threatening overhang. 'I just—ouch!'

As she moved her arm she felt a fierce jab from her funny bone and the hot sting of scraped skin on her forearm. She flexed cautiously, finding no screaming pain from any of her other limbs, no sickening grate of broken bone, although the ringing in her head made it difficult to concentrate on the messages coming in from the rest of her body. 'I think— I'm OK…just—bit stunned…' she advised threadily.

The girl bent over, her hands on her hips in a pugnacious pose that Anya recognised from their previous encounter. 'That was *such* a dumb thing to do—I could have killed you!'

Anya gaped up at the scowling face framed in its distinctive dye-job, the spikes of gold-tipped black hair standing up in defiance of gravity, the ring in her nose matched by two smaller ones in each ear. The words were spoken in relief rather than anger, she thought, and with a strong Australian twang.

'Stopped—you—hurting yourself,' she panted out in between whistling breaths, in defence of the scolding. At any other time she might have been amused at the role-reversal.

'Yeah, and it's probably going to cost me, big time,' was the disgruntled reply. Anya decided to try and sit up, but the girl dropped onto her skinny haunches and planted a surprisingly strong hand on Anya's collarbone, holding her flat against the uneven bricks. 'No! Don't try and move yet. I'll go and get some help—'

Anya suddenly remembered where she was. 'No, really, I'm OK—' she protested weakly. 'I can feel everything…' She wiggled her toes to prove it.

'Just *wait*!' The young voice, formerly shrill, had now sunk back to its natural husky register and carried an amazing amount of authority for one so young. 'Jeez, lady, don't be in such a hurry. Please—don't try and get up until I get someone to help. I don't want you dying on me. I'm too

young to have that on my conscience. I'd be traumatised for
life!'

Anya doubted it. Not with that resilient sense of humour.
'You…didn't mean to…do it,' she huffed, gracious to a fault.

'No, well…' The blue eyes sparked with a devilish light
that plucked a familiar chord in Anya's mind. 'Be a real mate
and hold that thought for me, will you?'

'What—?' But she was already gone, sprinting like a black
gazelle towards the back of the house, leaping and hopping
from leg to leg as she whipped off her running shoes along
the way, dangling them by their laces as she ran. Did she
think she was faster in bare feet?

Anya remained spread-eagled on the ground, not because
she was following instructions but because she felt slightly
giddy when she lifted her head, and her breathing was still
catching unpleasantly in her chest. She would get up in slow
stages, she decided, carefully straightening in her limbs in
preparation to rolling over and pushing up on her knees.

She thought she was starting to hallucinate when she suddenly saw the girl's head and shoulders poke out of the self-
same dormer window high up under the gabled roof. The
weirdly skewed sense of *déjà vu* was shattered as the girl
gave her an encouraging wave and launched into a series of
ear-piercing screams. Her head abruptly disappeared back inside the room and Anya was left staring blankly upwards,
thinking perhaps she *was* unconscious after all.

To her confused mind it only seemed bare seconds later
when the girl came dashing back up to her prone body, this
time from the direction of the front of the house and closely
trailed by a babble of voices wanting to know what was going on. One of them, deep and resonant, made Anya utter a
fatalistic cry of pained frustration.

'What the—?' Scott Tyler's exclamation was cut short as
he dropped to his knees beside her, his large hand going to
her forehead to brushed away a few crumpled leaves. In his

dark trousers and casual open shirt he looked younger and less ruthlessly constrained than he did in his elegant suits.

'What on earth have you done to yourself?' he muttered, running his eyes rapidly over her body, looking for clues. Over his shoulder Anya was dismayed to see the curious faces of Sean and Samantha, his niece and nephew, falling into startled expressions as they realised who it was lying on the path.

'What are you doing here, anyway?' he continued, 'I didn't see your car parked out front.'

'I—I walked over,' she said, watching Sean turn around and hurriedly slope off while his sister craned forward.

'Did you trip and hit your head on the bricks?' he said, sliding his fingers around the back of her skull and feeling for any telltale sponginess.

'No, I—' Anya tried to pull her head away from his touch and saw the young girl looking down at her with pleading eyes, her hands steepled under her chin. '—I fell,' she finished lamely. The girl silently folded her hands to her heart in a mime of swooning gratitude.

'Not watching where you were going?' murmured Scott Tyler, his dark brows drawn together as he bent over her and placed his flattened palms on either side of her neck, making her pulse jerk. Dark hair flopped across his forehead and she could see the pulse jumping at the base of his own throat through his open shirt-collar.

'The bricks on this path *are* very uneven, and the steps do tend to sort of blend in,' chipped in the cause of the accident with inventive flair.

'I was looking up at the house,' Anya said truthfully, gasping as his big hands smoothed over her shoulders and arms, and down her sides, his fingers trailing over the front of her ribs. 'What do you think you're *doing*?' She squirmed as his hands kept going south, moving over her hips and down her legs.

'Stop writhing about,' he growled.

'You're tickling,' she complained, and blushed when his dark lashes flicked up so that he looked directly into her eyes. Could he tell she was lying?

'Well, at least you don't appear to be suffering from any loss of feeling,' he said drily. 'And your colour seems to be coming back.'

'I had the wind knocked out of me, that's all,' she said, putting a hand to her scooped neckline, drawing his attention to her yellow knitted top.

'You look like a wilted buttercup,' he murmured, 'mown down by a summer breeze.'

Anya was flustered by the unexpected whimsicality of his words. Was that a poetical way of saying that she was a weakling? How would *he* fare on being struck by a human cannonball?

'If you move out of the way I'll get up,' she said gruffly.

She began to hoist herself up on her hands but he remained where he was, tilting his head to frown at the scrape on her arm below her bunched sleeve. 'I think it was a little more than a winding, but lying there on the damp ground certainly isn't doing you any good.'

To her shock he slid an arm behind her shoulder blades and one under her knees and stood up in one fluid movement, tipping her high against his chest to readjust his grip under her thighs before he turned and began to retrace his steps, Samantha and the other girl trailing behind him, whispering to each other.

She pushed at his shoulder with a gritty hand, leaving a smudge on the front of his pale blue shirt. 'Put me down...you can't carry me—'

'Why? Don't you think I'm strong enough to handle a fairy-weight like you?'

She could feel the play of muscles across his chest and abdomen and the tensile pull of sinews and tendons in his arms as he moved effortlessly over the ground. He wasn't even breathing hard as he mounted the steps to the open front door. There was no doubting his strength; it was the *handling* part that Anya was worried about…

'I'm perfectly able to walk—'

'But evidently not without falling over.'

He stepped into the hall and there was a muffled giggle behind him. 'You just carried her over the threshold, Uncle Scott,' Samantha Monroe informed him, her bubbly voice pregnant with meaning.

'I doubt Miss Adams is feeling in the least bit bride-like at the moment,' he answered repressively. 'Go and get a bowl of hot water with disinfectant, and some cotton wool swabs would you, Sam?' He raised his voice above the sound of her chunky sandals clattering off across the polished hardwood floor. 'And while you're in the kitchen getting the bowl, ask Mrs Lee to make some tea.'

'That girl has marriage on the brain.' He sounded sorely harassed. 'Her sole aim in life seems to be how to snag herself a boy.'

'Actually, from what I've seen at school, it's the boys who want to snag *her*,' Anya told him. 'Samantha's interest in marriage is probably partly self-defensive. Even fifteen-year-old boys realise that pretty girls who are misty-eyed about marriage are going to be the type to want commitment, and not likely to put out for whoever happens to be that night's date.'

'And people call *me* a cynical manipulator,' he murmured, glancing down at the woman in his arms as if surprised by the rawness of her perception.

She tilted her chin. 'No, do they really?' she marvelled, widening eyes the colour of the sky on a rainy day.

'Cat!' he said, carrying her down the wide hall towards the living rooms. The interior walls and high, moulded plaster ceilings were the colour of whipped cream, and in daylight the impression of lightness and space was markedly different from the effect of the dark-stained panelling and densely-patterned wallpaper that Anya remembered from her childhood, or the garish coloured lights from Saturday night. The rooms off the hallway were carpeted in wheat-coloured wool which from the pristine look of it had been professionally cleaned since the party. She hoped Scott Tyler was making his nephew work off the cost.

'I thought I was a buttercup,' she countered.

'A buttercup doesn't have claws. I trust that this simple act of human kindness *isn't* making you feel bridal?' he enquired mockingly.

'Homicidal, more like,' she said, remembering the purpose of her visit. She kicked with her legs to signal her displeasure. 'You can put me down now.'

'All in good time.'

As they passed the former dining room she saw it was fitted out as an office and next door she caught a glimpse of something that genuinely widened her eyes. 'You have a piano!' she blurted.

His mockery turned sour. 'Why so surprised? Did you think me too great a Philistine to own such an icon of high-brow culture?' He turning into the living room opposite, reading the answer in her all-too-revealing flush. 'Ah, I see…you've been listening to your loose-lipped cousin. Well, of course, it's only there for pretentious show—or thumping out pub songs—whichever you think is the most offensive to good taste.'

Anya stiffened at the implication that she was a cultural snob. 'As a matter of fact, Kate's hardly mentioned you to me at all,' she snapped. And then only in answer to direct questions.

His eyes gleamed as if he read her mind. 'How frustrating for you,' he said with a silky smile, lowering her onto a deep couch upholstered in cream-coloured linen.

She sank back into the plush cushions as he picked up her ankles one by one and calmly unzipped her boots, his hand cupping the backs of her calves as he slid them off her stockinged feet, ignoring her protest that there was no need for her to lie down.

'Humour me,' he said, allowing her to wriggle up so that her back was propped against the arm of the couch. 'I don't want to leave you any excuses to sue.' He turned to accept the steaming bowl that Samantha had carefully carried into the room, along with a plastic box adorned with a red cross.

There was a high-pitched burble and Samantha snatched up the cordless telephone from the coffee table before it could ring a second time, her flawless complexion pinkening as she responded to the voice at the other end, twirling at one lock of golden-blonde hair around a manicured finger as she answered.

'Oh, hi, Bevan...Yes, it's me...Oh, nothing much, just hanging around here...Well, I don't know—Angie and Sara want to go to the beach later...' She wandered out of the room, the little domestic drama eclipsed in her mind by the pressing demands of a teenage social life.

Anya suffered a closer inspection of her minor bumps and grazes and clenched her teeth as they were meticulously bathed clean and the stinging patch on her arm was treated and a small dressing taped into place over the raw skin. She never would have thought that Scott Tyler could be so gentle, she thought, keeping her eyes fixed on his fingers so she didn't have to look at the face so uncomfortably close to her own. Strangely, his deft gentleness made her feel more, rather than less vulnerable to his aggressive personality.

'I'm using hypoallergenic sticking-plaster because I'm guessing that you have very sensitive skin,' he said, pressing down the final piece of tape and running his thumb down the tender, velvety-smooth inside of her arm to linger over the blue veins in her fine-boned wrist.

'Mr Tyler—'

'Miss Adams?' The prim way he said her name made her feel foolish for her attempt to reassert a formal distance between them. 'You'd better call me Scott. A woman should be on first-name terms with the man who carries her over the threshold.'

The threshold of what? she thought darkly and was chagrined when she realised that she had muttered it out loud.

His eyes picked up the blue of his shirt, making their colour more intense than ever. 'I guess that's the lady's choice.' He looked down at her where he touched her. 'I'll bet you bruise very easily—*Anya*.' He broadened the initial 'A', the way it was meant to be pronounced but seldom ever was by anyone outside her family, making it sound seductively foreign.

'Yes, but I heal very quickly, too.' He was stroking tiny circles at the flex-point of her wrist, proving his theory about her sensitivity. Anya could feel the hairs all up her arm rising as if swept by a fine electrical current.

'Then you're a lot more resilient than you look.'

'I thought we were agreed that appearances could be deceptive—*Scott*,' she said, and his fingers tightened briefly on her wrist and then released it to brush the specks of brick dust on her hand.

'I'm surprised you don't have any defensive grazes on your palms. Most people instinctively fling out their hands to try and break a fall…'

Anya's hands had been raised to catch the girl who was now hovering at the other end of the couch, her gaze darting between them, a thoughtful wrinkle forming above the bridge of her strong nose.

'And oddly enough it looks as if you're going to have a bruise here.' He lightly touched the reddened skin over her breast-bone just above the neckline of her top, his eyes puzzled as he traced what he didn't realise to be the outline of a bony knee.

Fortunately the owner of the knee interrupted him before he noticed Anya's spontaneous reaction to his feather-light stroking.

'Aren't you going to ask *me* to do something to help, too?' she said, with a rather challenging look at the man now rising to his feet. 'Or am I surplus to requirements?'

To Anya's surprise he didn't react to the sarcasm with his usual swift retort. He seemed momentarily at a loss, and the pair of them stared at each other across the couch, two sets of blue eyes exchanging a silent message that neither seemed able to interpret. In fact, had Anya been given the choice, she would have picked the youngster as the marginally more confident of the two.

Finally Anya couldn't stand it any longer. 'Perhaps you'd like to see if the tea's ready?' she suggested brightly, swivelling her legs off the couch. 'I could really do with something to drink.'

Scott ran a hand through his hair, suddenly released from his tension. 'Good idea. Could you go and ask Mrs Lee for the tray, and bring it through here? And you may as well take this away,' he added, giving her the bowl of water floating with used swabs. 'Oh, and Miss Adams's boots, too, please, Petra,' he said, picking them up and handing them over. 'Put them out on the shoe stand by the front door.'

'Oh, right! So now I have to do *every*thing,' the girl griped, with a roll of her expressive eyes.

This time Scott grinned, relaxing even further. 'Well, you *did* ask. And I doubt if you were doing it just to be polite, because politeness doesn't seem to be one of your strong points.'

'I can be polite,' came the pert reply.

'Then how about demonstrating your manners now? In spite of the dramatic manner of your meeting, you two haven't yet been introduced.' A furtive glance between the two females was smoothed into polite expectancy on both sides. 'Miss Adams, this is my fourteen-year-old daughter, Petra Conroy—*temporarily* attending Hunua College from the start of the new term. Miss Adams teaches history, Petra.'

'Yeah, so Sam told me. Hi, Miss Adams!'

Petra patently enjoyed the shock in Anya's murmured greeting, giving her a huge grin before strolling out the door. As she stepped into the hallway, Anya realised the reason for her dance to take off her shoes. Her bare feet made no sound on the wooden floor. She would have been silently fleet up the wooden staircase and deliberately rowdy thundering back down. A girl with a great deal of natural wit and cunning, she thought. I wonder where she inherited *that* from?—probably the same person who had given her those forget-me-not eyes.

'You have a daughter?' she couldn't help saying. 'I didn't know you'd ever been m—' she stopped, biting her lip, but he was quick to embarrass her over her near faux pas.

'Married? I haven't. I hope you don't make that conventional assumption about the parents of your pupils at the college; a lot of them come from painfully fragmented backgrounds.'

'I know that.' Anya repudiated the criticism. 'I meant that I hadn't heard that you had children—'

'*A* child, and I don't "have" her. She's lived with her mother in Australia since before she was born,' he said, dropping into the armchair opposite the couch, his outstretched arms dropping over the padded arms, the casual sprawl of his legs a direct counterpoint to her neat, straight-backed, knees-together, ankles-crossed pose.

'Oh,' she said, searching for the proper response to such a statement. 'You must have been quite young yourself when she was born—'

'Eighteen.' He saved her the maths. 'She was conceived

while I was still at school.' His daughter wasn't the only one with a propensity to shock. Anya tried to control her expression but some of her involuntary disapproval must have leaked out because his mouth drooped sardonically. 'And no, I didn't carelessly get my teenage girlfriend pregnant. Lorna was thirty, and she was the one making all the decisions about our relationship, including the one to have and raise a child on her own.'

Anya's mouth fell open and the corner of his mouth ticked up in satisfaction.

'What's the matter? Aren't I conforming to the stereotype image you've created of me?'

She was so stunned she instinctively spoke the truth. 'I…you— I just have difficulty thinking of you as a…a junior partner in any relationship,' she stammered.

'Everyone has to get their experience from somewhere,' he told her, and for one horrible moment she thought he was going to demand to know where she had got hers. She tried not to think about Alistair Grant any more, except in his capacity as her parents' agent. Anyway, she was sure that her limited experience was of no interest to Scott Tyler.

'Are you saying you were a—' Suddenly she realised what she had been going to ask and her whole body suffused with heat. It was no business of hers. How could she even think of asking such an intimate question of a man she barely knew, a man she had come here to angrily confront?

'A virgin?' he said with explicit clarity, relishing the sight of her fiery blush and the embarrassed flutter of her guilty grey eyes. 'Perhaps not physically but emotionally it was certainly a first for me.'

'You were in love with her?'

'I was flattered by the attentions of a very attractive, intelligent, older woman,' he replied with exquisite evasiveness. He might want to slap her in the face with the raw facts of life, but he evidently wasn't prepared to reveal the secrets of his heart.

Anya moistened her dry lips. 'H-have you been able to see your daughter very often?' She ventured onto what she thought was more conventional conversational ground.

'Not since she was a baby. Lorna wanted it that way. She didn't want any financial support and in exchange I agreed not to involve myself in her child's life.' He shrugged at her indrawn breath. 'I was eighteen…what did I know? As Lorna pointed out, I had no money and at least four years of law school ahead of me. I wasn't ready for parenthood—she was…'

There was more to it than that, Anya was sure of it; his whole attitude was simply too nonchalant. 'So what's Petra doing here now? Has something happened to her mother?'

'No. Petra decided that it was time she tracked down her biological father. After an argument with Lorna about it she ran away from home, hopped a plane—booked with her mother's credit card—and turned up on my doorstep last week.'

'Good lord…!' Climbing out of a second-floor window was probably a breeze compared with what she had already risked.

'After some discussion Lorna and I agreed that since Petra felt so strongly about it she should stay here for a few weeks and get to know her paternal relations—as long as she doesn't miss her schooling. History is one of her subjects and since you may find her in one of your classes I thought it might help you to know a bit about her background.'

'Talking about me, Dad?' Petra waltzed in with a laden tray which she set down on the coffee table with a cheerful rattle.

'Who else? You *are* the current hot topic around here,' said her father drily. He looked down at the tray and raised his eyebrows. 'Three' cups? Nice try, Petra. If you go back to your room right now we'll only add—' he checked his steel watch '—another half an hour onto your sentence to make up the difference.'

'But Dad—I was rescuing someone. I should get time off for good behaviour!' Petra had the grace to flush when she looked over and saw Anya's lowered brows. 'OK, OK,' she amended hastily. 'But this sucks. All I did was tell Sean what I thought of his brain-dead friends.'

'In language I'm more used to hearing in police holding cells than at my own breakfast table. And throwing food is *completely* unacceptable.' Anya looked at him through her lashes as he was laying down the law, hiding her amusement. He might know nothing about parenthood but he was obviously a fast learner. 'None of us are used to living with each other, but if we act civilised and respect each other's boundaries we can all get along. My house, my rules, Petra—and I don't think a couple of hours of time out is unreasonable punishment. You spend more time than that plugged into the stereo in your room every day. In fact, why don't you take up that book about New Zealand I was going to lend you? In a couple of hours you could learn some of the things you may need to know in school next week. Why don't you pour Miss Adams's tea while I get it?'

There was a small silence after he left the room until Petra rushed into speech.

'Hey, thanks for not dobbing me in!' She picked up the china teapot and poured out two cups, pushing one across the coffee table to Anya and carefully sugaring and stirring the other before positioning it within easy reach from the vacant chair.

Anya watched this small, telling act with a softening heart but she wasn't going to be bamboozled by her emotions.

'I fell for a good con job,' she chided in her cool, clear voice. 'But it won't happen a second time. What you did today wasn't reckless, it was just plain stupid, and really dangerous. The fright your father got when he saw me lying there was *nothing* to the anguish he would have felt if it had been you. You might not have died, but you could have had to live the rest of your life unable to function as an individual, with your father blaming himself for not taking better care of you. If nothing else, at least have consideration for the feelings of others before you give in to your selfish impulses.'

She found herself being regarded with unexpected awe. 'Wow!'

'What?' she demanded.

'Nothing.' The girl shook her head, but then blurted: 'You wouldn't think to look at you but you're real good at making a person feel bad.' Her husky voice dropped into quiet sincerity. 'I was just sneaking out to prove that I could—I won't do it again, I promise.' She pulled a wry face. 'I knew as soon as I got out there that it was a dumb thing to do but I couldn't get back in, so I figured it was better to go down as quick as I could so there was less far to fall. I thought it was too dorky to yell for help. I really am sorry.'

'You had to yell for help anyway,' Anya pointed out.

'Yeah, but it's cool to do it for another person,' the girl pointed out with unarguable truth.

When her father came back with the promised book she was quick to beat a retreat.

'She probably won't even open it,' he grunted, sitting down and reaching for his tea.

'Uh, Petra's already done that for you,' said Anya when he ladled in a another teaspoonful of sugar.

He paused in his stirring. 'Then why didn't you stop me?' he said, irritated.

'I'm sorry my reactions weren't fast enough for you,' she replied astringently. 'I didn't know I was supposed to police the sugar bowl. For all I know you could need all that extra sweetening,' she added in a dulcet tone, taking a sip of her own, unadulterated tea.

He shoved the over-sweetened drink back onto the tray and poured himself another in the spare cup, adding a sparse teaspoon of sugar, then sat back in his chair and regarded her with a threatening attentiveness.

'So, to what do I owe the honour of this visit? Or were you simply strolling by and decided to "trip" in for a neighbourly chat?' His ironic inflexion stressed the fact that she had never made any such neighbourly gesture before.

'I walked across the fields because my car battery is flat,' she told him, to disabuse him of any notion that she was in the habit of skulking around his property. 'And you must know why I've come!'

'Must I?' His eyes were steady over the rim of his cup.

'Don't play word games with me!' Her fingers tightened on the edges of the delicate bone-china saucer as she forced herself to calm down. 'I'm talking about your phone call last night to Mark Ransom. You made absolutely no effort to contact me to get my side of the story about Saturday night, so I quite naturally assumed that you had got the full truth out of Sean. Now I find out that without even bothering to give me the chance to explain you've complained to the college—'

'Actually, I did try to contact you last night to warn you what I was doing, but I was unable to get through,' he interrupted, taking a fraction of the wind out of her sails. 'And this morning I've been tied up in conference calls...'

Anya had been careless hanging up after Kate's phone call the previous night and hadn't discovered the receiver was still dislodged from the cradle until early this morning. That still didn't excuse what he'd done. She set her tea down on the coffee table with an angry rattle.

'You wanted to warn me that you were going to stab me in the back with unsubstantiated lies? Mark is coming to see me and I don't even know what kind of slanderous allegations he's going to throw at me!' She had the satisfaction of seeing him frown. 'What exactly did you say to him? Do you have *any* idea what you've *done*?'

'Calm down...'

'*Calm down?*' She was outraged. 'This is my career we're talking about!'

He waved a dismissive hand. 'I know *exactly* what I've done. And I haven't made any allegations or complaints about you or your conduct. I merely informed Ransom—*as a friendly courtesy*—that there was an unauthorised party here on Saturday night and a lot of kids from the school were here with illicit alcohol and that you also were here at one point, collecting some partygoers—'

'—and prancing around in my underwear,' she finished his sentence bitterly.

He kept his gravelly voice even. 'I didn't mention your state of dress—or lack of it. I was purposefully vague. Ransom knows you, you're friends—he's not going to automatically assume the worst.' As *he* had! 'I told him that Sean was being appropriately punished—fortunately his memory of the evening is pretty much a total blur—'

'Fortunately for *Sean*, you mean!'

His mouth thinned but he held onto his patience. 'For *both* of you. The only things Sean recalls of the latter part of the night is you chewing him out for what was going on, and him throwing up. After that everything's a blank. He doesn't even remember *me* arriving on the scene, let alone what he said to me, or what you were or weren't wearing at the time...'

Anya felt a brief pang of dizzy relief. 'Then why on earth did you have to go telling tales to Mark?'

'Because word has a way of getting round, and it's easier to attack with the facts than defend against rumours,' he told her, his blue eyes persuasively intent on her stormy face. 'Sean says that the party was supposed to be just for his rugby mates and their girlfriends, but it became an open secret around school and more and more people kept turning up on the night.'

He picked up her cup and handed it back to her, still holding her captive with his compelling gaze, and she automatically began drinking, the hot liquid easing the angry tightness in her throat. 'I had a few calls from concerned parents yesterday about the state their children had arrived home in after what they had been told was an evening of watching videos. The phones have been running hot amongst the kids and before I warned him to keep his mouth shut Sean had already told a few of his mates that you had caught him with "some rich chick", and no doubt they told a few of *their* mates, probably embellishing as people tend to do when they're telling a good story. There are probably others, too, who'll remember seeing you when you arrived at the party and start wondering why…'

'Oh, no…' Anya sighed, beginning to perceive the enormity of the problem in which she was entangled.

'Oh, yes. Trust me on this, Anya, it's my own field of expertise: it's always safer to be the source rather than the victim of information. If rumours are flying around, we definitely don't want it to look as if we've tried to cover anything up, because that implies that there's something *worth* covering up in all this. As it is, only you and I know what happened in that bedroom, and as long as we corroborate each other's story there won't be problems about it. I'm sorry I couldn't wait for your prior approval, but it was imperative to make a pre-emptive statement before any whispering campaign got started that could affect you in the classroom, or some parent formally approached the school.'

Trust him? Anya swallowed another mouthful of tea. She supposed she didn't have much choice, and everything he had said *did* seem to make solid sense.

'Well…' Suddenly she realised the most important point she had almost overlooked. She straightened. 'So you now admit I was telling the truth about what happened? That you were wrong about me.'

'You can't blame me for—' He halted as she gave him the haughty-eyebrow routine. He inclined his head. 'On *this* occasion, yes...I was wrong,' he conceded, with an obvious difficulty that made the admission all the sweeter as far as Anya was concerned. He picked up the decorative plate of home baking which had remained ignored on the tray, and offered it as a blatant distraction.

'Biscuit? Mrs Lee has a very light hand with brownies.'

'Thank you.' She took her time selecting one and then continued to press her advantage in the same, insistent tone. 'And, of course, you take back all those terribly insulting things you said to me...'

His eyes narrowed and he put down the plate with a thump, giving her a sharkish smile. 'I'm afraid I'm not prepared to give you a wholesale retraction. Why don't you be a little more specific? You tell me what each insult was, and I'll either agree or disagree to withdraw it.'

And in the process make her repeat every embarrassing one. Anya bit down on her biscuit with unnecessary force and nearly choked on the crumbs that exploded onto her tongue.

He watched her splutter for a moment, her eyes watering as she washed down the crumbs with the dregs of her tea, and leaned forward, his smile shifting into shocking suavity and his voice deepening to a sexy throb. 'I am, of course, deeply sorry to have caused you any degree of discomfort whatsoever and hope that you'll accept my most humble apologies for having the temerity to doubt a lady's word...'

'Oh, very prettily done,' she said, outwardly unimpressed while inside her bones were resonating to the rich vibrancy of his tone. 'A for effort and acting, but you get a definite F in sincerity.'

His suavity was discarded as he burst out laughing.
'You're a hard woman.'

'I'm glad you finally realise it.'

'Then I needn't worry about putting you through this next
ordeal, though I think we both understand that it has to be
done...'

The 'ordeal' turned out to be an apology from a very subdued Sean Monroe who, with his uncle standing with folded
arms behind him, trotted out a few stilted words that didn't
quite conceal a lingering hint of truculence.

'I don't remember whatever it was I'm supposed to have
done, but Uncle Scott said I acted like an obnoxious little
kid so I guess I'm sorry for that, and whatever...and thanks
for helping me when I was sick...'

Anya didn't prolong his agony, accepting the olive branch
with a casualness that she hoped wouldn't leave any lasting
feelings of resentment. She could see no hint of a smirk in
his brown eyes which would indicate that the blank spots in
his memory were anything but genuine.

'Very clever to make him feel he made a fool of himself
behaving like a silly little boy instead of a bad, macho stud,'
she commented to Scott when his nephew had slouched out.
'Maybe he won't be so keen to let himself get out of control
in future.'

'Maybe. He wants to be a professional rugby player and
he has talent, but whether he has the long-term application
and the temperament, I don't know. His problem is that he
enjoys being the sports superstar too much and expects it to
earn him special treatment off the rugby field as well.'

He had accompanied her to the door, where she slipped
on her boots. 'At the moment he's bitter because I've
grounded him for the next three weeks, which means he'll
miss the first two weeks of rugby training when he gets back
to school. I suppose *you* think I'm being too lenient.'

'Actually I think you're wise not to go overboard,' she

said mildly, perceiving in his acid comment an underlying doubt that appealed for her professional reassurance. 'Except possibly—' she hesitated, then forced herself to confront the worrying issue '—except where drugs are concerned...'

His face took on an expressive grimness. 'Don't worry, he and I have dealt with that as an entirely separate issue. I'm inclined to accept his claim that it was a one-off, because he's obsessive about smoking or anything that might affect his fitness, but it's still something that his parents are going to have to look into when they get back.'

Their new and tentative peace accord was almost breached when Scott refused to let Anya walk back home alone in spite of her insistence that she was perfectly recovered from her small accident. Under the threat that otherwise he would walk her home himself, step-by-step, she found herself bullied into his prowling silver Jaguar, which ate up the distance in no time flat.

Being enclosed in a small space with him heightened her unwilling physical awareness until she was responding to every drawn breath and slight shift of his body, and she began to quietly fret at the thought that he might choose to linger when they arrived at their destination. She couldn't very well refuse to invite him in if he asked, but she knew that once he had been in her home his pervasive image would be even more deeply imprinted on her consciousness.

To her mingled relief and disappointment he merely dropped her at her front gate as she requested, with a glance at his watch and a brief instruction to answer Mark's questions without going into unnecessary detail, and to try to sound casual and amused rather than angry or shocked.

CHAPTER FIVE

'YOU'RE going to *what*?' Anya cried, leaping to her feet in angry disbelief, jarring the two cups of coffee on her small kitchen table.

Mark Ransom held up his hands, surrendering to her vivid shock.

'Look, it's nothing formal, it won't go on your official record or anything—'

'You're *suspending* me!'

'No, no, nothing like that,' he hastened to reassure her, his brown eyes regretful. A thin, wiry man of average height, he didn't make Anya feel small and vulnerable when she stood beside him, like someone else she could name! At thirty-seven he was young to have the headmastership of such a large school and had cultivated a gravity beyond his years. Anya liked him for his seriousness of character and dedication to his students, and when his small kindnesses had begun showing signs of becoming more personal in nature she had been cautiously optimistic about a future relationship.

Until now!

After Scott had dropped her off she had checked her letter box, and although it was too early for the mail she had found a handwritten note from Mark.

Anya, I called while you were out. Couldn't wait. Phone me ASAP on my mobile.

ASAP had been underlined twice, and after she had changed out of her grubby clothing and slipped into a skirt

83

and blouse that covered most of her bumps and scrapes, her response had brought Mark back to her doorstep as soon as he could conclude his lunchtime appointment.

'It's damage control, that's all. I just want you to be prepared if I *do* have to ask you to take a bit of time out over the first few days of term,' he clarified, standing up and smoothing down his tie under his suit jacket in a characteristic gesture of nervous impatience. Since he and Anya had never had a disagreement he was unused to her arguing with his authority. 'But it probably won't come to that, because by the time school goes back this will all have sorted itself out—'

'*Probably?*' Anya said in a frustrated voice, pacing around her small kitchen. 'You said that Sc— Mr Tyler told you it was a private party and I've explained why I went there. I don't see why it has to be made into such a big deal.' She hadn't mentioned Liz's call, or her hasty visit to The Pines that morning, and of course it hadn't occurred to Mark that she might have tried to take the initiative.

Mark ran a hand through his close-cropped sandy hair, looking as harassed as he sounded. 'It won't be if I can help it, Anya, but unfortunately Adrienne Brinkman has already been on the phone to me this morning to quietly warn me that she's had to discipline two Eastbrook girls who said they were taken to a wild party by boys from Hunua's first-fifteen team—'

Anya spun around. 'Those girls were on a *school camp* at the time, but the Hunua kids were on holiday—there's no way the college can be held responsible—'

'Not quite true,' Mark interrupted gloomily. 'I did have one other parent phone me this morning—a regular busybody, as it happens, but this time I'm afraid she has a point. Apparently her son, who came home drunk, found out about the party from the college's Internet bulletin board, so the school *is* involved. We have to find out who hacked in and posted that message, for one thing. And she also wanted to know why, if there was a teacher from the college chaperoning the party, the alcohol wasn't confiscated?'

'But I wasn't *there* to chaperone the party—'

'I know, but this is obviously the kind of thing that's going to bubble up unless we satisfy everyone that the situation is being properly looked into,' said Mark, unknowingly echoing Scott Tyler. 'You know how careful teachers have to be about hints they're leading students astray. It's a question of retaining moral authority…'

Much as she hated to do it, Anya felt driven to play the personal card. 'Surely the fact that *you* can vouch for my integrity must count for a lot? For goodness' sake, Mark, we're going out together—'

'Yes, well—that's actually part of the problem, don't you see?' he said awkwardly. 'If I casually sweep this under the carpet people might think that it's because of our personal relationship. In the circumstances it's very important that I'm *seen* to be acting impartially.' He looked at her from under furrowed brows. 'You *do* understand?'

She was afraid she did. 'Does that mean you won't be picking me up for dinner tonight after all?' she asked drily. All their other dates had been casual, but this time Mark had booked them to dine at the gourmet restaurant of the country hotel on the other side of the Ranges.

He thrust his bunched hands into his hip pockets, looking uncomfortable. 'If you don't mind…I think it's best not to, just at this point in time—don't you think?'

She kept her thoughts to herself, her polite smile pinned firmly into place as she nodded. 'It might look as though we were colluding.'

He looked relieved at her easy agreement. Perhaps after her outburst he had expected her to throw a tantrum.

'Ridiculous, of course, but you know how paranoiac some

people are.' He looked down at the half-finished coffee on the table and Anya could see him already mentally edging towards the door. 'I'll keep you posted but, as I said, I think this will all fizzle out, especially if we divert attention to finding and making an example of this hacker, whoever he or she is...'

At her front step he turned to deliver a last piece of gratuitous advice. 'By the way, it might help if you tried to get on with Scott Tyler instead of being at loggerheads with him all the time. If people know you're feuding with him they might be tempted to wonder if you went to that party *intending* to stir up some trouble for him. I know he gave you a rough ride at your interview but don't be too sensitive about it, that's just his way—I'm sure it was nothing personal. In our own best interests, we need to present a united front on this one.'

Of course, it had to be *her* injured sensitivity and not Scott Tyler's prejudice that was at fault, simmered Anya as she let the door swing closed behind him, tempted to give it a swift kick.

She swept the neglected coffees off the table, dumping the cold liquid down the sink before walking into her cosy living room, her arms wrapped around her waist. So her wonderful new life in the country had hit another hiccup, more serious than some of the others—so what? She would survive, as she had always survived the rough spots in her life.

She looked around at the sunlit room she had sweated to scrape down, paint and paper before she moved in, the second-hand furniture she had stripped, polished and otherwise refurbished to create the warm, natural, lived-in look that she associated with a real home. Nothing to remind her of the soulless modernity of a hotel, or the makeshift clutter of a student flat, or the regimentation of a school boarding house. Everything here was hers and no one else's...except the big chunk of house that was mortgaged to the bank, she amended, and time would correct that unavoidable hitch.

Provided, of course, she could keep up the payments, which were geared high in order to see off the mortgage more quickly. A teacher's salary was nothing spectacular but it was a regular income from doing a job she loved. If her reputation was so damaged that she could no longer find work in her chosen profession she might find herself in much lower-paid work and struggling to make the mortgage payments.

She wasn't going to let that happen!

Spinning around with her fists clenched in determination, Anya looked out through the French doors and saw that Mark hadn't yet left. He was leaning out of the window of his car talking to two people who had walked up the drive as he backed out…Scott Tyler and his daughter, the distinctive silver Jag parked in the street behind them.

She hurried outside, trying not to look self-conscious as both men turned their heads to watch her approach. Had Scott let the cat out of the bag about her visit?

'I was just telling Mark that I thought it was a good idea for you and I to bury the hatchet,' he said before she could open her mouth. 'I wanted to apologise in person for getting you innocently embroiled in my nephew's problems, and my daughter was fascinated to know you were the cousin of a world-renowned classical pianist. Petra takes piano lessons.' He nudged his daughter forward with a large hand.

'I'll leave you to it, then,' said Mark, giving Anya a smug look, as if he had personally conjured up this fortuitous happenstance, along with a subtle jerk of his eyes towards Scott that she supposed was both a warning and encouragement to mend her fences.

Anya was still off balance at the unexpected reference to Kate, and barely noticed Mark drive off.

'What are you *really* doing here?' she asked suspiciously, shading the sun from her eyes with her hand as she looked up at Scott, the neat circular coil of hair on the top of her head glowing like a halo in the bright light.

He seemed to have no problem with the glare, his perceptive eyes studying her tense expression. 'How are you? Have you found any more injuries?'

'No. Is that why you came back—to check I hadn't developed whiplash and decided to sue?'

He sighed. 'It seems to be in danger of developing into a boring habit of mine, producing relatives to deliver their apologies. Go ahead, Petra.' He turned and walked back to his car, where he opened the boot and began to fish inside.

Anya transferred her gaze to his daughter, who shrugged, and gave her a cocky grin. 'Sorry. He found out. I guess I knew he would, but it was worth a try.'

'You confessed or he found out?' She could see Scott coming back up the drive towards them out of the corner of her eye.

'A bit of both, really…'

'I went back to look at the path in case there was a real safety hazard that needed to be tidied up, and noticed all the fallen leaves, and damage to the creeper all the way up to her window,' supplied her father as he rejoined them. 'Since you're an unlikely candidate for a cat-burglar, it didn't take a genius to work out that Petra had decided that a simple closed door was the modern equivalent of Colditz—'

'What's Colditz?'

'A World War II POW prison for chronic escapees, you appallingly ignorant child,' was the drawling reply. 'Haven't you ever studied the World Wars at school?'

'Yeah, but I usually listen to my Discman in the boring classes…you know, run the earphone wire from my bag up under my sleeve and sit with my head propped on my hand—' she flattened her hand over the side of her face and ear.

Anya recognised the characteristic pose and hid a grin while Scott growled, 'Have you made your apology yet?'

'Actually she already did that, back at your house,' Anya said. 'Spontaneously. *Before* your other relative trotted out his rather more forced effort.'

He glowered at her. 'You told me you'd fallen.'

'I did. I just didn't happen to mention it was because Petra landed on top of me.' She could see he was busting to take her to task, but she wasn't going to provide him with any more ammunition. Her eyes fell to the object he was carrying. 'What's that?'

As a distraction for both of them, it did nicely. 'A new battery for your car.' He hefted the weighty cube as if it was a feather. 'I picked it up from the garage for you on the way over.'

She noticed the tools in his other hand. 'Thank you, but I've already arranged for the mechanic to come and put one in,' she said sharply.

'Not any more. I told Harry to cancel the call-out. Why pay for something that you can get done for free?'

She looked dubiously at him, knowing she should be annoyed at his high-handedness, but overcome by curiosity. '*You* know how to change a battery?' He wore the same dark trousers, but had exchanged his shirt for a tight-fitting, v-necked, navy top which was casual yet obviously expensive. He didn't look like someone who spent much time under the hood of a car.

'All men are born knowing basic car maintenance. It's in the genes.' Her contemptuous snort produced a crooked smile. 'In my case, literally. My father was a mechanic until my mother died and he took up boozing as a career; then he relied on me to keep the family crate running.' He began heading for the open doors of her garage. 'Why don't you take Petra inside to entertain you with more of her grovelling while I do the swap…?'

Petra was already heading up the path before he finished speaking and Anya hesitated before darting after him. 'What do I owe you for the battery?' she demanded to know.

'Nothing.'

'Nothing is for nothing,' she pointed out

He stopped and turned in the shadow of the garage. 'My daughter's life—is that *nothing* to you?'

She took a step back at his fierceness. It occurred to her that he'd only known Petra for a week and, although he might have accepted in abstract that he had been a father for the last fourteen years, he had been utterly unprepared for the huge emotional impact she had on him. He was discovering within himself depths of emotion that he hadn't realised existed, or which had been long suppressed in order for him to survive. Even though he had been cynically off-hand in his telling of the circumstances surrounding Petra's birth, Anya had sensed a powerful retroactive resentment of the way he had been totally shut out of his daughter's life. At the time he had been made to feel that he had nothing of value to offer his own child and somewhere deep inside him a little of that fear probably still lurked.

'I only meant that I don't want to be beholden to you—' she said, uneasy with the unwelcome insight.

'Do you think I like feeling indebted to *you*?' he asked tightly, his eyes cut-glass brilliant as they scored her face.

'I don't know,' she said, fighting a sudden light-headedness. 'I don't think you do, either. Since Petra arrived I think you're not quite sure what you're feeling about anything any more.'

'Stop trying to get inside my head,' he growled. 'I'm not one of your students—'

'Thank God!'

'I'm a full-grown man and right now I'm going get my hands filthy doing a man's job, so why don't you run along and flitter about the kitchen or whatever it is prissy ladies do while someone else does their dirty work for them?'

Anya's eyes flashed. 'Why, you sexist pig! I didn't *ask* you to dirty your hands for me.'

'No, you're certainly like your cousin in that respect. Kate never *asked* but she always managed to make it clear what she *expected*, and those expensive hands of hers never had to get soiled because someone else ended up paying for the privilege of meeting those haughty expectations. If she hadn't had the papers to prove it, I never would have believed she'd grown up on a farm.'

She flinched at the accuracy of his vivid word picture. 'My life and expectations are totally different from Kate's, so don't you dare start comparing us!' she said in a voice shaking with repressed anger. 'I may not be able to change a battery, but I can change a tyre and check the oil and water, which is as much as most car owners can do. And I am *not* prissy!' she was unable to resist adding in a fierce hiss.

She knew she had made a mistake when a slow, taunting smile curved his mouth and twin blue devils danced in his eyes as he leaned closer and murmured: 'You always look prissy to me. Even in sexy green underwear with your pretty little breasts begging to be kissed you looked more naughty-but-nice-Miss-Adams than sultry and wicked Miss January. Not that prissy can't be just as much of a turn-on to some men...'

Anya's face was still bright red as she slammed into the house and found Petra flicking through her CD collection in the living room.

'Is something wrong?' Petra looked up at her, the small gold ring in her left nostril glinting as she turned her head.

'Yes! That...that *man*!' Anya's hands clenched and un-clenched by her sides.

Petra looked around, alarmed. 'What man?'

'Your *father*!' It was rendered as the grossest of insults.

'Oh.' Petra's blue eyes brightened with curiosity. 'What's the matter? I thought he was doing you a favour.'

Anya breathed carefully through her nose. 'He is. He just doesn't have to be so—' she searched for some relatively innocuous phrase to express her seething annoyance '—so odiously *superior* about it!'

'Well, I guess it's hard for him not to be…him being such a superior kind of guy and all…'

Anya stared at her for a blank moment before she realised she was having her leg gently pulled. 'You know, when you use that sarcastic drawl you sound just like him. You want to be careful; it's not good for someone your age to be too cynical.'

'You really think I sound like him?' Petra asked with a touch too much nonchalance.

'Sometimes. You have his eyes, too. What's your natural hair colour?'

Petra pulled a face. 'Brown. Too ordinary. Mum went spare when I did this—' she tugged at her locks '—but I want to be *different*.'

'I think we can safely agree you've achieved your goal,' Anya told her with a small smile of understanding. 'On the outside, at least.'

'Oh, I feel different on the inside, too.' It was said with a quiet determination that was at odds with her impulsive brashness.

'Different enough to make you want to run away from home?'

She shrugged. 'Mum would never talk to me about Dad. Even my birth certificate didn't have his name on it. I wanted to see him but I knew she wouldn't help, so I looked through her old stuff and found a letter from before I was born. It asked for photos of me as I grew up but she never did send him any—I asked him. When Mum makes up her mind about something that's it—you can't get her to change it. Once I had his name it was easy to track him down on the Net and find out that he wasn't some sleazebag of a loser that I was worried he might be—did you know that his law practice even has its own website? I didn't let him know I was coming because he might have got Mum to stop me. I figured once I was here he'd *have* to see me, even if just to get rid of me, but it turned out that he'd wanted to meet me, too…'

'You still took some pretty horrifying chances. Lawyers can be sleazebags too, you know. You could have just written him a letter—'

'And risk it being binned or waiting ages for a reply, or Mum finding out? I had to see him *now*.' Petra modified her urgent tone with a quick grin, 'Before I started having a serious identity crisis that could screw up my entire adulthood. I'm glad he didn't freak out on me or anything—he's a bit heavy-handed with the new Dad thing but otherwise he's real cool, don't you think?—and pretty hunky for an old guy.'

'He's not old,' responded Anya automatically.

Petra gave her a knowing look. 'So you think he's *young* and hunky?'

Anya wasn't falling into that sly trap. 'I try not to think about him at all,' she said. 'Do you want to put one of those on?' She pointed to the CDs.

Petra accepted the change of subject with a shrug. 'I was wondering whether I could borrow these four of Kate Carlyle's. Dad said she's your cousin—does that mean you get freebies?'

Anya laughed. 'I did when Kate first started recording but now she's become so blasé she doesn't usually bother to send them to me any more.'

'Bummer. So most of these—' she ran her fingers over the rack '—you had to go out and buy them full-price like everyone else?'

'Well, yes. But I do get lots of free opera recordings from my parents—see.' She showed her the tapes and CDs.

Actually it was Alistair Grant who despatched them to her, usually without an enclosure. 'My mother is a guest soprano at leading opera houses all over the States and my father travels too, as a conductor.'

'Wow, so music was real important in your family. I bet you got all the music lessons you wanted from the time you were little.'

'The trouble was I *didn't* want them,' she admitted ruefully. 'I showed no musical aptitude whatsoever, thereby convincing my parents they had a changeling in the nest. I would have sacrificed all my lessons for a bit more of their personal attention. Fortunately for their hopes of a musical dynasty, Kate came to live with us and showed herself to be such a piano prodigy it took all the heat off me.' Petra was looking at her as if she couldn't believe her pierced ears. 'I take it you're enjoying *your* piano lessons?'

Petra's face closed up. 'Yeah, but Dad only pays for one hour a week so I babysit to earn the money to pay for an extra lesson.'

'Your *father* pays?' Anya was taken aback. 'But— I thought that there wasn't any contact between Scott and your mother?'

'Not *Scott*. My *other* Dad—Ken—who's married to Mum.'

'I didn't realise your mother was married,' she murmured, wondering uneasily if that had been the case at the time of her affair with Scott.

'Yeah, they just had their tenth anniversary last week,' said Petra, banishing the disturbing spectre of adultery. 'I've got two little brothers.'

Anya thought she saw the light. 'Is that a problem for you? Ken being their real father but not yours?'

'Nah… Lots of my friends have more than one set of parents. The boys are pests, but they're OK. And Ken's an OK guy—he owns a sports store.' She shrugged. '*I'm* the problem, not them.'

Anya was about to ask what she meant when a prickling of the hairs on the back of her neck made her turn around. Scott was standing inside the door with a stillness that suggested he had been there for some time, listening to their conversation.

'You were quick,' she said, thankful that his eyes were resting on his daughter as she remembered the words he had used to chase her inside.

'I told you I knew what I was doing. Can you show me somewhere I can wash up?' He spread out his oily and grease-grimed hands. He'd pushed his sleeves up past his elbows and she could see a few nicks on his wrists. It hadn't been such a straightforward job after all.

'Of course.' She could have told him where the bathroom was but she was so flustered she led him along the hall and into the green and white bathroom. She indicated the pedestal basin but he was looking around at the deep, claw-footed bath—big enough for two—the extensive collection of ornamental glass containers of bath salts and oils decorating the window sill and the fat, scented wax candles dotted on saucers around the room.

His speculative eyes moved to her warm face, intense masculine curiosity forming in the depths.

'Don't you dare say a word,' she warned him.

'Not even to ask you if you have any chemical cleansing cream?' he asked, with an injured innocence that didn't fool her for a moment. He nodded at the sea-shell of miniature soaps on the pedestal. 'I don't want to besmirch your pretty little soaps, sitting on their dish,' he purred.

…*your pretty little breasts, begging to be kissed*…

He was deliberately trying to embarrass her all over again.

'I think there's some in here.' Anya reached past him to open the mirrored bathroom cabinet mounted above the basin. He didn't move out of her way, allowing her arm to brush across his chest, nosing with interest into the contents of her cabinet as she looked for the elusive tube of cream.

'Do you mind?' she said, as he tilted his head to read the prescription off a box of pills.

'You can tell a lot about people from their bathrooms,' he mused. 'For instance, you're obviously healthy, except for a little hay fever now and then. You don't like taking pills any longer than is strictly necessary, you prefer the silky-smoothness of a wet shave to the mechanical kind, you're currently celibate, very protective of your delicate skin, and—' this with a provocative glance towards the bath '—you like to keep yourself very, *very* clean.'

Currently celibate? That slyly buried piece of effrontery was obviously based on the absence of any form of contraception in her bathroom cabinet, but it could only be a wild guess because lots of women kept their contraceptives in a bedside drawer, thought Anya. *She* had, during the holiday in New York after her graduation when she had naively believed that Alistair was going to be the love of her life, before Kate had blazed across his firmament and Anya's flattering attentions had suddenly become an embarrassment.

Anya grabbed the cream and slammed the door shut, almost clipping Scott's nose.

'Be careful, I've had that broken once already,' he said, throwing up a protective hand.

'Disgruntled client?' she enquired tartly, unscrewing the lid and handing him the tube.

'Angry father.'

She had been about to leave, but he must have known that she wouldn't be able to resist the tantalising lure of that brief statement.

'You and your father had a physical fight?' Was that how he had got the scar on his mouth?

He dropped the plug into the basin and nudged the hot water tap on with his forearm, vigorously working the non-foaming cream into his oil-streaked palms. '*He* fought—I dodged…most of the time, until I got big enough not to have to run.'

Her heart dropped into her boots and she felt a familiar, helpless anger. 'You were abused as a child?'

He picked up the nail brush in the shape of an iridescent green fish and began to scrub the tips of his fingers. 'Not until my mother died of cancer when I was ten. Dad had a lot of anger inside him after that, and when he got drunk, which was pretty often, he let fly with his fists. He never touched my sister, though—Joanna's always been the spitting image of Mum—and when I got as big as he was he stopped. Never stopped being angry at the world, though.'

'Didn't anyone ever realise that you were being hurt?' asked Anya.

His shoulders moved dismissively. 'I wasn't hurting half as much as he was. At least I had an escape—a future to run towards. He couldn't break free of the past. He was locked into his pain until the day he died.' He pulled the plug and let the dirty water drain away, rinsing the basin and his raw hands under the cold tap.

'I'm sorry…'

'Pity him, not me.' He turned, holding up his dripping hands like a surgeon waiting for a scrub nurse.

Anya hurriedly passed him the sinfully fluffy green bath sheet from the towel rail.

He dried his hands and then lifted the plush pile to his cheek, turning his face inwards to inhale the faint body scent which lingered in the fibres from her bath the night before. 'Mmm…sumptuous. You're really a closet sensualist, aren't you, Miss Adams? Or, should I say, a *bathroom* sensualist?'

'I thought you were going to call me Anya,' she said, choosing to confront the lesser of two evils.

'I've decided I like Miss Adams. It sounds so…'

She knew what he was going to say and her hand flew up

to cover his mouth, trying to smother this latest outrage. 'Don't say it!'

His eyes slitted wickedly above the blade of her hand, accepting her foolish dare.

'Prissy…' The word was muffled, his lips pursing briefly against the centre of her cupped palm in a sibilant kiss.

She removed her hand and scrubbed it down the side of her skirt, but that didn't rid her of the intimate heat of his mouth.

She glowered at him as he threaded the towel neatly back onto the towel rail. 'You needn't do that. It's going straight into the wash, anyhow.'

'Afraid I've contaminated it?' he murmured, pulling his tight sleeves back down to cover his wrists. He noticed a dollop of grease perched near the hem of his shirt where it hugged his broad hips, and pulled out his handkerchief to dab it off, cursing as it smeared deeper into the thin, breathable material.

'That'll probably never come out now,' Anya told him.

He threw his ruined handkerchief into her bathroom bin and took hold of the bottom of the shirt. 'You're an expert on emergency spills. Shall I take it off? Maybe if you run it through the wash for me straight away…' He curled it away from his skin, giving her a teasing flash of a tanned, washboard stomach and a deliciously furry navel.

'I'm not doing your laundry!' she said, backing to the door. 'I presume that's one of the reasons you employ Mrs Lee.'

'It's just an excuse, really. I thought you might welcome the chance to see me half-naked…sort of even the score between us,' he murmured, prowling after her.

Oh, wouldn't he just love to know she had already seen him stark naked in her fantasies in this very room?

'If I want to even the score I'll just sue you for all the pain and suffering you and your family have caused me,' she hit back, aiming deliberately below the belt. 'If I've already lost my job and my reputation I've got nothing to lose by taking you to court, have I? I bet I could gouge enough out of you to keep me in clover for the rest of my life!'

The threat of legal action had a very satisfying effect. The arrogant smile was wiped off his face, his shoulders straightening, eyes narrowing and jaw jutting. As she moved back down the hall he slipped in front of her, his arm shooting out to slam against the opposite wall, barring her way. 'What do you mean, lost your job? What in the hell did Ransom say to you?'

'That I might be suspended from teaching as part of the school's ''damage control'' if things get messy,' she said.

He swore. 'You're not serious!'

His anger spurred her own. 'Do I *look* as though I'm joking?' She succinctly laid out all Mark's arguments. The sound of Kate playing a Chopin 'Impromptu' had started up in the living room but she still kept her voice low, not wanting Petra to overhear. 'If things do go much further I can probably wave goodbye to my career. An official investigation goes into my teaching record and, even if I'm completely cleared of any wrong-doing, that kind of mud sticks. Even if it *doesn't* get that far I still might find myself struggling to re-establish my credibility—'

His hand fisted against the wall. 'Dammit, why the hell isn't Ransom taking my lead and playing it low-key? I thought you two were supposed to have become *close*—'

'That's why I can't expect any special favours,' she defended Mark, choosing not to make an issue of the insinuating emphasis. 'He has to be above suspicion.'

He made a disparaging sound in his throat. 'Doesn't he realise that it's *his* actions that'll give the thing legs? It'll run all the way to the newspapers if he's not careful.'

'Well, that'll just up the amount of compensatory damages you'll have to pay, won't it? Maybe my neck *is* stiffing up a bit after all. A neck brace has got to be worth a few extra thou.' Anya cupped hand to her nape and flexed her neck with a theatrical little groan.

He dropped his arm. 'Don't issue threats you're not prepared to back up,' he said, his tone containing a little sting of contempt.

'I can back them up and you know it,' she flared. 'You've admitted liability with your apologies. I don't even need a good lawyer to bring a civil suit; I could practically take the case to court myself and win!'

His professional pride recoiled. 'The hell you could!' he exploded quietly. 'I'd eat you for breakfast in any courtroom in the country. You could have the judge in your hip pocket and you still wouldn't be able to screw a red cent out of me.'

'Who's issuing threats now? Did you really think that you could buy me off with a few paltry apologies?'

At first she had merely been taunting, to teach him a lesson, but now Anya wondered whether there wasn't a grain of truth in what she was saying.

His eyes searched hers, an experienced predator looking for the slightest hint of weakness in his prey. 'I thought you didn't want me comparing you to your cousin. You're making it pretty difficult. This is just the kind of stunt I'd expect from her—'

Her steady grey gaze didn't falter. 'Is asking for justice a "stunt" unless *you* happen to be the one doing it?'

'You can dress it up how you like, but this is extortion, pure and simple!'

'I prefer to call it compensation for pain and suffering, both mental and physical—and so will a judge.'

'This is just a bluff,' he guessed shrewdly. 'If it came to the crunch you'd fold. Turn tail and run, like Kate did when things threatened to get sticky. You won't dare take me on. You're bluffing!'

She was amazed and alarmed at her own temerity, but his

assumption that she would never have the guts to stand up for her principles made her dig her heels in. She knew that if she blinked first she could count herself the loser.

'Maybe I am, maybe I'm not.' She folded her arms and raised her eyebrows, the only movement in an otherwise poker face. 'Are you prepared to risk it? The money, the publicity…the implication that your guardianship has been negligent? Or are you willing to settle quietly out of court for an undisclosed sum? Tell me, what's your best offer, Counsellor?'

For a moment she feared he was going to explode, but then the background music paused before the start of Kate's second 'Impromptu' and Scott seemed to use the brief silence to rein himself in and let his astute brain make a lightning reappraisal.

His capitulation, when it came, was calculated and un-equivocal.

He folded his arms and raised her another pair of brows.

'OK. Here's the deal—a one-time, non-negotiable, yes-or-no offer: forget suing and I'll use all my personal influence and financial and legal muscle on your behalf to make sure that you emerge from all this with exactly the same reputa-tion, status, job and prospects that you had going in—'

'You think you can do that?'

'Let me finish. If I succeed, you get no cash—apart from the extremely generous rate I'm prepared to pay you for pri-vately tutoring Petra while she's under my roof. This will not only give out the signal that you have my full support and confidence as a teacher, but also help Petra do something about the appalling grades her mother tells me she's been getting. Lorna thinks she needs more individual attention—of the kind that I doubt she'll get in her regular classes at the college—and, Lorna having once been an excellent teacher herself, I'm prepared to take her word for it.'

Anya's head was whirling. 'Your— Petra's mother was a teacher?'

'Oh, haven't I mentioned it?' he said smoothly. 'Her career came to a rather abrupt end when she admitted she'd been having an affair with a senior student who was doing a scholarship year at the private boys' school where she taught. She was allowed to resign rather than being fired, in order to hush it up...'

Anya felt as if she had swallowed a golf ball. 'Are you saying—when you and she...that she was *your teacher*?'

'Maths with Statistics. The lovemaking was strictly extra-curricular. I got ninety-seven per cent in my final exam—to the relief of the school—and she got to have the baby she'd been wanting—which the school never found out about—so I guess you could say it was a mutually beneficial relationship.

'With a precedent like that you can see why I might have overreacted to the circumstances in which I found you and Sean at the party. Women teachers *do* sometimes overstep the moral boundaries, Anya.'

'I—yes, I suppose so...' she faltered, knowing full well that he had blindsided her with his startling revelation in order to soften her up for the kill, and sure enough he moved ruthlessly in.

'So, what's your answer? Do we have a deal?'

'You only mention what happens if you succeed.' She - struggled to rise above the turmoil of her emotions. 'What if you fail?'

'If you don't come out of this smelling like a rose, then you can name your own figure.' Her eyes widened at the rashness of his words but he arrogantly disabused her. 'But it's not going to happen. I never fail. Remember that, Anya. When I set out to achieve something, I never give up and I never give in. One way or another I get what I want. So make your choice. Yes or no?'

CHAPTER SIX

'YOU know, if you can express yourself like this, I don't understand why you're getting such low marks in subjects that require essay-writing,' said Anya, laying the handwritten page she had just read beside her on the dappled grass. She leaned back on her hands and studied the girl sprawled on her stomach in front of her. 'Your grammar and punctuation are a bit sloppy but you seem to have bags of creativity.'

'Too much, my teachers say. My ideas are too radical for them, though I don't see why I shouldn't liven up the facts when they get too boring,' Petra replied cheerfully, in between bites at the apple which she had plucked off the tree above them and polished against her ubiquitous black top.

Scott had insisted that the tutoring take place under his own roof, but over the past three days Anya had discovered that the conventional use of table and chairs and structured lessons were not always conducive to Petra's concentration. Sean had been conspicuous by his avoidance, but Samantha had gaggles of friends coming and going and Scott, too, was a powerfully distracting presence. Anya had found it more productive to find a peaceful spot amongst the orchard trees where the casual surroundings caused Petra to relax and open up rather than regard their discussions as a dismal chore.

Every now and then they would see Scott disappear off in his Jag, presumably for court appearances or meetings with clients, but for the most part he seemed to be working out of his study—or *trying* to.

'It's because of me,' Petra had brashly confided on the second day. 'Sam says she hardly used to see him before I came, because he was always at work, but he's sorta trying to hang out around here for my sake. You know—*be there* for me. He bought this *parenting* book, for God's sake—I saw it in his study: *Bringing up a Teenager in the New Millennium* or something equally dorky.' The rolling of her eyes hadn't quite concealed her sneaking satisfaction.

'I don't think I "thrive in a formal classroom setting",' said Petra now, rearing up to hurl her core accurately over the fence into the depths of a bank of low-growing shrubs.

Anya smiled wryly at the direct quotation from one of Petra's report cards. She had said much the same thing to Liz Crawford when she had dropped by the school office to pick up a copy of Petra's timetable and some texts and syllabus information.

'She obviously has intelligence, she just doesn't choose to focus it. Music is the only subject where she appears to score consistently high marks.'

Liz shook her dark curls as she handed over the requested photocopies. 'You're a glutton for punishment. First that camp and now this. I thought you were going to be selfish with the rest of your holiday…work on that essay of yours.'

'I can do that in the mornings—I don't go over to The Pines until after lunch. Anyway, I *am* being selfish. I'm doing this to allay people's fears that I'm *persona non grata* with the board's legal eagle and a bad influence on their kids. It's starting to work, too. You'd be amazed at the number of parents I've run into, or acquaintances who ring me up, and happen to mention that they've heard I'm teaching Scott's daughter—'

'Hah! That's only because they're trying to pump you for information,' was the cynical reply. 'Scott Tyler turning out to have a fourteen-year-old daughter nobody's ever heard of is big news around here. I hope she handles attention well, because she's going to get quite a bit of it on her first few days of school…'

'Oh, I think she'll handle it,' Anya had murmured and,

looking at Petra now, she wondered whether 'craves it' might have been a more accurate description. The girl was certainly no shrinking violet.

She waved away a lazy fruit fly that was trying to land on her bare knee. The Indian summer was still rolling on and she had worn a sleeveless sundress to cope with the heat. 'Maybe if you tried looking on essay-writing in the same way that you look on music—as containing a set of classical conventions that need to be followed in order for you to fully express your ideas in the medium, in a way that your audience can understand and appreciate—'

'OK, OK, I get it,' said Petra, selecting and buffing up another late-season windfall. 'You think I'm paying too much attention to one subject. So does Mum. She knows what I want to be, but she keeps saying I can't put all my eggs in one basket, that I'll need qualifications to fall back on if I can't make it as a musician.' She shrugged her thin shoulders, tipping the apple from hand to hand—drawing attention to the wide span of her palms and long, flexible fingers. 'She and Dad—my other Dad—think that if I cut down on my piano lessons I could put more energy into my other work, but it doesn't work like that.'

She tossed the apple into Anya's lap, amidst the pattern of dark red flowers which decorated her simple shift.

Bingo! thought Anya. Was this part of what had brought her winging across the Tasman Sea? 'It *is* a very tough profession,' she cautioned. 'You need a lot of luck as well as loads of talent and a ton of ruthless ambition.'

'I have talent. I'm ambitious.'

'No kidding?' Anya held up the shiny but misshapen and skin-blemished fruit. 'You're not trying to bribe the teacher into taking sides, are you?'

Petra grinned. 'Would it work?'

Anya crunched into the sweet overripe flesh. 'Not a chance.'

Petra's eyes suddenly brightened and she sat up, then tried to look nonchalant as she waved a casual hand. 'Hi, Dad.'

'Mind if I join you, or am I interrupting the lesson at a critical juncture?' Since Scott was already plunking himself down between them on the grass he considered the question already answered.

'Nope. Miss Adams was just complimenting me on my terrific essay,' said Petra, confident that Anya's mouthful of apple would give her a few moments' grace before the inevitable qualification.

Anya cupped her hand over the spurt of juice which chose just that moment to run down her chin. Unfortunately she had left her handbag in the house and she surreptitiously felt for a spare piece of paper to serve as a napkin.

'Here, allow me.' Scott produced a handkerchief, but instead of passing it to her to use he tilted up her chin with his knuckles, nudged her hand aside and mopped up the glistening moisture himself, paying particular attention to the primly tucked corners of her sticky pink mouth, his eyes sparkling with amusement at her chagrin.

Some of the juice ended up on his fingers and he licked at them unselfconsciously with a limber tongue.

'Mmm, sweet yet tart…just the way I like it,' he approved, his lazy-eyed look making Anya think of everything but apples. She mistrusted him in this kind of whimsical mood. She had earlier seen him in a grey suit, dictating to someone over the speaker phone in his study, but now he was in jeans and a blue Hawaiian shirt—purpose-dressed for lounging out in the open. He hadn't just wandered out here for a passing hello.

'Thank you,' she muttered grudgingly, as she swallowed the rest of her mouthful. She looked down at the apple in her hand, suddenly having lost her appetite.

'Fair exchange.' Scott laid his handkerchief over her sticky hand and took the apple, taking a slow bite from where she had left off. He stretched out on his side, propping his chin on his hand, and Anya hurriedly curled her bare legs the opposite way, tucking the hem of her dress securely around her knees. 'So, what have you two been talking about?' he asked, watching her smooth the dark green fabric down over her slender thighs.

Predictably, Petra chose not to talk about schoolwork. 'Miss Adams has been telling me how she used to come here when she was little and this was her uncle's farm. She got to feed pigs and see them get born, and milk cows with her hands and stuff like that.'

Scott didn't demand to know what that had to do with the fourth-form syllabus. He grinned at Anya from behind his apple.

'I see the sophisticated young Sydney-sider isn't sure whether to be impressed or grossed-out.' He squinted at her as he took another bite and she knew he was going to say something provocative. 'So…you were a pink-cheeked milk-maid before you became a teacher…'

His smile mocked her with the clichéd traditional image of a plump, glowing-skinned young woman of earthy good humour and easy virtue.

'I was only a child at the time, but actually I wouldn't have minded being a farmer,' she reproved him, sprinkling her tacky fingers with water from the bottle which she had lain in the shade of the tree-trunk, and wiping them dry with his handkerchief.

'Or a farmer's wife? Is that why you moved out here to the country, to improve your prospects with the local yeo-manry?'

'I don't happen to see marriage as a valid method of achieving my career goals. I have more respect for the spirit of the institution than that,' she told him, tilting her nose and for once having the luxury of being able to look down on him.

'Huh?' Petra's gold-tipped fringe tickled her wrinkled brow.

'Miss Adams holds to the romantic view—she wants to marry for love, not money,' her father extrapolated. 'Though I suspect, like most people, she might find mutual respect and liking a more durable prospect.'

'That's a very cynical view—'

'As you've pointed out before, I'm a product of my experience—as you're obviously a product of yours. I take it your parents still have a strong marriage…?'

'As far as I'm aware, yes,' she said firmly, wondering if he was going to pick on her privileged background again as he had at her interview. 'They spend a lot of time apart because of the demands of their careers, but it doesn't seem to have weakened their relationship.'

'All that travelling and performing can't have left much time for bringing up a child.'

'Miss Adams had a nanny and tutors and music teachers from when she was a baby 'til she went to boarding school,' supplied Petra eagerly.

'Accelerated learning?' murmured Scott, and Anya gave an involuntary laugh.

'Not in my case. My parents realised pretty quickly that I was never going to set the world on fire with my genius.'

'Did you want to?'

She shook her head. 'No. No…funnily enough I never did. I was shy, and often sick when we were travelling. All the fuss and emotional drama that my parents created wherever they went made me happy to be left in the background. I was glad not to be trotted out to show off my budding accomplishments. The only thing I was any good at was reading, but, as I was telling Petra, if you love books then the world is your oyster.'

'I used to read with a torch under the blankets,' said Scott, and Anya slipped him a surprised smile of fellow-feeling.

'My nannies always used to search my bed before they turned the lights out.'

'You had more than one?'

'Only one at a time. But, as I said, we moved about a lot, and my mother was always very…*particular* about personal staff. They had to have the right vibes. She always seemed to be in the throes of hiring or firing someone.'

'But you didn't bring a nanny whenever you came here?' said Petra, waving at the house.

'No, my aunt and uncle looked after me.'

'And Cousin Kate…' murmured Scott in a neutral voice that made her give him a wary look.

'Cousin Kate soon worked out that I thought it was great fun to do the farm chores that she hated,' she said lightly.

'Don't tell me…she had you whitewashing the picket fence.' Scott surprised her with a rich chuckle, adding to his mystified daughter, 'If you want to know what we're talking about, I suggest you try reading some Mark Twain.' He finished off the apple and tossed the core in the same direction that Petra had chosen, but to a considerably greater distance.

Anya watched with a poignant sense of wistful yearning as he and his daughter talked, fascinated by the mixture of boldness and tentativeness on both sides, the hunger and hesitation that tangled their lines of communication.

A little while later, encouraged by Scott's relaxed responses into further reminiscences about life on the farm and how, a few years after her aunt and uncle's death, she had been happy to come back to boarding school in Auckland while Kate had remained with her parents in New York to continue her intensive music studies, Anya suddenly realised that she had just been the victim of a very subtle form of cross-examination.

'I'm sorry, you shouldn't have let me run on like that,' she said, reaching for a taste from the drink bottle, her dry throat telling her she had been doing far too much talking and too little listening.

'So you and your cousin were sort of born to the wrong set of parents, and then you swapped lives, except that *you* never got to live at Riverview again until now,' Petra worked out.

'You obviously had a far greater sentimental attachment to the farm than Kate,' said Scott quietly. 'It must have been quite a wrench when she sold it, but at least you knew she still owned The Pines up until five years ago.' He sat up to face her with a smooth tightening of his internal muscles, draping one long arm over a bent knee, his other leg still outstretched. 'Did you ever consider the possibility of buying the house yourself when she told you she was putting it on the market?' He watched her grey eyes skate away from his and performed one of the intuitive leaps that made him such a formidable lawyer. 'Or didn't she tell you until after the deed was done?'

Anya shrugged, her finger tracing one of the dark red flowers at the hem of her dress where it was drawn taut across her knees. 'It wasn't as if I could have afforded to pay what she was asking, she knew that—'

'But she was family.' Petra hit the nail on the head. 'Wouldn't she have sold it to you on the cheap or something, if you'd told her you wanted it?'

'It would have saved her several thousand in real estate fees for a start,' commented Scott. 'Did you ever ask her to give you first refusal, or hold the mortgage for you, Anya?'

'It was her inheritance from her parents. I couldn't expect her to forfeit that. At the time she sold she was facing a hefty bill for back taxes; she needed the money up front—'

'You offered what you could, but it wasn't enough,' he guessed shrewdly. 'Wouldn't your parents help you out? They must be loaded.'

'The lifestyle they lead is also extremely expensive to

maintain. I've been self-supporting since I left school and I like it that way. Of course they've paid for trips for me to visit them, and are generous with gifts, but my parents and I inhabit completely separate lives. Anyway, regardless of how much money they have, it's appallingly bad manners to treat one's parents as if they're a bank—' She missed the flash of discomfort on Petra's face, preoccupied as she was with Scott's infuriating expression of knowing sympathy.

'So you asked, but the folks turned you down.'

'Will you stop trying to turn me into Little Orphan Annie?' she said in exasperation, stiffening at the slight hint of sympathy. 'They would have given me the money towards an apartment in the city, but I didn't want that. I'm perfectly happy in the house that I've got! The Pines would have been way too big for me, and I never could have afforded the renovations it obviously needed on top of everything else—'

'So you don't resent me for owning it?'

'That would be as pointless as you resenting me for being related to the person who sold it to you.'

'Touché.' He saluted her with a finger to the centre of his broad temple.

'When you used to stay here, which was your room?' asked Petra, looking up at the wall from which the creeper had already been pruned ruthlessly back to first-floor level.

'The upstairs has changed around since I was here—there were never any *en suite* bathrooms for a start—but Kate and I used to share a corner room where that gable looks out over the back, one with a trapdoor to the attic.'

'Sam's room,' said Scott, saving her from the frisson it would have caused her to know that it was now his.

'This house has an attic?' Petra said. 'Cool! What's up there?'

Anya could feel the blood throb guiltily in her veins. She had tried to push Kate's problem to the back of her mind, but every now and then it loomed oppressively large in her thoughts. Scott had provided her with both alibi and opportunity when he had invited her to tutor Petra, but the moment Anya moved to act on her cousin's request she would be crossing an invisible line, violating a code of ethics that was integral to her self-respect.

'A lot of dirt, cobwebs and boring old furniture, I expect,' Scott replied. 'That's all that seemed to be up there when I did my first tour of inspection and I never bothered to have it cleaned out. I suppose the builders added a bit of extra debris of their own.'

A series of high-pitched squeals and boisterous splashing rose from the other side of the house and Petra heaved a huge, martyred sigh.

'It sounds as if Sam and her friends are having a good time in the pool. Why don't you go around and join them?' suggested Scott.

She had leaped to her feet even before he'd finished his sentence, but then she hovered briefly, looking at Anya.

'But what about Miss Adams?'

He smiled and a small shiver went up Anya's spine. 'I'll look after Miss Adams.'

Petra's pang of conscience evaporated on the instant. 'OK. Thanks, Dad. See ya!'

'See you tomorrow, Petra. And don't forget to read that biology chapter!' Anya called after her.

'I won't!'

'Will she?' asked Scott settling back. 'Perhaps accidentally on purpose?'

Anya shook her head. 'She's been pretty good. Once she sets her mind to something she does it. She's very quick on the uptake.'

Scott's mouth adopted a wry twist. 'I've noticed.' He watched his daughter round the corner of the house. 'She's incredibly sophisticated in some ways and terrifyingly naive in others. I just don't get why she needs all that defensive bravado—the black clothes, the hair, the ears, the *nose*, for God's sake. I suppose I should be grateful that she isn't sporting a tongue-stud and tattoo!'

He turned his head and glimpsed the tail end of Anya's secret smile. 'What?'

She shook her head, starting to gather up the books that were scattered on the grass. 'Nothing.'

Her blatant nonchalance made his eyes narrow. 'Yes, it is. You're wearing that damned Mona Lisa look. You know something that I don't. What is it?'

'Mona Lisa?' Anya murmured, her grey eyes wide.

His hand closed around her arm as she reached for a folder, his expression dangerously playful. She had learned to beware that devilish look. 'That enigmatic smile that tiptoes around your mouth when you think you have me at a disadvantage. What aren't you telling me that I ought to know?'

'I really couldn't say—' she began demurely, and then squeaked as he tumbled her backwards onto the grass, pinning her wrists on either side of her head.

'Are you ticklish, Miss Adams?'

A horrified giggle of nervous anticipation bubbled up in her throat as she looked up into his teasing face. 'No!'

He had lowered his hard body to press against her side, and registered her ripple of tension at his question.

'I think you're lying,' he murmured, his eyes insufferably smug. He slowly drew her wrists above her head, gathering them into one of his large hands. The other he allowed to trickle lightly down her ribs. 'Shall we test my theory?'

Anya bit back another betraying giggle. 'This is highly inappropriate behaviour,' she said sternly, as he stilled her squirming by sliding a heavy calf across her ankles.

'Inappropriate to what?' The smell of crushed grass mingled with the spicy scent of warm male skin, overlaid with a tang of sweet apple as his face hovered sinfully close.

'T-to our relationship,' she quavered as his fingertips

stirred against her ribs, and watched as a sultry spark began to smoulder in his blue eyes. Now it was his body that was invaded with tension, chasing out some of the playfulness.

'And what exactly *is* our relationship?' His words whispered across her lips. 'Partners in a hostile deal? Co-conspirators? Combatants? Friends?'

'I—we—' The stirring of his hips against her slender thigh brought her faltering to a stop, her smoky grey eyes filling with a fatal curiosity that was irresistibly alluring to the predatory male who held her captive.

'Perhaps it's time we found out...'

His hand contracted with deliberate intent, surprising a gasp of laughter from her that parted her lips for his sensuous pleasure and he immediately settled in to stake his claim, his hand stroking back up her body to cup the side of her face, guiding her deeper into the kiss, his chest crushing her breasts as he moved over her, slanting his head to seek greater access to her silken surrender.

Anya's fingers curled helplessly into her leashed palms as her curiosity was stunningly satisfied, and then swiftly transmuted into a fierce craving that arched her trembling body against his dominating weight. She murmured under his mouth and he recognised the heated encouragement of a woman desirous of greater pleasures, his nostrils flaring at the piquant scent of her startled arousal, his tongue dipping further into the moist interior, delicately teasing the slick satin walls of her most sensitive inner surfaces, his hand relaxing on her captive wrists, sliding sensuously down her slender bare arms to fold them one by one around his powerful shoulders.

The sun shone through the leafy branches overhead, creating a dancing dazzle against her closed eyelids as Anya sank beneath rippling waves of ever-widening pleasure, utterly open to his demanding passion, her breasts aching as they rubbed against his chest. Her short, sensible nails dug desperately into the back of his polo shirt and he seemed to know instantly what she needed, his big hand seeking out the slight weight of her breast, cupping it through the thin fabric of her dress, his long thumb circling the hardened nipple, teasing at it until her breath sobbed in his mouth and he rewarded her eagerness with a gentle twist of thumb and forefinger that sent a gush of hot pleasure pooling between her thighs.

In spite of her enthralment she felt a tiny nudge of shock at the intensity of her feelings. For the first time in her life she appreciated the validity of the excuse 'swept away by passion'. Her eyes flew open to glimpse his, brilliant with reckless male triumph and a slightly dazed wildness that made her heart melt.

'Scott—'

His hard mouth curved against her lips. 'Hush…I know…it feels good, doesn't it…?' She could taste his rising hunger, hear the husky rasp of his breath, feel the urgent thrust of his desire as he nipped and suckled at her lower lip, his hands moving down to shape her slim hips to his need, his fingers curving into her soft bottom.

It felt more than good. Anya pushed at his shoulders. 'Stop… We can't do this,' she panted.

For a moment she feared that he wasn't going to pay any attention to her protest, but then he rolled off her with a groan, lying flat on his back in the grass, his eyes closed, his chest rising and falling in a shallow, uneven rhythm.

Anya sat up, shakily rearranging her twisted dress and tidying her hair.

'Why don't you take it down?' Scott had opened his eyes and was watching her with unblinking curiosity. 'What's the point of having long hair if you never wear it loose?'

'It's cooler like this,' she said.

'You mean more schoolmarmy. If you think you're turning

me off you're mistaken. Or maybe you're trying to remind me of my historical weakness for schoolteachers?'

His sly reference to Petra's mother made her flush and his chuckle was low and taunting.

'You don't look in the least cool any more. You look deliciously hot and bothered.'

'You shouldn't have grabbed me like that—'

'Why?' He pushed himself up on his hands. 'We both enjoyed it, didn't we? Where's the harm in a couple of adults having a little harmless frolic in the sun?'

Harmless? Anya felt faint.

'You have impressionable teenagers around,' she told him severely. 'What would their parents say if some of them went home and told them that they'd seen you…that you….'

'Were rolling in the grass with some brazen hussy?'

'We're trying to rehabilitate my reputation, not give people even *more* to gossip about,' she reminded him.

He tilted his head. 'Then you shouldn't have kissed me back with such enthusiasm.'

She was stumped for a crushing answer. 'I—you took me by surprise.'

He shouted with laughter. 'I see, so when you're *prepared* to be kissed, you don't kiss back. That must make your dates with Mark Ransom pretty disappointing for the poor guy.'

How he would crow if he knew they had only got as far as a swift peck on the cheek! 'What makes you think that *he* doesn't surprise me?'

He ticked her a lopsided grin. 'He's the boy scout type— he'd make sure you knew what was coming. I bet, to Ransom, every woman's a lady…'

'Whereas to you…?'

'Every lady is a tramp,' he said with typical provocativeness.

'And you have the nerve to wonder that your daughter sets out to shock!' she scoffed, beginning to gather up the books again. 'I hope you weren't including your mother in that crude remark.'

Her pointed barb missed its mark. 'My mother would have laughed if I'd called her a lady,' he told her. 'She was a barmaid—frank and full of beans, always seeing the bright side of life and the best of people. We lived in a pretty tough part of west Auckland and she worked long hours at the pub, but she always managed to find something to laugh about. She brought us up rough but right.'

So that was where his strong sense of justice came from, and his preference for defending the underdog, for taking on cases that other lawyers considered to be lost causes.

'Speaking of rough, are you going to tell me what you were smiling about, or do we get to have another torrid tussle on the grass?' he said, scattering her empathetic thoughts.

Anya sighed, hugging the books defensively to her breast. 'It's fake.'

He looked bewildered. 'What is?'

'Petra's nosering. It's a clip-on.'

'*What?* Are you sure?'

She took advantage of his stunned reaction to rise to her feet, flexing her cramped legs. 'Trust me. I worked at a school where unauthorised body piercings were an expelling offence, whereas jewellery-wearing only merited confiscation. I had a drawerful of the things.'

'The little devil!' He stood up beside her, eyes gleaming with wry admiration. 'She *knew* I was biting my tongue not to criticise it—or her mother for letting her have it done.'

'She's testing you.'

He bent to pick up her water bottle and fell into step beside her as she walked towards the house, intending to collect her handbag which was being looked after by the taciturn Mrs Lee.

'I suppose I lose points for things like sending her to her

room when she's rude to Sean and making her take extra lessons.'

'Actually, I think it makes her feel safe with you. She's obviously used to discipline at home, because she has very good manners when she cares to display them, so when you demand a certain standard from her you're indicating that you care about her future. She's also secretly impressed that you're making the effort to work from home so you can be with her.' She slipped a sideways glance up at him and was startled and amused to see him blushing to the tips of his ears.

'Yes, well...I don't know how much longer I can keep it up,' he gruffed in an attempt to hide his pleasure. 'I can't continue pushing cases off onto my partners, but I don't want her to think that now the novelty of her arrival's worn off I'm abandoning her.'

'I don't think there's any danger of that. She'll be starting school in a few days, and if she's bussing with Sean and Samantha she won't be home herself until half-past four.'

'And then she'll have a couple of hours under your supervision...' he murmured, busily constructing himself a mental timetable. He saw her step falter and gave her a frowning look. 'You agreed to the bargain. Even if everything works out for you as smoothly as I planned, I still expect you to continue with the tutoring. You've seen for yourself how much Petra benefits from individual guidance and you've already established a close rapport. She needs you.'

Petra wasn't the only one. Over the next several days Scott continued to invite himself to join them, and although Anya took care not to be left alone with him again, she soon realised that she was being utilised by both father and daughter as a kind of emotional buffer, a neutral third party through whom they could filter their curiosity about each other without directly confronting their feelings.

On Saturday evening Mark rang Anya just as she was putting the finishing touches to her essay on the cultural impact of taste and consumerism, to tell her that the head of the Information Technology department had tracked down the hacker who had posted the party invitation on the bulletin board. It had turned out to be a student who was already on probation for serious misuse of the school's computer system. A suspension had been handed down and the trouble-making parent's threatening rumbles had been considerably dampened by her son's identification as the purchaser of several bottles of hard liquor for his under-age friends.

Once back at college Anya found that she had to fend off intrusive remarks and irritating jokes from staff and suffer back-chat from more than the usual number of smart-mouthed kids, but by clinging to her usual good-humoured tolerance she rode out the initial flurry of interest and thereafter the fresh scandal of the hockey coach who was having a not-so-discreet affair with the wife of the caretaker took precedence in the collective imagination.

She and Petra adjusted their schedules and for two hours in the early evening, while Sean sweated on his uncle's fitness machine in the pool-room to compensate for his lost rugby training and Samantha breezed through her own homework between phone calls, Anya went over any problems with that day's lessons and helped Petra with her homework. The only thing that stumped Anya was the maths, but fortunately Samantha had an aptitude for the subject and proved willing to revisit some of her previous years' work with her younger cousin. Just before the two hours were up there would be the throaty purr of the Jag in the driveway and Anya would shortly find herself sitting in the living room sipping dry sherry or a frosty lime-and-tonic while Scott nursed a vodka and Petra plied him for the lurid details of his latest case in between swigs of Coke.

Late Friday afternoon, as she was leaving school, Anya

received an unexpected dinner invitation from Mark. Caught off guard, she instinctively demurred but he was flatteringly persistent and, remembering that Petra had said that her father was going out for the evening, Anya suddenly decided to set aside her recent disenchantment with Mark and defiantly enjoy their delayed date.

Deciding to get the day's tutoring over early, so she had plenty of time to get ready, she called in at The Pines on the way home from school instead of popping home first, as she usually did.

Sean answered the door, no longer flinching at the sight of her, and saw her glance at the line of suitcases against the wall. She had forgotten that he and Samantha were due to return home today.

'Mum and Dad flew back from LA last night,' he confirmed. 'Mum's on her way over now, to pick us up.' He wasn't looking overly enthusiastic, probably anticipating his parents' reaction to the reason for his not yet being back at rugby training.

She murmured an appropriate response and he jerked his head in the direction of the closed door along the hall in response to her enquiry about Petra.

'She's in there...banging away at the piano or listening to CDs, I guess. She spends ages shut in there by herself. Screams blue murder if you try to sneak in and listen to her playing,' he groused.

Perhaps Anya's knock was a little soft accidentally on purpose. The sound-proofing of the room was so good she could hear the music only by putting her head close to the panelled wood but when she quietly opened the door the sound of a Bach 'Partita' spilled into her ears in all its exquisite clarity. She stilled when she realised that the superb technical skill and luminous delicacy of emotion wasn't flowing from any stereo speakers but from the young girl seated at the piano, her face intent on her flying fingers.

Anya stood by the partly open door, not moving until the vibrant humour of the final *gigue* faded into silence. She didn't applaud; she was too full of admiration and anger. 'You're good.'

Petra quietly put down the lid of the piano. 'I know.'

Anya moved to sit beside her on the edge of piano stool. 'No, I'm mean *you're good.*' Her voice carried a gravity that extended beyond mere words. 'I may not be able to carry a tune myself but I've lived amongst musicians; I've listened to greatness and I know pure, raw genius when I hear it.' She took the girl's restless hands in hers and looked down sternly into the piquant face. 'Both of us know what it takes to play the way that you do. The dedication it takes, especially in one so young. So what are you doing here, Petra? And I don't mean that stuff you gave your dad about wanting to know the other half of your heritage. What is it that you *really* want from him?'

Petra's grip tightened to the point of pain, her blue eyes dangerously overbright. 'Mum and Dad can't afford for me to go overseas to study. They just haven't got the money— not with Brian and David to provide for, too. Even if I win a scholarship, I'd still need extra money. I could work and save up, but I can't wait that long. I need to go *soon*, Miss Adams. I don't just want to be good, I want to be *great*. But I'm already fourteen; if I'm going to reach my full potential my teachers say I need to start intensive full-time study *now*.'

Petra's face was pale but determined. 'When I found out about my dad—my real dad—I thought he could help me. You know, if he got to know me first, and like me and everything…'

'And then you'd spring a guilt trip on him that he owes you the money because he didn't stick around when you were born,' said Anya, aware that the child had been hoist by her own petard. She might have come looking for a financial backer for her talent, but she had found so much more. And now she was feeling thoroughly torn by her conflicting feelings.

Petra's short nails dug into the backs of Anya's hands. 'I know he was just a kid back then, but he's not any more. In spite of what Mum said, he *wants* to be my dad. He can afford to help me, and I know he would want me to be the best that ever I can be. I *know* he would!'

'Yes, he would,' sighed Anya. 'But, please, for his sake, try and put it to him diplomatically.'

'As soon as I found out that Kate Carlyle was your cousin I knew you'd understand!' Petra burst out, bouncing to her feet. 'You think he should give me the money, too, don't you?'

'For God's sake, don't tell your father that!'

'Don't tell me what?'

Scott, tall and intimidating in a dark pinstriped suit, had slipped in the door. The man had the most incredibly awful timing. He was always turning up when and where Anya least expected him.

Petra grinned, unable to hide her hyped-up state, and Anya knew she was going to blow the whole thing wide open.

'That I came over here to ask you to cough up for me to study at the best music school that I can get to accept me as a student!'

Scott's head whipped around to Anya, still sitting on the piano stool. 'Is this your idea?'

Petra shook her head emphatically, intercepting his steely look. 'Nah, she only listened to me play and realised how good I am.' It was said completely without boastfulness or irony. 'She didn't want me to hurt your feelings—like, make you feel all twisted up that the only reason I wanted to meet you is so that I could screw money out of you.'

'And was it?'

'Well, yeah,' she admitted, lifting her pointed chin. 'But that was before I met you...'

'God knows why, but I find myself understanding that incredible piece of contorted reasoning,' he murmured. 'Ambitious, aren't you?'

Even though he wasn't showing the glimmer of a smile, Petra heard the rueful pride in his voice and her cocky smile returned. 'It's in the genes.'

'Like being cunning and conniving.' He grinned back, and something inside Anya relaxed with a slithery sigh.

He was tough, both inside and out, and, most fortunate of all for Petra, he was a realist and a consummate game-player himself. Conniving and lying he could understand—even respect—if it had an honourable purpose; it was hypocrisy which he despised. And Petra had never pretended to be anything other than what she was—his bold, wilful and outrageously different daughter.

'I only learned to play the piano as an adult, so it's impossible to compare any genetic similarity there. Exactly how much of a prodigy are you?' he quizzed. 'Whenever I suggested you play for me you acted like you weren't in the mood or were too shy…' And he would have been too wary of alienating her to insist, thought Anya, and secretly hurt that his daughter didn't appear to want to share with him the one area in which she was an achiever at school.

'Because that would have given the game away,' Anya told him. 'You would have instantly realised that she was holding out on you. Her sort of talent would turn ''Chopsticks'' into a bravura performance.'

Petra immediately sat down and flipped up the keyboard, producing a sizzling set of variations on the simple, plunking rhythm that made them all laugh. She then segued into some Mozart, and her whole attitude changed, her head drooping, her face becoming tense and absorbed as she concentrated on the moving intensity of the difficult passage.

When she at last folded her hands in her lap, Scott turned

to Anya with a dazed look that reflected her own feelings when she had first heard Petra play.

'What do you think?' he asked thickly.

He already knew. The room was lined with rows of bookcases filled with books, but also an eclectic collection of records, tapes and CDs from country and western to a large block of classical recordings. So either Kate had lied about Scott saying he didn't like classical music…or he had lied to Kate.

'I think you should be proud of her. You have an extremely gifted child.' His blue eyes were glittering as he struggled against an upsurge of emotion, moved not only by the music but by an overflowing sense of paternal pride. 'And I think you and your daughter should talk about what she intends to do with her gift. Alone.'

He and his daughter looked at each other and Anya held her breath. She wasn't sure who moved first, but suddenly Scott and his daughter were hugging each other, and he was pressing a kiss on the top of her ruffled head, his eyes squeezed closed as his arms contracted around her skinny frame, burying her snuffling nose in his jacket. Anya swallowed a lump in her throat as she backed out of the door. This was no time for anything as mundane as schoolwork. It was the first time she had seen the pair of them spontaneously touch each other and knew that another important barrier had been breached—in the politically correct world it had become practically taboo for an older man to show physical affection towards an unrelated female child, and that was how they had both been acting. But now Scott and Petra were truly father and daughter, bonded in trust as well as in blood.

She was wiping the moisture away from the corner of her eyes as she reached the front door and almost cannoned into a big, chestnut-haired woman coming up the front steps.

She knew Joanna Monroe by sight from her volunteer work in the school's tuck shop, but had got the impression

she was a little stand-offish for all her air of bustling con-
geniality so she was taken aback when the woman lifted the
sunglasses from her nose to reveal pale blue eyes and beamed
her a wide, friendly smile.

'Hello, Miss Adams. Or I suppose I should call you Anya
now. Scott told me when I rang last week that you were
helping him sort out his daughter's problems. I must say, I
was as mad as a wet hen when Gary insisted I go and play
corporate wife on his conference trip just when Scott needed
me! Of course, I knew he had a daughter, but none of us
ever expected her to drop in unannounced like this, least of
all Scott! I hope he's not too shell-shocked, poor lamb, what
with my two to look after as well. Not that *they're* likely to
give him much problem, and he does have Mrs Lee here six
days a week—' She had said it all with barely a pause for
breath and as she hesitated to draw her second wind she
noticed Anya's repressed smile.

'What? What did I say? Am I running on like an idiot?—
sorry—I tend to do that. I'm sorry I never said hello to you
before but I didn't realise you and Scott were on such *friendly*
terms.' She gave Anya a disconcerting wink. 'He did try and
act close-mouthed on me but I can always winkle these things
out of him, even though he got rather tangled up in his own
tongue when he talked about you. He said you were infuriating but you made him laugh and I thought *Oh, good*, at
last because it's ages since he's had any real *fun* in his life.
In his job everything is so depressing and serious, and Scott
has such a highly developed sense of humour—well, you'd
know that, wouldn't you? It's just a pity you're related to
that *wretched* woman—sorry, she's your cousin and I know
I shouldn't say that—'

'You mean Kate Carlyle?' interrupted Anya, in fear that
Joanna Monroe was never going to run down.

'Yes, and I know I shouldn't say any more because Scott
will kill me but—well, one minute she's cuddling up to him

all lovey-dovey, and rabbiting on about giving up her career for him and the next—bang! She's gone without a single word. Not even a Dear John letter to tell him why she went, just a note from her agent about a concert booking. She dumped poor Scott two weeks later by e-mail—*e-mail*, can you believe it!'

Anya could, and she couldn't.

There was a pain in her chest so intense she could hardly breathe. Scott and Kate had had an *affair*?

'Are you saying that Scott was *in love* with Kate?'

'Well, I don't know about *in love*. Scott always plays his cards pretty close to his chest. But he must have been fairly deeply involved to be so devastated by her leaving. He virtually stopped dating for a whole *year* afterwards, and since then he's never even come *close* to finding a suitable woman to marry. Sometimes I think he never will…'

CHAPTER SEVEN

'WHAT a coincidence, look who's sitting over by the window—it's Tyler with Heather Morgan. They must have arrived while I was ordering drinks. Why don't I go over and say hello and see if they'd like to come and join us…?'

Anya almost dropped the menu she had been studying, her body stiffening with horror, her eyes rigidly fixed on the man across the table. 'No, Mark, please, I'd rather it was just us—I hardly know Miss Morgan—'

But Mark was already getting to his feet, smiling and nodding in the direction she refused to look. 'It's too late now, they've seen me. Besides, you should see it as a chance to get to know her better. It's good politics to be friendly with people like the Morgans…'

'They're on a date; they'd probably much rather be left alone,' said Anya desperately, but she was talking to thin air as Mark strolled across the busy restaurant to the table where the other couple were being fussed over by the head waiter.

Coincidence? Anya would rather call it horrific bad luck. The old-fashioned pub restaurant was popular with people from Riverview because it was halfway between the town and the motorway which was the main commuter corridor between the city of Auckland and all points south, but she wouldn't have thought it stylish enough for Heather Morgan's tastes. She was certainly among the most smartly dressed, in a glittery red cocktail dress, while her companion—leaning back in his chair to speak to Mark—was more subdued but no less elegant in a dark suit, where most of the other men in the restaurant were in sports jackets or shirt-sleeves. His eyes flicked past Mark to capture Anya's unsmiling gaze, and she felt a rush of panic, jerking her eyes back to her menu, her heart thumping uncomfortably in her chest.

She bent her head, staring unseeingly at the ornately printed words, silently cursing herself for her foolish reaction. She should have smiled and coolly inclined her head instead of acting like a frightened ostrich. What she had done had amounted to an outright snub. She didn't dare look up again and almost melted in relief when Mark reappeared, alone.

Relief turned to dismay as he moved around to grasp the back of her chair. 'Come on—Scott's invited us to be *his* guests for the evening. I tried to protest but he insisted—he said their corner table is much better suited to conversation.'

That was what Anya was afraid of! 'But we've already ordered our drinks—' she protested feebly.

'The waiter's sorting that out. He's happy because we're freeing up a table for more customers.'

Anya tried not to resent Mark's guiding hand on her back as she walked towards the flames of hell. He wasn't to know that she was still shell-shocked by Joanna Monroe's devastating revelation. For some reason Joanna had seemed to think that Anya was now part of Scott's intimate inner circle, and naturally assumed that she had known about the turbulent affair.

She stretched a smile across her face as they reached the table, conscious that her unadorned black slip dress with its filmy, beaded overtop was no match for the other woman's dramatic flair, and wished she had worn her hair in a more sophisticated style than the simple French braid that hung down her back. She had always believed that the inner person mattered more than the outer one but it would be nice, just once, to be able to out-dazzle the opposition.

Scott had risen to his feet and she was forced to briefly look him in the eye during the exchange of greetings, pretending not to notice the threatening determination she glimpsed in his studied politeness. His tigerish smile told her he was highly satisfied with the turn of events, while Heather's tight, brief effort suggested that she held the opposite view of the disruption to her evening.

Etiquette demanded that Mark sit next to Heather while Anya sat beside Scott, which at least saved her the nerve-racking prospect of having to converse with him face-to-face, but the table's banquette seats made the brushing of arms and legs inevitable when sharing with a man as tall and broad as Scott, and Anya's nerves soon began to hum at the suspicious frequency with which he was casually rearranging his limbs.

'Having trouble with your contact lenses, or do you need those to read the menu?' drawled Heather, and Kate put a hand up to her face and realised that she was still wearing her driving glasses.

'I use them for long-distance—like when I'm driving.' Annoyed with Mark for not mentioning them before, she quickly whisked them off with fumbling fingers that bounced them onto Scott's bread and butter plate.

'And in the classroom—to keep your eye on the delinquents and troublemakers who always try to hide themselves in the back row,' Mark jokingly reminded her.

'*I* used to sit in the back row,' Scott murmured, picking up the spectacles and folding them up.

'Why am I not surprised?' It came out a little tarter than was strictly polite and was rewarded with instant punishment.

'They must make you look even more like the quintessential schoolmarm,' he said, handing them back for her to stuff in her purse, his eyes wickedly bland as they reminded her of his supposed predilection.

Heather Morgan chuckled sympathetically at what she assumed was a disparaging remark. 'Did you use them to drive here tonight?' Her speculative brown eyes shifted from Anya to Mark. 'I thought you two were here together...?'

'I got called out to a fire alarm at the college, so I wasn't able to pick Anya up as we'd planned,' Mark told her. 'It turned out to be a false alarm, but with vandalism as rife as it is we don't like to take chances, so I got the fire department to do a full check of the premises.'

'We had other plans, too.' The diamonds in her ears glinted as Heather tossed a mildly reproachful look across the table. 'We were supposed to be going to a Law Society dinner in the city but Scott got caught up in some fresh drama with his little daughter that he's not talking about, didn't you, darling?' The clipped consonants indicated a hint of over-strained patience. Anya had already gathered from Petra that the girl's arrival was viewed as a tiresome but temporary blip on Heather Morgan's personal radar. Her condescending interest had not endeared her to Petra.

'I did suggest that you could go without me,' drawled Scott, as the waiter served their drinks.

'But of course I wouldn't *hear* of it, even though the dinner was honouring the achievements of one of my colleagues in the firm,' Heather continued with an attractive little moue of her glossy carmine mouth which emphasised the extent of her self-sacrifice. 'Since I'd skipped lunch in anticipation of a big dinner, Scott decided he'd better feed me at the nearest decent local eatery.' She opened the folder in her hands and studied it with critically raised eyebrows. 'It's quite an extensive menu, but a little on the unimaginative side.'

'It's excellent food, though,' said Mark. 'They have a live band on Friday and Saturday nights, too. Not the head-bashing stuff they have in the public bar, but a good blend of dance music...'

They ordered their meal and Anya, who had not felt much like eating anyway, now found her stomach churning at the thought of anything on the menu. She finally opted for the blandest thing she could find—consommé followed by grilled fish and a green salad.

The talk was blessedly impersonal for a while, with Anya

valiantly keeping up her end of the general conversation in spite of some distracting asides from Scott which were designed to force her to turn her head, or risk seeming spectacularly rude to the man who was paying for her meal. When the wine list arrived and Mark deferred to him as host, Scott consulted Anya's opinion on his choices and she had to confess her ignorance.

'If I like the taste, I'll drink it, but the only thing I really know anything about is champagne—'

'You mean the local bubbly?' Heather interrupted, her voice nasal with disdain. 'They're not allowed to call it champagne any more, it has to be *méthode champenoise*.'

'Oh, I meant Krug and Dom Perignon,' Anya was startled into saying. 'Champagne is the only alcohol my mother ever touches. She says it's good for the throat. Even as a child I was given a small glass and expected to toast her success.'

Scott unwisely chuckled at Heather's ill-concealed chagrin and earned himself a chilly look. He explained about Anya's background, adding several details that he could have gleaned only from Petra. The thought that she was an object of conversation between Scott and his daughter gave her an odd frisson.

'Why didn't you go to an American private school if your parents were living in the States?' Heather wanted to know.

Anya could imagine the supercilious reaction if she said that to her parents she had been a woeful distraction from their joint careers. They'd despaired of what to do with the quiet little cuckoo in their moveable nest, and had been relieved at her naively expressed desire to live in Auckland, 'near where Aunty Mary and Uncle Fred used to live'.

'Because she considers New Zealand her spiritual as well as her birth home.' Scott spoke for her with a lazy blend of amusement and approval which suggested a degree of familiarity that made Heather's face turn even more frosty, and retaliate by shifting the main focus of her attention onto Mark.

Her cold-shouldering had no effect, and instead of competing to recapture her interest, as he was supposed to, Scott was left free to torment Anya with his full awareness. Heather's displeasure became even more pronounced when, over their main course, Mark made a passing remark about the college's reputation for equality and fairness and Scott swiftly took him to task for his lack of recent fairness to Anya, countering every excuse he presented.

'Well, Anya has sure got you on her side,' said Mark ruefully, when Scott had manoeuvred him into admitting and apologising for his over-zealousness.

'Doesn't that present you with rather a conflict of interest—seeing as you're the college's legal representative?' Heather pointed out acidly.

'Naturally I couldn't have advised her myself—but Anya would have had excellent grounds for suing if Mark had suspended her on the speculative fear of a future rumour rather than any eye-witness testimony of wrong-doing…'

The others had finished their mains and Scott watched as Anya pushed the salad around on her plate to disguise the fact she'd hardly touched her food.

He leaned over so that his shoulder touched hers. 'Not hungry?' he asked softly, under cover of the talk on the other side of the table.

'I *was*,' she lied pointedly, in a correspondingly low tone. 'But something in the vicinity seems be turning my stomach.'

Instead of being chastened, he chuckled. 'Let's see if we can't do something to exercise your appetites.' He began to shift across the banquette, nudging her off the bench seat with the hard pressure of his hip and thigh.

'You two carry on with your conversation—Anya and I are just going to try out the band,' he said, and had her in the centre of the small group of slow-dancing couples on the dance floor before she or anyone else had a chance to express an opinion of his manners.

'Your girlfriend is not amused at your behaviour,' said Anya, helpless to prevent her body shivering against his when his arm contracted across her back, enfolding her in the wings of his open jacket, his other hand cupping hers against the smooth weave of his shirt instead of in the correctly polite position. Her head was turned to one side, to prevent her nose being buried in his snowy breast, the top of her head barely reaching his collarbone.

'Then it's as well I'm not her court jester. I'm not any more amused at her mood. And she's hardly a girl,' he said, turning her so that she could no longer see their table, his foot pivoting between hers, his knee briefly kissing the inside of her thigh.

'That's right…your taste runs to older women, doesn't it?' she jabbed breathlessly. 'You're such a champion of the underdog, I suppose you're used to handling bitches.'

To her fury he laughed. 'I think I've got my hands on one right now. And to think I thought you were too soft and tender-hearted. What's got you clawing and biting? Or need I ask? Your cousin is younger than I am but she certainly ranks as a bitch.'

She stiffened in the circle of his arms and the hand on her spine moved, capturing the end of her plait and wrapping it around his wrist so that he could tug her head back and look down into her stormy face. 'I know that my sister, in her inimitable motor-mouthed wisdom, welcomed you into her acquaintance by spilling the beans about Kate and me, so let's stop the sniping and get it out in the open—'

'Oh, so *now* you want to talk about it? Well, maybe I don't!' She jerked her head to try and free her hair, the sharp tugging on her scalp bringing tears to her eyes…or so she wanted to believe as he instantly unwrapped his hand and smoothed the plait down her spine, allowing her the freedom to avert her gaze. She tried to increase the distance between them, but he had reached the limits of his tolerance and bracing herself against his controlling arm merely arched her body into greater intimacy.

'You're angry with me for not telling you?' he said, his eyes on her pale profile. 'I might point out that Kate obviously didn't tell you either.'

He wasn't going to get away with making her sound unreasonable and illogical. She had every right to feel searingly betrayed. She knew exactly why Kate hadn't told her—because it might have made Anya even more reluctant to take any risks on her behalf to know that she was dealing with one of her cousin's ruthlessly discarded lovers.

'Yes, and I'm furious with her, too.'

He had reduced their steps to a bare shuffle, the better to protect the intimacy of their exchange, his head bowed over hers. 'And since she's not here you're going to take it all out on me?'

'Yes!'

'That isn't very fair,' he murmured. 'What happened between Kate and me isn't relevant to this relationship—'

'Isn't *relevant*? You had a love affair with my *cousin* and didn't think it worth *mentioning*?'

'There's a certain etiquette involved in discussing one's past liaisons—particularly when they're with well-known people. When I realised that Kate hadn't told you, I was presented with a dilemma. How could I betray something she clearly wanted held in confidence? Would you respect me if you knew I was the kind of man to kiss and tell?'

'From what your sister told me, it was a hell of a lot more than *kisses*!' hissed Anya, conscious of the relaxed looseness of his body as it teased at her stubborn rigidity.

'It was also five years ago. Well in the past. And I'd prefer it to remain there. I don't make a habit of discussing my past lovers with future partners. That's not my style.'

Future partners? Anya went weak at the knees, telling herself he was just toying with her. She knew she was totally different from the other women he had had in his life. 'And we all know what *your* style is,' she said, catching a glimpse of Heather's haughtily aloof face.

'Oh? What's that?' he asked, again turning her back into the thick of the dancers.

'Sophisticated, successful, beautiful…'

'—and don't forget bitchy,' he had the nerve to tack on with a hint of laughter in his voice, his hand pressing hers into the warmth of his chest, making her aware of the springy cushion of hair under his shirt.

'Elegant women who wouldn't dream of…of—'

'Rolling around on the grass with me under the trees?'

He was definitely laughing at her. Her hand clenched into a fist underneath his palm. 'I bet you didn't roll Kate around on the grass!' she accused raggedly.

'God, no…she hated being ruffled. Your cousin was moonlight, champagne and caviar and silk sheets…everything had to be first class all the way.'

While she was strictly economy, Anya thought bitterly, refusing to acknowledge the sardonic self-contempt that was invested in his words. 'And I bet you loved every minute of it,' she said.

His jaw brushed her brow, his voice unrelenting as he uttered the confidences that she had demanded from him but hadn't really wanted to hear.

'As you say, she's a very beautiful woman, but suffice it to say that I didn't do the chasing. I was single and unencumbered, and I wouldn't have been a man if I hadn't been seduced by her passionate declarations. I admit, I temporarily lost my head. For all of eight weeks she had me convinced I was central to her happiness and I was arrogant enough to actually start believing that she meant it when she said she loved me, that we might be building something special. It was quite a kick in the ego when the attraction didn't last—on *either* side. It was an affair, certainly, but in retrospect I don't think I'd classify it as a *love* affair…

'Five years ago I might have mistaken glister for gold but my tastes have matured since then. Maybe I'm discovering that I prefer to lose my head over the simple pleasures of life—sunlight and laughter, apples and grass, and a pair of eyes as clear and refreshing as a cool drink of water…'

His hand had somehow insinuated itself under the filmy fabric of her little cropped top, his fingertips resting on her silky bare skin above the low-cut back of her dress. Not caressing, or doing anything indecent, just *there*…as seductively enticing as his words.

'You must have been pretty serious about Kate at the time,' she tortured herself. 'Your sister said you didn't date for a *year* afterwards—'

He snorted. 'Jo is a dyed-in-the-wool romantic. It was actually longer than a year. I was building up my practice as fast as I could and at the same time supervising all the renovations being done on The Pines both before and after I moved in. For a long time I simply didn't have the spare energy to devote to a new relationship. My sex drive was sublimated in work. I didn't have *time* for another woman in my life—'

'But now you do,' Anya said tartly, her feminine hackles rising. She stopped moving, glaring up at him. 'Do you know how arrogant that sounds?'

He kept his arm firmly around her, their bodies touching from chest to knee. 'What about you? You obviously haven't had much time for men if you think Mark Ransom is going to make you any kind of decent lover.'

She clenched her teeth. 'There's nothing the matter with Mark!'

'I didn't say there was…only that he's not right for you. He's too conventional. One look at your kinky underwear and he'd be blushing like a vicar instead of ripping it off you.' He grinned at her expression and began dancing again. 'You're a buttoned-up little thing who needs a man who won't be put off by those snooty boarding school manners—'

'And you're a white-collar professional with a big chip on your shoulder!' she snapped, her body unconsciously obeying his lead, moving in perfect unison with his changing step.

'Do you blame me? My one year at private school was an education in the corruption of privilege,' he said, undermining her anger with his sudden gravity. 'Because I was a scholarship boy I was automatically an outsider to the boys who had been there since kindergarten. My language, my mannerisms, my lack of money, my aggressive desire to succeed, they all marked me out as different and threatening to the status quo. And when I found warmth and acceptance in the one place that it seemed to be freely offered, I found that trust was also a flexible commodity. I trusted Lorna when she said she loved me, but she traded on that trust to deny me the true realisation of what it means to be a man.

'I trusted your cousin, too, to be honest about her emotions and open about her intentions, but Kate wasn't capable of that much unselfishness. Her claims of love were just flashy pyrotechnics, full of noise and dazzle but utterly ephemeral. So don't ever think that there's any way that I'd want your cousin back, or confuse you with her…or her with you…'

His words lingered in her head for the entire weekend, during which she cravenly stayed home and gardened. Heather had been sitting in glacial silence by the time they had got back to the table and Anya had quickly invented a headache which Mark had accepted with relief as a reason to excuse themselves from dessert and coffee. Anya had had the feeling that if she hadn't been driving herself she would have had to listen to a lecture all the way home in the car. As it was she had escaped with only an irritated comment that in being submissive to Scott's domination she had only succeeded in being rude to Heather.

Submissive? If only he knew!

She was not feeling at all submissive on Monday afternoon, when the final bell dismissed her last class and Petra bounced into her classroom towing her father.

'Hi, Miss Adams. I hope your headache's better because Dad and I've got a fantastic surprise for you!'

'Oh, really?' said Anya, moving behind her desk, taking off her spectacles and making a business of putting them in their soft leather case in order to avoid Scott's hooded gaze. He doubtless knew very well the reason that she had not tutored Petra over the weekend was because she had not wanted to face him. Her headache had not been organic.

'Yes—look! Dad's got us tickets to go to a concert at the Auckland Town Hall tonight.' Petra released her father's hand to excitedly pull the tickets out of their printed sleeve. 'They've apparently been sold out for *weeks* but Dad managed to get three review seats from a friend at one of the newspapers.' She pushed the tickets across the desk to Anya, pointing out the name of a famous Russian pianist appearing 'For One Night Only'. 'He's playing Beethoven's "Fifth Concerto"—the "Emperor",' she exalted. 'This is just going to be *so* fantastic!'

'Tonight...?' said Anya faintly, folding into the chair behind her desk, frantically trying to think up an excuse.

'You already have a date?' asked Scott, his eyes no longer hooded but blazing with challenge. He was going to pin her to the blackboard behind her if she tried to refuse, she realised.

'Well, no, but...it's a school night,' she faltered, rolling nervously at the fine gold chain exposed by the open collar of her yellow blouse.

'Oh, that's OK, we're not going to be out too late—Dad's booking a hotel suite so we don't have to drive all the way back home tonight.' Petra was almost dancing with glee at the idea. 'We can take everything we'll need for tomorrow and Dad'll drive us home in the morning and drop us right here at school.'

'The perfect plan,' purred Scott, and something in his voice alerted Petra because her face fell with ludicrous speed.

'You're not going to say *no*, are you, Miss Adams? I've never been to a concert where someone famous is playing— just free ones and symphony matinées…'

Anya had picked up a pen from her desk, instinctively trying to retreat behind her professional facade.

'No, Miss Adams is definitely not going to say no,' her father said in that same, silken voice, leaning both hands flat on the edge of her desk. 'She wouldn't *dream* of disappointing you. She's delighted that I'm thoughtful enough to want to ensure that she's bright-eyed and bushy-tailed for school tomorrow. She's going to thank me nicely and say that she feels privileged to be able to attend a concert by a former Tchaikovsky prize-winner in the presence of a *future* Tchaikovsky prize-winner.'

'Oh, *Dad*!'

'Well, if you're sure there's no-one else you'd rather invite,' Anya murmured. 'Someone in the family. Or perhaps Miss Morgan would like to hear the "Emperor"…' she felt driven to suggest.

'Miss *Adams*!' Petra stared at her, eyes rounded in horror at this unthinkable betrayal.

'Miss Morgan thinks the "Emperor" is a giant penguin,' drawled Scott, sending Petra into a fit of hysterically relieved giggles. He leaned further across the desk, his tie brushing Anya's open text-book as his deep voice provided a counterpoint to the high-pitched giggles. 'She also thinks that I no longer fit her profile of a desirable escort. I've apparently changed for the worse since I became an active father—I've become selfish, rude and indifferent to a woman's needs!'

He certainly gave the lie to the first two criticisms that evening as he escorted a lady on each arm into the concert chamber, Petra minus her nosering and wearing a new dress—black of course—bought from a screamingly trendy boutique near the hotel and Anya in a silver lurex top and long black skirt. They had dined at the hotel, Petra in transports of delight at the sight of the luxurious, three-bedroom penthouse suite, confiding that she'd never stayed in a hotel before.

Petra sat between them at the concert, leaning forward in her seat in the centre-front of the circle, her hands gripping the ledge, while Scott lounged back in his seat, his arm extended along the back of her seat towards Anya, occasionally exchanging smiling glances with her behind his daughter's entranced back.

Petra remained utterly still through the entire performance and during the slow movement in B Major Anya even suspected her of holding her breath so as not to make even the slightest sound that would interfere with her blissful appreciation of the adagio. Her expression was filled with such soul-wrenching purity and sublime yearning that Anya felt doubly moved by the music and blinked furiously to dispel the tears in her eyes.

A touch on her shoulder had her turning her head and seeing the corresponding glitter of Scott's eyes as they shared a moment of perfect emotional communion. With his daughter's coming the cynical, hard-bitten lawyer was rediscovering the joys and sorrows of vulnerability, was able to reveal the tenderness and sensitivity which didn't detract from his toughness but merely added depth and breadth to his character. Her heart fisted in her chest. Perhaps what it really meant was that he was opening himself up to love…

The rousing final rondo brought the audience to their feet and Petra clapped and stamped and cried for encores with a glorious abandon that had the people around her laughing indulgently and leaning over to compliment Anya and Scott on their enthusiastic daughter. When Anya blushingly attempted to correct them, Scott swapped seats with Petra and told her not to be silly, and stayed there his arm draped around her for the brilliant short encore that again had Petra shouting herself hoarse.

Outside the Town Hall they strolled across Aotea Square, to a theatre restaurant where they ate a late supper and let Petra begin to wind down from her excitement, her feverish chatter eventually fading into a dream-like contentment.

Back in the hotel suite, Petra yawned her way into her bedroom and re-emerged in the heavy-metal T-shirt that passed for night attire to give Anya an unexpected hug, followed by an exuberant leap into her father's arms. He whirled them both around, turning her babble of thanks into a shower of choked giggles. When he set her down she didn't let him go for a moment, and when she did it was with a fierce kiss and a passionate little speech.

'I know you pretended that you'd wanted to go all along, but you did this for me. I'll never forget that. I'll make you proud of me, Dad, I promise!'

'I already am.' he said gently. 'Let's make a date for the first time you play Carnegie Hall—I'll bring the flowers you bring the piano!'

She laughed, her incipient tears vanishing.

'Go on, sleepy head,' he said. 'To bed—and if I don't hear another peep out of you until morning, I'll let you order breakfast on Room Service!'

After her door had closed behind her he stood still for a moment in the centre of the room, his head bowed, his face pale above his black dinner suit and white silk shirt, his hands flexing at his sides. 'I don't see the point of dwelling on what can't be changed, regrets are so futile—but I hate how much I've missed of her life,' he said hoarsely. 'I hate that I was so ignorant and uncaring that I never got to hold her as a baby or see her first step, or her face the first time she ever touched a piano… And now there's another man whom she obviously loves and is happy to call Dad—her everyday Dad, who's a bigger part of her life than I'll *ever* be…'

'You may have been ignorant; you *weren't* uncaring,' said Anya compassionately. 'Just human. We're all entitled to make mistakes, especially when we're young.'

'Are we?' His shoulders relaxed under the smooth jacket, the jut of his jaw easing as he lifted his head. 'And what heinous mistakes did *you* make when you were young?' It was said in a wry tone that doubted she would have any to confess.

'I fell madly in love with a man whom I thought truly appreciated and accepted the real me. Unfortunately the real me was too boring, both in bed and out, to sustain his interest and he graduated to a very exciting, very public fling with my cousin.'

'Ah.' That rocked him back on his heels, as she had meant it to, but he recovered quickly. 'So you and Kate have issues about men…?' he murmured, walking over to the bar and uncapping a bottle of whisky.

'*An* issue. And we resolved it. I decided Alistair wasn't worth loving after all, and she dumped him.'

He winced. 'Drink?' He tilted the whisky bottle to show her the label and she shook her head.

'I'm still feeling the effects of the Irish coffee I had at supper,' she said, watching him pour two fingers for himself. 'I don't think I can take any more artificial intoxication.'

Scott raised the crystal glass to his mouth, then stopped, looking at her over the rim.

He set the glass back down on the bar behind him. 'You're right—natural intoxication is infinitely more preferable,' he said huskily. 'It gives you a much more sustained high.' He shrugged out of his unbuttoned jacket and stripped off his black tie, tossing them onto the white leather couch. He stretched—a long, slow flex of his big body—and then strolled towards her wide-eyed figure, pulling his shirt-tails loose and lifting his chin. 'Would you mind?' he murmured as he came to a halt well within the limits of her personal space. 'The collar is so tight and the buttons so small, my big clumsy fingers always have difficulty manoeuvring. Would you undo them for me?'

He waited passively, his big, clumsy fingers innocently hanging at his sides, and after a brief hesitation Anya reached up, going on tip-toes to see what she was doing so that she could comply with his request as quickly and efficiently as possible. He turned out to be right about the buttons. They were devilishly playful little things and she was aware of his warm breath stirring the hair at her temples as she slid her fingers inside his snug collar to help work the fastening loose, her knuckles massaging the hard column of his throat, the unique, spicy scent of him rising from his warm shirt as he lifted his arms, infusing her with familiar longing.

Suddenly she became aware of the reason that he had moved. The strategic pins anchoring her elegant French twist were plucked out and her hair tumbling in a silky, sun-streaked spray down her back.

'What did you do that for?' she demanded, struggling with the second and last tiny button as his arms fell back to his sides.

'You were frowning and I thought that maybe your hair twisted up like that was giving you a headache,' he said innocently. 'You don't wear it up at night, anyway, do you?'

He meant in bed. 'Sometimes,' she lied.

'But not tonight,' he said with a bone-melting satisfaction.

'There!' She tried to step back but he caught her hands.

'You haven't finished…' Holding her eyes, he moved her fingers down to the first button below his collar. 'Please…' he said softly, and, mesmerised by the smouldering desire in the blue gaze, she undid it for him, only to have him slowly guide her hands down to the next button, and the next, and the next…each act of compliance acknowledging his bold intention to seduce.

'Do you recognise it?' he murmured, as they reached the last button and her fingers brushed against the betraying bulge that pushed at the front of his trousers under cover of the loose shirt.

'Recognise what?' she said, blushing furiously, recklessly tempted to trace the outline of that intriguing hardness.

'My shirt…it's the one you borrowed that night to cover your peek-a-boo charms,' he murmured, sending a fresh flush of awareness through her body. 'I've discovered I like having something that you wore next to my skin. It's as if you're wrapped around me, caressing me with your featherlight touch every time I move…'

His shirt was fully unbuttoned now, exposing his powerful chest with its masculine pelt of crisp, dark hair arrowing down over the hard ridges of his abdomen to a thin tracing below his navel. He placed her hands over his hard, flat nipples.

'Would you like to do that to me, Anya?' he invited in a whispering groan. 'Would you like to touch me, stroke me, wrap yourself around me and move with me, on me….' His hips shifted as he spoke, pushing at her skirt, teasing her with their mutual awareness of what she was doing to him.

His skin was hot to the touch, taut and seductively smooth under the roughening of hair, she discovered as he released her hands to roam in helpless fascination over his upper body. It was as if she had never touched a man before, and she hadn't…not with this combination of excitement and fear, hunger and yearning, not with a mingling of love and bittersweet resignation, knowing that there was not even the pretence of love in return and not caring… For the moment it was enough that he wanted her, that right here, right now, she was the most desirable woman in the world to him.

When her fingernails scraped over his nipples he shuddered and let out a thick groan. The harsh sound in the quiet luxury of the lounge startled her and her confidence faltered. Was she mad? What had made her think she could handle an affair with such a formidable man?

'I—what if Petra gets up?' she said, backing away. He shadowed her with a smile that had her skittering nervously towards the two adjoining doors on the opposite side of the suite to Petra's room. 'I think it's time I was in bed—'

'You're right, of course,' he agreed smoothly, looming up behind her and putting out a hand to cover hers as she grasped the first door handle. 'Wrong room,' he purred in her ear, his other hand sliding around her waist, drawing her back against his naked chest.

'I—it's very late,' she tried.

'Yes, it is…far too late for either of us to back out.' He nuzzled the side of her neck through the fine veil of her hair, nibbling at her tender skin and licking at the tender lobe of her ear. 'I've been thinking about this all night…and so have you,' he said, compressing his swollen shaft against the soft curve of her bottom. 'About what we were going to do when we were finally alone together. You've been readying yourself for me, honey…I can feel it, taste it, smell it on you…'

Her head fell back against his shoulder. 'I don't think I'm cut out for this kind of affair—' she gasped as his hand slid up under her lurex top, to dip into her lacy bra and toy with her stiff little nipples.

'How do you know what kind of affair it's going to be until you give it a chance…?' he said, pulling her hand away from the door and drawing it back against the rigid muscles of his hard flank. 'Give *me* a chance to make love to you and you might find that our *affair* is exactly what you need.' He spun her around in his arms and picked her up, carrying her into his room and dropping her down in the middle of the huge bed. He locked the door and swiftly stripped off the rest of his clothes.

Big, hard and naked, he approached the bed where she was still kneeling in a state of delicious confusion. 'Take a good look, honey, it's all yours,' he drawled at her furiously blushing face, and she seemed bewitched by the bold arousal that jutted from the dark thatch of curling hair between his strong thighs.

She moistened her dry lips. 'You're—you're very—'

'Well-endowed?' He grinned wickedly.

That, too! 'I was going to say arrogant,' she said shakily, unable to tear her eyes away from his glorious nudity, beguiled by the supreme naturalness of his attitude to his flagrant sexuality. 'Whatever happened to the slow dance of seduction?'

His smile was a slow sizzle. 'Afraid I'm going to rush you? Not a chance! I still have you to unwrap and I know that's going to be the most fun of all...' He crawled onto the bed, prowling towards her like a sleek, glossy-skinned predator, enjoying the game as she retreated up against the stacked pillows, snatching up the handmade chocolate which had been placed on the turned-down covers and holding it out to him in laughing protest.

'You think that's enough to satisfy my sweet tooth?' He licked his lips and took a bite of the chocolate, following it up with a swift lunge and a bite at her mouth. His hands cupped her face, the velvety-smooth chocolate melting on their mingled tongues as he spilled her backwards across the width of the bed, his leg pushing heavily between hers as he plundered her willing mouth.

All Anya's former doubts and fears vanished like mist under the blazing sun of his hungry passion. The willingness to love was a strength, not a weakness, and it was worth all of the pain she was probably storing up for herself to have this chance to express her love in its most intimate physical form, to be at one with the man to whom she had secretly lost her heart. No, not lost…*given*. Even if Scott didn't know it, tonight he was going to be truly well loved in the fullest sense of the words.

He held her beneath him, protecting her from his full weight by the strength of one arm, his initial urgency reining back to a lazy exploration of the tender crevices and most pleasure-sensitive areas of her face and throat. For a long time there was only the hush of whispered praise and the soft susurration of sighs and kisses, the rustle of clothes against skin.

There was something fiendishly erotic about being pinned, fully dressed, to a bed by a naked male, and soon it was Anya who was frantically trying to hurry the pace, stroking her hands over his chest and back, drawing her nails up through the hair on his thighs and caressing his lean, muscled buttocks. Her mouth released from bondage to his, she squirmed down to taste the musky hot skin of his chest, but it wasn't until her tongue brushed his bronzed nipple and her tentative touch fluttered against his satiny-hot manhood that Scott exploded into passionate action.

He peeled off her tight lurex top, his eyes searing her with his approval as he traced the edge of her scarlet quarter-cup bra with his tongue and kissed and nipped his way over the soft mounds that swelled above the cups, paying special attention to the nipples that peeked at him over the indecently low-cut lace. 'Tell me you were thinking of me when you put this on,' he growled against her creamy flesh, hooking his finger into the underwire between the padded cups and dragging the fabric down so he could suckle at both cherry nipples unhindered.

'I…yes…you…' Anya struggled for coherency as he abraded the moist, glistening tips of her breasts with the light stubble on his jaw before unclipping the frothy concoction and tossing it away, the better to enjoy his delectable feast.

'Oh, God…Scott…'

'Aren't I going slow enough for you?' he taunted, and drew back to flip off her dainty black sandals, his hands sliding up under her skirt, groaning with pleasure as he discovered the silky bare skin at the top of her thighs. 'Stay-ups!' he sighed, running his fingers around the elastic top of her stocking. 'Doncha just love 'em?'

His mingling of passion and humour was as seductive as his sultry provocation and so obviously such a startling new concept to Anya in bed that he delighted in turning their love-making into a joyous romp that left her both breathless and quivering on the edge of completion as he stripped off the tiny, damp thong that barred his entrance to the moist haven of her desire and settled himself heavily between her slender, stockinged thighs.

Then the laughter was swept away in the power and glory of his surging possession and Anya could only cling to the rock-solid shoulders, her fingers slipping in the sweat of his shuddering exertions as he thrust deep into her wet, creamy depths, establishing a driving rhythm that exploded into a mutual rapture of the senses, his mouth drinking in her help-less cries of ecstasy as he claimed her heart, soul and body for his own…

CHAPTER EIGHT

ANYA opened her eyes just as dawn began to filter in around the thick curtains that protected the penthouse suite from the importuning world. She lay on her back, her blonde hair spread out in a wild tangle on the pillow, the ends tickling at the chin of the naked man who lay sprawled on his stomach beside her, his arms cushioning the pillow under his head, his face relaxed in deep, satiated sleep.

If she had been inclined to disbelieve the evidence of her eyes there was the evidence of her body to attest to the mind-blowing fact that Scott Tyler had spent the night in her bed…or, rather, she in his. She ached in the sweetest of ways in the wickedest of places. The crisply laundered white hotel sheets were wildly rumpled, draping low across their bodies, and, looking down, she could see the tiny bruises and abrasions of love on her breasts and stomach.

Carefully easing over onto her side, she studied the sleeping man, blushing to note that he, too, had reddened marks on his shoulders and back, as if he had been attacked by a fierce small animal…as indeed he had! His hard mouth was relaxed and slightly swollen, throwing the small scar into prominence, and that, along with the break in his arrogant nose and the tousled hair and strong growth of his beard, made him look rakishly disreputable and utterly desirable.

She knew that she would never have any regrets about giving herself to him because he had given of himself so generously in return… He had made her feel more like a woman in one night than Alistair had in all the time she had known him. He had been fierce, dominating and passionate, but exquisitely gentle too, and when she had cried after the sheer intensity of that first time he hadn't embarrassed her by asking her why, had just held her trembling body against his and kissed away the tears, and then shown her other ways for them to find pleasure in each other that were less unrestrained but no less satisfying, until she had once again been ready to fling herself into the lightning-storm of emotion that accompanied his tumultuous possession.

It hadn't taken him very long to recognise her lack of experience, and she felt a tingle of excitement prickle over her bare skin as she remembered how much he had enjoyed teaching her the different ways in which her body could accept him, excite him and bring them both to rapturous completion. He had liked to watch the shocked delight appear on her face each time he'd given her a new kind of caress, to coax her into using her hands, her hair, her mouth to make his body quicken and see her shyness melt away in a ravishing eagerness to torture and torment him until he was wildly out of control.

Oh, no, she needn't have worried that he would find her too *ordinary* in bed. He seemed to have no concept of the word. With Scott she had been made to feel supremely special, unique, exquisitely fashioned to satisfy his desires in a way that no other woman ever could, or would...

A smile stole across her lips as she lovingly studied his sleeping face, resisting the temptation to brush the dark strands of hair off his brow and kiss the faintly pouting mouth. So wary and mistrustful when awake, he was determined not to let himself be vulnerable to love. His daughter had cracked the self-protective shell around his heart, but the small breach wasn't wide enough to admit anyone else, had merely thickened the scars created by past betrayals.

Scott had been extremely vocal in the throes of passion, but not a word had been permitted to pass his lips that Anya could mistake for a profession of love. The profound sense of completeness that she had experienced in his arms was a gift that she couldn't acknowledge without jeopardising their relationship. Well, he might not be interested in *her* gift of love, but there were other things that she could give him that would bring him a joy that he *was* prepared to accept.

She began to ease back towards the edge of the bed, sliding out from under the covers, taking care not to awaken the sleeping tiger. Her feet soundless on the thick carpet, she snagged his shirt from the chair as she passed and scampered into her room, where she had a quick shower and donned the items that she had secretly purchased while Petra had been choosing her dress. She cleaned her teeth and ran a brush through her hair and emerged from her bathroom intending to tiptoe back into Scott's room, to find him sitting on the end of her bed dressed in a hotel bathrobe, a resolute expression that was distinctly unlover-like tautening his face.

'For a moment I thought our night together had been a figment of my imagination,' he said roughly. 'Didn't your good manners tell you that it's not the done thing to flee your lover's bed without at least the courtesy of a farewell?'

Oh, God, was he remembering the way that Kate had taken off without a word? Did he see it as a rejection of everything that they had shared? Did he think Anya was ashamed of what they had done and was seeking to pretend it hadn't happened?

Suddenly his sweeping gaze took in her feet and he did a shocked double-take that would have made her giggle if she hadn't been so unnerved by his brooding words. His widening eyes travelled with excruciating slowness up from the white ankle socks to his barely buttoned silk shirt veiling her delicate curves, the shadow of a triangle at the juncture of her thighs and dusky circles at the centre of her breasts making it obvious that she was wearing nothing at all under the tissue-fine fabric.

'I was just coming back to give you your wake-up call,' she said huskily, emboldened by the flare of his nostrils and the nervous jump in his throat as he swallowed, his incredulousness turning into smouldering recognition. 'But I wanted to get dressed first…as you can see.' She extended a leg, wriggling her toes in the white sock, allowing the silk to flirt slyly between her thighs.

She began slowly walking towards him, shaking back her long hair, causing a rolled-up sleeve to slide off one bare shoulder, revealing the paler skin of her breast.

'Oh, God, I think I've died and gone to heaven,' he murmured thickly, but she hadn't finished with him yet.

'I think there's still a price-sticker on my socks,' she said sweetly, coming to a halt between his spread knees. 'Would you mind peeling it off for me?' She lifted her leg and placed her foot daintily in his lap, just below the loosely tied towelling belt, her heel parting the edges of the bathrobe as she leaned forward.

His spine snapped back as the tender arch of her foot settled into his groin, cupping his rapidly growing arousal. He groaned and grabbed her ankle in a vice-like grip, his other hand stroking up over her smooth knee. 'I don't see any sticker,' he growled.

'You're not looking in the right place.'

He was staring at the tantalising shadow where the tail of his shirt draped over her hips. 'I'm looking exactly where you intended me too, you little minx.'

She felt deliciously wicked. 'What an old-fashioned term. I thought you were a ruthlessly modern man,' she teased, curling her toes against his thrusting resistance.

'Hussy!' he said, holding her foot securely in place, tilting his hips to increase the pressure on his engorged fullness as his other hand continued to creep up her thigh. 'If you're deliberately trying to drive me wild, you'd better be prepared to take the consequences.'

She veiled her smug smile of satisfaction with coyly fluttering lashes. 'How was I to know you were kinky for white socks?'

'Because I told you what a turn-on they were,' he purred. 'And obviously not only for me...' His fingertips had stirred through the fluff at the top of her thighs, finding the dewy feminine flower they were seeking, and he watched her eyes glaze over as he delicately stroked apart the moist petals and insinuated himself into her velvety sheath, his thumb playing lightly over the swollen bud bursting forth from its protective hood.

Anya's insides turned to hot syrup. Her teeth sank into her lower lip and her supporting leg began to tremble, her head suddenly too heavy for the slender column of her neck as sensation rioted through her body.

'Not so sassy with me now, are you, darling?' he murmured, deeply gratified by her extravagant response. He withdrew his glistening touch to pull her astride his powerful thighs and smothered her mewed protest with his hungry mouth, his hands wrenching open the buttons of the shirt and helping her to push aside his bathrobe so that he could crush her bare breasts against his hot chest. He fumbled in the pocket of his bathrobe and she had a dizzy moment to appreciate his forethought before he was ready for her, tilting his pelvis as he cupped her hips, teasing her with a few blunt nudges of his rigid shaft before forcing her slowly down onto his engorged length, merging them into one indivisible being.

Anya moaned at the blissful stretching of her body, winding her arms around his strong neck, trying to burrow further into his kiss. He reefed his fingers through her hair to tilt her head, running his hands down her back to settle at the base of her spine. 'It gets even better,' he whispered. 'Lean back for me...' And when she did he feasted at her breasts, tugging wetly on the nipples as he timed his powerful thrusts to perfection, grunting as her fierce convulsions ignited his own orgasm and they peaked in a wild conflagration of the senses that would be burned into Anya's memory for ever.

'Mmm,' he said lazily as they lay panting in exhaustion on the covers, still damply entwined, amongst a tangle of silk and towelling. He licked at a tiny bead of perspiration on the side of her desire-softened breast. 'We've made love in the bed, the shower, the chair and on the floor in my room...so I suppose we should do the same here.'

Anya's stomach quivered. 'We haven't got time. Petra will probably be awake soon.'

He propped his head on his hand. 'The door is locked. And I can be quick as well as slow. You seem to like it either way.' He chuckled as she pinkened.

'I still think we should be careful. Your— Petra's mother wouldn't like it if she was exposed to—'

He cut her off with a kiss on the mouth. 'Petra's a very intelligent and perceptive girl. She likes you and she's already picked up that I'm attracted to you—or, rather, have the "hots" for you, as she so tactfully puts it. As long as we act naturally about it, she's not going to be traumatised if she realises that our relationship has advanced to the level of being openly affectionate.'

His mouth was being more than affectionate! 'You said you were taking the hotel room so I'd be bright-eyed and bushy-tailed for school today. At this rate I'll be falling asleep in class,' she chided him.

'Ah, but I didn't say that it was *sleep* that was going to brighten your eyes or fluff up your tail,' he teased, riffling the cluster of curls below her flat abdomen with his knuckles.

'You're a very conniving man,' she said, pushing away his hand.

His blue eyes crinkled. 'But would you call me selfish, rude...indifferent to a woman's needs?' he asked slyly.

'*Extremely* rude,' Anya told him, her lips trembling into a smile that made her muted grey eyes glow. He knew very well that she couldn't criticise his performance on the other counts.

'But not offensively so,' he said, startling her with a hint of seriousness. 'I didn't hurt you in any way, did I? I wasn't too rough?'

She couldn't account the damage done to her heart. 'Of course not—'

'It's just that you're rather little, and I can see I bruised you,' he brooded, touching a tiny dark shadow on the upper curve of her breast with a gentle finger.

'You didn't exactly come out unscathed yourself,' she said lightly. 'You don't need to feel inhibited because of my size—'

'*Inhibited?*' That sparked a smile. 'I thought it was my *lack* of inhibition which might have been a problem.'

'Well, it wasn't. I may be little but I'm not brittle.'

'No, you're as pliant as a young willow,' he agreed. 'Quite astonishingly flexible.'

'Don't you ever think of anything but sex?'

'Not when I'm lying on a bed next to a beautiful naked woman—'

'I'm not entirely naked,' she pointed out mischievously. 'I still have my tiny little white socks on.'

He groaned. 'Don't remind me.'

'And you don't have to pretend that I'm beautiful, either,' she told him gravely. 'I'm happy with who I am.'

'So am I,' he said, tucking a strand of hair behind her ear. 'Because who you are is a lovely, complex young woman full of grace, candour and wit, and with an inner strength and intrinsic goodness of heart that makes me feel guilty for taking advantage of her...'

Her breath caught in her throat. 'Is that what you're doing?'

'I wanted Petra to see the concert but my primary reason for inviting you along was to give me the opportunity to seduce you,' he said flatly, almost as if he wanted her to recoil in disgust.

Anya widened her eyes in droll surprise. 'No, really? And here I was thinking that you were the kind of man who *always* carried that many condoms around with you!'

He scowled. 'If you were expecting sweet-talk and romance from me, you certainly didn't get it.'

She actually thought he had been extremely honey-tongued, but she knew what his words were intended to convey. He was warning her against seeing him as love's young dream.

'You must be confusing me with someone who cares about those things,' she said steadily. 'Someone who prefers glamorous trappings to the real thing.'

He reacted with defensive speed. 'If you're talking about Kate, you're wrong. I told you, I could never confuse you—you're as different as day and night. I knew that if you heard about the affair that it would taint your whole attitude towards me—'

'Is that the main reason you kept quiet about it? Because it might have made me suspicious of your motives for seducing me?'

His scowl darkened, his blue eyes sullen. 'You might have thought I wanted to revenge myself on her by taking you to bed,' he admitted reluctantly.

Anya's brow wrinkled, as if the idea had never occurred to her. 'I don't see quite how that would work. I'd think that she'd be more likely to pity you for trying to replace her spectacular self with her drab little cousin—'

He jerked up to brace himself over her body on bunched arms. 'Dammit, stop running yourself down like that! I hope you're not one of those people who excuse any behaviour on the grounds of genius. However brilliant and famous Petra becomes I would still expect her to be considerate of other

people's feelings. Can't you see you're a thousand times better than that selfish bitch, Kate?'

'Well, *I* can...but I thought you might be a little hazy on
the exact figures,' she murmured, secretly stunned by the
genuineness of his anger.

He blinked, his temper stopped in its tracks by her gentle
ribbing. A brief expression of uncertainty flitted across his
face and her glowing smile widened.

'I don't expect real life to meet the standards of a romantic
ideal, Scott,' she said, reaching up to touch his firm mouth.
'Besides, romance means vastly different things to different
people...especially men and women.'

'What does it mean to you?' he asked curiously, settling
back down against her.

'Well, great music and great sex are a pretty terrific beginning...' she said, straight-faced.

He laughed. She loved to make him laugh. All the harsh,
straight angles of his face tilted into slants and curves.

'What does it mean to you?' she dared.

'Right now?' He lowered his head and nudged her nose
with his to tilt her mouth up for his kiss. 'Why, you, of
course...'

Fortunately Petra slept soundly until Scott went in to wake
her, and she was too busy enjoying the novelty of a room
service breakfast and emptying the snacks out of the mini-
bar to notice Anya's self-conscious air as she buttered her
croissant and poured the coffee and tried to carry on a politely innocent conversation with her wickedly unco-
operative lover.

She couldn't *help* but notice, however, when the Jaguar
slid to a stop at the school gates and, after turning his head
to say goodbye to Petra in the back seat, Scott leaned over
and gave Anya a leisurely kiss on the mouth in full view of
the school crossing patrol.

'Uh-uh—no tongues, you guys. Remember my fragile juvenile psyche!' she snorted, slinging her bag over her shoulder and opening the door.

'Your psyche could be marketed as a bullet-proof vest,' replied Scott drily, sending her off covered in grins while he kindly tilted the rear vision mirror for a flustered Anya to repair her smeared lipstick.

'A pity it doesn't taste as good as it looks,' he remarked. 'I like you better totally *au naturelle*. Except for the cute socks, of course,' he added, just for the pleasure of watching her blush. 'I've got them in my pocket. You can put them on for me again later…'

She sternly repressed the hot thrill his words gave her. 'You shouldn't have kissed me like that,' she told him, putting the lipstick case back in her bag with a little snap.

'How should I have kissed you, then? I hate to disappoint.'

As if he could! 'Didn't you see them all *looking*?'

'Who? The kids? We're a couple. Couples kiss each other goodbye.' *We're a couple.* The phrase sounded much less transitory than *We're lovers*, thought Anya wistfully. Some couples who never got married nonetheless stayed together all their lives.

'Everyone's going to find out about us anyway. Don't expect me to skulk around with you like Ransom did—'

'We never *skulked*.' She roused herself to say with dignity. 'We were discreet.'

'Although you're employed by the Board he's effectively your boss,' he went on, shaking his head. 'Office affairs are a legal minefield. Ripe grounds for sexual harassment suits, disputed promotions, unjustified dismissals and all sorts of other nasty complications…'

She realised he was enjoying himself. 'We were *not* having an affair.'

'But you were heading that way. Why else would he take you out to dinner on Friday night?'

'Perhaps purely for the pleasure of my scintillating conversation. Men and women *can* simply be platonic friends, you know.'

His lawyer's ear detected a subtle inflection in her tone and instantly pursued it. 'Is that what he told you? That he wanted to keep it platonic? When did he say that—before Friday night—or afterwards?'

'During,' she sighed, knowing he wouldn't rest until he had dragged it out of her. As soon as they had been seated in the restaurant Mark had revealed that the purpose of his invitation had been to tactfully define the limits of their relationship. He didn't want to lead her on, he'd said, and his friendship was all that he could ever offer.

'Much as I really like you, Anya, it just puts me in too much of an awkward position, ethically speaking, to get romantically involved with anyone on the staff,' he had explained, with just the right touch of regret. 'I don't want to go through something like this again. And neither, I suspect, do you...'

Since Anya had been going to say much the same thing herself, she'd hardly been able to get up and walk out in a huff as he had rambled on about how much he valued her as a friend. After all, she wouldn't even have agreed to the date with him at all if she hadn't been jealous of the fact that Scott was going out with Heather Morgan.

Of course, she didn't tell Scott that part. He was already looking far too smug.

'So we both got dumped by disillusioned suitors on Friday night.' He grinned. 'Leaving no untidy loose ends to get in each other's way. We are well matched, aren't we?'

So much so that the next three weeks were a revelation to Anya. Scott might deny any pretensions to romance but he was intrinsically aware of how to make a woman feel special, and being the target of his exclusive interest made her increasingly self-confident, her heart soaring with hope in spite of her attempts to keep her feet firmly on the ground. She didn't get hearts and flowers from him, but she did get hand-made chocolates and pretty scented candles and flourishing seedlings for her garden—small tokens of his caring that she cherished more than diamonds.

At first Anya tried to hold back, wary of encroaching onto forbidden emotional ground by appearing to require more of his attention than he was able or willing to give, but he would have none of it, his innate curiosity and natural possessive-ness coming powerfully into play as he responded with re-newed determination to conquer any hint of restraint in her manner.

That first night he had driven over to see her after Petra had gone to bed—having paid Mrs Lee an exorbitant amount to stay on and babysit—and had ended up banishing the fe-vered memory of her bathtime fantasy by replacing it with even more ravishing reality. Sleek and playful as a seal in her steaming bath tub, Scott had proved her willow-like pli-ancy and his sexual athleticism to their ultimate satisfaction, and the detriment of her bathroom floor!

That had set the pattern of their relationship. Most nights of the week she either went over to The Pines for dinner with Scott and Petra, or he visited her later in the evening. They didn't always make love, although the passion between them grew rather than diminished with familiarity. Sometimes they would merely talk, and in the process Anya learned more about him to love. She found out that he donated large sums of money to a scholarship fund to enable some of Hunua College's poorer students to go on to further education, and that he provided free legal counselling to a woman's refuge. She discovered that he had spoken to Lorna and Ken to assert his right to provide his daughter with a trust fund for her education and music studies, and that he was dreading the rapidly nearing date of Petra's departure.

'It feels as if I'm losing her all over again, just when I'm starting to really get to know her,' he said, as they drank coffee on the couch in her living room, Anya curled up against his side, after an exhausting weekend showing Petra the sights of Auckland, including a ferry-ride out to Rangitoto Island in the Hauraki Gulf and a steep walk up to the top of the volcanic cone for a look at the view.

She leaned her head comfortably on his shoulder. 'It's not like last time. You're not really losing her. You've both made a binding connection, you'll see each other again.'

'Yes, this time Lorna's not going to have everything her own way,' he said grimly.

The only point of real conflict between them was Anya's adamant refusal to stay the night at The Pines, or even allow Scott to make love to her there. Neither frustrated argument nor seductive persuasion could pressure her into changing her mind. Her heart longed to make itself at home in *his* home, but she was afraid that in doing so she would be overwhelmed by the intensity of her feelings and relinquish the last remaining thread of control that she had over the progress of their affair. She used Scott's need to concentrate on his daughter in the short time they had left together as the reason for her reticence, but they both knew that it was more than that, and that when Petra had gone she would no longer be able to hide behind her altruistic excuses. The moment of truth was fast approaching—not least because she was also piling up increasingly querulous e-mails from London and Paris.

It arrived far sooner than Anya anticipated. One Saturday morning Scott had to respond to a call for an unscheduled court appearance for one of his remand clients and urged her to stay and keep Petra company while he was gone.

'I shouldn't be too long. By the way, do you know anyone called Russell Fuller?'

Anya shook her head. 'Is he a local?'

'He's a freelance journalist. He rang me earlier to ask if he could come and see the house and pick up some information about Kate Carlyle's time here—'

'Oh!' Her heart nearly leaped out of her throat.

He looked at her, eyes narrowing at the sight of her contracted pupils. 'So you *have* heard of him?'

'*About* him…just that some journalist was doing a big cover piece on Kate. She warned me that he'd probably be coming round,' she said dully.

He frowned. 'Well, I certainly don't want to rake over old ashes, but evidently Kate told him I bought The Pines from her. God knows what *else* she saw fit to tell him. He was fairly insistent that I could help him on the phone, so I thought it wiser to agree to see him and find out exactly what he wants rather than encourage his persistence by turning him down cold. I made an appointment for him to come over this afternoon. It's up to you whether you want to be here or not…'

He kissed her warmly before he walked out of the door, misreading her feverish clutch of desperation for one of entrancing eagerness, leaving her standing on the brink of a deep, dark chasm.

She should have told him…but she hadn't. She had been afraid to destroy the precious trust that had been built up between them. And now it was too late. Her period of grace had run out.

Did she owe her first loyalty to Kate—selfish, brilliant Kate whom she had known all of her life but found difficult to like? Or to Scott—a man whose true complexity she was only beginning to appreciate but whom she already loved? Family or lover? Whichever way she chose someone would be hurt. The question was, which choice would wreak the least damage on the least number of people?

The chunky wooden ladder into the attic still creaked at the metal joints as it unfolded from the pull-down trapdoor, and the attic itself was as dirty and cobwebby as Scott had suggested it would be. Anya's hand shook as she climbed into the cramped, dusty, stifling room, holding up the candle that she had stolen from the dining room to illuminate her way. She hadn't wanted to ask Mrs Lee for a torch, but matches had been a fairly innocuous request that hadn't raised any awkward questions. She hadn't even had to tell any fibs to Petra, because it would take an earthquake to distract the girl from her morning piano practice.

She stepped carefully across the timber beams, ducking to avoid the cobwebs and the low cross-beams that prevented her from standing up. The attic itself was big, running the full length of the house, but only a small proportion of it had been used for storage. Anya didn't bother to look under the bulky, shrouded shapes, holding the candle low to look for the small metal trunk that Kate had described.

She found it tucked against a beam and set the candle carefully down on a peeling paint-pot as she opened the lid, coughing at the cloud of dust that puffed into the air. Kate's green hardback journal was on the top, and she took it out and began rifling quickly through the albums, loose photos and papers, extracting anything in Kate's distinctive slanting hand, occasionally lingering over a half-remembered photograph or amusing piece of family history. Suddenly conscious that the time was slipping away from her, she hurriedly closed the trunk and gathered up her armful of contraband.

As she turned to leave she knocked over the candle, snuffing it out, and realised she'd lost her matches somewhere in the dark. Fortunately the chinks in the roof tiles and the square of light from the open trapdoor guided her stumbling steps back to her starting point and she slithered down the ladder on trembling legs, dropping Kate's journal with a crash on the floor. It fell open and several pieces of paper flew out of the pages, and when she gathered them up her eye was caught by the medical letterhead of a consultant gynaecologist.

She had never meant to read any of Kate's personal papers, feeling that she had already sinned enough against her own honour, but she couldn't help seeing what was right in front of her eyes.

Kate had had a pregnancy test done at the Manukau City doctors' office five years ago. The result had been positive. In view of Miss Carlyle's excellent physical and mental health, she'd had no grounds for abortion under current New Zealand law, even though she was only a few weeks into her pregnancy. If she wished to go ahead with a termination it would have to be done overseas.

Kate, who believed that having babies was the real reason that so few women achieved greatness in the world. Kate, who in the five years since her affair with Scott had recovered from her tax problems and brief career hiccup by fulfilling the promise of her youth with an unbroken string of concerts, recordings and festivals with no more than the odd weekend or two out of the public eye.

No *wonder* she had been panicked at the thought of Scott going through her papers!

'What are you doing?'

Scott looked from the attic ladder to Anya's agonised face. 'My case was called off—the judge was ill,' he explained absently, looking puzzled but not yet suspicious. 'Mrs Lee said she thought you were somewhere upstairs. I heard noises on the way up—I thought we had mice in the ceiling. Was that you? What were you doing up there?' He raised his eyebrows curiously at the untidy stack she was holding against her chest. 'What have you got there?'

In the silence that followed, her treacherous fingers went utterly numb, and the damning piece of paper floated down onto the top of Scott's shoe.

He hesitantly bent to pick it up, along with the fallen journal, alerted by her stillness.

When he saw what he had in his hands he went stark white.

He looked at her again, his eyes pure blue devastation, and she knew that she was looking at the death of a dream.

CHAPTER NINE

SCOTT didn't say a word. He didn't have to. The dead look in his eyes said it all. Anya felt sick. She could have defended herself against his anger, but his pain defeated her. She knew him now, knew the shocked revulsion he must be feeling at this further evidence of betrayal by someone who had claimed to love him.

He turned and walked away from her, the letter still crumpled in his white fist, the diary in his other hand, moving in a stiff-legged gait down the hall to turn into the master bedroom at the head of the stairs.

Anya went after him. She could do no less. He hadn't shut the door but she didn't take that as any form of encouragement; he was simply functioning on automatic, homing in on his private territory to lick his wounds. He was standing on the far side of the bedroom by the open sash window, flicking through the green journal, sending motes of dust rising to dance through the shafts of sunlight.

Anya had forgotten the burden she was still carrying, and hurriedly set the rest of the letters and papers on the table by the door, her trembling hands smoothing down the sides of her pale pink shirt-dress.

'Scott, I'm so sorry—'

'So Kate left a few incriminating pieces of personal property in storage when she took off, and after what she'd done she didn't have the guts to ask for them back,' he said in a grey monotone, as if he was reading the words off the page. 'Instead she got her sly little cousin to con her way under my guard and see if she could whip the goods out from under my nose.'

His head lifted, his eyes blazing at her from behind their film of blue ice, his intelligence rapidly shaking off his shock. 'How frustrating it must have been when you found I was working from home and Sam was using the room you needed to get into. No wonder you refused to sleep here. The last thing you wanted to encourage was an over-zealous lover who might be inclined to hover inconveniently over every move you made. What a sucker I was to fall for that shy will-she-won't-she act of yours! You were waiting until Petra went home to give you the run of the house. And I thought you were being cautious about committing yourself to something you weren't ready for, when really you were just baulking at the idea of prostituting yourself any more than you had to...'

Anya's throat tightened. This was far too reminiscent of another confrontation they had had, only this time she didn't have her cloak of innocence to protect her.

'I never slept with you for any other reason than because *I* wanted to,' she told him hoarsely. 'All right, so Kate *did* ask me to try and get some things that belonged to her without you knowing about it—'

'And this was your first opportunity to do anything about it? Why risk it now, while Petra was still here?' His face hardened as something clicked in his brain. 'Or perhaps you were afraid this was going to be your *last* opportunity... Ah, yes, of course—' he laughed bitterly '—the magazine article; *that's* the reason for the sudden urgency. My God, Kate knew what kind of dynamite *this* would be if it ever fell into the wrong hands.'

He held up the fisted letter and shook it at her. 'She had the bloody termination, didn't she?' he grated. 'That's why she disappeared so suddenly. She fled to some overseas clinic and aborted my child without even telling me she was pregnant, didn't she? *Didn't she?*'

Anya laced her trembling hands over her sick stomach. 'I really don't know…I can only presume so—'

His mouth contorted into a savage twist of contempt. 'You *presume*—you know damned well she did. She accidentally got pregnant and Kate, being Kate, only thought of how it affected *her*. God forbid she be trapped into any connection with me after I'd already passed my use-by date. I was simply a fling to while away the time while she waited for her agent to get her out of the financial jam she was in—'

'I didn't know anything about it until I saw that letter, just now,' said Anya shakily. 'She simply told me there were diaries here that she didn't want you or the journalist to find…'

'And you accepted that without question?' he sneered. 'Do you think that your gullibility excuses you? You didn't see anything wrong with what she asking of you? The thought that it was underhanded, dishonest, didn't bother you—?'

She moistened her pale lips. 'I—of course I knew it was wrong, but she's family. I may not have been entirely open with you, but I never lied to you, Scott—'

'Oh, come on, actions can lie as easily as words. I knew you were holding back on me but I didn't know *why*. Now I do—*this* was in the forefront of your mind the whole time we were together.' He threw the book and crumpled ball of paper contemptuously onto the floor. 'Dammit, if she'd simply *asked* me I would have been happy to be shot of any reminders of her,' he said bitterly. 'Is she really so arrogant that she imagines I care either way about her any more?'

Of course she was.

'She said she was afraid you might use anything you found as payback—'

'Kate, afraid? Face it, Anya, she was using you, and you knew it and still went along with it. She was demonising me out of guilt, but why didn't *you* trust me enough to be honest? Or is that part of the reason you were holding off—hoping to build up the illusion of trust between us until I was sufficiently softened up to *give* you whatever you wanted, instead of you having to find it yourself?'

He reeled around and spread his arms wide against the sides of the sash window, leaning his forehead against the glass.

'My God, what is it about me and the women I—?' He faltered briefly, his voice harshening. 'The women I seem to attract? First Lorna, then Kate…now you. I've had two lovers who stole children from me and a third who conspired to cover up a dirty little secret. And don't try and tell me that it's a woman's right to choose what happens to her own body—maybe it is, but if it's a principle worth fighting for why do it the way Kate did? With no discussion, no question of choice on my part, or joy for the miracle of life we created together—just get rid of my baby as if it was some kind of minor biological inconvenience. At least Lorna had the decency to consult me about her pregnancy and give me the *semblance* of a choice about my child's destiny.'

She felt his searing words like a brand upon her heart.

'Kate could have just had a miscarriage—' Anya offered up the faint hope. She moved across to stand behind him, the rigidity of his body making his navy suit sit as stiffly across his shoulders as an expensive suit of armour. Unable to resist the urge to comfort him, she laid a gentle, compassionate hand on his unyielding back. His iron-hard muscles contracted even further at her touch.

'You don't believe that any more than I do.' He wiped an angry hand across his face before spinning around. 'By God, Anya, if you're pregnant don't even think of trying to get away with not telling me about it,' he said savagely, his eyes shining with a ruthless intent. 'You may not think I'd make a very good parent but you're not going to be the third woman in my life to deprive me of being a father to my own child.'

'I would never do that,' she said thickly, over the tears in her throat.

'How do I know what you're capable of doing? For all the time we've spent together I don't know you at all, do I?' he countered jaggedly.

'You can't believe I'd ever do anything to harm a baby of yours,' she said, her grey eyes soft and pleading, her hand going instinctively to her stomach in an unconscious gesture of protection that sent a tormented spasm across his angry face. 'And I have no doubt at all that you'll make an excellent father one day. I'm sorry that I let Kate mix me up in her problem, but I honestly didn't know how to resolve it.'

He had been struck a blow to the very foundations of his pride. She took a deep breath, knowing that only by baring her own heart to him could she go some way to healing his wounds, and salvaging her self-respect.

'It wasn't lack of trust that stopped me from confiding in you. It was lack of faith in my own feelings. I believed that I owed my first loyalty to my own family but then I fell in love with you and everything got confused—'

'Love?' The word was uttered in loathing. 'You and your cousin say that so easily, yet you don't begin to know the meaning of the word...'

He thought this was easy for her?

'The more I loved you the more angry and jealous I felt of Kate, until I was afraid that my judgement was being clouded by malice,' she pushed on unsteadily. 'So I dithered over what to do until it was too late. I can only say I'm sorry for deceiving you. I love you and I was afraid of losing you, so I pretended to myself that nothing was wrong. I hoped that you might come to feel something for me, too.' Her voice cracked a little but she didn't stop. 'I was so afraid of doing or saying anything that might shorten our time together that I was a coward. I'm ashamed of what I did, but nothing can make me regret loving you...'

'Nothing?' The acid bite of the word warned her that worse was to come. He wanted to hurt her, as he had been hurt, and she had just handed him the perfect weapon. She only hoped that she was strong enough to survive the attack without permanent scars. 'Are you sure about that?'

She lifted her chin, slim and defiant in her silky pink dress, her arms straight at her sides, her fingernails digging into her palms. 'I'm not ashamed of how I feel about you.'

'Prove it.' His eyes glittered with cruelty as he threw down the gauntlet. He walked over to the door and kicked it shut, turning to lean against it with folded arms.

She licked her dry lips. 'What do you mean?'

'You know what I mean. Give me a demonstration of these so-called loving feelings. Let's see how unashamed you are. Take off your clothes. I want you to make love to me as if you really mean it. Show me how much you *love* me.'

She swallowed, refusing to be shocked by his sardonic crudeness, knowing that was what he wanted. 'I won't let you cheapen what we had—'

He shrugged, shouldering away from the door. 'I knew you wouldn't do it. Love has its limits as a form of manipulation, doesn't it, Anya? People have a nasty habit of expecting you to back up your words with actions.'

He stopped in his tracks as Anya's trembling hands went to the top button of her dress. He watched her as she undid the first button and then the next two, revealing the lacy white camisole she wore underneath. They were both breathing hard by the time she got to the button at her waist and he suddenly caught her wrists in both of his with a savage curse, preventing her from going any further.

'Are you really prepared to humiliate yourself like this? For what? It won't change anything,' he railed at her, dark blood flaring on his cheekbones.

'I thought you wanted me to prove my feelings for you,' she said, a tremulous hope stirring at the knowledge that he had stopped her from abasing herself. She bent her head and kissed one of the hands that was gripping hers. 'How can loving a man I respect and admire be humiliating for me?'

He wrenched his hand away and plunged his fingers into her pale, silky hair, pulling up her head to snarl in wounded fury, 'All you're going to be proving is that we don't need to trust each other to have good sex.'

He dragged her against his chest and crushed her mouth under his in a lustful, passionless kiss. Anya remained passive as he ran his hands over her open dress, fondling her braless breasts through the satin camisole and stroking her thighs with a clinical expertise and calculated lack of feeling that made her long to weep.

Instead, her heart aching, she lifted her hands to tenderly cup his angry jaw. At her delicately tentative touch he groaned a harsh protest, and suddenly the quality of the kiss was changing, from aggressive and punishing to a sensual, hungry meshing of mouths, his bullish stance shifting to support her softening body, his hands moving more slowly, a different kind of heat and tension beginning to build up in his big frame. Anya shuddered and uttered a soft cry as he stripped off her dress and began feasting on her soft flesh, shrugging out of his jacket and shirt and tearing at the fastening of his trousers.

'This doesn't change anything,' he groaned again as he pulled off her clinging panties and pushed her down onto the bed.

'I know...I know it doesn't,' she reassured him huskily, welcoming him with parted thighs as he came heavily down on top of her, offering him the only kind of love he was willing to accept. Passion flared and, conscious of the banked anger that had intensified his naturally dominating sexuality, Anya yielded ardently to his every command, their coupling hard and fast, yet deeply satisfying.

Afterwards, instead of lying with her in his arms in the

sweet aftermath of their love-making, he got up before the sweat had cooled on his body and silently tossed Anya her clothing. They both dressed swiftly, Scott substituting casual trousers and a clean shirt for his suit, Anya stealing glances at his unrevealing face, and when they were ready to leave she was stunned when he detained her at the door.

'Are you forgetting something?'

He turned to get Kate's untidy stack of belongings and handed them to her, including the journal and crumpled piece of letterhead.

'Isn't that what you came here for?' he said coldly, as she looked at him uncertainly. 'Take them. They're of no interest to me. They're a dead issue. Just like your cousin.'

And me? She didn't dare ask. At least he was being civil…barely. Surely that was a good sign?

'What are you going to tell the reporter?' she couldn't help asking as they walked down the stairs.

His knuckles whitened briefly on the banister rail. 'As little as possible.' They reached the foyer and he shot a cuff and looked at his watch. 'He's due at two. Tell Petra I'll be out until then.'

'Where're you going?' asked Anya involuntarily. She had hoped they might talk.

He looked at her and she saw a glimpse of tightly smothered rage. He had expended some of his anger in bed, but the rest was festering inside. 'I'm not answerable to any woman, least of all you,' he crunched. 'Don't think your *feelings* give you any sway over mine.'

'I wasn't suggesting—'

'Good. Don't.' He yanked open the front door.

'Would you still like me to stay with Petra?' she scraped up the courage to ask, taking heart from the fact he was still talking to her.

'You're a glutton for punishment, aren't you?' he rounded on her roughly. 'What do you want me to say? What I would *like* is for you to get the hell out of my face! Right now I don't want you anywhere near me, my home *or* my daughter. Is that explicit enough for you?'

The slam of the door reverberated through the big house.

'Jeez, did you and Dad have a fight?' Anya turned to see Petra frowning at her from the door of the music room.

Anya simply nodded, massaging at her temple

Petra padded up the hall. 'A bad one?'

'Pretty bad.' Anya was afraid she was going to burst into tears. 'Your father said to tell you he'd be back around two. I'm afraid I have to leave—would you mind telling Mrs Lee for me?'

She rushed to find her handbag, juggling the papers against her chest as she hunted out her car keys.

Petra followed her out to her car. 'But you will be coming back some time, right?'

Anya's fingers tightened around the keys. 'I'm not sure…'

'You're still going to be doing my tutoring, though?'

'I'm not sure about that, either. I don't know if your father will want me to do that any more.'

'You mean the fight was *that* bad?' Petra was shocked. 'You guys aren't going to break up, are you? But Anya— you can't. I'm going home next week. What about Dad? You know he's going to be all bent out of shape about it. And if you're not here he'll be left all alone…'

Anya was having difficulty seeing through the growing blur. Why wouldn't the key go in the lock? She took a wild stab and to her relief it finally fitted. 'Your father's a grown man. He lived here quite happily by himself before you came along, and he has plenty of friends.'

'Yeah, but he's sorta got used to having people hanging around—you know, like a family.' She caught the car door as Anya got into the driver's seat. 'And what about the puppy we chose?'

Anya looked at her foggily. 'Scott is giving you a *puppy*?'

What a ridiculous gift to buy a child who was about to fly back to Australia. Or was it supposed to be a lure to bring her back for future visits?

'Not me…you! Dad said you told him that you were thinking of getting a dog so he and I went out and bought one for you. But we couldn't give him to you yet because he has to stay with his mother until he gets big enough to be on his own and Dad wants it to be a surprise for you. He's real cute and cuddly, but he has a pedigree and everything, and Dad's even got you a collar and doghouse and a bowl and stuff. He'll still give it to you, won't he?' Petra worried.

A puppy? Scott had gone out and chosen a warm, cuddly squirming puppy for her?

That was the warm, squirming thought that kept popping into Anya's mind throughout a sleepless night and the long, dreary, lonely, grey Sunday which followed.

Giving someone a puppy wasn't like handing them a box of chocolates, she told herself. An animal required a serious commitment from the gift's recipient and that implied serious intent on the part of the gift-giver. That Scott had cared enough to want to buy her a pet to love and laugh and romp with in the grass surely meant that he had more complex feelings for her than he had been willing to admit. Otherwise, why bother? She had made it quite clear she had been happy with chocolates and candles. And doggy people were warm and loving. You didn't give a dog to someone unless you felt they were trustworthy enough to look after it properly.

At that point in her tortuous thinking she always came to a painful cropper. You could have trust without love, but it was impossible to love someone that you couldn't trust. And she was afraid that she had now indelibly associated herself in Scott's mind with the other two women in his life who had badly abused his trust. Sure, once he had thought it over he would probably understand why she had acted the way she had, and hopefully even forgive her, but it was bound to have a negative impact on their relationship. If she had told him that she loved him *before* he had found out what she was doing, things might have been different, but why should he believe someone who had already perjured herself by her actions and omissions?

No, whatever slim hope she had had of persuading Scott that she was worthy of his love was probably gone. But, as he had cruelly demonstrated, a lack of trust didn't stop him having sex with her. If she indicated she would accept such a one-dimensional relationship he might be willing to oblige. The idea left a bitter taste in her mouth. For her, sex and love had always been two sides of the same coin. She hadn't required Scott to return her love before she shared her body with him, but she *had* needed his respect to balance the emotional scales. Now she was afraid she didn't even have that.

Several times her hand hovered over the telephone, but if she rang him, what could she say? *I was thinking about you?* He must already know that. *I want to talk to you?* He would know that, too. As difficult as it might be, she had to wait for him to make the next move. And there would be one, because he wouldn't be able to leave the loose ends dangling. If nothing else he would have questions he wanted to ask, for in the heat of anger he was the one who had done most of the talking. He might have told her to leave, but he had stopped short of telling her never to darken his door again. He also knew all that he had to do was crook his finger and she would come eagerly running.

There was Petra, too; she was bound to be strongly partisan on Anya's behalf...

Her violently see-sawing emotions left her feeling tense and miserable, and by early Monday morning she was so firmly in the grip of a depression that she did something that she had never done in her life—she threw a 'sickie'. So it seemed like fate when, not long after leaving a message on Liz Crawford's answer-machine to explain that she was unable to come into school, she had a phone call from Russell Fuller and found herself talked into being interviewed later in the morning. She would have liked to fob him off with her supposed illness, but she decided gloomily that she might as well get it over with.

Talking to him reminded her she hadn't responded to any of Kate's nagging e-mails, so before he arrived she sent off a terse message to say 'mission accomplished' and ask if Kate wanted her to courier the package or send it by registered mail. Anya would have been quite content to throw the whole lot in the fire.

Russell Fuller turned out not to be the sleazy, ferret-faced scandal-monger she had feared, but a stocky, russet-haired man who not only recorded their conversation on microcassette but also took meticulous notes in his own form of shorthand in a lined notepad. He showed her the faded photo albums he said had been found for him at The Pines by Scott Tyler, after Russell had convinced him that Kate had said they were probably still in the attic of her childhood home.

Anya breathed a sigh of relief as he had immediately moved onto his list of questions, most of which were directed at identifying old photographs, and eliciting anecdotes of Kate's childhood on the farm and in New York. Anya kept her answers brief and to the point when the journalist moved on to her cousin's adult life and personality, but it was his final, casual, off-the-cuff question as he switched off his tape recorder that totally threw her.

'So…this is a kind of circle of fate thing with you and Scott Tyler—him being the owner of Kate's old home?'

'I beg your pardon?' she said warily, wondering if this was some cunning journalist's trap.

'Well, you and Tyler are in love, aren't you? I thought it would be a natural progression.'

'Who told you that?' she asked sharply.

He tucked his tape recorder in his briefcase. 'Tyler did, on

Saturday. He was very co-operative about letting me look around The Pines. Told me Kate had been a sharp negotiator over the price of the house, but he seemed more interested in talking about you than her.'

'He told you I was in love with him?' she asked numbly. A total stranger, and a reporter at that? The bastard! He must have still been rawly furious when he got back from wherever he'd driven.

'Ummm, no, not exactly—actually I think it was the other way around,' he staggered her by saying, leafing pedantically back through his notebook to the reference.

Anya nearly fell off her chair.

'What—*exactly*—did he say?' she asked tensely.

'You want the full quote?' He consulted his notebook. 'Here it is…ummm…' He pondered his squiggles, making a few seconds seem like several centuries. 'Ah, yes: "Kate was certainly a stunning woman, but it's her cousin I fell in love with. Anya has a kind of quiet grace and inner beauty that hits me square in the heart every time I see her. I think some part of me recognised that on the day we met, and I loved her even before I knew I was capable of it." Not a bad turn of phrase. The guy could be a writer himself.'

'But he said that to you off the record, right?' she said in a strangled voice.

'Nope. Got it on tape, too.' He tipped her a sly grin. 'Why? Would you like me to make a copy of it for you to replay to him every time you have an argument?'

He had been clearly looking forward to the offer of a second cup of tea, but instead found himself unceremoniously bundled out of the door.

Anya's finger was shaking as she punched in the numbers on her kitchen telephone from the business card in her wallet. 'I'd like to make an appointment to see Scott Tyler, please. Today. My name is Anya Adams.'

The businesslike voice on the other end was professionally

regretful. 'I'm afraid Mr Tyler is working reduced hours at the moment and he doesn't have any free appointment slots for the rest of the day. He's booked right through until he leaves at four o'clock.'

Anya clutched the phone with both hands. 'But he *is* in the office?'

'Oh, yes—but as I explained, Miss Adams, he doesn't have any spare—'

'Thank you.' Anya quickly put the receiver back in the cradle, cutting off a hasty cry.

'Oh, wait—Miss Adams—'

Remembering the adage about dressing for success, Anya took the time to select her clothes carefully and took extra care with her make-up and hair. She got into her car looking what she hoped was serene and confident, but tension and excitement took its toll and her cool became slightly unravelled in the hour it took to drive to the huge Manukau City shopping centre where Scott's chambers were located. It was another anxious fifteen minutes before she found the tower block she was looking for and somewhere to park, and in the express lift her stomach seemed to arrive at her destination well before she did.

The professional offices of Tyler & Partners weren't as intimidating as she had expected—the reception and waiting area actually showing the impact of natural good taste rather than cutting-edge interior decoration. The atmosphere, too, was informal and, by the look of the comings and goings and the number of people flicking through glossy magazines in the waiting room, business was good.

Squaring the jacket of her classically cut powder-blue suit, she approached the reception desk, eyeing the politely enquiring face, calculating whether haughty assumption or confiding friendliness was going to work better.

But when she opened her mouth, the young receptionist spoke first.

'It's Miss Adams, isn't it?'

'I—yes.' Was it someone she should know? A former pupil, perhaps?

'Julie!' The receptionist waved another, older woman over. 'This is Miss Adams.' She mouthed the next two words rather obviously. 'For Scott.'

'Oh, yes, of course.' Anya recognised the voice she had spoken to on the phone. 'Thanks, Melissa. Miss Adams? This way, please.'

Anya found herself whisked along to the end of the corridor, unprepared for the ease and rapidity of her progress.

'But, I—don't—'

'—have an appointment. I know.' The woman gave her an amused look. 'Scott came in just as I was telling you he was all booked up. I must say he described you to a "T".'

Anya frowned. 'You mean he's expecting me?'

'Well, if he wasn't he will be now. Melissa just buzzed him to get rid of his client.'

Anya clutched her cream handbag. 'I don't want to put anyone out. I thought you might just manage to squeeze me in when he had a few spare minutes…'

It was too late for cold feet. She was already being ushered into a large office to see Scott closing an adjoining door, spinning around on the plush green carpet to face her.

He looked wonderful, she thought fretfully. While she had been suffering from a thousand cuts of guilt he had been burnishing his skin and glossing his hair and generally making himself look like a million dollars. And there was no sign of joyous welcome in his eyes, just a watchful reserve.

'Crime obviously pays,' she said drily, looking around the office.

'The defending of it certainly does. It's a growth industry. Did you come here to assess my net worth?' he drawled.

She bit her lip and gripped her bag harder, reminding her-

self that she had it on very good authority that she hit him
in the heart. Unless he had been making an ironic joke.

'No. I'm sorry; I don't know why I said that.'

'You're nervous. Sit down.' He indicated the chair in front
of the desk, but instead of going around to the leather swivel
chair when she had seated herself, he sat on the edge of his
desk, legs relaxed, extended and casually crossed at the ankles, arms folded across his chest. He didn't look as if he
had a nerve in his big, gorgeous body, damn him!

'Why aren't you in school?'

'I called in sick.'

He dropped his hands to the desk, gripping the edge on
either side of his hips. 'You're ill?' he asked, searching her
delicate face.

Sick with love. She looked away from his penetrating gaze
and shook her head. 'I just felt like a day off.'

'And you've come to spend it in my office? Or have you
come for my professional advice? If you're going to take up
housebreaking as a full-time job you'd better put me on a
retainer. You don't seem to have much talent for the job.'

Her heart quickened at the wry amusement in his voice. If
he could joke about it...

'Russell Fuller came to see me a couple of hours ago.'

'Did he, indeed?' A lazy eyebrow rose, but she noticed
with another skip of her pulse that his fingers were tightening
under the overhang of the desk. He wasn't any less nervous
than she; he was simply better at disguising it.

'Yes, he did. And he told me certain things. Things that
you said to him. About me and you,' she said defiantly.
'Were they true?'

'What do you think?'

She looked at him in silence, torn by hope and fear. Suddenly she was tired of being brave and feisty, and her eyes
began to sting.

'I think if you have to go through a third party to tell me

what you feel, that doesn't bode very well for our future relationship,' she whispered, a tear spilling down her cheek.

He instantly lunged forward. 'Oh, God, no—don't cry—' He grabbed her out of the chair, and drew her into his strength, rubbing up and down her back with his big hands. 'Please—don't cry— Of course they're true, Anya. I was wilfully blind not to see it before. Of course I love you. That's why all this hit me so hard. When I was talking to Fuller it just suddenly all fell into focus, and then I spent the rest of the weekend agonising over it, figuring out why I'd been so anxious to lash out, to push you away, and blame you for things that weren't your fault. You said you were afraid of losing me—imagine how terrified *I* felt. This is all new territory for me. I've never, in my whole adult life, had anyone to *belong* to, or belong *with*—I've always felt like a loner. And then Petra came along, and you burst into my life—you, who'd been hovering around the edges of my mind for months, making me feel itchy and angry and *aware*. I built you up in my mind as someone I couldn't want, but then I wanted you anyway. My heart was already setting me up for the fall. Even when I seduced you I knew that you weren't the kind of woman to sleep with a man without feeling some deep emotional tie, but I couldn't help myself.'

His arms tightened possessively around her, as if trying to absorb her into his very being. 'And you turned out to be the best thing that ever happened to me. The one who made me feel that I *wanted* to belong—I wanted to be a husband, a father, and I wanted to be those things with *you*. Deep down I knew you were nothing like Lorna or Kate—it was just a form of panic, the shock realisation that you could hurt me far more than they ever had—it was the old protective reflexes kicking in. But I can't live in that kind of vacuum any more. I need you to love me, and I promise I'll learn to be more open about the way I feel—you can teach me. So please, stop crying now. I didn't mean to make you cry,' he said, pressing desperate kisses all over her damp face.

'Well, what did you expect me to do?' she sobbed into his chest.

'I don't know—yell at me, slug me one, laugh…' He groaned. 'I thought you might find my way of telling you I loved you quirky—romantic—'

Her head jerked back. *'What!'*

He smeared a tear away from her cheek with his thumb. 'You know—like sending a troubadour, to serenade you…' he said ruefully.

'Are you *crazy*?' she demanded.

'Yes, of course I am—crazy over you. Why else would I do such a stupidly juvenile thing? Fuller told me on Saturday he was intending to try and see you on Monday so I rang him last night at his hotel and *asked* him to tell you what I said.'

'Why didn't you just come over and tell me yourself?' Anya was trying hard to be angry him, but it was difficult with so much joy in her heart.

He bowed his head against her shoulder. 'I was ashamed,' he confessed, his voice muffled in the curve of her neck. 'You'd told me you loved me and I'd thrown it back in your face. I called you a prostitute, and then treated you like one. I used sex to try and show you that you meant nothing to me. I thought you might hate me for that and I was afraid to face you. I thought: How can she possibly love a man who treats her that way?'

She sniffed, shaken yet reassured by the depth of his anguished self-doubt. 'It's a dirty job but somebody's got to do it.'

He lifted his head to receive her glowing smile of benediction. 'And that someone has to be you,' he vowed. 'Only you.'

'Hmmm.' She spread her hands across his chest and

looked up at him, her nose pink, her rain-washed grey eyes loving. 'What are the pay and conditions?'

'No pay, but plenty of rewards. As for the conditions: you have to marry me, come and live at The Pines, let me seduce you out of your scandalous underwear every night, have my babies, be a stepmother to my brilliant, smart-mouthed daughter and fill my house with all the love and laughter it can hold.'

'And a puppy?' she bargained slyly, plucking at a button on his waistcoat. 'A family isn't complete without a family pet.'

He hesitated, a secret smile in his voice as he conceded, 'Maybe a puppy. But only if you're good.'

She tilted up her face to him, her hands sliding down under his jacket to settle down around his hips as she insinuated the centre of her body against his, pushing him back against the edge of the desk. 'Oh, I'm very, *very* good...' she purred.

His eyes smouldered and his mouth came down on hers, and as she allowed herself to be swept up in his loving passion she blissfully contemplated just how very badly she was about to misbehave....

MILLS & BOON®

Live the emotion

Modern
romance™

THE HIGH-SOCIETY WIFE by Helen Bianchin

Gianna and Franco Giancarlo went into their society
marriage to create an alliance between their powerful
families and to dispel gossip. A year on Gianna finds
herself in a state of emotional agony. Because she has
done what she vowed she'd never do – she's fallen in love
with her husband…

THE VIRGIN'S SEDUCTION by Anne Mather

Eve Robertson is just getting over her turbulent past.
However, her new-found stability is threatened with the
arrival of Jake Romero… Jake is tall, dark – and dangerous.
And he wants virginal Eve. His touch leaves her aching for
more – but there are things she just can't tell him…

TRADED TO THE SHEIKH by Emma Darcy

Emily Ross thought she'd escaped an evil drug baron
when she fled his yacht. But now she's the prisoner of
Sheikh Zageo bin Sultan al Farrahn – and he seems to
think she'll trade her body for her freedom! Only time
will prove Emily's innocence – and time is something she
just hasn't got…

THE ITALIAN'S PREGNANT MISTRESS
by Cathy Williams

Italian millionaire Angelo Falcone always gets his way. But
when he suggested to model Francesca Hayley that they
make their affair permanent, she turned him down. Three
years on, his anger still rankles – and now Francesca is in his
power and in his bed. This time Angelo won't let her go…

On sale 3rd February 2006

*Available at WHSmith, Tesco, ASDA, Borders, Eason,
Sainsbury's and most bookshops*

www.millsandboon.co.uk

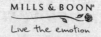

BEFORE SUNRISE
by Diana Palmer

Enter a world of passion, intrigue and heartfelt emotion. As two friends delve deeper into a murder investigation they find themselves entangled in a web of conspiracy, deception...and a love more powerful than anything they've ever known.

THE BAY AT MIDNIGHT
by Diane Chamberlain

Her family's cottage on the New Jersey shore was a place of freedom and innocence for Julie Bauer – until tragedy struck…

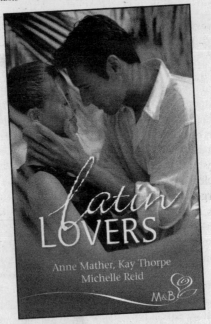